It stitches together, with brilliant storytelling, superbly crafted characters, a vibrant plot, the woes of modern life and a past that keeps delivering a legacy poisoned by secrets and betrayal. Gripping yet tender, it mirrors the devastation of the natural world with a moving exploration of prejudice, belonging, and otherness.

BYDDI LEE, AUTHOR OF *BARREN*

Blending the genres of murder mystery and historical fiction, yet set firmly in a modern Ireland on a warming planet, The Planter's Daughter is a clever, compelling read.

Beautifully written and ripe with intrigue, this is a compassionate, evocative book that expertly weaves in themes of climate change, gender identity and race, against a backdrop of Ireland's troubled history and our deep, ancient connection to the land.

MICHELLE MCDONAGH, AUTHOR OF *THERE'S SOMETHING I HAVE TO TELL YOU* AND *SOME OF THIS IS TRUE*

A book that will not only tug at your heart strings, but also make you ask bold, important questions. Gripping, compelling and written with a deft touch.

THE PLANTER'S DAUGHTER

SUSAN LANIGAN

IDÉE FIXE PRESS

To place the land of Ireland in the hands of the Irish is to invite ruin and rebellion.

LETTER TO THE TIMES (LONDON), 1881

I don't think we can mitigate for climate change…if we get into a position where we're going to challenge every single thing, saying it's against the climate, we're going to divide society fairly fast …

MÍCHEÁL MARTIN, TAOISEACH OF IRELAND, IN AN INTERVIEW FOR THE *IRISH INDEPENDENT*, SATURDAY OCTOBER 11, 2025

A NOTE ON THE TEXT

'Sadhbh' is an Irish name, pronounced Sive. 'Muintir na hÉireann' means 'Folk of Ireland' and is pronounced 'mwincher na hairann' while 'Coláiste Íosagáin Naofa', the fictional school, is pronounced 'kuh-lawsh-ta ee-sa-gawn nay-o-fa.'

Contains scenes featuring transphobia which some readers may find distressing.

PART 1

PROLOGUE

Knockalisha Hill, near Skibbereen, West Cork, June 1921

Harry Keating stood for a moment on the uneven stone floor, hands on his hips, wishing to God that Michael Savage would keep quiet and stop bleating. The fool was getting pushy now, ever since the young fella they'd captured had made fun of his lisp – or so Michael claimed. Harry had not heard Theodore Drummond doing any such thing, but Michael was thin-skinned and tended to hear mockery in everything. He was also the kind of young man whose family were of rising importance locally, but who would resent anyone who came from a better class than himself. Harry didn't care a rap for such things and was only dedicated to the cause; he now regretted bringing Michael with him on this operation. But there were few enough men he could trust in the middle of this war on their oppressors, and Michael knew the man with the truck, so Harry had to lump it.

Harry's captives, Arthur and Theodore Drummond, father and son, sat close together, tied up and shivering. The corpse of their relative lay in a bloodied, unlovely heap in a corner.

Harry had pistol-whipped Herbert Frost himself, then shot him. Herbert had looked him in the eye. Harry would give him that – if not much else. Herbert was a Great War veteran with the original British Army before Kitchener's lot. Like Harry, Frost knew how to keep it professional.

It was past midnight. The truck which had brought the three men up the hill was parked outside, but in that dark cave on the hill, it might as well have been on the moon. They couldn't hear the owl hoot, or the fox scuffle, or even a cart go by, as it sometimes did, if the horses could manage the gradient up past the woods. The air was heavy and cold, and in the sky outside, the moon itself was heavy with solstice. You could light a cigarette or a candle, but no warmth would penetrate through to the cave. It was a handy place for the IRA to keep its prisoners.

'Are ye going to let that young strip make fun of me?' Michael Savage's face was flushed, and he was sweating. That garish silver religious medal he wore around his neck, the Children of Mary or some such name, flashed in the torchlight. They were all about church that family. Harry could smell the salt and sourness on Savage from a few feet away. He could smell the fear of the captives too, darker still.

'They have no respect, them people,' Michael growled. 'No respect. I won't let them make a mock out of me. I'm well thought of in this town!'

Your father *is well thought of,* Harry thought. Which was not the same thing at all. But he saw that Michael would not be assuaged, and he was a dangerous fellow to cross.

'All right,' Harry said, 'let's pistol-whip 'em too.'

By the time they were finished – Michael sighing with pleasure at each blow and the prisoners' cries of agony echoing through the cavern in the flickering torch light – Harry's disquiet had deepened. Unlike Michael, he took no joy in this. Theodore was only a young lad, and he was crying now, gulping huge sobs of pain and fright, begging to go home. Theodore had not shot poor Stephen Rooney to death on the lawn of Liss Ard in cold blood like Herbert Frost had done. He was just collateral in a nasty, intimate fight.

'All right—' Harry said, about to tell Michael he was going to let them go. But then he heard a click beside him and felt his chest tighten in alarm.

Jesus, Mary and Joseph, the fool had gone and loaded his gun.

There was no way Harry was going to let Michael Savage fire a bullet at the Drummonds. He wouldn't know where to start and would leave a mess behind. The peelers would be after them right quick. This was Harry's operation, and he needed to take control.

He had kept his weapon loaded throughout, so with a swift, clinical movement, he turned the torch on the prisoners with one hand, and raising his pistol with the other, shot them both before Michael Savage realised what was happening.

They did not die immediately, of course; there was flapping and gurgling and groaning, and that unspeakable fear in the boy's open eyes as he rasped his last breath – but it was as fast and as kind as Harry could manage under the circumstances.

Michael jumped back with a pig's squeal of fear, even though he'd been about to shoot them himself. It did not take long for the fear to be replaced by indignation. 'They made a mock of me and ye wouldn't let me near 'em!'

Harry did not dignify Michael's complaining with a response. Instead, he directed him in a low mutter to help him load the bodies back on the truck. Within ten minutes, they had driven halfway down the hill and dumped them into a clearing by a stream. The Drummonds' corpses fell softly onto the forgiving earth, hidden from the road by fronds of willow and fern.

As they drove away towards the town, Harry saw Michael sliding angry, resentful looks at him with those puffy eyes of his. He had wanted to kill the prisoners himself; he would have enjoyed it, but Harry hadn't let him. Harry would not be quickly forgiven for that.

There will be a price to pay, Michael's glare said.

Harry knew Michael was right. But he also knew that he and Michael were not thinking of the same price – or the same thirst for payment. In the cool early dawn, as the truck jiggled and jarred along the boreen and the silence thickened between them, Harry felt deep in his bloodstream that this was not the start of something, but the end.

ONE

Knockalisha Hill, 3 May 2021, 10 a.m.

The forest fire had been brutal. The route Clodagh Duffy took in her Toyota truck shielded her from seeing the worst of the devastation all at once, but even the glimpses she had were enough. The entire top of Knockalisha Hill was now black and brown – the gorse, and all that sustained life from it, gone. So intensely burned that even the rocks were scarred. Where magnificent Scots pines and birches had once stood were now blackened, charred tree stumps.

Even as Clodagh's truck turned downhill towards the lake, she could still see the upper reaches, well below the treeline, where the hillside looked like a war zone. She wound down the window. The horrible smoke had dispersed, but the dry, polluting ash still gathered in her nose and throat. Grabbing the stiff handle, she wound the window back up again.

Forestry was doing well, they kept saying, but still no money to buy new trucks. And Clodagh's area was expanding all the time as forest managers retired and no one replaced them. At this rate, at the age of thirty-four, she would be managing half the Munster forestry estate and would hardly have time to inspect the Sales Proposal land parcels, let alone control anti-social behaviour. Or hill farmers.

All over Ireland, forests were burning. Assets going up in smoke, as hill farmers broke the law and burned their gorse and cooked the eggs of the stonechats and marsh warblers and didn't care a rap for the consequences. The recent coronavirus lockdown had given the lie to the claim it was tourists causing the fires. There were no tourists, and still the uplands burned.

'Fuck you, Tom Keating,' Clodagh hissed at the steering wheel. 'You malicious little bastard. Twice! Was once not enough?'

On a relentlessly sunny day such as this, the inadequate little car park at the forest entrance would usually be full of day-trippers and picnickers, eager to avail of the marine lake's pleasant warm water. But today only one other car was in evidence, so there was plenty of room for Clodagh to reverse in. She put on her boots and stepped down from the truck. Even though it was only ten in the morning, the air hit her like a warm wave. Usually, it would be cooler; usually there would be the sound of the wind in the trees; but there was little of that this morning. No wind, and far fewer trees. Nothing to break up the oppressive warmth. No cloud to gently interject itself into the unbroken blue of the sky.

She recognised the other car – a battered blue Ford Fiesta. It belonged to Philip Moulton, the Forestry Department's ecologist. Like Clodagh, he would be here to inventory a loss: hers commercial, his environmental. To her, they were one and the same. She was the closest thing to a mother these forests had. She had cried when Tony Geoghegan, the local Fire Brigade chief, had told her one of his men had rescued a baby rabbit and given him a drink from his water bottle. She tried not to think of the rabbits, stoats and hedgehogs that hadn't made it.

That had just been the first fire. That scum Keating, emboldened by local silence and the lack of a swift arrest, had lit a second one a week after that and any wildlife that had hung around had surely now been obliterated. No, say the words: *burned to death*.

'Bastard,' Clodagh hissed again. 'Bastard from hell.'

'He is, isn't he?' Philip's doleful voice sounded from somewhere behind her.

Clodagh turned on her heel. Typical bloody Philip to be hidden behind a tree. Occupational hazard of working in forestry, she supposed, but he made it an art. If he weren't so amiable and non-threatening, he would have made an excellent stalker.

'Tom Keating, yeah?' Clodagh called out.

'Whatever his name is.'

Philip emerged, and Clodagh could see his shirt was stuck to his skin. His straw-coloured hair had darkened with sweat. He must have been working away for some time.

'You just going? I'll see you later, so.'

Philip shook his head and took a swig of water. 'It's bad up there, Clodagh. You shouldn't do this alone.'

Clodagh was relieved. Documenting exactly which units of land had been burned to a crisp was always going to be a devastating task. Having Philip there would be better than going through this alone.

'OK. Thanks, Phil. Let's go up and get it over with.'

They set out on the wide forest road, walking past the gate which said FOREST OPERATIONS – NO ADMITTANCE. Families and visitors would often creep up the narrower, log-ribbed paths, taking shortcuts through the canopy of Douglas firs, but Clodagh and Philip were not here for pleasure. They took the main road and ascended in silence.

Still there was the smell of pine and the soft cover of needles. Still, from time to time, dappled light and shadow fell over the road as they walked. But not a whit of birdsong was to be heard, not a scuffle from the depths. Silence, except for Clodagh's and Philip's boots as they trod on the road's rough surface.

Tom Keating's second fire had proved far worse than Clodagh had feared. Half the forest looked gone, the tree branches bare and black, signalling their end like ghostly semaphore in a scorched desert. The light on the bare, dry ground was bright and hot; the further up they went, the more damage they found.

Clodagh needed to take it all in. She needed to see the big picture before taking out her field data management device – that handy little gadget that mapped every forest by layering maps one on top of the other, back to the oldest map which dated from 1912. Then she could carry out her accounting more dispassionately.

They stopped just fifty metres short of the top of the hill, at the end of the treeline. The scorched slopes allowed Clodagh and Philip a view they should not have had at that point: of Lough Ine lying far below, sparkling blue-aquamarine, with one solitary canoe making its way across to the small channel between the tranquil lake and the Atlantic. From where they stood, the canoe made its way along the surface like a water boatman on a river. The hum of the ocean was distant and peaceful.

Neither of them spoke; they just silently drank their water. Clodagh drained the bottle she had picked up the garage that morning and crumpled it in her fingers. The plastic made an angry, cracking, recalcitrant sound when she crushed it – and even when she threw it on the ground and stamped on it, she could not flatten the thing.

'I'm picking it up,' she reassured Philip. He, of course, had his own bottle which he had pre-filled before going out.

'It's OK. Hard to see a beautiful place like this destroyed.' His voice was soft. 'Especially when it's your second visit in a week, and the hen harrier nests are all burnt to a crisp.'

'Yeah.' Clodagh stuffed the bottle in her backpack where it bulged out, the cap peeking out from the side pocket. Then she took out her scanner. One grim advantage of the trees being gone – she would have no problem finding a satellite. In dense cover, the signal could be twenty metres out. Not today, though. It was right where she stood. God bless the US military and all the junk they put into the sky. And God damn the Irishmen who couldn't control their burning.

'I'm gonna start now,' she called out, descending into the first set of skeleton trees, scanning carefully, noting 'Fire Damage – Tree Destroyed' in her reporting fields.

Area 12, Sales Proposal 12–1, 12–2, 12–3 … For a while, numbers took over. As Philip stood on a rock under the sun, hands in his pockets, Clodagh worked diligently and slowly, left to right across a ten-foot line, then the next line, then the next, until she began to approach living forest cover, and switched her reporting field.

But then she stopped.

Something dark and strangely shaped, an abnormal shadow, lay under a young oak that had by some miracle escaped the ravaging horror Tom Keating had set. It looked like … Why surely it couldn't be?

'Philip.'

Metres away, he heard the urgency in her voice and slid down the slope with surprising speed, loping the remaining yards between him and her until he was right at her side. When he saw what she saw, he sucked in his breath.

'Stay back.' His tone was quiet and urgent, his arm up blocking her. He treaded carefully towards the tree, whose leaves were singed. But he was hardly a foot away when he recoiled so violently, he fell backwards, his arse hitting a bare branch.

'Jesus Christ!'

Clodagh had to look. Now drawn to that spot, she ran past Philip, even though he called loudly for her to stay back.

She saw what he had seen, and a powerful wave of dizziness and nausea rose in her. It took her several seconds to scream.

TWO

Cork City, 3 May 2021, 1 p.m.

Detective Inspector Rosa Keane was asleep when her phone went off. At first, she blinked and turned over, but like a trapped fly, the phone kept buzzing, slowly vibrating its way towards the edge of the nightstand until it fell over onto the carpet. Rosa swore softly and reached out for it.

Work. *Shit*.

'Keane here.' Her voice sounded even more hoarse than usual, while a lock of curly hair stuck obstinately to her forehead. The digital clock that had been with her through three house moves – the last one turbulent – flashed the time. It was past one in the afternoon.

'Ah, good. You're about.' It was Superintendent Eames. His northern accent was sharp. 'Need you to come in. Sorry, but it's urgent.'

Rosa blinked again and swivelled into a seated position on the edge of the bed, her nightgown rucking up at her knees as her bare feet hit the warm floor. Her tongue felt dry against her mouth. 'It's my day off.'

'I know. I'm sorry,' Eames said briskly. 'But there was a second wildfire over in Knockalisha forest yesterday and the forestry lads found a body this morning.'

Rosa padded over to the window and lifted the thin curtain. Even in her small, dark townhouse on South Douglas Street, the sunlight was unforgivingly bright. Unforgiving enough to show the dust on the sills and nightstand and where the carpet needed a good hoover.

'Wasn't that the place where the Fire Brigade gave a baby rabbit a bottle of water?'

'I don't know.' Eames was short. 'They haven't got a time of death for us yet, but not more than two days ago for sure.'

'Caught in the fire?' Rosa massaged her temple. 'Christ. Who is it?'

'Preliminary tests indicate the victim is a thirty-six-year-old woman. We believe it's Sadhbh Drummond. Her husband reported her missing on Sunday evening.'

Somewhere in the back of Rosa's mind a bell rang, faintly but firmly.

'And everything points to her not being caught in the fire. Dr Moran will be down later today to confirm, but between you and me, we're already treating it as suspicious.'

Rosa sighed. 'OK, I see.' She badly needed a shower. She would turn on the water after she got the Super off the phone, hear the hiss of the water tank as it rumbled into life. She would let the hot water pound her clean.

'I'll see you at three, Super.'

'Two.' It was clearly not a request.

'OK.' Rosa hung up and cursed for the third time. So much for the shower. She would barely have time for a pee and putting on her clothes. And she had fallen asleep with her make-up on again. The pillowcases would be ruined.

She cleansed her face and dressed hurriedly. Her suit was

unremarkable, the Garda ID and the little Smith and Wesson pistol discreetly tucked into the inside of her jacket.

Passing down the dark, narrow hallway, lit only by a small fanlight, she nearly missed the small white envelope lying on the doormat, name and address neatly typed and postmarked Dublin. Her heart began to beat a little unsteadily. Had it been there since Friday, and she hadn't even seen it? Was it the appointment?

She had gone to a GP. Not the one they went to in Glanmire, God no. Someone in the city, a South African man who after many years of locum work had joined a large primary care centre in Togher. Dr Naidoo knew nothing of Rosa's background, and expressed little emotion at her request. All he did was to hum and tap his notepad with a pencil, finally announcing 'I must refer you to a psychiatrist.' The psych, in turn, had put her on the waiting list for an appointment, 'but heads up, it might be a little while.' That had been six months ago, and now here it was: the date a week on. Not the end, hardly even the beginning, but an important step forward all the same.

Some people had to wait years.

Rosa could hardly believe her good fortune, but she didn't have time to savour it. She had to get a move on.

She walked out into unrelenting heat. In that dank little place that flooded at the mere suggestion of a cumulonimbus in the sky, you usually couldn't imagine a heatwave. But even for early May, it was blazing hot.

'Climate change,' Rosa thought absent-mindedly, as people do about things that they believe are not their concern. And then she remembered where she had heard the name Sadhbh Drummond before.

THREE

It had been nine years ago at the mass demonstrations against the incinerator. When built, it would be the biggest thermal waste unit in all of Ireland. The planning board approved its construction over near Seven Heads and the entire county rose in rebellion. Rosa and her colleagues had been busy for weeks trying to keep the peace: managing riots, standing by in demonstrations, even making the odd arrest here and there when people invaded the site.

She hadn't arrested Sadhbh Drummond, but Rosa remembered how badly, how *intensely*, that woman had wanted to be arrested.

They had come down to Courtmacsherry in the squad car, responding to the frantic call from one of the outnumbered security men. The site had been a heap of disarray: bits of shale and rock scattered everywhere, building materials and a small prefab hut over in the east side. The prefab was deserted, locked, its window barred on the inside. A reinforced cardboard sign saying THIS SITE IS PROTECTED BY 411 SECURITY, with a picture of a bulldog on it, had been knocked to the ground, half-submerged in a puddle from recent rain. Due south of the entrance, a hillock of earth had been disrupted by the beginnings of works on the site.

Sadhbh Drummond stood on that hillock, her arms outstretched, her long hair unfastened and blowing in the wind. Young, vibrant, powerful, glorious. Her clear, cultured accent, with just a trace of Cork, rang out like a bell.

'If you want me off this site, you'll have to arrest me first.'

She was surrounded by a group of admiring men. Two of them clasped her hands on each side, and the rest linked hands in a line – Sadhbh, of course, in the middle. The winter sun shone on them all without a scintilla of warmth, but the eco-activists were high on their own moral crusade while the guards, Rosa included, shivered in their jackets. Briefly, Rosa thought of the Yeats poem that bored her so much in school she had thrown paper planes at the English teacher: *beauty like a tightened bow … high and solitary and most stern …*

'No Second Troy', that's what it was called. Hell, Sinead O'Connor had even done a song with the poem as lyrics. Rosa remembered that eerie melody leaking through the door of her sister's bedroom, and how she wanted to borrow that cassette tape and play it herself, but didn't dare ask.

'Arrest me first,' Sadhbh repeated. Her wide, blue-violet eyes seemed to Rosa to zero in on her.

Although she was not the superior officer, Rosa spoke up. 'No need to worry. All people like you want is attention, and we don't have the time to satisfy your vanity.'

To this day, Rosa had not known where those mean, parsimonious thoughts had come from. Her every sympathy that day should have been with Sadhbh. Nobody wanted this damn thing. The planning men from Dublin had, with practised arrogance, bypassed the local authorities and politicians and Tidy Towns and public will. There was already a judicial review brewing.

But something in Sadhbh's look had floored Rosa – this beautiful stranger, unabashedly feminine, seemed to size up Rosa and see the awkwardness of her physical frame, how her shoulders hunched, the secret estrangement Rosa had with her own body. *That woman has the measure of me,* Rosa thought, and a wave of bitterness at Sadhbh's glance, which seemed to leave Rosa naked, had both loosened and sharpened her tongue.

For a moment, Rosa thought Sadhbh flinched a little at her remark, and that the energy in the activist line flickered and weakened. But if she did, it was brief.

'All I care about is that this abomination does not go ahead, and if vanity and attention-seeking make that happen' – here she was interrupted by cheers from her comrades – 'then I'll happily indulge in both, Garda Keane!'

That Sadhbh had known her name unsettled Rosa too. She was nobody and nothing back then. Sadhbh must have studied up. Afterwards, as Rosa suffered a thorough bollocking back at the station from Detective Sergeant Mahon for opening her stupid mouth, she reflected again on Sadhbh's beauty and charisma. Mesmerising, that was the word for it. Dangerous, too. That look she had given Rosa, one of amused pity and understanding, had scared the bejesus out of the young guard.

In the end, the waste company pulled out. Resistance made it too expensive for them to continue. Sadhbh had galvanised public opinion far enough that it became politically unappealing to push on. She had won that battle.

But nine years later, she had lost the war.

FOUR

Anglesea Street Station was an unlovely building designed in candy-rock shades of white and marshmallow pink, both of which had aged badly over the five decades of its existence. The station was on the corner of a junction, flanked on two sides by a car park mostly full of white Garda patrol cars, with a few anonymous, unmarked vehicles dotted between them. Rosa put her mask on and headed inside. Past reception, she took a right through a pair of auto-locking double doors into a long corridor lit by panels over the office doors to her left and right. Eames's office was near the end.

In its anteroom, another detective, Kevin Xiao, sat typing up notes. Xiao was not local, meaning solely that he was not from Cork; he had been transferred from Dublin three months ago, and since then, had barely left the office. Rosa had heard rumours about tribunals, and accusations of racism being flung around at his colleagues. He'd been on sick leave and come back, but after all the unpleasantness, he had been transferred to Cork, it seemed, in disgrace. Rosa herself wondered what he thought about sitting there under the

Super's eye, typing up notes, sorting files, while being kept away from anything resembling normal Garda business. But Xiao, head down so that Rosa could see his black, gelled, neatly parted hair and the curve of mask elastic around his ear, typed away diligently, ignoring Rosa and everyone else. Beyond Detective Xiao's typing station was a half-and-half style wall: glass-panelled on top, with a dado style below. Beyond that, Rosa could hear Eames on the phone. 'We'll get someone up to Kildorrery. This talk of killing bats is a bit lunatic. It might seem minor, but if we have an elected councillor making a nuisance of himself … Yeah. OK. Oh there's Gerry.'

Eames had spotted Rosa, and motioned her in, waving at her from behind the semi-opaque glass. Rosa took a seat while Eames continued his call. The office smelled of newspapers and mint gum. The photos on the wall behind him she knew well: the black-and-white reproduction of the RIC barracks down the road at the Bridewell; the colour one of a social evening on Harrington Street for Eames's father's retirement. His grandfather had been one of the founding members of the Garda Síochána, a holdover from the old RIC before Ireland became independent. Before independence, he'd come south from Carrickfergus with its Lambeg drums and grim castle, to start his new posting as a constable, but after the changing of the guard, he stayed on and got promoted all the way up to superintendent, before retiring and heading back north. His grandson had made the return journey and was proud of the endeavour.

'Sorry again, Gerry.' Eames said once the call ended. 'I know you're not thrilled to be here.'

'Not really, but let's move on.'

Eames made a mock gesture of being punched. 'Oooof. That bad, eh? Coffee? Water?' Rosa shook her head to both.

'Right. This just happened this morning. Press will be all over it, so we'll release details this evening.' Rosa allowed herself the most frigid and smallest nod. 'The fellows in Skibbereen are already fingering a local for her murder. A neighbour, it seems.'

'I know who Sadhbh Drummond is,' Rosa said. 'Met her once before, on the incinerator site. You remember that whole controversy?'

Eames chuckled. 'I do. I heard you gave her some lip too.'

Rosa bent her head. 'Anyway,' Eames recited from his notes, 'Sadhbh Drummond comes from landed gentry. Her ancestral house was burned down in the War of Independence and much of the lands were sold off afterwards. She was a geography teacher in the local CBS, married to the headmaster of the same school. Ronan Furlong. Eight years married with two children. Stepmother to two more from his first marriage.'

Rosa recalled the superintendent himself was twice divorced; up North these things were more common.

'The local lads told him this morning and Roisin is with him now.'

Roisin Malone was one of four Family Liaison Officers in the county. It was her job to comfort victims' relatives and guide them through the police process.

'Sadhbh was a teacher, as I've said, but she was also one of the most notorious eco-activists in the entire Munster region. As you are probably aware from your encounter with her. She was kicked out of the Environment Party two years back for being too extreme and has been campaigning independently ever since. She stood for local election but failed to get a council seat. The neighbourhood had turned against her by then.'

'I'm not surprised,' Rosa said. 'If even the hippies couldn't handle her.'

Eames took a sip from a plastic tumbler of water. 'You're talking about a government party now. Perhaps don't write them off as hippies before you've even spoken to them.'

Looking at him made Rosa thirstier, but she'd left her bag with the water bottle in the cloakroom.

'And they're sure it's murder, Super? She couldn't have been going for a walk and got caught in the fire?'

Eames shook his head. 'Nope. Maura Casey in in pathology told me that when a person burns like that, their arms and legs contract and stiffen, as if they're curling. Sadhbh Drummond was found lying on her side, and her legs were straight out. She'd been left there dead and was burned later. They're still trying to narrow down time of death – it's tricky when there's so much fire damage, you can't ascertain it from skin and lividity – but Sandra's certain that she did not burn to death.'

As Eames's words faded into the air, Detective Xiao hit the space bar with what sounded like decided venom. Rosa began to feel a little faint. Her underclothes were too tight and constricting. She felt the lack of that shower very acutely. 'Could I get some water now?'

Eames nodded, and Rosa filled up a plastic cup at the water cooler outside. When she returned, she sensed that Xiao was watching every move she made, though he didn't even glance her way.

'The guys in Skibbereen reckon it's a local man, Tom Keating. He's a hill farmer with land next to the Drummond family estate. He's been in trouble with the local environmental groups over the past two years for burning gorse and cutting hedges out of season. Sergeant Connolly down in Skib told me they didn't have enough evidence to arrest him, even when the Forestry Department lads had him on their drone footage building a pile of timber next to his gorse.'

'They've got drones?'

'They do, apparently. A lot of angry farmers burning down forestry in the past few years, and they decided it was time to invest in the latest technology. But drone or no drone, folk don't tend to interfere with Tom Keating's business. By all accounts he's got certain ... connections.'

'IRA?'

Eames nodded. 'Several generations back. Not so active now, but his grandfather Harry was very prominent in the War of Independence. He's fanatical about his land, and the locals are scared enough of him not to cross him in any way. There was talk of a national waymarked trail back in the late nineties, and a proposal to put a yard of it through one of his fields with a CPO ...' Eames smiled wryly. 'It ended up with two Belgian hikers being threatened with a shotgun. The council shut the whole thing down after that.'

'Jesus.' Rosa shivered. 'He sounds reasonable.'

'He's part of the reason we want you on this.' Eames looked very serious now. 'We need somebody who isn't from the area and won't suffer consequences for it. When you've had your station firebombed with a note that your children are next, it makes a man thoughtful, y'know?'

'Keating did that?'

'He did. Though they've never been able to pin it on him. They *do* have him for starting the first gorse fire, though he'll only have to pay a fine for that and maybe lose his subsidy, because the powers that be still don't take that kind of thing seriously, even with the Environment Party in government.' He grimaced, and Rosa recalled his conversation about the bats over the phone. 'The other drone they had flying around that day got downed by a golden eagle, of all things. Bird-watch Ireland's pride and joy.'

'I take it Keating's been arrested?'

Eames shook his head. 'We don't have enough on him yet. And we need to keep an open mind on this. There's too much history in that part of the world of ... let's say ... trying to find a suspect without using the proper ways. I don't want Mary Fehily having another field day with this.'

Rosa nodded. They both knew the notorious case he was talking about, that German woman beaten to death fifteen years ago out near Barleycove. The local gardaí had arrested a man based on an unreliable witness who later retracted her statement, and the whole thing had collapsed. Mary Fehily, a roving journalist who liked nothing more than a good juicy scandal, had excoriated the Gardaí, accusing them of carrying out a cover-up. She'd even insinuated the actual perpetrator was a now deceased senior guard with a rep for beating up prostitutes. Rosa was not one to put her colleagues on any sort of pedestal, but the fact that Fehily declined to provide even a hint to the man's identity led Rosa to suspect he did not exist. Still, they had to tread carefully. Fehily might have been a right-wing conspiracy shill, and yes, she may have been madder than a box of frogs, but she had a small but dangerous following, who would do only God knows what in her name.

'I want you to take a car directly down to Knockalisha Forest Park. Rob Whelan is the investigator there, so you can have a chat with him. Dublin is already working on getting you the phone records to find her last movements. We haven't been able to locate her phone, unfortunately.' He smiled grimly. 'No surprise there; the murderer has likely chucked it into the Atlantic Ocean. Likewise the drone. I doubt it's going to provide anything of value, so I wouldn't waste too much time over it, but you never know.' Eames shuffled a few papers on his desk. 'I'd like you to see the husband out in Toe Head in the family home. As soon as you can. Really get to know Sadhbh Drummond. Who she was and who might have wanted her dead.'

'Yes, sir.' Of course, the husband would always be a suspect. 'Oh and take a partner. I'd say Darragh McClure, but I'm after sending him up to Kildorrery to do battle with a county councillor who's been trying to kill bats with a shotgun, God help us.'

'That's Darragh?' Rosa exclaimed in surprise. Darragh McClure was the closest thing Rosa had to a friend in this place, and she knew well that his usual beat did not include bat conservation. Surely murder was surely more important than bats?

'They're a protected species, you know.' Eames drummed his fingers on the table. 'We're getting a lot of flak for letting people off the hook for animal cruelty. Not to mention cyclists. Bloody cyclists, do they ever stop moaning?' He took another gulp of water. 'You could take Bailey, maybe? A bit junior, but how else do you learn except by being on the job?'

Rosa thought for a second and then gestured at the glass panelling. 'I'd like him, if I may.'

Eames frowned deeply. 'Kevin Xiao?' He lowered his voice. 'Are you serious?'

'Why shouldn't I be?'

Eames leaned in so far that Rosa had no choice to do likewise, and their foreheads almost touched. 'You know why he's here?'

'Yes. He worked with a bunch of racists, took them to tribunal, and won, didn't he?'

'Racists?' Eames sounded annoyed. 'Colleagues, you

mean. People who never had the chance to put their side of the story against somebody who played the race card against them.'

Xiao stopped typing. *Christ,* Rosa thought, *had he heard them?*

'Sir,' Rosa said, 'you specifically asked for a person who didn't have sufficient ties to the area. Sounds like he fits the bill, to be honest.'

'Fine,' Eames said, his annoyance evaporating suddenly, as it tended to do. 'Have him if you insist. Though I'll never get anyone else in the force with a seventy words per minute typing speed.'

They stood up and Eames called out, 'Xiao! Come in here a moment. I've got some news for you.'

FIVE

3 May 2021, 4 p.m.

The drive from Cork City to Skibbereen should have taken an hour and a half. Instead, it took nearly three quarters of an hour to get from Anglesea Street to the roundabout on the city's ring road. The interior of the ageing car was broiling in the heat. *Isn't it hot?* Rosa wanted to say but didn't dare.

When Eames called Kevin Xiao into his office and explained he would be partnering Rosa on the Drummond case, Xiao merely responded with a curt 'Sir', not even looking in Rosa's direction. He had been silent all the way to the car and on the journey thus far. Rosa didn't pluck up the courage to speak to him until they reached the inevitable queue at the Wilton roundabout. She asked him what his Chinese first name was. Indicating deftly onto the round-about's middle lane, Xiao replied 'Kevin.'

'I mean your real name.'

'There's no point.' Xiao indicated off the roundabout, and they left the city behind. 'People can't pronounce it. Kevin is fine.'

'But—'

'I guarantee you won't be an exception.' His voice was both deep and metallic, not inviting further conversation. From there to Leap, another hour down the road, he and Rosa did not exchange another word.

At least he hadn't asked Rosa to give hers in return. That was a relief.

With a heatwave in full swing, even in lockdown, the traffic was as bad going out as returning. The road was jammers with people heading out of Cork towards the coast on a bank holiday Monday. As the traffic ground its way through Innishannon, Bandon and Clonakilty, Rosa wondered if she should phone Glanmire. She had been hoping to get on the phone and negotiate a visit with her two children, maybe visit them at their home – but no, better not risk it. Not when her phone had in the last twenty-four hours received five angry, abusive messages from Lou, their other parent. There seemed to be nothing Rosa could do to assuage Lou's anger; any attempt at contact only seemed to aggravate things further, reminding Lou of the initial hurt, the betrayal. It had been months since Rosa had last seen the children, and nothing could be done about it. She sighed and put the phone down into the small well under the handbrake, where it nestled with an old used tissue and a half-eaten packet of Polo mints.

West of Clonakilty, the air cooled a little, the land got poorer, and the hedgerows more resplendent with ever-present fuchsia spilling out among the brambles. Once they reached Rosscarbery, passing the Celtic Hotel on the causeway, Rosa felt her spirits rise and a sense of anticipation in the air, as wide and open as the estuary they had just crossed. She remembered holidays here as a child, taking the exact same route, until they reached that small white cottage just by the beach. The sharp prick of seashells on the soles of her feet, the net in her hand as she went shrimping … Life was simpler those days. Except even then, she knew she was not the person they thought she was.

She leaned back and closed her eyes.

A few moments later, Kevin woke her suddenly by pulling into the small car park outside Connolly's pub in Leap village and disappearing. Rubbing her eyes, Rosa looked blearily out the half-open car window. Xiao was heading for the co-operative shop up the road. Closing her eyes again and switching on the fan, she was soon interrupted by a knuckle tapping on the window: Kevin, holding a 99 ice cream in each hand.

'You got some with Flakes,' she exclaimed in happy surprise.

Xiao looked at Rosa as if she had two heads. 'Who on *earth* buys a 99 ice cream without a Flake?'

Good point.

Xiao slid back into the driver's seat to eat his own cone, while Rosa wound her tongue around the glorious vanilla spirals, biting into the Flake and spreading the chocolate fragments across the ice cream with her tongue, the same way she had done when she was a child. It had been years since her last 99.

Xiao finished his quickly and turned on the radio. It was tuned to a soccer talk show, but he pressed the buttons until a familiar rhythm and a smooth bass vocal chanted Barry White's deep bass prologue to 'My First, My Last, My Everything'.

Before Rosa could comment on the selection, her mobile rang. She licked a dollop of ice cream off her fingers and hit Accept, leaving a slight smear on the glass.

'Keane.'

'Howya, it's Tony Cawley here.'

Rosa put him on speaker. 'Superintendent Eames told me you were working on the Drummond case, and I was to get the phone information for you from her mobile. Christ, is that Barry White? Haven't heard that song in ages.'

Xiao switched it off. Rosa thought she saw a fleeting grin. 'That's right. We're on the case,' Rosa said.

'I just sent you an email, but I thought you might like to know about it as soon as possible so I thought I'd give you a ring as well.'

'That would be great, Tony. I've got my colleague here too, Detective Xiao.'

'Kevin? Oh I remember him well from the Shankill branch. Nice lad. Give him my regards.' Tony's voice held genuine warmth and pleasure. Obviously not everyone who dealt with Kevin Xiao had disliked him. 'Anyway, we struggled to narrow it down. There's sweet FA down there when it comes to phone masts. But I can tell you this. At half past five her mobile pinged a mast in Skibbereen town, just near the SuperValu at Mardyke Road. Then nothing until 7.50 p.m. when she was within at least a kilometre of mast CK1504 at Tragumna beach. That was the last we traced of her. Phone was deactivated about an hour later. We tried getting GPS data, but what with privacy issues and not having the phone with us – no luck so far. Though, for what it's worth, I think 'location' was switched off because no GPS data was available all evening.'

'Thanks, Tony. And any info about messages?'

'I was just getting to that. We've obviously been concentrating on the last messages received on the phone. And the number she was using was one that came up quite frequently over the last few weeks. Usually at odd hours – like in the middle of the working day or late at night. The last message she received that evening came from that number. She got it at the point where she pinged Skibbereen, or just before, at 5.21 p.m., and replied straight after. Then she sent another text to her husband's mobile. That was the last message she sent to anyone.'

'So, she must have gone there straightaway,' Rosa said, 'if she went of her own free will.' The familiar excitement she felt when constructing a narrative had begun. Callous as it was, taking the fragments and making a story out of them was one of the things Rosa enjoyed most about her job.

'Perhaps,' Tony said neutrally. 'Anyway, we traced the number back to a Peter Ludwig. He lives at Hunter's Cross between Skibbereen and Ballydehob. I've emailed you on his address and particulars.'

Peter Ludwig. Why did that name, too, ring a bell?

'And what's the story with *his* phone? Is there more traffic on it after that?'

'Yup. But not till about midnight that night. Several texts and even a call, all to Sadhbh's mobile. No response, though.'

'Any other numbers of interest?' Rosa was thinking of Tom Keating.

'Not really. Unless you widen the timeframe a bit. But Sadhbh wasn't texting anyone else in the two hours before she disappeared. Hubby never replied to her last note.'

Peter Ludwig. As Rosa was racking her brains to recall where she had heard of him, the ice cream began to slide down the cone and all over her fingers. With her free hand, she rooted around for the ancient piece of tissue, but Xiao tutted and stopped her by swiftly handing Rosa a fresh one.

'Oh crap. Sorry, not you, Tony. The ice cream I'm holding is melting on my fingers.'

'Right you are, then. Ring me if you need more, but it should be all in the email.'

'I will, Tony. Thanks a million, that's very helpful.'

'I'm only sorry it wasn't even more specific. You can get great results these days, but only if the privacy nutters don't try and sue you.' Rosa sensed Tony was about to launch a rant, so she smoothly thanked him again and hung up, then hoovered up the last of ice cream and crunched the cone in her mouth.

'Sorry,' she said, mouth still full, 'I know I'm being disgusting.' She wiped her fingers. 'So, what do you think?'

'Hold on a moment, I'm looking something up.' Rosa saw Xiao open Maps on his phone and key in a place name. Then he put the phone back on the bracket, put his hands on the steering wheel and stared ahead in silence for a long moment.

'I just looked up her address. If she passed the second mast they mentioned, that's very close to where they live. She could have told the other man no; she could have gone home. But then again –' Kevin frowned – 'it doesn't take more than two hours to get from Skibbereen to there. So maybe she was just saying she would be late.'

'Well, she *was* late,' Rosa said. 'She never got there.'

Even though it was still balmy out, something felt a little colder, and it wasn't the ice cream. Soon they were on their way south again, passing the turn-off to Glandore and Unionhall.

Rosa looked Peter Ludwig up on her phone and got several images: a handsome, truculent youth, with a fringe that swept across his forehead and wide, soulful eyes. One had him standing next to Sadhbh Drummond and both were holding placards: DIRECT ACTION AGAINST BRUTAL FISH FARMS. It was a newspaper photo, dated just the previous year, detailing how Sadhbh had been cautioned and Peter arrested for breach of the peace near a fish farm. It was clear that its author did not approve of the antics of either 'Ex-Environment Party activist Sadhbh Drummond' or

'German self-styled eco-warrior Peter Ludwig'. Why mention his nationality, Rosa thought, unless it was to foment ill-will against him? Mind you, from the look of him, Peter Ludwig probably managed to do that very well himself. He had his arm draped around Sadhbh's shoulder in a proprietary fashion, and she looked more than a little uncomfortable. As well she might, considering she was married to someone else.

Another search brought up a website called West Cork Action for Planet Earth. It was rough and ready, little more than a blog. Peter Ludwig appeared to be its sole author. The briefest of scans indicated that his attitude towards the Environment Party ('sell-outs') was virulent; he firmly believed that all mainstream politics were corrupt and the only way to save the planet was to replace late capitalism with violent revolution. But he reserved his most venomous attacks for the guards. In one recent entry – imaginatively entitled 'Fuck the Police' – he wrote:

I refrain from referring to them as pigs. The pig is the tenth most intelligent animal in the world!

Oh, I know your type, Rosa thought to herself.

The app directed them to turn left off the main road. After Kevin took the turn, the route on the app headed vertiginously uphill, with hairpin bends that required grinding gear changes. Kevin Xiao accompanied these manoeuvres with several words of Cantonese which Rosa guessed were not suitable for polite company in China, but entirely fitting for negotiating L roads in Ireland. With each turn the terrain got rougher, until they were bouncing along a narrow boreen with grass growing down the middle and three-metre-high hedges, whose thorned arms grew out and brushed against the windows like zombies from a horror movie. The foliage was so profuse it made everything dark. As they crawled along, they could hear the chatter of birds and insects from somewhere deep inside the laurel border.

'Are you sure this is the right way? This road doesn't seem to be going anywhere.' But even as she spoke, Rosa spotted a little recess by the side of the road where a few slabs of rock were laid into a well. They were driving slowly enough that she could take a good look: a rowan tree grew over it, and from its branches hung pieces of coloured paper and small baubles. Picked wildflowers wilted at the well's base and painted pebbles lay at the tree's root and around the well's circumference. Someone had put a small, plastic statue of the Virgin Mary just above where the water poured into an underground stream. A holy well. Rosa remembered it from her childhood.

'The old ways are still there,' she murmured. Then, louder, 'We're on the right road. We'll be at the lake soon.'

'Some road,' Xiao said. 'It's barely a cow track.'

'It's a famine road.' Rosa shivered as she recalled what her father had told her. 'The British authorities paid starving men to dig a useless road past that well, so the men could feed themselves and their children. They stole our food and then said we were weak of character and needed to be employed with good works. Like this pointless road.' Rosa stopped, winded, shocked. Where had that anger come from? When it was all so quiet and peaceful now, a small set of wind chimes on one of the rowan tree's branches gently tinkling in the breeze, the little prayer sheets fluttering?

Xiao seemed to understand, though. He stopped the car and switched off the engine, so they were swallowed in the quiet. 'Man-made famine. We had that back in the sixties. I lost family in it. They called it the Great Leap Forward.' The metallic edge of his voice was dark, bitter. 'Shooting sparrows and digging up stony soil. Crops failed, ten million dead.

Sparrows all gone. Every time I hear a sparrow now, I think about it.'

'Jesus.' Rosa said softly. 'Ten million.' The wind chimes sang again. They sat in silence, listening to the wind sough through the laurel and cypress hedges. Clouds covered the merciless sun for a moment, and Rosa felt as if it was just the two of them, the trickle of the well, the wind chimes and the famine road. They were in a timeless place: even the car could be swallowed up by grass, thorns, moss and become part of the landscape. There was a rage in that land, a poison at the root.

But then the sun returned, the spell dissipated, and the wind brought an acrid, unmistakable smell. Of ash and dust and the burning stubble of devastated forest. The smell of crime. Xiao wrinkled his nose. 'We must be near.' He turned the ignition.

They lurched on until the boreen ended at a junction with a proper road. 'Turn right,' chanted the satnav, but by now they could see the glorious aquamarine of Lough Ine, as it glinted tantalisingly below them, and what was left of Knockalisha forest directly above.

Xiao took another steep right up the hill until they reached the forest gate at the back of the estate. Rosa got out to lift the gate, and then they drove along the wide forest road, their journey ending at a clearing, where piles of logs stood and a bent sign hanging off a fir declared WAR FOR OPERA. It should have been 'Warning – Forest Operations' but Rosa liked the truncated version better. She usually liked forests in general, even when they were crime scenes – which, by their nature, they often were – but the skeletons of trees and the smell of death overcoming the sweet odour of pine cast a cloud over this place which was more than just literal ash.

They parked up close to where Rob Whelan was waving

at them, at the edge of an overgrown plantation path. With his prematurely balding head and long, pasty face, Rob reminded Rosa of that fellow who'd been in *Bachelor's Walk*, except that Rob would probably have been in rompers when that programme was on. He was in civvies now, out of his crime scene overalls, a lit cigarette in his hand. They must have interrupted his smoke break, but he didn't seem to mind.

'Howyiz,' he greeted them, taking a drag.

'Rob. Good to see you again.' Rosa introduced Xiao and the two men shook hands. Rob waved at them to follow, and they treaded warily through the forest.

'Are we not disturbing evidence?' Xiao murmured, but Rob must have heard because he said, 'That's the very reason we picked this route. The usual way has footprints in the dried mud and even some tyre tracks. This one's clean. We've a bit of a walk yet before we get to the scene. It's quite high up.'

They toiled in the sun, the heat barely broken by the forest cover. Xiao's head was bent, but Rosa could see he was struggling – as was she. Fair play to the foresters, that they could grow and harvest trees on a slope like this!

They broke out past the treeline and blinked in the light. Here, activity was visible: the crime scene tape sagging in the windless heat, the investigators in their white boiler gowns and gloves, moving here and there. A makeshift path of steel plates led from the Garda-painted Ford Fiesta down to the tree where a white tent had been set up.

'This is as far as ye can go,' Rob said. 'Body's already been moved on to the coroner's office.'

'This was once a beautiful place,' murmured Xiao, putting his hand to his forehead to take the sun out of his eyes.

'And it will be again,' a voice said hoarsely behind them.

'We won't let them win.' Turning around, Rosa saw a woman, probably in her early thirties, with long, straight hair, freckles, and a small mouth. She wore work dungarees and fawn hiking boots, and an N95 mask dangled around her neck. 'This is Clodagh Duffy,' Rob said. 'She's the area forest manager. She found Sadhbh.'

'That was this morning?' Rosa said. Clodagh nodded. She looked dazed, and Rosa wondered if anyone had taken care of her. Seeing a body in the condition Sadhbh Drummond was found would be a shock to anyone.

'I'm sorry you had to come across that,' she said.

'She won't leave,' Rob said in a low voice, 'even though we've told her there's nothing more she can do here.'

'It's my forest,' the woman said defiantly, raising her chin. 'Everything that happens here is my responsibility.'

'You can't be responsible for murder,' Rosa said gently.

'They're saying that's what it is, all right.' Clodagh folded her arms and looked ahead. She was adopting a tough stance, but it was clear she was shaken. 'And so near their own land.'

'She means the Drummond estate,' Rob cut in. 'We were just talking at lunchtime about the land around here. Most of Knockalisha is state-owned, taken over and run by the Forestry Department. But just on the edges down the other side of the mountain still belongs to the Drummond family, after all these years. Except for Tom Keating's bit, which is right next to it. I think they were tenants but then bought it out. That all used to be Drummond land, since the eighteenth century.' He encompassed the land in a wide gesture. Rosa remembered then that Rob was local to the area, living near Drinagh, and knew the ins and outs of it all.

'That's interesting,' she said, 'when we've been told that Tom Keating and Sadhbh Drummond were at odds with each other over hedge cutting.'

'It didn't start with hedges,' Rob said. 'It's been going on a long time, that dispute.'

'And they've destroyed our forest in the middle of it.' Clodagh was bitter. 'The first fire, we could regroup, treat some of it as clear-felling, and plan. The second fire, that was pure spite. So much needless destruction, just to stick it to the man. I hope you lads have arrested Tom Keating,' she added. 'Rob keeps telling me Sadhbh mightn't have been killed on this plantation, but I'm willing to bet no matter where it happened, Keating did it. If he's cruel enough to do this twice over' – she gestured around – 'he's more than capable of murder.'

'Clodagh.' Rob stubbed out his cigarette, loped over, put a hand on her arm. 'Take it easy.'

'No, I won't,' the woman cried, suddenly animated with rage. 'Tom Keating has terrorised the whole area long enough. He should have been arrested a long time ago, but everybody is too scared to talk against him. He burns his gorse whenever he pleases, never mind the birds and their nests and the hares and rabbits – and the forests that have been there hundreds of years. And he walks around town, cock of the walk. He's well known for raising his fists to his own wife. He's your man, Guard. He needs to be put away for good.'

'Clodagh, I can assure you we take this very seriously. We want justice to be done as much as you do. That's why we're interested in knowing exactly what happened.' Rosa felt pity for Clodagh but didn't want to touch her. Her rage was too present and bright. 'We heard you had drone footage connecting him to the first fire, but not the second.'

She shook her head, sniffing. 'That's right. Got taken down by one of our golden eagles. I can only presume the bird knocked out the camera. God only knows where the drone is now.'

Xiao, who was making notes, looked up. 'I know people who fly those. Is there any chance the connectivity might have been knocked out, but the camera stayed running? It's usually mounted on one of the arms of the drone, so it would be fairly robust.'

Clodagh wiped her eyes with her sleeve, breathed heavily and replied, 'I imagine it's *possible*, yes. But unlikely. The bird would have seen it as prey and taken it down. They don't give up, those eagles.' There was a hint of pride in her voice, but then it grew dull again. 'Just a pity our lads found the bird poisoned near Mount Gabriel just an hour ago. They've reintroduced falcons in Wales and eagles in Norway, but never mind that, some have-a-go farmer thinks the rules don't apply to us, and we can poison every living being in radius.' She lifted her face to Rosa's, fresh tears in her eyes. 'Tell me, Guard, why are we Irish so fucking backward?'

SIX

Skibbereen Garda station was a small, unprepossessing breeze-block bungalow with pebble dashing straight from the seventies: a squat island in a worn asphalt lake. The blue door with its Garda insignia on the lintel was ajar; Sergeant Sean Connolly would be there to meet them. Rosa had phoned ahead. She'd got through to Sergeant Connolly straightaway. He had been eager to emphasise, in his deep West Cork accent, that it was all 'action stations', and that he'd come in personally to see them and make sure they were set up and looked after.

'We're very eager to put this one to bed,' he told Rosa over the phone. 'It's heartbreaking. And Sadhbh, of all people. Such a beautiful girl, so full of life'. Rosa was startled to hear his voice breaking. 'Do you know she has two young children? A woman like that, in her prime. I can scarcely believe it, Inspector.'

Rosa replied, 'I worked in the DV unit for a few months. I can believe it all too well.' Something in the sergeant's tone put her off. 'A woman in her prime.' As if Sadhbh Drummond were a piece of meat.

Now as they crunched their way across the gravel, Rosa tried to ignore the grumbling in her stomach that the ice cream had failed to assuage.

'Let's get this over with quickly,' she said to Xiao as they walked to the door. Then, without thinking, she added. 'God, I'm starving. I could murder a Chinese.'

Xiao stopped and raised an eyebrow.

'Oh Christ. I didn't mean that like it sounded.'

Shit.

'I mean – I was hungry. That's all. I was thinking I would like some Chinese foo— Oh crap!'

'Inspector,' Xiao interrupted.

'Oh God, I feel so stupid ...'

'Inspector!' A bit sharper this time. 'You're blocking the doorway. And breaking the two-metre rule.'

And now she saw the familiar yellow markers in that narrow corridor, indicating the two-metre distance. Probably more honoured in the breach than the observance, but Xiao was right. Rosa sorry-sorried herself out of his way and followed him in at the sanctioned interval.

'Will ye have tea?' the sergeant asked. He wore a mask, but with his nose sticking out, nullifying its purpose. Reluctant to correct him, Rosa shoved her cloth one further up her face instead.

Xiao, his arms folded, showing a muscular set of biceps in short sleeves, shook his head. 'Not hot. Iced, maybe.'

'Iced tea? Ah, we don't have that. Orange juice?' Xiao nodded and a rinsed glass was duly produced, filled with a viscous liquid that reminded Rosa of the Kia-Oras of her childhood. Xiao lifted his mask and downed the congealed-looking stuff in one gulp, setting the glass down on the table.

Connolly had a manila file in each hand; one slim as an

envelope, the other a big bulky yoke that looked as if it would collapse and the sheets of paper inside it fall to the ground. He sat down, sighing as his backside hit the chair and passed both over the table.

'One of these is the file we have on Sadhbh Drummond. The second is the one we've just opened on her.'

Rosa saw immediately what Connolly meant. 'The first one being the complaints she brought to us. The second being on her murder.'

Connolly nodded. 'I'm sorry to say this, because I thought she was a fine woman – but there is *no* shortage of people who would have it in for her. This is a big oul' file.'

'I heard she was politically active, all right.'

'Now that,' Connolly laughed, 'would be an understatement. There was nothing that went on in this neighbourhood that girleen wouldn't campaign about. You couldn't take a piss in the river or throw out a plastic bottle without her hearing about it and slapping an EPA complaint on you. She was an utter scourge.' Connolly managed to convey both exasperation and affection. 'She had this daft idea of local people donating a patch to a 'rewilding project'.' He waggled the quotes in the air with his fingers. 'Mother of God, as if you could persuade any Irish farmer to part a scrap of his land for *money*, let alone for free!'

'And was Tom Keating one of those farmers?'

'Yes. I've just this last half hour sent a lad to bring him in.'

'To the station?' Rosa was sharp. 'For murder?'

Connolly rose and plugged in a large fan that had been lurking in the corner. It whirred to life and slowly whapped as he talked. 'No. Arson, though. We surely have him for that this time. I was thinking we could question him about the murder when he gets here.'

'I heard he's threatened you in the past.'

'He might have done.' Connolly was evasive, crossing his legs and looking away. 'There's a lot of talk in this town; doesn't always translate into action.'

Oh Lord, if only he would pull that mask up over his nose! Rosa had to restrain herself from leaning across the table and doing it for him.

'But from what I've heard, Keating was ...let's say, well affiliated with certain individuals.'

Connolly shifted uncomfortably from foot to foot. 'Yeah, but like, you can only play the Ra card for so long.'

He meant the IRA, or whatever local scumbags were operating in their name.

'This could change things. Word on the ground is, he's becoming a liability to them.'

You wouldn't think it from the way Sadhbh's complaints went unanswered so long. But Rosa wasn't here to criticise Connolly's slowness to act.

'Best we get a plan,' she said briskly. 'As well as Tom Keating, we need to speak urgently to a fellow called Peter Ludwig. He was the last person to message Sadhbh Drummond at twenty past five on the evening she was murdered. As far as we know, Sadhbh took a route south pretty much the moment she got that message, and she never communicated with anyone else after that.'

Sergeant Connolly frowned. 'Him? Now that's a surprise.'

'I've got his address—'

'Oh, no need. Everyone around here knows Peter.' Connolly picked up his phone and dialled a number. 'Niall? You free? Can you get the car and head out to the crusties in Abbeystrewry? We need to pick up Peter Ludwig.'

'Just to clarify,' Rosa interrupted, 'there's no suggestion of any wrongdoing. Yet. We just need to know what the story is with his phone.'

'Oh no?' Connolly looked disappointed. 'I'd love a chance to drag him in here. Would you believe the things he says about us? Why he once said—'

'I know. I read his blog.' Rosa wanted to shut down Connolly's indignation. 'Can you ask Niall if he can swing by here and take us with him?' Connolly added the instruction and hung up. When he sat down Rosa said casually, 'I see our colleagues in Bantry arrested them last year. Sadhbh and Ludwig.'

'Oh yeah,' Connolly sighed, 'the fish farm. But I told the Bantry guards to let her go in the end. She said she wouldn't leave the station unless they let him go too, so we ended up releasing the two of them. She's nothing like as bad as him. For all her faults, she's local.'

'But so is Peter, if he lives nearby.'

'Ah, hardly. His aunt and uncle, now, they're long settled. The Heilgers. Came from West Germany originally. Odd as two left feet, but very successful. There's been a German community around here for a long time, and they all know each other. Peter's come over every summer since he was a child. Then two years ago he decided not to bother going back. Apparently, he was in England and got arrested for something similar and decided to beat a retreat before Brexit.'

Rosa sighed. They could be here all night if they worried about Peter Ludwig's track record. It was time to get moving.

'Have you anything that would work for an incident room?'

'Eh, there's a whiteboard somewhere, I think. And markers. We're always running out of markers. They dry out fierce quick.' Connolly scurried about.

'Right, well, whatever's to hand will do.' Rosa said impatiently. 'Kevin, can you sit down with Sergeant Connolly and interview Tom Keating once they've brought him in? I'll drop in on Peter Ludwig, see what the story is, then talk to the husband. Also, Sergeant, if you have a list of people who associated with Sadhbh in any way, friend or foe, it would be of enormous help.'

'I do, indeed. It's in the file, right at the front. I've even put in into 'friendly' and 'hostile'.'

Rosa flipped it open. As suspected, the 'hostile' column was longer than the 'friendly'. She took it out of the file and handed the rest back to Connolly. 'I'll keep this, if you don't mind.'

'Not at all.'

'Right—' Rosa started, but they were interrupted by the sweep of car on gravel and the sight of a short, heavyset man with thick dark hair, a horsehair jacket and a florid mouth being dragged in by two uniforms. He was shouting and roaring obscenities, but when he caught sight of Rosa and Xiao with the sergeant, his eyes narrowed, his brow darkened, and he declared in a voluminous roar: 'Will ye listen to me? For the last fuckin' time, I'll swear on me grandad's life, I DIDN'T START THAT FUCKIN' FIRE!'

Tom Keating had entered the building.

SEVEN

'Sadhbh Drummond is dead,' Kevin Xiao told Tom Keating. Keating heard him all right, but did not so much as raise an eyebrow. His face unmasked but unreadable, he looked away, squinting at the spinning fan in the corner. Kevin guessed he was trying to focus on the moving blade to calm his agitation. Sadhbh's death appeared to be news to him. Kevin glanced at the fan, reached over, and switched it off.

Tom Keating's eyes lit up with rage. Good.

'I expect you're pleased. You hated her, didn't you?'

Tom said nothing.

'It's on record. Have a listen.' Kevin had his phone ready on a small stand, the video clip loaded. The second clip Eames had sent them, recorded earlier that year. Sadhbh was standing for local, not general, election and there were no Environment Party posters with their characteristic 'Vote the Green Machine' slogan. She'd been expelled from the party by then. Nor was there any sign of her husband. She looked quite alone.

No banner behind her, nothing more than a bare wall –

and yet, even filmed through a camera held by hostile hands, she was still vibrantly beautiful. She wore her hair loose, along with a fitted olive-green tunic shirt. The colour suited her, too.

'I have already prepared the section of land that belongs to my family up on Knockalisha Hill,' she said, 'and I come here today to ask for your participation. The Not in Our Lifetime project is an act of reparation. Lough Ine is a nature reserve, but the delicate marine life is disappearing because farmers are letting run-off and nitrates into its waters. Our beautiful river Ilen has been killed by the Office of Public Works. The ecosystem is wrecked with concrete culverts. And all because farmers were allowed to pollute because of nitrate derogations, developers built houses on a flood plain and farmers and landowners let them.'

A restive mutter surged through the audience.

Then a man stood up. Tom Keating. 'I think ye've said enough. Ye know nothing about nitrates or flooding. You in yer ivory tower, while people in the town are two feet deep in wather. Families losing their homes and livelihoods!'

'I know enough about flooding to know building on a flood plain is a bad idea,' Sadhbh responded with spirit. 'Flood plains are for rivers to flood safely. That's it. With the onset of climate change, flooding will be more frequent—'

'Will ye cop on with yer fuckin' climate change?' Tom leapt to his feet. 'I'm bored out of me hole hearing about it. I'm tired of *you people* using it as an excuse for stealing our livelihoods! Haven't you done enough damage?'

The audience cheered loudly.

Kevin paused the recording with Tom's fist in the air. '*You people.*' He fixed his gaze on Tom.

Tom folded his arms. "I'll shed no tears for the Ascendancy.'

'Let's play some more.'

Sadhbh was retorting, 'Well, I'm not surprised to hear that from *you*, Tom Keating—'

But Tom wouldn't let her finish. 'Rewildin'! A land grab, that's what it is. Ye're talkin about puttin' hogweed and knotweed and the divil knows what on *my* land! You and your rules, saying I can't keep sheep, or burn gorse, I can't cut me hedges, can't mow the fuckin' grass, can't drive me diesel tractor, can't spray me bits of corn! After all yiz did to my people? You're not gettin' it back, you stuck up Proddie bitch!' And then they were all standing up, gesticulating, roaring, whistling and booing. Shortly after that the filming had stopped.

When Kevin was a child in Fuzhou city, his mother had told him about the Speaking Bitterness sessions the Communists organised against the landlords of the previous regime. Tenant farmers and peasants could attend these meetings and roar abuse at their employers and landlords for hours on end, even beating them up if they didn't respond. Tom Keating, it appeared, was speaking enough bitterness for a small district.

But then again, he wasn't just 'speaking bitterness' any more. He was speaking motive.

'You hated her. You wanted her gone. That Proddie bitch in her ivory tower. Your words, Tom.'

Tom kept his arms folded and started humming, looking at the ceiling.

'She took everything from you,' Kevin continued, as Tom droned louder and louder like a vacuum cleaner. 'But you could handle all that. Until Luke. He chose her over you, and that was the last straw. Wasn't it?'

The droning stopped. Tom's face clouded over. 'How do ye know about that?' The pain in his eyes was unmistakable.

Kevin felt a twinge of pleasure at unearthing the hard man's weak spot.

'Your son made a complaint to us about you for common assault on –' Kevin checked his notes – '13th May last year, along with a complaint that you cut your hedges out of season in contravention of the Wildlife Act 1976. He alleged that you threatened to cut her up with a large tree saw. He said you physically threatened her with the tool. He later dropped both charges. Under pressure from you, I'd imagine.'

But he had made them. For a woman to come between a son and a father, that was a serious vulnerability for a hard man like Tom. 'A chink in his armour, one might say.' As Kevin could imagine Detective Sergeant McGuinness back in Kilsheelan intoning with meaningful emphasis, before hastily adding, 'Oh, but we can't say anything like *that* around here any more, can we?' Then the knowing sniggers around the galley kitchen.

'The woman had no decency,' Tom spat. 'She was a stain on the community.'

'I see.' Behind his mask, Kevin smiled. 'And what do we usually do with stains, Mr Keating?'

'We—' But Tom broke off, realising where the detective was going.

'We remove them, don't we?'

Tom lapsed into sullen silence once more.

'Where were you between the hours of six and eight p.m. last night?'

Keating looked at the floor. 'At home,' he muttered. Then, before Kevin could prompt him: 'Ask my wife.'

'Anyone else?' Tom said nothing. 'Just your wife?'

He looked pleased with himself, Kevin thought, given his

alibi was thinner than the cheap toilet paper in the men's cubicles in Anglesea Street.

'If ye had anything on me,' Tom said, 'you'd have charged me by now.'

'You're charged with arson, and we've footage to prove it.'

Tom made a gesture of brushing something away. 'Them drone things aren't gonna tell them nattin' of use. The Department of Agriculture aren't going to do anything to me for what I do on my land.'

Kevin wanted to roll his eyes. This fellow was a nightmare. 'We're talking to your wife as we speak.'

'Talk away. She'll tell ye nattin' more than the truth.'

'And the fact that the tyre prints near where Sadhbh's body was found match your van?'

Tom roared laughing. 'You're goin' to get me on tyre tracks? Are you mad? Sure tyres are all the same.'

'We're all over that van, Tom. And we're all over your wife and house.'

'Jesus.' Tom spread his hands on his haunches, breathing deeply. 'I didn't start that fire that burned over the weekend, and I never laid a finger on that Drummond woman.'

'So, your son was lying,' Kevin countered, 'when he said that during the encounter in May last, you 'brandished your electric chainsaw in front of her face and legs, then aimed it at her groin, while shouting at her',' – Kevin read from his notes in a monotone – "I'll kill you, you fucking bitch?"

For a moment, Tom's fists curled inwards, his nostrils flaring. He leaned forward, his weight on his knees. His eyes were light and wild with pure rage. He looked as if he were about to start a fight. Well, let him try. Tired racist stereotype it may be, but Kevin's martial art skills *were* excellent. Not that he'd bother with those when it came to a man like Tom Keating. He'd just flatten the prick.

But Tom loosened his fists and sagged back in his chair. 'That boy hates me,' he observed in a bleak tone. 'He told me to go fuck myself.'

After that confession, Tom Keating folded his arms and refused to say another word for the rest of the session, no matter how much Kevin persisted. Later that evening, he was charged with arson, and released on bail thanks to the duty solicitor.

EIGHT

Abbeystrewry was a townland just outside Skibbereen across the old Ilen bridge. Perched on a steep hill just above the road, it contained a famine graveyard where a third of Skibbereen's population had been interred in the dead of night in a mass, unmarked pit. They did it by night because of the shame, Niall told Rosa. They did not want it known fever or hunger had entered the house.

Just above the graveyard was the old road out from Skibbereen, a narrow, hilly boreen with low hedges, mercilessly clipped since spring, their blossoming hampered even in May. Yet when Rosa and Niall pulled into the small gravel entrance and stopped, that scent of escallonia and honeysuckle still wafted through the air, the waxy leaves themselves leaving a signature scent too. Even with the fading light and the sun going down, it was what Rosa's father would have called 'a pet of a day'. Though, these days, Rosa's father did not return her calls.

Just past the gravel the terrain was dried muck, and it widened out into a grass clearing containing several caravans on blocks. Each one was surrounded by large geranium pots, and the entire assembly was protected from the wind coming off the hill by a large hedge of vibrant blue hydrangea. At one, a man sitting on the steps quickly dropped and extinguished whatever he was smoking, grinding it with his heel. Rosa waved at him not to bother. She and Niall were not interested in his cannabis intake. A bicycle lay on its side near one of the caravans, which Niall nodded at. 'That's his.'

They approached the caravan, which was smaller than the others. The blinds were drawn on the windows. Rosa banged on the door with her fist. Silence. 'We gonna break in?' But Niall tried the handle, and the door swung open. Immediately Rosa was assaulted with a smell that was all too familiar: sweet, cloying, metallic. Blood.

'*Shit!*' She sprinted into the main room and saw a trail of blood leading the other way. Niall, in the bedroom, shouted 'Here!' and Rosa joined him.

Peter Ludwig lay on the single bed, blood all over his clothes and the sheets, more dripping onto the ground. Flinching at the sight of his open wrists, Rosa put two fingers on the artery in his neck. Alive, barely. Still warm, just about. But that would change if they didn't treat him fast.

Niall was already calling for an ambulance. Meanwhile Rosa tugged at the sheet to try and make a tourniquet, almost slipping in the blood, swearing as she tried to rip up the fabric. Finally, she managed it, once then twice, and bound his wrists tight.

'What do we do?' Niall said.

'Wait for the ambulance. We can't leave him.'

'We'll get nothing out of him now.'

'I'm … not so sure about that.' On the bedside table under the window, Rosa had just spotted an envelope with some writing on it. 'I think he's left a note.' She picked it up. 'It says

'To whoever may find me'. Hmmm.' She took the note out of the envelope and squinted at it in the gloom. 'Any chance you can stick on the light?' Niall flicked the switch several times. Nothing. Rosa moved closer to the window and scanned through the closely written cursive. Then she threw the note down on the table. 'Tells us nothing. Other than he loved Sadhbh and wanted to go away with her, and without her he has lost his reason for living.'

'It tells us that he knew she was dead pretty soon after they found her,' Niall pointed out. 'If not before. Could be a murder–suicide jobbie.'

'Yes, but why not admit it in the note?' Rosa said. She suddenly wanted to get out of there, that teeming, unventilated caravan stinking of blood. She wanted to stick her head out in the fresh air.

'You see all sorts of things when people are not in their right mind,' Niall responded. 'The ambulance has to come from Bantry, so it'll be a good hour. We're stuck. The emergency services here are woeful.'

'I tell you what,' Rosa said, 'why don't you stay here, and I'll call Sergeant Connolly for a lift and get out to Toe Head. No point the two of us hanging about.'

Niall's response was not enthusiastic, but Rosa called the station, and Sergeant Connolly told her he'd be out in a jiffy. Rosa left Niall to stand guard in the caravan and wiped her bloody soles on the grass while watching the sun set over the Ilen river. She felt bad leaving Niall on his own with Ludwig, but she was desperately hungry and had to eat something before she went mad.

NINE

Alone in the car, Rosa allowed herself a belch. She had, in the end, thoroughly murdered a Chinese.

The indiscriminate slaughter began with a starter of innocent wontons, continued with the frantic assassination of an angelic chicken chow mein with cashew nuts, and ended with a small flimsy box of banana fritters which she ate with a plastic spoon. The crime scene was all over the passenger seat, which was covered in paper bags, takeaway cartons and small round plastic containers with satay and sweet chilli sauce.

She had received several updates from Kevin and Niall since being dropped back to the station, the most significant of which indicated that Peter Ludwig was at that moment in an ambulance en route to Bantry, but with no update on his condition. There were still traces of blood on her shoes and she wished she had time for a shower, but the Furlongs lived out on Toe Head – a promontory which was miles from anywhere, with gorgeous cliffs and useless for buying a pint of milk in a hurry – so she had to get moving.

She was glad to have a full belly at least, to get rid of the smell of blood that kicked back from her nostrils so strongly, she felt she could taste it. Seeing Peter Ludwig like that had rattled her. So much blood ... He had been in a bad way, all right. He could still die before the ambulance got to Bantry hospital. You came across scenes like these in your line of duty, of course. But it didn't mean you got used to them.

She opened the car window. The route was not particularly scenic, curving through mostly agricultural land, yet the promise of the Atlantic lingered everywhere, the smell of it, its presence beyond each bend.

Heading south, the countryside grew thinner, stragglier. Gorse replaced grass; rocky hills took over from fields. Rosa couldn't help but wonder at Sadhbh Drummond's choice of home, so far away from any urban centre. Hardly the sustainable ideal she had been aiming for.

Rosa missed the house at first. It was below the road, on a bend, surrounded by trees. By the time she saw the two gateposts and the little wooden signpost pointing to The Wanderer's Rest, she was a few yards past it. Reversing, she saw below the title, painted in red, sans-serif capitals, 'ORGANIC FARM AND SCHOOL'. Presumably another thing Sadhbh Drummond had tried her hand at. She could see that a field behind the fuchsia hedge had been partly turned to cultivation, though it was too dark to tell what had been planted. Over a small wrought-iron gate, Rosa could see a garden with a large stump in the middle of it. It jarred with Rosa, that stump. Looked out of place with everything else.

She had to turn in sharply, then execute another hairpin turn down a steep, gravelled driveway lined with overgrown viburnums and flowering montbretia. At the front of the house, two cars were already parked, taking up the available space. Unable to do a three-point turn, Rosa reluctantly squeezed the car into the remaining space, apple blossoms scattering on the bonnet as she switched off the engine, and made her way to the front door, breathing in the silence of the darkening indigo sky. The house was made of the same stone as the gateposts: a pleasant grey sandstone. Small, wooden-framed windows dotted the walls in a traditional farmhouse pattern, though on the left-hand side was a box-like extension with floor-to-ceiling tinted windows. Rosa's glance travelled to the roof, which was covered with silver-glinting solar panels, and to the right-hand side, a large rainwater barrel collected water from the gutter. The front porch was tiled terracotta red, and the oak front door was flanked by two small earthenware pots out of which grew geraniums, their scent heady in the summer air. And just under the nearest window, a wooden-seated tricycle lay on its side, front wheel up. It was always important to remember, Rosa told herself, that above everything else, Sadhbh Drummond had been the mother of two small children. Her killer had torn that family apart.

When she rang the doorbell, the sound of wind chimes gently clamoured through the hall. Rosa shifted from foot to foot, but she didn't have long to wait. The door opened only fifteen seconds or so later, and a thin, middle-aged woman in a green turtleneck top and flared trousers greeted her.

'Oh Guard, so glad you're here. We've been manning the fort for poor Ronan. It's been bedlam all day. I'm Ronan's sister, Catriona.' She smiled at Rosa. 'The younger children are off at their granny's. They don't understand yet, poor little loves. Poor Ronan, he's devastated.'

Rosa followed the woman through a hallway filled with boots and inspirational posters to a large kitchen area, which abutted onto the glass-filled extension Rosa had seen earlier. 'His wife's with him now.'

'His what?'

Catriona put her hand over her mouth. 'Oh my God, I'm sorry. Of course you're one of the lads they brought down from Cork City. I meant Jeanne, his first wife. Come on, come through.'

Ronan Furlong was sitting on a long, padded window seat, head hunched forward. A large mug of tea provided for him lay untouched on a broad, low, timber coffee table. In the kitchen, a middle-aged woman and a girl of fifteen or so also sipped tea. The girl was overweight and shy-looking, her head a mass of dark curls. The woman looked up at Rosa with an affable smile and said, 'Hello, Guard. Come on in. I know you'll want to talk to Ronan, but he's not quite up to it yet.'

Jeanne Furlong was fifty-odd, jowly and heavyset, with small, brown-hazel eyes. Around the neckline, her skin was a mixture of sunburn and freckles, and her thick mousy hair was in a blunt cut bob. It almost suited her, Rosa thought, if only she had a bit more chin to carry it. The daughter looked far less comfortable. In black jeggings and a long, shapeless knitted sweater with batwing sleeves, her gaze focused on the mug she held in front of her like a shield.

'I'll put the kettle on.' Jeanne said briskly. 'And empty Ronan's cup. He's hardly touched it, poor man.'

The girl lifted her chin. 'He won't let me sit with him. I've tried.'

'Sinead,' Jeanne said reprovingly, 'your dad needs to be alone right now. Apart from answering the guard's questions, of course.'

'But I'm family. His daughter. He should let me sit with him.' The resentment in her tone was unmistakable. But Jeanne shook her head at Sinead and clicked her tongue, and the girl relapsed into morose silence.

Rosa surveyed the kitchen. Along with the coloured mosaics and children's drawings above the counter, as well as the recessed LED lights and meticulously labelled bins – 'Plastics', 'General', 'Organic – No Meat Here!' – she could see a large flask on the counter labelled 'Hot Water'. The kettle next to it was a cheap white yoke you'd pick up in Home Store + More. It looked like nothing else in the kitchen. Jeanne must have brought it with her.

Rosa watched Jeanne as she opened the upper press and pushed aside a worn mug with 'GREENPEACE – RAINBOW WARRIOR' on it, picking out a more nondescript one and slipping in a teabag. Never mind Rosa could see clearly, on the shelf, a grey-brown pewter teapot as well as an ample selection of loose-leaf teas. Jeanne Furlong had brought her own kettle, her own teabags and very possibly even her own milk, effectively erasing her dead rival from her own kitchen.

Rosa could not help but be impressed.

The rest of the room was a typical kitchen–living area: from a shelf near a recessed television, Sadhbh and Ronan smiled back at her from a cheap gilt frame. In another, larger one, the whole family – the second – were posing in a studio backdrop. Another one of Ronan and Sadhbh had them standing, in profile, shadowed, their foreheads touching, Sadhbh heavily pregnant.

Jeanne shuffled toward her with a mug of steaming tea. 'There you are, Guard. Get that down you now. I didn't get you biscuits, I don't know what kind are kept here.'

'For God's sake, Jeanne!'

Ronan Furlong was standing in the space between kitchen and conservatory, his face livid and pale, cheeks sucked in, eyes burning and huge. About the same age as Jeanne, he wore it better, his smooth, tanned skin going well with those eyes, his greying hair attractively clipped around his temples, neatly trimmed beard a similar shade. But his blue, V-necked pullover hung loosely on him that night. Handsome as he was, at that moment he looked a bit wild. The shirt collar and cuffs were rumpled, and Rosa wondered if he had slept in them. 'We can talk in the front room,' he said tonelessly. She followed him through a door into a corridor. 'Here,' Ronan said, opening another door into a drawing room with a brick-arched fireplace and glass-doored cabinets that reminded Rosa of her friends' living rooms in the eighties. The light was already on. Ronan sucked in his breath. 'Wasteful.'

Rosa sat down opposite him on a chintz couch that nearly swallowed her up, like a soft Venus flytrap. She took a tentative sip at Jeanne's tea. It was sugared more than Rosa would have cared for.

'Mr Furlong, as you probably know by now, your wife was murdered.'

Ronan Furlong sat up very slowly, in a creaking, discontinuous motion. Even seated, he was a tall fellow. He looked down at Rosa, his blue eyes all blazing attention.

'Your family liaison person already informed me of that.' He pressed his lips together. The wild look had gone; he was all cold and collected now.

Rosa pressed on. 'Right now, it's very much an open investigation.'

'Really.'

Did Rosa detect a note of sarcasm? Either way, she ignored it and interlaced her fingers.

'We need a picture of your wife. A narrative, if you will. What I'm asking is, do you know of anyone who would have wanted your wife dead?'

Ronan Furlong laughed shortly. 'Only half the town.' When Rosa pressed him to elaborate, he just shrugged. 'Use your imagination. What do you think it was like for a woman like her in a place like this?'

'Would you like to be more specific, Mr Furlong?'

Ronan Furlong straightened his long back and looked down his long nose at Rosa. 'Well, for a start, you can look at Tom Keating. My in-laws' neighbour. He exhibits what we in education call 'oppositional defiance'.' There was an accompanying tone of 'Of course, you don't know what that is', but Rosa couldn't be bothered rising to the bait. It was all testimony, Furlong's behaviour. People grieved in different ways, true; but his eyes were dry and the wild look she'd seen in his eyes was one she had seen before in domestics. Abusers had that kind of arrogance; the false concept that they were untouchable.

'Sadhbh's family had land next to his,' Ronan continued. 'Sadhbh was using a portion for her rewilding scheme, right next to his boundary. He isn't just a thug, Inspector. His hatred is ideological. Sadhbh challenging him so often didn't help.'

'And did you not challenge him?'

'I prefer to take the softly-softly approach when it comes to local disputes. We're both Environment Party members but Sadhbh was not always ... temperate.'

Rosa decided to move on. 'And you say there were others?'

Ronan opened his mouth and seemed poised to say something. Then shut it again. Then after a pause: 'Deirdre Twamley was another one. The Muintir na hÉireann local rep. She was particularly poisonous. I could well imagine her capable of anything.'

'Sadhbh had issues with her too?' Deirdre's name had also come up on Sergeant Connolly's list, Rosa remembered.

'Sadhbh considered this area around Toe Head to be a

special conservation zone. As did I. But she would go off to County Hall and get the names of everyone applying for planning permission to build in the area, so she could lodge an objection. You just don't do that.' A crease of exasperation appeared on his brow. 'People weren't happy. We got a lot of threats. Notes. Bricks through the window.'

'Did you warn her she was playing with fire?'

'Oh God, I tried.' The first trace of emotion. 'She didn't care.'

He looked straight at Rosa now, his eyes gone all small like those of an eagle. 'Do you know 'Beautiful Lofty Things'? I take it you don't.' He stood up and started pacing about, reciting: 'Augusta Gregory seated at her great ormolu table. 'Yesterday he threatened my life. I told him that nightly from six to seven I sat at this table, The blinds drawn up."

The curtains in the room they were in were not drawn either. Rosa could see the moon coming out from behind a cloud, shining on the cars, the whitethorn and fuchsia branches painted into sharp relief. The evening had taken a rather dramatic turn, she thought, with him getting up and reciting poetry, but perhaps Furlong would loosen up a bit as a result.

'Last month they came out here to picket our house. Deirdre Twamley organised it. She and her stooges stood outside on the road waving signs and every time either of us drove out, they'd shout and bang on the car windows. The little ones were so scared. Sadhbh kept up a front, but she was frightened too. She was right to be.' Ronan looked at the nondescript carpet.

Rosa remembered looking at that first YouTube clip Eames had sent her. Sadhbh was standing at a dais, miked up, though she hardly needed it, her voice was so clear and carrying. All around were Environment Party posters as well as some that read 'Stop the Incinerator'. It helped, no doubt, that she had to command the attention of a class of teenagers. Even in the poor quality phone footage, she was crazy beautiful, Rosa thought. Her eyes were full and shining, her hair too, falling down her back.

Then the camera rested on a thin, lanky man of about forty, standing at the back, leaning against the wall in the shadows. Ronan Furlong. Younger then, wearing denims and a blue, knitted polo shirt, with a smart blue-checked collar peeking out of the polo. He continued to stare at the figure on the stage, his every limb nerved and energised, his gaze, even only in profile, rapt and full of need. Somebody interrupted him. As his hand moved, the flash of his wedding ring caught the overhead fluorescent light.

The voice behind the camera had interjected: 'That's our principal, Mr Furlong. Used to teach me history. He's a strict oul' bollocks. But even he can't resist Miss Drummond.'

Rosa continued. 'I have to ask you this, Mr Furlong—'

'I was at home. All Saturday evening.' Another pause. 'Catriona – that's my sister, you'd have met her – dropped in at about seven thirty, but until then, it was just me and the kids.'

Seven thirty. That would have given him more than enough time, had he murder on his mind.

'And when did you last see Sadhbh?'

'Just after two. She'd been at the farmer's market in Skib and was just dropping off a few things at home. She was popping out again for … I think she said she was going to swing by her parents and then meet her friend Ola for a coffee. I asked where, given the place was in the middle of another lockdown, and she snapped at me.'

So, Sadhbh had lied to her husband about where she was

going. 'How did she seem to you? You say she snapped at you. Was she disturbed, upset, in any way? Distracted?'

Ronan did not reply.

'Mr Furlong. Please. We need you to tell us everything.'

He sat back down. Still not looking at Rosa, he muttered, 'We had an argument earlier that day. Sadhbh wanted to cycle into town. I told her it wasn't safe.' Seeing Rosa's surprise, he added, 'She wouldn't wear a hi-vis.'

'She'd hardly need one in summer.'

'She wouldn't wear a helmet either. Said it was victim-blaming and that drivers should behave better. A woman on her own, going out on the roads at all hours, with the crazy traffic, and half the town against her.' He was animated now, momentarily forgetting he was picking a fight with a ghost. 'She wanted to bring the children to school on the bike with a flimsy trailer. I said absolutely not. I told her she would *not* endanger them with her reckless views. I was already dealing with protesters outside our house and the fallout from the Board of Management. She could put herself in harm's way well enough, without involving Oisin and Fionn. Every single day she starts up about that bike and how controlling I am.' He looked shocked at his own emotion, and not a little disgusted. 'God. I'm still fighting with her. She's gone.'

You certainly have a need for control, Rosa thought.

'Can we talk about the school Board of Management? I imagine that didn't help matters. They dismissed your wife, your colleague, on very spurious grounds.'

'They didn't dismiss her,' Ronan Furlong said. 'I did.'

Rosa nearly dropped her notebook. 'I beg your pardon? You dismissed Sadhbh?'

'They forced me into it after that last board meeting. I had to do it formally, in my office. I looked her in the eye the whole time. I owed her that much.' His mouth was fixed in a grim line.

'God almighty,' Rosa said in a soft whisper, 'why would they ask you to do such a thing?'

'You might ask Staunton Davies that – and Diarmuid Savage.'

'We will.' Rosa wrote the names down on her pad. 'I recall the name Staunton Davies – he's the local Progressive Ireland TD?'

'Yes. And a wealthy dairy farmer. He's got land up near Drimoleague for his seven hundred cows, and his fancy house down here. As for Diarmuid Savage –' Ronan laughed harshly – 'he's a local insurance broker. Among other things. And my brother-in-law. First one, I mean. Jeanne's his sister.'

Rosa took note. 'He didn't like Sadhbh, I take it?'

'No.'

'Because of the marriage break-up?'

'Partly.' Ronan Furlong rubbed his right eye, which was twitching. Rosa remembered the grainy footage of him at the back of that community hall, how his wedding ring flashed while he drank in Sadhbh Drummond's every word, every gesture. It was not hard to see why his first wife's family would bear a grudge.

'So that was enough to have him push you to fire your wife?'

Ronan shook his head. 'Not entirely. I mean, he disliked Sadhbh for that, but he's quite thick as thieves with Tom Keating recently. Of course, that makes sense given the history.' He said no more, as if he expected Rosa to know what he was talking about. And she did – because that was how history worked in this country; it seeped into the ground and rose up like radon gas, so you breathed it in and it slowly contaminated you. You didn't even have to name it. It became odourless.

Rosa discreetly checked her phone: quarter past nine. It was getting late; the solar-powered lanterns dotted around the driveway outside were now providing useful light. She rose. 'Mr Furlong, thank you very much. You've been very helpful to us at a difficult time for you.'

Ronan Furlong barely acknowledged her thanks.

'One question. Do you know a Peter Ludwig?'

His expression darkened. 'He's a scumbag.' The word from his precise, particular mouth sounded unintentionally hilarious. 'I'd say he never did an honest day's work in his life. He was a bad influence.'

'On Sadhbh?'

Ronan Furlong rose to his full height, a good seven inches on her. 'Inspector, you understand how things get done in this country, yes? Horse-trading, deals, patience. It's infuriating, but you need to move incrementally. That is, step by step.'

Rosa wanted to tell him she knew full well what 'incremental' meant. He was such a teacher.

'You entertain the likes of Staunton Davies, who wouldn't know biodiversity from a combine harvester. You smile, empathise. Ludwig didn't bother with that. He just pulled stunts. Sadhbh fell in with him and the Extinction Rebellion crowd, and she got more extremist. Sadhbh was always too black-and-white in her thinking, and she got worse after meeting him. Then the party kicked her out.' He was morose. 'I told them I'd leave with her, but Isabel Connolly phoned me personally and asked me to stay.'

So, he was on close terms with the Environment Party leader. He must have influence there. Something to follow up, maybe. Rosa made a note to contact Isabel Connolly as soon as possible.

'I must ask. Were they close, Sadhbh and Peter?'

Ronan Furlong responded with a long, pointed shrug. 'You wouldn't be asking me if you didn't already know, would you?'

Rosa did not reply. Behind the arrogant, cold front, she could sense his anguish. And jealousy could provoke a man's rage ... In someone so controlled as Ronan Furlong, once their rage broke, it would surely be like a roaring river.

'It hardly matters now,' he said. 'I can't fight for someone who's gone. I can't persuade them to see sense. It's too late.' His energy was gone, his face bleak and emptied out. The ceiling lamp, a discoloured shade of wicker rattan, reflected its pattern in the single-glazed window. They must have run out of funds for a retrofit.

'We will find whoever did this.' Rosa intended her words to hover over the gap between reassurance and threat, but Ronan looked unexcited.

He shrugged again. 'That's as may be.'

Rosa let him open the varnished pine, glass-panelled door back out into the corridor. Seeing her out, Ronan paused briefly, his eyes tawny as they focused on her.

'I'd have changed nothing.'

'Eh?'

'Meeting Sadhbh.' His face contorted and he turned away. 'I knew it would be hard. I gave it all up for her. My marriage, my reputation, everything. For someone who never needed to compromise. Her position in society was always guaranteed. I married the planter's daughter, and I paid the price.'

Again, Rosa was silent. She sensed he was quoting again, but could not tell from where. Nevertheless, it seemed to her that the opposite was true – that he had kept his job, his status, his income, while hers had all gone, much of it at his hands. And he was intelligent, so he was surely aware.

After a decent interval of time had passed, she said, 'You do understand we will have to execute a search warrant here?'

At that Ronan Furlong opened his eyes wide and allowed himself a sarcastic smile. 'Are *you* unaware we were broken into just two weeks ago? Surely you should have had this information?' He had that clipped, annoyed tone now. 'Why am I the one having to tell you this? When I insisted on reporting it to Sergeant Connolly myself?'

'What was taken?' Rosa took out her small jotter.

'Nothing.' Ronan cut across her thoughts. 'Nothing that we could see. They just left our study in a mess.'

Rosa straightened up at that. 'So, this was not a regular burglary? They were looking for documents, I take it?'

'I said all this to the sergeant.' Ronan folded his arms and leaned against the wall. 'I would have thought he'd have passed it on to you.'

Oh God, this man with his 'I would have thought' and 'Surely, you're aware'. The verbal equivalent of picking at the flesh around a cuticle.

Ronan sighed, realising he would have to repeat the information. 'I don't know what they were looking for. Nothing of value was missing. My guess would be something legal, given they messed up that section of our filing cabinet and threw out half the folders. But I don't know. I think Sadhbh knew quite well, though.' His lips thinned. 'She was not at all eager to go to the guards. Hardly said a word in the station. I had to manage it all.'

Rosa remembered the voluminous file of Sadhbh's complaints Sergeant Connolly had shown him earlier. 'From what I've been told, that wasn't like her.'

Ronan gave her a disapproving look. 'Is that supposed to be a joke, Inspector?'

Rosa's cheeks burned. They'd been both standing in the corridor for several minutes, Ronan leaning one shoulder against a wall, Rosa trying to stay straight when she was bloody tired of being interrogated by someone she was supposed to be interrogating.

'Is there any way I can access her laptop? Her files?'

He gestured at another similar door. 'Through there. It's our office.'

'Any passwords or tips I need to know?'

'No.' Ronan Furlong turned his back on Rosa and disappeared back into the kitchen. He obviously hadn't liked that question. Had he put on that surprise? Was he just a good actor?

There was something about his manner, something standoffish, that originated in a mood deeper than grief.

Chief suspect.

TEN

Rosa was surprised to feel a blast of cool air as she went into the Furlongs' office. Closing the door behind her – feeling it drag on the carpet – she switched on the light. A fluorescent bulb groaned, switched, hummed, then blinked on.

The strip was just above the ancient-looking desktop computer monitor, while the keyboard was on a pull-out table. But where was the laptop? The sooner they got it to HQ where they might find a password breaker, the better. Ronan hadn't known the password for Sadhbh's laptop. Not knowing must have been a reminder of Sadhbh concealing things from him. Rosa had seen the look in his eyes when she had mentioned Ludwig: that dull, angry flash. He had not been happy.

Eventually, Rosa found the laptop under a shoebox of papers, which she duly sifted through. Then she spotted the Post-It note. Virulent purple, barely hanging onto the monitor table. If she flicked at it with her finger, it would give up the ghost and float away to the nearest carpet or dustbin. Right in front of her, how could she have missed it? Username: sadhbh1. Password: realtinfionn16.

If this were it, Ronan needn't have worried about Sadhbh being secretive after all.

Could it really be that easy, though? Well, she would find out. Slipping on a pair of gloves, she flipped open the laptop. *Welcome, sadhbh1, please enter your password.* Bingo. She was in. And better still, Sadhbh's open browser immediately popped up. One of the tabs said 'Inbox (7)'. Seven messages their intended recipient would never now read. Funny how dead people could have something approaching a second life on social media: auto-tweets from their account saying who had unfollowed them, the username on Teams still there in your chat history, a small grey 'x' beside their name the only indicator that they were offline – permanently.

Offline. But not gone. Unfinished business, still.

Of the seven unread messages, one of them was a subscription renewal notice for *Irish Wildlife* magazine, the next a circular from the Secondary Teachers' Union of Ireland. The remaining messages were bundled under one 'conversation' labelled 'Edward, me'. The latest date stamp was Monday at 3 a.m. So Edward, whoever he was, must have written it. His full email address was ejf72966@gmail.com – an address, Rosa guessed, he had created for the sole purpose of corresponding with Sadhbh.

She scrolled down to the beginning. No greetings, just:

Why did you leave that message on my phone? I played it back and heard your foul language and defamatory statements. It was a highly inappropriate communication. Only out of consideration for your current mental health circumstances I shall stay silent, but do not provoke me again. Leave me alone – and leave my wife alone. E.

Good Lord. This was some turn-up for the books. Sadhbh's reply:

I left a message to avoid an email trail. Good luck suing me for slander – I've got all the letters saved. And the airline ticket to Liverpool. You'll be glad to hear I'm flight-free now, Edward. I know you were responsible for getting me kicked out. I heard it from the horse's mouth. You destroyed my life once, and I kept quiet, but now you want to do it again?

Sadhbh

PS. Don't you think it's a bit late in the day to be worrying about your wife?

Holy shit. Rosa grabbed her phone. Kevin had given her his number earlier that day, before they left Cork. She rang it immediately.

'Inspector.'

'Kevin, can we do a search and see if we can identify everyone in Sadhbh's circle who might know someone called Edward?'

'Just Edward?'

'Yup. And someone who knew Sadhbh some time ago, it seems. There may have been a pregnancy involved.' Privately, Rosa was sure there had been. Anyone who had lived in Ireland before 2018 knew exactly what 'airline ticket to Liverpool' meant.

'OK.' Kevin hung up, and Rosa kept on reading. The correspondence went on in similar vein: Edward blustering and threatening, Sadhbh growing ever more bitter.

Sadhbh's last communication to Edward was dated April 29th. He'd said to her:

You need to move on with your life and stop making these hysterical threats. I love Jane. Live with it.

So, Edward was married to someone called Jane. That … didn't narrow it down much. Rosa rang Kevin again.

'He's married to someone called Jane.'

Kevin, to his credit, didn't tell her to get stuffed. 'Jane. OK. I'll make a note. Bye.' Beep.

Sadhbh's reply:

That's cute, Edward. Nice to know, if irrelevant. I've rung that journalist. Told him everything.

Edward had not been happy at that one. His response was, to put it politely, vituperative and of no evidential value. Except for the time sent – barely fifteen minutes after Sadhbh's reply. Whatever Sadhbh had on him, she had him good and rattled, that was for sure.

A knock on the door, which was then pushed open before Rosa could say yes.

'I thought you might like some more tea, Guard.' Jeanne entered with a tray and a packet of biscuits.

Not now, for fuck's sake! Rosa hit 'Minimise'.

'I'm in the middle of something,' she snapped. Jeanne put the tray down with a small, pointed thud. Then a tut, and an indrawn breath, as she produced a tissue from her sleeve – who did *that* any more? – and wiped up the slop from the inevitable spill.

'Sorry for disturbing you, Guard,' she said, while continuing to disturb. 'Poor Ronan. It's been terrible for him.' Rosa said nothing. 'I'll go now, then.' She hovered a few moments longer and then – finally! – went out, leaving the door just that little bit ajar. *At last, thank Christ.* Rosa got up and closed the door, before returning to the screen.

There was little else to read, but the date stamps told the whole story.

Sent: May 1, 2021 00:11 p.m. UTC

Sadhbh, I have emailed my solicitor. Expect a letter shortly. Do not continue with this course of action. I'm warning you.

Sent: May 1, 2021 03:15 a.m. UTC
Sadhbh – answer now!
Sent: May 2, 2021 09:20 a.m. UTC
Due to the bank holiday the letter will be sent on Tuesday.
Sadhbh, can we talk? We can discuss this, and I can ask David
to recall the letter. E.
Sent: May 2, 2021, 10.01 a.m. UTC
Sadhbh – are you there?
By then, of course, it was too late.

Rosa took pictures on her phone, closed the laptop, and
decided she would bring it with her. She blinked a couple of
times. It had been a long day since the Super's phone call.
She'd been on the go for most of it, and she was seriously
flagging. She'd get back into Skib and be done for the day.
Perhaps ask Ronan Furlong who this Edward fellow was.

As she was preparing to leave, Rosa heard an almighty
crash and some shouting and roaring. Female voices,
imploring and crying.

'You're very cruel, Ronan.' Jeanne, tearful. Then steps on
the gravel, *crunch, crunch*, the sound of a car starting. Then an
unnatural, high-pitched roar that surely could not come from
the lank, supercilious teacher she had just interviewed.
Surely?

Rosa ran to the kitchen in time to see Ronan Furlong fling
one of the kitchen presses open and pull out a frying pan.
Lifting it high in the air, he crashed it down on the kitchen
table, shouting unspeakable curses. And like a mantra he
repeated: 'I'll kill you. I'll kill you.'

Rosa, entirely forgotten, stood in the doorway, watching in
horror. This man was mad. Dangerous.

It seemed to go on forever, though in reality, it probably
wasn't more than two minutes. What broke the trance was a
low vibration whose source Rosa could not divine. Until

Ronan Furlong came out of his trance and looked at his watch. God almighty, he was wearing a Fitbit! How come she had not noticed that before?

'Mr Furlong.' She approached him, tentatively. They were alone, him, her and the frying pan. And the Fitbit wouldn't save her. Intense activity recorded.

'I heard something. I ... was checking to see if you were OK.'

Ronan blinked and then looked at Rosa as if she'd mortally offended him. 'What are you still doing here?'

'I ...' Why did she feel awkward when *he'd* just had a freakout?

'Leave.' He gripped the counter. The fury had returned; it was there in his eyes like a cold flame. The fridge broke into a hum, a false reassurance; as if everything were normal; as if this household hadn't been shattered in a weekend.

'Mr Furlong, I'm sorry about this, but might you know who Edward is?'

Ronan swayed. 'Edward?' he gasped. 'I'm sorry, Inspector ... I haven't a clue.' From the look of him, he seemed to be telling the truth, though Rosa reckoned he'd prevaricate with Pontius Pilate.

'OK. Mr Furlong, would you mind handing over that Fitbit?'

Ronan Furlong's eyes seemed to shrink until they were all pupil. With a cold look, he slowly unbuckled the watch and handed it over to Rosa without a word.

'And your phone as well, please.'

'No.' He drew back.

'We need the phone to examine the data from the watch.' Of course, Ronan knew all this. 'I could always get forensics to pick it up—'

'Over there.' He pointed at the kitchen counter. It started

vibrating. Rosa grabbed it and saw 'Jeanne' flash up. Ronan shook his head imploringly and she pressed Reject. The vibration stopped.

'Thank you.' Ronan sounded tired.

'No worries.' She didn't know what else to say.

Then he turned away and Rosa knew she would get no more out of him.

ELEVEN

The hotel bar was serving, but Covid regulations and the warm night had all the drinkers outside, sipping from large plastic pint receptacles on plywood benches and tables. These overflowed the footpath, a risky endeavour given the amount of through traffic on the route, but there was a good crowd, including Kevin and Rosa, who had just been served two sloppy Carlsbergs by a paper-masked bartender standing by a half-door on the river side of the building.

'A wet pub,' Kevin commented. He was in civvies: black short-sleeved shirt and tan trousers. With his arms folded and a silver watch around his left wrist, he looked handsome in a solid, blockish way. He meant: no food.

'What a phrase,' Rosa laughed. 'Conjures up all sorts. How did you get on with Keating?'

Xiao wiped a bit of head foam off his upper lip with a tissue. 'No luck. We had to let him go. He denies he set the second fire, but his only alibi for the night of Sadhbh's murder is his wife. He was at home, he says.' Xiao was meticulously clean-shaven, Rosa noticed, so much so that the pores on his lip were visible.

'So, what did he say about Sadhbh Drummond?'

Xiao smiled thinly. 'It was obvious he hated her. He was very obsessed about his land. Said she wanted to take it away from him again, and he would set himself on fire before he'd let that happen.' He swigged back a mouthful of beer and exhaled.

'He's a great one for setting things on fire.'

'Allegedly.' Kevin Xiao lifted his pint once more and his watch panel caught the glow of one of the overhead street-lamps. A volley of laughter from a few lads in football shirts erupted into the air. A little breeze got up, and Rosa felt surprisingly chilly. She wished she had a shawl to wrap around herself.

'Forensics are running tests on the van prints,' Xiao's deep, metallic voice interrupted her thoughts, 'so I wanted to keep him until they came through, because if it's his van, that's a game changer. But Sean said we needed to charge him with arson and let him go, for the file.'

'He's got a van?'

Xiao nodded. 'White Ford Transit.'

'Bloody hell,' Rosa said, 'why is it always a white Ford Transit?' Kevin was about to tell her, so she added, 'Rhetorical question.'

They downed their pints, and it was Kevin's round. More of the same, Rosa requested, and Kevin duly waved down the passing waiter.

'I had the devil of a time with Ronan Furlong,' she said, after the waiter had left. 'He's a slippery fish and he's got a nasty, violent streak.' Rosa told Kevin of what she'd seen and heard, the demented, unblinking rage of the man banging a frying pan down on a kitchen table.

Xiao was wide-eyed. 'Why did you not arrest him?'

'Believe me, I considered it. But it's not a crime to smash up your own kitchen.' Rosa shook her head. 'If it's him, he'll break cover eventually. They always do.'

She checked her phone. It was almost one in the morning, and she had no messages. Much to her relief.

'Two Carlsbergs.' The waiter put them down, leaning over Rosa to set them on the table, not very socially distanced.

'Oh yeah,' she said, picking up her second pint, 'about that guy, Edward, did you—' But before she could finish her sentence, their table clattered and half of Rosa's beer was gone, slipping between the timber slats until it was on the ground like a pool of wee.

'Jesus!' Rosa swore, righting the glass and saving the last quarter of beer. 'What the ...?'

'Begod, I'm so sorry.' The speaker was a well-built elderly man who wore a peaked tweed cap and loose trousers. He was a bit red in the face, the light from the brazier showing the coarse veins of someone who might have drunk too much at some time in their life. With his chalky-blue cardigan and loose twill trousers, he looked like something out of a John Hinde postcard. But in the crook of his arm, he held a very smart-looking hardback with a glossy jacket.

That must have been what had upended Rosa's beer.

'Can I buy you another one?'

'I'm fine, thanks.' The last thing Rosa needed right now was for this fellow to sit down and join them. Xiao, however, was looking at the book with some interest.

'*Ghastly Crimes of the Night*,' he read out in his characteristic monotone. "A Telling of the Struggle Between Harry Keating and the Drummond Family, and the Protestant Murders of 1921.' By Denis Geraghty.' He half-turned to face the old man. 'Is Harry the grandfather of Tom Keating?'

'He is indeed,' Dinny Geraghty said, 'and you can have the book for your trouble. Go on, it's my present.' Before Xiao could object, the large oblong item was there in front of him, lined up beside his pint. 'Have a read of it there now, while you're at it.'

The detective dutifully opened the book. 'Nice finish,' he commented, running his finger down the title page. 'Glossy.'

'Oh, I only wanted the best.'

Dinny sat down beside Rosa, and she could smell a mix of pipe smoke, musty clothes and body odour. 'None of this 'lash out a couple pages and stick it up on Amazon' foolery. And I'll hazard a guess too why you're enquiring about Tom Keating. That rat-bastard up the hill—'

'Are you at it again, Dinny?' Another of the waiters interrupted him, hand in the air with a tray of empty glasses. This man was older, in his thirties, with wide blue eyes, blond hair and an Eastern European accent, tinged with a bit of Cork. 'Bothering the customers? We've hardly been open a week since lockdown.' But he was laughing, and Dinny loudly declared that he himself was a customer, he was bothering nobody, and he would buy two …? Carlsbergs for his new friends.

Rosa, very aware she was still on duty, could not help but cringe. Three pints, well, two and a half thanks to Dinny Geraghty, was wandering into hangover territory, and she'd need her wits about her tomorrow.

When the waiter left, Dinny leaned in and said in a much lower tone, 'The dogs in the street know why you're here. It was all over the news this morning. Poor Sadhbh. I've known her family all me life; used to chat to her when she was knee high to a grasshopper and I was working out the fields. Fished on their land and never a bad word from them when I got the odd trout.' He sighed. 'You reckon it was Keating?

He's a bad lot. I wouldn't be surprised. Not at all happy about my book. Told me he'd sue, God knows what for. Everything his grandfather did is on the public record.'

'We are keeping an open mind at the moment,' Rosa said, wishing the waiter would come back. Kevin Xiao was still absorbed in the book, slowly turning the pages. Dinny put his hand on Rosa's elbow.

'Listen, Guard. Before you know anything else, you need to know this about Sadhbh Drummond. You've probably seen photos and videos and the like, but never the woman herself in her true beauty. There was a Traveller woman, Mary Bird, long since passed on now, once told me that when she saw Sadhbh walking up Market Street, she fell to her knees, the girl was so beautiful. There was once a poem, 'twas only a short one, but it said it all. 'O, she was the Sunday of every week.' You know it, I'd say. 'The Planter's Daughter.''

'I do.' Rosa felt a shiver go down her spine. 'I married the planter's daughter,' Ronan had said earlier. The unnatural stillness about that holy well and the Virgin Mary with the coloured ribbons. The famine road. The old hatreds, buried with the dead who must have fallen down, starving, in their droves trying to build that pointless road. She did not tell Dinny that she had met Sadhbh before.

'I was terrible shook up to hear about what happened to her, but not altogether surprised,' Dinny went on. 'She fought for nature, and that's fine and noble, but it made a lot of people angry.' His eyes were wet. 'Guards, if you can do one thing, read that book. Youse can have it free, gratis and for nothing. I think when you read it, you will understand a lot about this town, and about Sadhbh Drummond. I think it might help ye both.'

The waiter came back with two more Carlsbergs. Rosa fumbled for her credit card as the waiter held out his machine, but Dinny assured them the drinks were on him, handed over a dirty twenty euro note, and as suddenly as he had joined them, took his leave.

'That's awkward,' Xiao noted as Dinny left, his shambling step brushing the edges of the table. 'He could be a potential witness and he's buying us drinks.'

'And you're drinking them.' It was true; Kevin Xiao had put the book down and was sipping away.

'I once had a murderer offer me a cup of tea. He'd just battered his wife to death in a drunken row and was trying to pass it off as an accident.'

'Did you drink it?'

Xiao shook his head. 'I didn't like the way he made it. Too much milk.'

After the third beer, Rosa and Kevin agreed to call it a night, donned their masks and went inside. The hotel was festooned with signs on the walls and arrows on the corridors denoting a two-metre distance. But they didn't encounter anyone else in the corridor. People were obviously still spooked by the lockdowns.

In spite of the deserted feeling in the hotel, the two rooms they booked had a shared bathroom. Rosa's room was a twin, with nondescript beige walls, red concertina curtains on the windows and an old-fashioned corner TV. From the brief glance into Kevin's room, apart from a double bed, it was the same. Eames must have penny-pinched, but surely the hotel owner could have managed rooms with en suites? Especially now when business was, of necessity, not particularly brisk.

But it was clean and quiet, and would do. Rosa changed into a nondescript T-shirt with the logo of a software conference that had been held an embarrassingly long time ago. The walls were thin and the bathroom separated the two rooms; she could hear Kevin Xiao running the tap. Too tired to get out and wait, she instead hastily brushed her teeth with the travel brush she'd brought along, swallowing back the foamy spit and wiping her mouth and brush with her fingers. That done she warily switched the phone on and hooked it into its charger. Hopefully, there would be no messages during the night either. No taunting little pop-ups on her screen with the name that chased her during the night. She liked that Kevin Xiao only called her 'Inspector'; that he kept up the formalities. Not because she was power-hungry about such things, no. It was because she did not have to hear that name: the one that was no longer hers but which she could not relinquish.

~~Gerry~~.

TWELVE

~~Gerry, Gerry, Gerry.~~

As the pipes in the bathroom clanked and the water heater inexplicably hissed in the middle of the night, Rosa sat up in bed, reached out for the glass on her nightstand, and sipped away at the brackish tap water. The sounds outside, with everyone dispersing, had faded now, until all that could be heard through the half-open upper windowpane was the intermittent howl of a fox near the riverbank.

Oh how she hated that name. Every time someone said it, she felt a little piece of her die. She wished that every time someone used it, something like the *Father Ted* scene would happen, where bells would ring and trollies would crash whenever Mrs Doyle's Christian name was mentioned, rendering it inaudible.

But it wasn't only the sound. The *sight* of it made her cringe too. Having to put that name at the bottom of every email she sent. If she could have typed it in an invisible font colour she would have done. Or strike it out completely, for once and for all. Scribble all over it until it was invisible. Write her new name in the margin as a correction.

Rosa had known she was a girl since she was five, but kept it to herself all those years, until she was discovered by Louise, her wife, who had found that secret diary Rosa kept, the one with a swirling moleskin cover from the V&A in London, with her true name on the inside flyleaf. In cramped, edgy writing, the pages described her longing to dress like a woman, the forbidden thrill of doing so. Louise, reading it, probably thought it was a fetish. It wasn't. The thrill was from authenticity. Being true to oneself.

Rosa would not forget that day in a hurry, how a once affectionate face she had known, kissed and seen through two births, had contorted itself into the contempt and rage she'd seen in black-and-white photos of white women booing black children entering white schools in the US. How she'd been given ten minutes to pack her bags and leave the bungalow in Glanmire she and Lou had lived in for the last decade. How she wasn't even let drive off but had to walk down the driveway and ring for a taxi. How any attempt to explain or plead mercy had only been met with 'I can destroy you with a single phone call.'

Worst of all, Lou was right. Why else had Rosa kept this secret for so long?

All her life:

Gerry, that's the girls' section.

Gerry, leave those scarves alone. You look weird stroking them.

Gerry, why aren't you trying out for the hurling?

She remembered the day she did try out, bare knees pimpling in the cold, hating the shiny shorts and the older boys with their masks and mouthguards, their faces gurning derisively at her. The feel of the smooth ash stick slipping through her hands, the rough jersey padding brush her palms. The damp chill in the air. Jim Delaney, the coach, yelling out all the rules. The deadening shriek of the whistle as she lumbered behind the others, the grass pitch churned to muck by their school runners.

She knew girls also played hurling, though they called it camogie. But there was a grace about them that she did not possess. She had ~~Gerry~~'s knock knees, ~~Gerry~~'s earthy, tangy armpit stink, ~~Gerry~~'s— But there was no need to go on. Rosa's first go at GAA try-outs had been her last.

She'd joined the Gardaí out of pure bloody-mindedness. Her father had looked her up and down and said, 'Are you sure you're able for it, ~~Ger~~?' With that provocation, she'd striven to prove them all wrong – most of all herself.

Training to get in shape, the entity known as ~~Gerry~~ could squat lift one hundred kilos, and deadlift nearly twice that. His sprints were four minutes a kilometre. He managed eight burpees in twenty seconds, almost enough to join the US Marines. Surely after all that, this thing in his head called Rosa would shut up and realise he was a man?

But no matter how many weights she put on that bar, lifting them above her head with a gasping roar, Rosa Keane was still a woman. And when she realised that fact, she wept. Because as well as joining the Guards, she had become engaged to Louise Brehony, daughter of the local solicitor.

There was no way out now. No way she could tell the truth. Ever. There were no transgender people in the small village she lived in near Clogherhead. The only trans people she knew about were Chelsea Manning and, well, Caitlyn Jenner. She would quash the knowledge forever.

But the truth had come out all the same.

In the middle of all the chaos, misery and pain after Lou had kicked her out, Rosa had been able to take the first tentative steps towards establishing her identity. The letter that had arrived just that morning was an appointment with the National Gender Service in Loughlinstown Hospital. These were like gold dust. It was a miracle she had got one that early.

On the other side of the coin, it hurt like hell not to be able to see her daughter. To hear the long beep of a terminated call. To not be able to explain why she had disappeared from their lives so quickly. There had been a few times when she had wept uncontrollably thinking about it.

'You cry like a woman,' her father used to mock her. She couldn't appreciate the comment, not even ironically. If her father held regular women in such contempt, what would he think of her, once he knew the truth?

Perhaps with this new Gender Identity process, Lou wouldn't have her over a barrel as she did now. Rosa could start to make things official. Perhaps even at work …

Rosa wondered what Kevin Xiao would make of it all. Perhaps he would be understanding. After all, he too knew what it was like to be different. But then again, she hardly knew the man, and he wasn't the one she'd need to placate. She could only imagine the Super's face if she told him. Mind you, if there was anything she hated more than being called 'Gerry', it was being called 'Gerry' in a Northern Irish accent you could strip paint off a wall with.

These thoughts during the small hours were all too familiar to Rosa. Especially when she couldn't sleep. Her unmentionables were sweaty, and when she turned on the bedside light, some insect slumbering there came to life, indignantly banging and buzzing against it.

For want of anything else to distract her, she picked up Dinny's book and flipped to the contents page.

And there was the chapter she was looking for. 'A Telling of the Struggle Between Harry Keating and the Drummond Family, and the Protestant Murders of 1921.'

THIRTEEN

June 1921

It was told that Harry Keating had been the first man at Soloheadbeg to kill a Black and Tan one-on-one. No guns, not even a knife, just his bare hands. Some even said he'd travelled up to Gort for the sole purpose of taking a potshot at Lady Gregory through a window. That particular story was a lie. Harry had no interest in killing an old woman, particularly someone who had written such beautiful plays as Augusta Gregory. Being neither a boor nor a philistine, he didn't particularly have an interest in killing anyone – he just saw it as part of his duty for the struggle for Ireland. Besides, if he'd been out to kill her, he wouldn't have missed.

But lies or truth, his name was feared and admired all through County Cork. So when Stephen Rooney's sorrowing mother came to him in the months just before the War of Independence came to a truce, he agreed with her immediately that something had to be done.

Harry didn't have to hear the story from her lips; it had been in the copy of the *Skibbereen Eagle* that Delia Minehane had brought him, along with his breakfast, just the day before in their safe house on the Elgin Road. The Minehanes were allied with the cause, and Harry could stay with them in the middle of the town and fear no betrayal. Just as well, since the peelers were out in droves, and the town was on heat with anger.

It happened like this: one night just that August, Stephen had sneaked into the grounds of Liss Ard and managed to break the lock on one of the sashed windows of the Drummonds' fine drawing room. Although surrounded by ornaments and priceless works of art, all Stephen Rooney wanted was to feed his family. There were nine children, and he was the eldest. Stephen's mother had had her latest baby two months ago and her milk was nearly drying up: the poor baby ailing and listless with hunger. All the acts of protection against tenants in arrears had done nothing for his family because his father drank away all the money.

Stephen had broken in, managed to find the well-stocked larder and pocket a hunk of cheddar wrapped in greaseproof paper. Then a jug of milk, poured into the first bottle he could find. Then the rush of cold air as the door opened, the flash of light and all those dark kitchen corners suddenly lit up.

In the doorway stood Herbert Frost, Penelope Drummond's grown nephew, in full military uniform, regimental flash glinting. Pressed against his shoulder, pointing directly at Stephen, was a hunting rifle. Frost's eyes were burning and blank at the same time.

Stephen was not to know that Herbert, barely three years after the Great War had ended, could still hardly sleep for nightmares about Germans and his own men being blown to bits in front of him; or that habitually he spent the early hours of the morning pacing the floorboards of his first-floor bedroom, wearing his colours, trying with each pace to walk away the piercing bayonet of guilt and hypervigilance that refused to let him be at peace for a single night. Stephen was not to know that Herbert, like a sleepwalker, both knew where he was, but did not know. Stephen only knew one thing: he had to run – and fast.

He lowered his head and charged at Herbert, knocking him over as he leaped up the stone steps, dashing out the front door, setting off Bran, the family Labrador, into a fit of barking and running about. It was dawn by then, and Stephen's figure was no longer a dark enigma as he fled across the huge expanse of front lawn, down to the driveway, the gateposts a marker in the distance. He was an easy mark, nearly hallucinating from weakness and a brutal stitch in his side, which he could not clasp, so laden down was he with foodstuffs. But he was almost there …

And then Herbert, poised and still on the granite front steps of Liss Ard House, his gun raised and his eye screwed into the sights, pulled the trigger.

A split second later Stephen was down, the grass rushing up at him, its scent sharp and sweet, everything hyper-real yet like a slow dream. The grass covered in spilt flour, the milk leaking from the broken bottle, soaking his flannel trousers. As he lay there, the blood started to gush out internally, darkening his skin, and he felt pain like he had never known before. Somehow he found it in himself to tear off a piece of his shirt, which happened to be white, or close enough to it, and wave it in the air. To make sure his assailant understood, with great pain and difficulty, young Stephen Rooney rose to his feet, his hands in the air, his makeshift, bloodstained flag flying.

Then Herbert fired again.

Stephen Rooney had no chance.

In the tumult that followed, with the squire and his lady

and their servants all out in their dressing gowns and slippers, Patrick the stableboy attended to Stephen as best he could, while Mrs Drummond telephoned a Roman Catholic priest to perform the last rites. Meanwhile, Herbert stood there like a stone, gun emptied, swinging from his shoulder, as if the bloody scene had nothing to do with him. Even when Constable Corcoran from the RIC barracks came up to put steel around his wrists, he neither complied, nor rebelled. He was back in a dark, dark world.

The inquest took place shortly afterwards. Herbert's lawyer declared he had acted in self-defence, and he was released. There was never a trial, because Herbert was of good family and had never offended before. The Rooney boy was notorious for stealing: he had a record as long as your arm. A low murmur of rageful dissent had broken out when the coroner announced the verdict. Stephen's mother wailed and wept, and then, with five of her younger children in tow, was advised to meet Harry Keating at a safe location. And Harry put his arms around her and told her he was sorry indeed for her trouble.

That was how Harry found himself, that late summer night, softly treading the drying grass on that same wide expanse of lawn where Stephen Rooney had fled and Herbert Frost had taken him down. He, Michael Savage and Sean Furlong crept along the lawn wearing balaclavas and carrying pistols, the truck parked a discreet distance away. Harry would not in all honesty have chosen either man, but the war had reached its apogee: Cork was still under martial law from the British, and the IRA was severely down on men all over the country. Many of his friends were in prison, in hiding or buried in unmarked graves. The truce was barely a week away. For a personal favour? Harry needed to take what he could get.

It was a warm midsummer night, the sky never fully black, not even at midnight. The three men forced the huge door open. Bran leapt up, but Harry, prepared with a Stanley knife in hand, grasped the Labrador's collar in one hand, and with the other, slit the dog's throat ear to ear, then dropped him to the stone floor to bleed out.

'Fine work,' Sean Furlong declared, regarding the dog's corpse.

'Well, it'll all be for nothing if you don't shush,' Harry replied, carefully wiping his bloodied shoes on the horsehair doormat. Christ, that stuff was sticky.

'Them Prods always love their animals,' Michael Savage said dolefully. 'They treat their dogs better than they treat us.'

'Will ye shut up?' Harry hissed. 'Let's get to work.'

On his mark, guns loaded, they charged up the stairs to the first-floor bedrooms and rushed the men out: Arthur Drummond, his young son Theodore, seventeen, and home from his first term at Oxford, and Herbert, who was in uniform once more, even at midnight. It was work Harry had done before, not often, but enough that he could approach it without either sentimentality or vengeful aggression. Ignoring the screaming women and children, stepping over the huge dog corpse, they bound and gagged the three males and dragged them into the back of the truck. The truck originally belonged to the Brits; Michael had told him that his father had recovered it from an ambush Liam Lynch's crowd had carried out down in the Nire valley a week back and you could still see bloodstains from the slaughtered Auxiliaries on the wooden slats at the truck's base. A likely story, Harry thought, but if there were any truth in it and their captives saw those traces in the faltering early light, they would surely be scared to death of what might be to come.

The truck had come with something else useful. Grenades.

On Harry's orders, as he and Michael drove out, Sean Furlong stayed behind and set each one off in an act of careful sequence. For all its granite finery and panelled smugness, Liss Ard burned as hot and hard as any house would: the flames searing out the windows, the roof falling in, the walls blackened with soot, the whole structure unrecoverable. As they drove away, parking up past the entrance and waiting for Sean, the glow of the fire threatened to cast them in stark relief. Old oaks that had been there since Elizabeth I's invasion were turned to skeleton and ash. The screams from Liss Ard would chill most men's blood, but Harry remained unmoved. This was necessary war.

But then, once Sean Furlong hopped on the back of the truck with Harry, Michael Savage and the captives, and they drove off to Knockalisha to deal with the Drummonds, things happened that were, to Harry's mind, not necessary. Not necessary at all.

Back in Skibbereen the following morning, once the truck had been safely parked and concealed, Harry and his pro tem comrades went back to the Minehanes and had a slap-up breakfast: sausages, rashers, black pudding from Clonakilty, all washed down with mugs of strong tea to keep them awake for the day ahead. It helped that Tom Minehane was the local butcher, and Delia was a fine cook. Harry would have preferred to dine alone, but the lads insisted on accompanying him, and given that he had importuned them in the first place, it seemed only fair to allow them enjoy the breakfast, even if it meant betraying his whereabouts. He didn't like to do that, endangering Tom and Delia – they were like mother and father to him. Having no children of their own and well into their forties, they had taken the volunteer boys to their heart and lavished all their affection on them.

Harry would not be going to Mass either. The events of

the previous night still troubled him. No confessional, no dithering Father Whooley whispering in a reedy voice to tell him his sins, would ease his mind about those Drummond lads, particularly Theodore. In truth, he'd shed no tears about killing Herbert Frost; shell shock was not an excuse that moved him any more, not after Captain Bowen-Colthurst shooting an unarmed Frankie Sheehy Skeffington like a dog in the street, and bleating shell shock in his defence afterwards. Bloodthirsty to a man, those war veterans, the Irish ones too. But Arthur Drummond ... And, especially, Theodore ... That was different. He was just a boy, a frightened, harmless boy.

Harry knew, too, that he was no longer safe. Not after such an audacious crime, and the peelers being on the move. Once the lads had gone, he would have to pack up and be on the move again himself. He would leave no note, he decided. Nothing that would implicate the Minehanes.

Harry Keating was not a man who kept many possessions, not after a year on the run. A letter from Noreen, his wife. A magnifying glass, to start a fire. His service pistol. Two pairs of briefs and an extra flannel shirt, a toothbrush, and a St Christopher medal – a gift from his late mother.

With any luck, he thought, draining the last of the tea, he would be out of the house before the Minehanes returned from Mass.

FOURTEEN

Extract from Dinny Geraghty's book

It was a miracle that poor Penelope and her children managed to escape that dreadful inferno, including young Hugh, just eight years old, who would become father to Eric, and grandfather to Sadhbh, Edith and Tom, though he died of cancer before any of his grandchildren were born.

PENELOPE MOVED *into a small dower house on the estate where her descendants still lived. She never went back to the old house, not even to visit its ruins. She said it would make her cry to remember, and Penelope Drummond was of old stock, who did not cry.*

FIFTEEN

Skibbereen, Monday, 3 May 2021, 4 p.m.

Timothy Jennings' phone started ringing just as he carried up the last box of files from his grandfather's practice to the top room of the Ludgate Building where the West Cork Historical Society kept its archives. He was seventy-two and there was no lift, but he had still managed to go up and down the stairs at a nice clip all afternoon. He cursed at the interruption, which for Timothy meant exclaiming 'Crikey', since he allowed himself nothing ruder. He'd specifically picked the bank holiday to avoid being interrupted.

'Yes?' he exclaimed, a little less courteously than usual, as he brushed down his lapels. The old law office had been dusty.

'Harry Keating's will.' The voice was brusque. 'Have ye got it?'

'Have I—? What, excuse me? Have you the right number here? I no longer practise.' Timothy Jennings had retired late from the law, just five years before. He had enjoyed his work as a solicitor in South Mall in Cork City, and now, having retired on a decent pension, he and his wife had moved out to their holiday home, and he was enjoying his retirement voluntary work with the West Cork Historical Society in Skibbereen.

'Ye need to help me.' The voice was panting now. 'I'm under a lot of pressure.' This annoyed Timothy. Thoroughly put him out. Here he was toiling away on a bank holiday and this fellow phones him with something resembling a threat. 'I just need to know if you have it, that's all.'

'I told you, I—'

'I was told to check with the historical society. And they gave me your number. Jennings, you see. The name of the solicitor given it after Harry was hanged for the Skibbereen murders.'

'The murders of Protestants,' Timothy added coldly. Though he was technically a Unitarian, who hadn't been to church in years. The last time he'd been there, they'd had a transgender Buddhist nun from Ballyphehane delivering the guest sermon, and he'd decided it was just a bit much for him.

'Big House Protestants. He was my grandfather, you see. And Mr Jennings the solicitor, was yours.'

Timothy Jennings realised who the caller was and something cold crept upon his heart. He'd heard enough about that family not to want to have anything to do with them. But, then again, refusing might bring trouble to his door.

'Your timing is good. I've just finished bringing up files from my grandfather, Ernest Jennings' office. I literally dumped the last one on my desk. If you believe there is such a file, I'll find it.'

'Can ye do it now?' It sounded like a threat.

'No, I can't. My grandfather kept the files in good order, but we had a flood a while back in the office – it's another

THE PLANTER'S DAUGHTER 99

firm now – and the priority was to get them out. Everything got lost and muddled in the haste. I'm certainly happy to start looking for you now, but God knows when I'll find it. If ever.' He put his fist to his mouth and coughed delicately. This place used to be a grain mill on the river Ilen, and now was a dusty hellhole.

'Well, do your best for me, yeah? I'll pay ye what I can.'

Mr Jennings assured him there was no need, and the call ended. He surveyed that last cardboard box and the mountains of tottering files and loose folio papers in front of the desk, not to mention the boxes that filled the shelves, all to be indexed and transferred to filing cabinets.

'Well, Harry,' he said aloud, 'let's see if we can find this will of yours.'

SIXTEEN

Skibbereen, Tuesday, 4 May 2021, 8 a.m.

Coláiste Íosagáin Naofa was a brown, two-storey building constructed in the seventies style, with long flat windows and blocks that funnelled the wind around corners. The entrance hall was poky and dark, with an inside window looking out onto a small spot of concrete courtyard. A couple of dandelions gamely held onto the margins, but other than that, the space was dead. As was the hall itself, containing only a statue of the Virgin Mary holding the infant Jesus, all encased in a small glass alcove. Two corridors extended from the entrance hall: one on the left, and one on the right, visible only through a pair of double doors with small, ruled glass panes. The hall and corridors were marked with the garish yellow of the two-metre warning stickers; school had hardly been able to start again before the most recent lockdown.

The clack of footsteps on a hard floor echoed from behind the double doors. A woman of about forty-five appeared, masked, with long, straight, dark hair showing a slight tinge of grey at the roots. Unremarkably dressed in a three-quarter length A-line skirt and buttoned cardigan, she had a sharp, angular chin that poked out from the mask and a wide forehead emphasised by a pair of huge spectacles that settled high on her nose and fogged up as she breathed.

'You've come about Sadhbh.'

'Yes. I'm Inspector Keane, and this is Detective Xiao.'

'Triona Costello. I'm the vice-principal. Obviously acting principal right now.' Her voice was toneless and heavy. 'Come with me.' They followed her down a corridor into a bright classroom with concrete brick walls painted a mixture of canary yellow and brilliant white. The place smelled of chewing gum and sweaty feet and the two-metre signs were everywhere, though how that could be implemented in a crowded classroom was anybody's guess. There had been no end of controversy about the decision not to restrict the classes at the end of the first lockdown. Not that coronavirus was the biggest problem they had right now.

All over the room there were collages and pictures. A poster of the Earth from space, a photograph this time, with a tagline by Carl Sagan, the one about everything being made of stardust or suchlike.

A diagram of a hydroelectric station. A blue sheet of paper with 'Our Projects' written on it with cut-out letters. Rosa could just make out photographs of compost heaps and greenhouses. Miss Costello pulled out hard plastic chairs from the wall.

'This is where she taught,' Triona Costello said thinly.

'You didn't take her posters down after she left,' Rosa observed, letting her gaze roam around the walls.

'We started,' Miss Costello said, 'but the students got upset. She was very popular with them, particularly the boys.' A disapproving sniff. 'There was a lot of bullying going on, particularly picking on Seanie Davies. Staunton's son.

And now, of course, there's no question of taking anything down.'

'We will want to interview other members of staff, and pupils,' Xiao said. 'We will get a few people in for that.'

'Of course. You must do as you please.' She was reminding Rosa of Ronan Furlong now, with that prim manner.

'Just in case you didn't hear, Miss Costello, but unfortunately we suspect foul play in Sadhbh's death.'

She dipped her head. 'I did hear something on the radio this morning. That you were 'treating the death as suspicious'.'

'Were you surprised?'

Triona Costello fished in her bag and pulled out an open packet of tissues. She pulled one out and blew her nose loudly. But her eyes were dry.

'I was, to be honest. With the circumstances, I thought it was suicide.'

'You mean her dismissal from the school?'

'Yes. It's fierce hard to fire a teacher usually; there's a lot of union stuff needs going through, even if they're totally useless. I had to break it at assembly this morning that she was dead, and oh, the quiet! It was if the room had sucked away every sound. Then Luke Keating got upset and ran out of the room. Of course, they all started. Crying and hugging, and the Lord knows what.'

Rosa perked up. 'Tom Keating's son?'

Miss Costello's face darkened. 'The very one. Some said he was obsessed with Sadhbh Drummond. That probably didn't help her case with the board. Might have helped if they'd been in lockdown longer. He might have got over his obsession if he'd just been looking at a box in a screen.' She sniffed once more, blew her nose, then scrunched up the tissue and threw it in the bin, laughing self-consciously. 'Y'know, I forgot for a minute and found myself looking around to see if she was there. Would she spot me throwing the tissue in the wrong bin? Now I can throw it wherever I like, God rest her soul.'

It was clear that Triona Costello's feelings about her late colleague were somewhat complicated.

'Can you elaborate on this case with the board?' Rosa asked. 'Why would Luke have any effect on things? Was Sadhbh's relationship with him inappropriate?'

'Not sexually, Guard. Politically.' Miss Costello's thin lips deepened into a frown. 'Look, I liked her well enough, but the last few weeks Sadhbh was here, she wasn't doing her job properly.'

'Meaning?'

'Meaning she spent the whole time upsetting the students with her proselytising about climate change.' Her cheeks reddened, her eyes shrinking to two pinpoints. 'We warned her. Well, Ronan did. Must have been hard for him, given it was his own wife, and a second wife at that.' Triona Costello's antipathy was becoming more unguarded, spilling out and contaminating the whole room.

Kevin Xiao leaned forward. 'Sadhbh Drummond taught geography, didn't she?'

'Sorry? What did you say?' Although Kevin had expressed himself perfectly clearly.

'Ge–o–gra–phy,' he repeated in an exaggerated tone.

'Yes. And occasionally civics.' Miss Costello's mouth was a thin line.

'But mostly geography.'

'Yes.'

'Then what's wrong with talking about climate change? Is that not a part of geography?'

'Not a proven part.' Triona responded instantly and angrily.

Oh, sweet Jesus on a pogo stick.

Rosa wanted to cut in then and there, but something in Xiao's body language stopped her. He was poised and prepared. He was a police officer pursuing a line of enquiry.

'I still don't understand how a teacher can be dismissed for teaching the curriculum. It doesn't make any sense to me. Please, help me understand.' Xiao was smiling warmly, as if he liked this woman and found her company enjoyable.

Triona Costello's hand flew to her hair, shiny and stiff as raffia. 'Well, Detective. It's not that simple. The Department of Education are very cautious about putting climate change on the geography curriculum. There's mention of it all right, but she was repeating it Every. Single. Class. And bringing the farming into it.'

'Farming?' Kevin Xiao was playing the simpleton with aplomb.

'A lot of people are dairy around here. You wouldn't think it with the land quality, but there you are. She was telling the children it was all their parents' fault for having the cows generating the methane. And that the older generation were stopping the transition to renewables and cutting down trees. Upsetting families, upsetting the community. You could see it was all going to end badly.' She shook her head, tut-tutting.

'Could you see that? Did you predict her murder then, Miss Costello?' All said with the same broad smile. Good man! Xiao would be smiling at this thundering weapon when he drove the spear through her heart. He was playing an absolute blinder.

'I did not,' said she, sucking her cheeks in with indignation. 'If you're going to make accusations like that, you'd better be careful. Spoil my good name and I'll sue you.'

'I assure you, I couldn't do something like that,' he said soothingly, allowing the ambivalent meaning to sink in.

God, Rosa thought admiringly, *Kevin Xiao could be a right bitch.*

'Well,' Triona Costello said, not mollified, 'after that nasty incident with Luke Keating's father, the board had to do something. Oh, wait' – and now she was in the ascendancy once more – 'you didn't hear about that either, did you?'

Rosa and Kevin sat silently as Triona Costello related the circumstances. Six weeks ago, after Sadhbh Drummond had given a particularly controversial class on hedge cutting during the nesting season – 'definitely not in the curriculum' – hadn't Tom Keating walked into her class and grabbed her by the arms and started shaking her, swearing and roaring, saying over his dead body would her clan ever get their hands back on his land.

'He was ranting and raving; he called her a Proddy bitch, and the young ones watching the whole thing.'

Miss Costello was finishing with disapproving relish just as the door opened and she jumped in her seat.

A straw-haired girl in a Coláiste Íosagáin uniform stuck her head around the door, then at the sight of the two Garda officers, quickly disappeared, head last, muttering an apology.

Rosa was troubled that this incident with Tom Keating had not been written up on Connolly's file. Something that was becoming a common motif. This town was pretty and scenic but liked to hide its nasty secrets.

'Were we not called in?' she enquired. 'That's assault in the workplace.'

'Sadhbh was yelling at the students to get Mr Furlong. Keating didn't like that at all, apparently. Threatened to strangle her.' Triona Costello nodded at their notebooks as if to say, 'Put that down.' Xiao dutifully started scribbling.

'Anyway, Mr Furlong arrived with another teacher, Mr Lowry, and they managed to get him under control. Sadhbh was all song and dance about pressing charges. Thankfully, her husband talked her out of it.'

'Why 'thankfully'? It's not a 'song and dance' to go to the guards when someone violently assaults you in your place of work. She had every right.' Rosa was angry now. What sort of place was this?

Miss Costello shook her head wonderingly. 'Do you really think Sadhbh Drummond could go and take criminal charges against a parent of a child in her school, and everyone would be OK afterwards? What effect would it have on the class? Tom Keating is a scunner, but some of the people he knows are dangerous.' She made a meaningful face. 'I was surprised the Board of Management came out in his favour, but … I'll get you a list of who's on the board and you can ask them.' She sighed. 'Will that be all, Guards? It's just that I have a class to go to in ten minutes and everything's at sixes and sevens this morning after what's happened with Sadhbh …' She spread her hands in a gesture of helplessness, as if Sadhbh Drummond's getting murdered had ruined her schedule.

'One last thing,' Rosa said. 'Did Sadhbh know or mention anyone called Edward?'

'Edward?' Miss Costello frowned. 'I … don't believe so.'

'And any Edwards in the school? Adults, that is.'

'Well. There's Ted Carey, who was teaching remedial maths last year, but nobody ever called him Edward, and I don't think himself and Sadhbh Drummond often crossed paths. No. I'm sorry.' She was sharp. 'It must be someone from her private life.' The slightly disgusted emphasis put on the word 'private' made it clear what was meant by the word.

'Christ,' Rosa said once they were well out of earshot, walking back down the linoleum corridor with its dark panels, as if emerging from the Big Brother house. 'That was something else.'

'It was enlightening,' Kevin agreed.

'She didn't even offer us a coffee.'

'If she had,' Kevin Xiao said with the ghost of a smile, 'it might have been poisoned.'

'You did good work there, Kevin. Well done.'

'I know.' Again, that slight smile. Cheeky Han bloody Solo. Perhaps she could trust him with her secrets. He still hadn't called her *that* name.

In the lobby the Virgin and child statue looked askance at them. 'You're not off the hook either,' Rosa said, waggling her finger at the impassive stone face. A nearby cleaner, wiping down the tiles with a bucket of water and a large carton of Cif, gave her an odd look, said something in Polish.

Back in their car, poring through the Board of Management list Miss Costello had printed out for them, they found the usual scattering of religious orders and county councillors. Pillars of the community, no doubt. Rosa clicked in her seatbelt. 'That TD fella Davies we could get later for sure. Let's go talk to the Drummonds first.'

'OK,' Xiao put out his hand to turn on the satnav and then paused. 'You said something last night about a Fitbit. Ronan Furlong?'

'Jesus,' Rosa said. 'I completely forgot about that. Thanks for the catch.'

'Will we go back to the station and review?'

'Sure, I have it here. Might as well check it now.' She pulled out the phone and entered in the passcode Ronan had given her. 'He was very reluctant to hand it over, so this might be interesting.' She turned to Xiao. 'Where do I go for heartbeat?'

'Scroll down.' Xiao squinted in the sun's glare. 'Put up the brightness a little.'

'It's already at max ... Oh, here it is.' Rosa selected the Heart section, which only had a line where the beat should be. 'Right. Day before yesterday. Six to eight p.m.' She navigated to the day in question and then jumped in her seat. 'Christ, look at this.'

Xiao leaned over. Starting at 6.30 p.m. and ending at 7.45 p.m., Ronan Furlong's heart rate had spiked. It was not regularly high, as it would have been if he were running, but sporadic high spikes, some plateauing, with intervals of lower activity.

'That's the heartbeat of a man who is in a fight,' Xiao said softly.

'If he wasn't killing Sadhbh, then what the hell else could he have been doing? And he's got no alibi.'

'That's true,' Xiao said, 'but we can't arrest him based on his cardiac stats. We need more than that.'

Rosa nodded. 'We do. Let's file it under 'things to follow up'. Quietly. If he's our man, he'll give himself away eventually.'

That agreed, the two officers headed out towards the dower house where Sadhbh's family lived under the shadow of the ruins of the Big House at Liss Ard.

SEVENTEEN

Skibbereen, 9.30 a.m.

They were travelling the same route that Harry Keating would have taken with Sean Furlong and Michael Savage that day in 1921. From the photographs Rosa had seen in Dinny Geraghty's book, much of the town was unchanged from those days. The draper's shop with its long, nondescript skirts and baby onesies all jostling for space in the window; the redbrick post office on the junction with Drinagh Road. There, Rosa was brought back to modernity by the sight of the out-of-town German supermarkets and hardware stores, parked cars gleaming in the sun.

They turned right and passed a camping site before seeing signs for Liss Ard Park. It was now in the care of the Office of Public Works in conjunction with the Forestry Department and people could go visit and even gawk at the ruins. It reminded Rosa of a trip she had taken to Coole, Lady Gregory's estate, when she had been on a Garda training weekend in Galway. The lake, the woodlands and Augusta Gregory's favourite catalpa tree were all still there – but the Irish state had demolished the entire house. The mansion where Yeats wrote poems and held court, where Synge, G.B. Shaw and O'Casey wrote their plays. A repository of literary life, all dismantled.

At least Harry Keating's actions had been motivated by war. Destroying Coole Park was surely motivated by nothing more than monumental parochial spite.

The dower house was up another road again. Xiao drove up a small hill, around a corner and the gateposts were suddenly there in front of them. Crafted from simple stone, they were overgrown with Virginia creeper and had long become part of the hedge of soft, sparse ancient pine and mountain ash that bent over the low stone walls. The car bounced and groaned over a potholed driveway, until the avenue widened out into a turning area. This was surrounded by a low laurel hedge interspersed with fuchsia and escallonia, flowering in dots of pink and red. They pulled up beside a light green Citroen hatchback. The paintwork was faded, and the registration year was ninety-nine. The Drummonds had been thrifty enough to keep it going for twenty-two years.

The air was heady with the fragrance of the escallonia and wild mint. It was hot, but a little breeze stirred about. At the far end of the hedge a small wrought-iron gate led onto a garden path; it squeaked gently as Rosa pushed it open. This led them past a mossy, uncut lawn with a small rose garden, and on to the house itself, which was substantial enough. Two storeys, five sashed windows across, with a chimney at each corner of the high roof.

'Pretty,' Xiao observed as he tugged at a small bell pull which clanged resonantly through the house. The door opened and a stooping, white-haired man in a short-sleeved blue cotton shirt raised his eyes and cried, 'Welcome! Please come in.'

The sudden cool of the stone-flagged entrance was a shock after the summer heat. 'Olivia! It's the guards. They've come about Sadhbh, you know.' From deep within the house, Rosa could hear the clash of crockery and the whoosh of a running tap.

Rosa could only wonder at Eric Drummond's composure, barely a day or so after his daughter's horrific death. He chatted away as he led them both into a pleasant back parlour, the sun streaming in from the south windows and a hint of blue sea out past the fields on the west side. The home smelled of biscuity warmth and had a cosiness absent from Ronan Furlong's house.

Above her chair, Rosa spotted a framed sketch of what looked like a Great Dane, in black-and-white pencil. The initials 'S.D.' were inscribed in the bottom right-hand corner, along with 'Dagda – In Memoriam 1993 – 2004.' Sadhbh was not a bad artist, Rosa thought. It was obvious she had been close to their childhood pet – if pet were the right word for a creature that size.

As Mr Drummond talked on about this and that of no conse-quence, about the weather and their journey, it soon became clear that what had sounded like friendliness was a nervous compul-sion to keep talking, lest in the silence, the weight of his loss would crush him. When his wife entered with a tray, wearing a pink, flounced apron, her face told a different story. It was blank, caved in, her green eyes watery and bulbous, her dark grey hair loosening out of its hairpins. The tray, by contrast, was well put together, covered with a pretty, floral oilcloth, bearing a pewter teapot and an assortment of biscuits and cake on a Dresden plate.

Olivia Drummond picked up the teapot and poured into

each cup. As she poured, her hands shook violently, and when she got to Kevin Xiao's cup, her hand slipped, and the hot liquid poured onto her fingers. Her reaction was to drop the cup with a wail and start sobbing hysterically as the tea flowed all over the carpet.

'Don't worry.' With a woman's instinct carefully learned, Rosa calmly and quickly took over. She guided Olivia to the large, dimly lit kitchen to run her hand under the cold tap. The cold water appeared to wake Olivia up from her trance of grief and she had presence enough of mind to direct, in a wavering voice, that Eric 'get the bicarb out, for God's sake, just scatter it around, it will deal with the stain quite nicely.'

Rosa and she exchanged a smile. The sisterhood, commiserating about male incompetence. But Olivia didn't know it was a sisterhood. All she knew was that she had a strange man in her kitchen, an officer of the law.

Back in the parlour, Olivia now took the initiative. 'So, Guards, Sergeant Connolly told us that Sadhbh was murdered.' Eric flinched at the word. 'They killed my girl and dumped her body on the side of Knockalisha Hill like an animal.'

'Olivia!' Eric remonstrated, taking his wife's hand.

'No, your wife is right,' Xiao cut in, the metallic edge of his voice deepening. 'Your daughter was murdered in an abominable way. There is no sugar-coating it. And we want to assure you that we will do everything in our power to bring her killers to justice.'

It was a cliché from every law enforcement drama, but coming from Xiao it sounded true and heavy. Rosa thought of Sadhbh at that protest with her companions, hair flying, all aglow. Like a statue, or a conduit of lightning. She recalled a visit to the Yeats exhibition in the National Library with her daughter a year ago, where they had looked at a photograph of Maud Gonne in her youth and Muireann had read out the quote placed alongside it from Yeats's poem, 'A Bronze Head', written when both Yeats and Gonne were old:

I saw the wildness in her and I thought
A vision of terror that it must live through
Had shattered her soul.

'We know that Sadhbh was a very principled woman,' Rosa began, 'and when you have fierce principles, it stirs opposition. We're trying to establish motive.'

Eric sighed and closed his eyes briefly. 'Sadhbh was always ... wilful. And a natural leader. From when she was a child. She always led the way and others followed. See, look at her.' He rose, and opened a glass cabinet, handing a framed photograph to Rosa, who turned it around. At the back of the frame '1999' was written in faded pencil. In the photo, Sadhbh was poised at the top of a ladder on the edge of an outdoor swimming pool; presumably abroad somewhere, as Rosa could detect a few palm trees and a hotel building. She would have been sixteen then. There was not a trace of adolescent awkwardness about her. She was looking directly at the camera, a slight roguish upturn of the corners of that generous mouth, the points of her nipples clearly visible under the fabric of her swimsuit. Her hair was a little unkempt, windblown; her entire frame broad and open, not hunched or half-turned. Only in her half-smile was there a hint of coyness. There was something disconcerting about looking at the photo of a dead woman – then barely a girl – and acknowledging that the girl was sexually attractive.

Rosa put the photo down on the table.

'We were in Madeira for the week, and of course, she got about three proposals,' Eric sighed. 'I remember worrying it was all getting out of control. And then one day when we had this enormous row, she just smiled and said, 'Don't worry, Daddy, I'm not going to go off with just anyone. Do you think I've no self-respect?" He broke off and inhaled wetly.

'And did she?' Rosa was gentle.

'Well, she married Ronan Furlong, didn't she?' Olivia broke in.

'Olivia.' Eric squeezed her hand. 'This isn't helping anyone.'

The clock in the hall struck ten, a pleasant fusillade of notes. *Au contraire*, Rosa thought. The real meat was coming. Again, Rosa felt an illicit rush of pleasure. She loved this point, when all the niceties faded away, the dirt would be dished, the narratives bent until they all converged, like tributaries of a fiercely fast-running river, and momentum would carry the enquiry relentlessly forward until it reached the unavoidable sea of conclusion.

Darragh McClure had once uncharitably accused her of joining the Guards to catch up on all the gossip.

'I never liked Ronan,' Olivia declared. 'I was pleasant to him for her sake, but he's a cold fish. And dragged Sadhbh into a big scandal, him having a wife and children and so much older than her. She was only twenty-six! Her whole life ahead of her.'

'But he married her too?'

'Yes, but the damage was done by then, wasn't it? Don't you tell me that it's a free-for-all these days and everyone's equal. He can go on with his life and nothing changes, while she gets talked about and judged. I tried to warn her of course, but she doesn't listen to me— Didn't.' Olivia took out a handkerchief from her apron and blew her nose. 'Never, all her life—'

'It's nothing personal, Mum,' a hoarse female voice said

from the door. 'She had a habit of not listening to women. Self included.'

The self in question was a girl in a camel fleece dressing gown that looked to have seen better days. Pale-skinned, with freckles and brown hair, she was sturdier than Sadhbh, her features less euphonious. She looked as if she had dragged herself out of bed, her cheeks and eyes puffy and her hair tapering off into rat's tails.

'You the filth?' she drawled, dropping into an armchair near the window with a flash of bare, plump leg slung over the arm. 'I'll have some of that tea. I'm wrung out.'

'Edith,' her father hissed, 'cover yourself, for God's sake.'

Edith carelessly tossed the corner of the gown over her lap. 'Now, now. You should thank me, Daddy. I came in just as Mum was about to embarrass us all by telling the nice policemen here that she was disappointed in Sadhbh for marrying a Papist.' She looked around, trying to gauge how much mischief she had caused. 'It's one thing to go off with a married man, but he could at least be a fellow traveller.'

Olivia's shoulders started to shake. Eric Drummond stood up. 'Edith. That. Is. Enough.' Then, turning back to Rosa and Kevin. 'I'm so sorry about my daughter. She's upset by this, as we all are, but it's coming out in totally the wrong way. We don't wish to offend anyone's religion.'

'Religion!' Edith's eyes danced with anger. 'Sadhbh is dead. Burnt to a crisp and stuck in the county morgue. I couldn't care less about religion.'

'I haven't got any,' Kevin Xiao said equably.

'Me neither,' Rosa agreed. 'Not any more.'

'But what's your last name?' Edith was staring straight at Rosa, ignoring Kevin. 'That's what it's about, not what you profess to believe. Your tribe. Your suitability.'

'Edith!'

Seeing that Eric was about to blow a gasket, Rosa stood up. 'Keane. Detective Inspector Keane.' She held her hand out. 'Pleased to meet you, Edith. And for the record I was baptised Catholic.'

And I'm much happier you want my last name rather than my first.

Edith took the proffered hand but ignored her father's continued entreaties to get dressed and make herself decent. Abandoning the armchair, she plonked down on the sofa beside her parents and grabbed a spare cup, filling it to the brim from the teapot and topping it up with so much milk from the little jug it was in danger of overflowing.

'Mummy's annoyed because Sadhbh married that long drink of water Ronan Furlong instead of someone like Professor Fitzpatrick. I mean, he was cute. Still is. Bit of a silver fox.'

'Miss Drummond … um, Edith, we actually wanted to ask about Tom Kea—'

Edith kept going, as if Rosa had not spoken. 'She lost the big fish and went for the yellow-pack version: the local school principal whose wife looked like a Friesian cow. There were a few guys in between, mostly political wonks, nothing serious. On her side, anyway. I doubt she was ever single.' Edith wrinkled her nose. 'Mum's right. She could have done better. And to add insult to injury, our prof did leave his wife eventually – for Jane Lombard, the history PhD who dresses like a pensioner with her shiny patent black court shoes and plays the college chapel organ on Sundays. Oh, what now?' She broke off, glaring at her father. 'You want me to shut up, is that it? How's that going to help Detective Inspector Keane and, um …?'

'Detective Xiao.'

'Xiao. OK. How does that help the detectives find out what happened to my sister?' Her voice wobbled. 'She's been murdered. Do you really want to waste time keeping up appearances with tea and biscuits when whoever killed her is free?' She wiped her nose on her wide, fleecy, dressing gown sleeve.

Rosa decided to get the discussion back on track.

'Look, first, we don't want anyone to 'shut up'. All these feelings are completely normal. What we'd like to know about are Sadhbh's movements on the day in question,' she said gently. 'I know it's a hard time for you all. But if you can cast your minds back just to Saturday. That was the last known sighting of her, and we had several pings later from her mobile.'

Eric thought for a bit. 'We last heard from Sadhbh that morning. I was driving into town to do a bit of shopping. I often picked up some bits and pieces for her, to reduce the carbon footprint of her driving in, you know.' Eric smiled but Edith tutted and shook her head.

'Fleecing you for shopping all that time, because Ronan was too strapped for cash with all the maintenance Moocow wanted off him.'

'You didn't like your sister,' Xiao cut in. There was a brief silence in the room. But instead of shouting back, Edith drew her knees to her chin and set her full gaze on Kevin Xiao. For a moment Rosa saw a trace of her older sister's beauty and poise.

'No. You're wrong. I loved Sadhbh. I just hate how her life turned out. She lost her degree. She lost her reputation marrying that headmaster. Then she got kicked out of the Environment Party. Then she lost her job. And now she's lost her life.' Edith was truly anguished. 'But look, what do I know? If you don't mind, I'll leave you to it. And no, I don't know where she was on Saturday.' Edith rose, sloppy tea in one hand, unlit cigarette in the other.

'You wanted to know about Tom Keating?' Eric said wearily after Edith left.

'Yes. We understand there is tension between your families.'

'Tension? Ha! That's one way of putting it.' Olivia laughed bitterly. 'You know what his grandfather did to Eric's family, don't you? Scum, descended from scum.' Her face was white with hatred. 'The first generation killed poor Arthur and Theodore, and now his effluent has killed our Sadhbh.'

'Olivia.' Eric put a hand on her knee. The room was getting hotter now, and nothing could keep it cool. Rosa was uncomfortably aware of the sweat gathering between her thighs and in her armpits. 'Tom Keating denies having anything to do with Sadhbh's death.'

'Well, of course he'd deny it!' Olivia snapped. 'You hardly expect him to tell the truth, do you? His lot would lie that white was black.'

'Olivia,' Slightly firmer this time. 'That's enough.'

'He thinks his grandfather's a hero,' Olivia's face crumpled. 'And that poor Theodore deserved to be tortured and shot. He was only a boy!'

Xiao shot a look at Rosa. *Theodore?* he mouthed.

'Theodore was my father's uncle,' Eric explained. 'He was killed along with Arthur, my grandfather, during the War of Independence.'

'By Harry Keating.'

Eric nodded. 'It was cruel and cowardly. Theodore was a young lad. He never harmed anyone. My grandmother never got over it. At least Keating hanged for it, that's some comfort.' He laughed bitterly. 'There was talk that Harry

Keating had left a will that returned his land to us. My grand-mother swore on her deathbed. But poor Granny was delirious by then. I'd say it was all nonsense.'

'Interesting nonsense, though. Given how attached Tom Keating is to his land,' Rosa said quietly. 'Is there any chance it could have happened? This will?'

Eric shook his head with a frown. 'Sadhbh was convinced the will existed, and that Tom Keating kept it. She was in some sort of legal dispute ... I don't know what it was about, to tell you the truth.' Eric ran his hand through his silver-grey hair. 'Convinced people were following her, out to get her.'

She wasn't wrong.

'Stop it.' Olivia glowered. 'Stop all your talk about wills and court cases. Excusing that vile man. He battered and tortured and shot poor Theodore, and his grandson did the same to Sadhbh. My poor girl! My poor, poor girl!' Olivia let out a cry of anguish and bent forward, collapsing into sobs. 'Why haven't you arrested him?' Her voice was harsh and edged like a silver knife. 'What are you still doing here, drinking our tea, eating our cake? While that animal roams free. How dare you?'

'Mother.' Edith's unexpected return startled Olivia out of her fugue of rage. 'They can't arrest him. They need proof.' She put her hands to her temples. 'Your wailing is giving me a headache.'

'It's all right, we won't keep you.' Rosa stood, followed by Kevin, but the latter seemed reluctant. He was looking mean-ingfully at her.

'What is it?' Rosa tried to hide her irritation.

'Edward,' Kevin Xiao responded quietly. 'You forgot to ask about Edward.'

'Mr Drummond, can I ask—' Rosa began, but she was interrupted by a peal of laughter from Edith. It was quite the most beautiful sound Rosa had heard since the birdsong in the bushes that morning.

'Edward? That's the prof! The one Sadhbh had her affair with. Edward Fitzpatrick. Head of Biosciences in UCC. Go ahead, ask me about him, I dare you.'

EIGHTEEN

An hour later, from the window seat in her room, Edith pulled up a knee, rested her chin on it, and watched as the guards pulled out of the driveway.

Her childhood bedroom had a view of the garden. With its single bed with wrought-iron curlicues at its head and foot, floral-patterned wallpaper, a rumpled patchwork counterpane hand-sewn by her grandmother, and a white vanity with a rather dirty mirror and smudges around the drawer handles, it was both a refuge and a prison. She always ended up back here, because she could not seem to sustain herself out in the world.

But now Sadhbh was dead. Murdered. Within a few miles of the house. She would never be safe here again. The old hatreds were still roiling in the ground itself.

When did you last speak to your sister? A week ago, she told the guards. The last Sunday in April, when the weather was still brisk and springlike, racing clouds and tumultuous showers, before this suffocating heat had drawn in. Sadhbh had been up at the house with the two kids. She hadn't looked well at all, her sunken cheeks and blazing eyes looking like the old days when maidens had consumption. She'd been angry, combative, picking fights with Mother. All Olivia had done was to tell her to be careful about the protesters who had been harassing her outside their gate. Perhaps if she withdrew some of her objections, things might get easier?

Sadhbh went down her throat. 'So, you're OK with what's happening here? One-off housing destroying the ecosystem, fish kills in the Ilen about every two months now? Rewilding legislation blocked by farmers every single time? The planet's dying, and I'm supposed to stop fighting for it and give in, because heaven forbid Rory English shouldn't be allowed to build five luxury houses in a special conservation area and get the road widened?'

It was absurd, really, and a little pathetic – that someone who had lost her job, her political party and whose marriage was in trouble should claim to be Earth's ultimate warrior. *Why don't you just pack it in?* Edith had beamed silently to her sister. *It's making you miserable.*

They had been mildly interested in that, the guards, but much more about Edward Fitzpatrick. Oh, they'd been all over her business once she mentioned him.

How long were they seeing each other? She wasn't sure, but it had definitely started mid-2004, when Sadhbh was in her third year of an undergraduate degree in Natural Science and was over by the time she received her unremarkable Bachelor of Sciences the following year. Was their relationship discovered? No, not as far as she knew. There were rumours, but that was about it. Is there any reason why he might have threatened her recently?

A pause. Then her answer: Yes. Several reasons.

NINETEEN

Western Road, Cork, January 2005

'You're preggers, aren't you? Edie, you absolute idiot.'

Sadhbh was regarding her with a mixture of fondness and exasperation, leaning her chair back a little, arms folded. Since they'd met for lunch at a café on the Western Road, opposite the gates of University College Cork, Edith had just returned from the toilet for the third time, wiping her mouth and looking green.

'Who? Oh look, it doesn't matter.' Sadhbh pushed away her unfinished latte. 'We'll sort it either way.'

Things moved quickly. The SailRail tickets, the fictitious biology tour –'We'll visit the museum if you're up to it, buy some postcards, OK?' – the appointment in the clinic. Everything. The procedure was done quickly and kindly by an Asian woman with scrubs and a hairnet who beamed when she saw Sadhbh – as if they had met before. All seemed fine until the return train journey, when Edith suddenly had stabbing pains so sharp she was bent double and moaning loudly, and they had to get off at Crewe. On that freezing, underserviced platform, Sadhbh caressed Edith's back and told her sister it would be all right.

'Trust me,' she said. 'We've got this far. Stay strong.'

Something nagged at Edith, beyond her own agony. The way that Asian lady had recognised Sadhbh. The way that everything had been arranged so quickly and smoothly.

'You've done this before.'

Sadhbh said nothing, but Edith could feel the hand on her back hand stiffen, feel her sister withdraw. But why? Edith would not judge her for helping others to have an abortion.

Not others. *Herself.*

Why, Edith wondered, when she's the clever one? The self-possessed one? Sadhbh wouldn't miss contraception for some casual encounter on the street like Edith had done. Sadhbh wouldn't *have* a casual encounter on the street.

'Who was he?'

'Edie.' The wind got up on the station platform, blowing a sandwich wrapper and Tanora can past their bench. The can rattled an empty tune. Sadhbh wouldn't look at her sister. Her hair blew across her face, the strands whipped up like a barrier.

Edith grasped Sadhbh's shoulder and pulled her round. 'Whoever he is, he must have a bit of money.'

Sadhbh still said nothing. Her silence stretched into minutes, until Edith lost her nerve and let her go. The next train pulled in.

A few weeks after the return to Ireland, she was on a smoke break with another business student, Mairead O'Connor. They hung out a bit when Edith made it to college. Mairead had narrowed her eyes and put her fag down in the ashtray. 'Did I see your sister get a lift from Professor Fitzpatrick this afternoon outside the science building? He turns up there in his Morris Minor and she gets in the front.'

'She's on a field trip,' Edith said. Sadhbh always seemed to be away on field trips from what she could tell. Going up the arse-end of the Burren to try and find a rare variety of borage or flax was not Edith's idea of fun, but to each her own.

'Well, I'd be interested in what sort of field,' Mairead had replied tartly, 'since I definitely saw her at half past three. And I'm fairly sure it was him. I mean, who else in God's name drives a Morris Minor?'

'That's a bit weird,' Edith agreed. 'But maybe she got back early or something. Took a lift from him somewhere.'

Professor Fitzpatrick was head of the Bioscience Department at UCC and was supervising Sadhbh's final year thesis in her bachelor's degree. Edith had only met him once, when Sadhbh had brought her around her department to introduce her to people. Sadhbh often did that, trying to get her to meet people, since Edith had few friends. She didn't know how to make friends really; when she made overtures, they were done wrongly or were too intense – she didn't know what it was exactly that put people off her, but it was dispiriting.

Sadhbh, of course, had none of these problems. Women wanted to be around her for her charisma and her ability to hand out random compliments to plainer girls, like scattering crumbs to a bunch of starlings. Very occasionally Edith had seen her shine her light on some randomer and declare, 'Wow, your shirt is gorgeous, I love the colours!' or 'That haircut is amazing on you,' and the recipient would light up, not just because of the compliment, but because of the eminent social superiority of the person who gave it. They would mistake the gesture as a spontaneous show of generosity and comradeship, but in reality, Edith knew, Sadhbh had no interest in them. They would approach her later, perhaps in the bar or under the colonnades in the Quad, eager for her friendship, and she would look at them blankly. It would take them a while to realise it had all been for show. An instinctive action to keep her feminist credentials intact. The reasons men wanted to be around her were more self-evident. But when Edith occasionally asked if she were dating this debating champion or that postdoc, both of whom had adoring sophomores halfway around the block, she would just shake her head and smile, repeating her mantra, 'No. They're just boys. I want to wait for someone worthy of me.'

After Mairead's insinuation, Edith began to wonder if that worthy person was indeed Professor Edward Fitzpatrick. It would explain the money Sadhbh would have to be able to terminate the pregnancy. He was in his late forties, older than Methuselah as far as Edith was concerned, but he was good-looking; she often saw him running on the Mardyke, his shorts showing off tanned sinewy legs that looked good with his greying hair.

She told the guards about that night in the Old Bar, when she was accompanying Sadhbh to a class table quiz. She hadn't wanted to go, but Sadhbh had implored her. Her girl friends, it seemed, were all busy.

'To be honest, Inspector, it occurred to me that Sadhbh didn't really have girl friends any more.'

When they crossed from the Boole theatre entrance that winter night and entered the packed bar, with its leatherette stools and retro carpet and smell of Guinness farts and some other odour, probably from the gents, Edith sensed the usual sudden lull she experienced whenever she entered a room in Sadhbh's company. Eyes fixated on the tall woman by the door, her flowing hair, her generous eyes, the tight, high-necked cotton polo neck which outlined her breasts. Hunger permeating the air, low and louring. An expectation. The boys nursing their pints either turning and staring, or resuming their conversation too loudly and hysterically, before petering out again, in the full face of Sadhbh Drummond's assertive beauty.

It was mad crack being the fat, pale, freckled, tomboy misfit sister beside her, so it was.

They sat down at their table and Edith braced herself.

'Sadhbh ... I heard something about you and—'

'And who?' She was smiling her 'how absurd' smile, like a cat.

'Professor Fitzpatrick.'

Immediately Sadhbh's demeanour changed, darkened. Those lustrous eyes flashed angry sparks, and she grabbed Edith's shoulders, nearly letting her pint fly. 'Who is telling you this bullshit?'

'So, it's true, then?'

Sadhbh laughed loud. 'Of course not.' But her laughter was hollow.

'Sadhbh – you can't.' Edith said, horrified.

'Do not tell me what I can and can't do.' The determination in her voice was chilling.

'He's married, Sadhbh. And he's supervising you. He's the one who's responsible for your final grade. And you ... going over to England? It was his, wasn't it?' Seeing the colour drain from Sadhbh's face was confirmation enough. 'Jesus, Sadhbh.'

'It's not like that, Edie.' Sadhbh's tone was strangled. 'That's such a tawdry way of seeing things.'

'Because it's a tawdry thing to do, Sadhbh,' Edith hissed.

'Only if you're narrow-minded and conventional. You want to look at it like some sort of *Daily Mail* journalist with a long lens and a peephole.'

'What?' Edith was trying to reconcile herself with what she thought she was hearing, but some lad was bawling in her ear with his Carlsberg breath: 'WHICH OF THESE TERRITORIES DOESN'T BELONG TO ANY COUNTRY?' and waving the sheet of paper in her face.

'Tell him it's option C,' Sadhbh responded in a bored tone. 'Bir Tawil, between Egypt and Sudan.'

'Look,' Edith said, exasperated, 'if he's shagging you, that's completely unethical of him. Do you really want to risk your degree for him? All your dreams?'

'He shares my dreams,' Sadhbh cried out. 'We want to form a party together – an organisation. He cares so much about the environment.'

'Hang the environment! The only thing he cares about is himself!' Edith burst out. 'Diddling his student while his wife looks the other way. Putting a pile of filthy notes in your hand so you can get rid of his baby and banging on about the environment? I never thought you a fool, Sadhbh.'

'Are ye going to be arguing all night or are you going to tick the fuckin' box, like?' One of Carlsberg-breath's mates, equally broad-shouldered and blond, waved the sheet in their faces. Edith, seeing Sadhbh was not going to move, scribbled 'BIR TAWIL' on the dotted line and slid it back across the table.

'Oh Edith,' Sadhbh turned around and sighed. 'You don't know what you're talking about. This isn't something that ends in a grotty episode in a train station in the north of England. This isn't something you can comprehend. But then again, your mileage may vary.' She smiled, as if she hadn't said something breathtakingly spiteful.

The chatter, the resumed music, the boys' braying; the way the tatty room swayed after two drinks and felt like a college building and not a bar any more; the dirty brown of decades of smoking on the walls, the gentle click of sick at the back of the tongue, barely swallowed back – all these swelled in Edith's brain with Sadhbh's casual treachery going around and around. And then Sadhbh, taking her wrist, 'Oh don't be like that, Edie.'

'Go fuck yourself,' was all Edith could manage, her tongue like a whale in her mouth, her hard palate sore and teeth singing. Then she got up and left, making it as far as the Quad before puking her guts out in a flowerbed.

'So,' one of the cops had asked her. 'Was it the real thing, then? Her and that professor? Was she right?'

'Oh. Well, no, she wasn't. Because he didn't leave his wife, and Sadhbh didn't get a First. She got a 2.2. So instead of doing a Masters in Botanic Science, she went to teacher training and taught geography back here in her hometown. And married Ronan Furlong.'

TWENTY

Wednesday, 4 May, 11 a.m.

'Ed. Hi.'

It was Isabel Connolly.

'Hey, Izz, what can I do you for?' Edward was leaning against the kitchen counter, while Jane sat by the window overlooking Fitzgerald's Park, crocheting beanies for premature babies in soft pastels. Her hands worked deftly, chaining the stitches, working through them in the round.

Edward never tired of that view from the window, the garden sloping down to the slow-moving River Lee. From his home in Sunday's Well, it was a less than ten-minute walk to the UCC School of Biology, Earth Science and the Environment, snappily shortened to BEES, where Edward had long held tenure as department head. He did not mind being so close to his workplace. It meant that he could wander in and out during the day when the academic year was winding down and there was less activity.

As the soles of his bare feet hit the floorboards, Edward felt the familiar expansive rush that filled him whenever he looked out the back bay window onto the sloping lawns, with their tea-roses and small cherry blossoms, and beyond onto the glistening, dappled river and the park on the other side, where couples sat on benches and families wheeled their buggies along the bank. He was lucky. There was no denying it. But now Isabel was talking.

'I've just got a call from Dave O'Meara, for the *Irish Examiner.*'

Edward smiled and mmm'ed in sympathy. Dave O'Meara was the new enfant terrible of the paper, constantly getting political party scoops to the maximum embarrassment of whichever party got caught with their pants down. Some accused him of being sloppy in his methods and research, in search of the scoop. But by then, Dave was so popular on social media that he hardly cared.

There must have been yet another row in the Environment Party. Like a royal courtier, smooth and practised, Edward was more than ready to provide his counterstrategy. Never complain, never explain. Keep your head down until they get tired of it – whatever it is.

Jane's Tunisian crochet hook moved steadily in gentle undulation as she approached the centre of the beanie in an ever-decreasing circle. The yarn was a glorious panoply of soft pinks, gentle blues, calm ivory. Edward watched her fingers. So elegant.

'He's about to break a story about you.'

What? His trance was broken by Isabel's words. 'I— Me? Um, wait a moment.' He motioned to Jane that he was heading into his study. Jane, who was just pulling yarn through the final row of stitches, merely nodded and took up her scissors to make the cut and sew the end in.

He shut the study door behind him. 'What on earth could interest O'Meara about me?'

'He claims you sent threatening emails to Sadhbh Drummond a few days before she died. And that after we expelled her, she threatened to go to the papers about an affair you had with her while she was your student in UCC. An affair that resulted in a pregnancy you forced her to abort.'

Jesus. Edward paced around the room, his light canvas shoes squeaking on the parquet floor, holding the phone so close it flattened his ear. 'That's lies, Isabel. Lies from start to finish. I can't believe you'd entertain this farrago of nonsense.'

'O'Meara says his source is sound.'

Edward leaned his hand on the corner of the desk. 'Well, we all know what he's like. He'll go off half-cocked with any third-rate rumour for attention and clicks.' His hand and arm jerked under the pressure and his legs felt loose and strange.

'He got it from the guards.' Isabel's voice was cold.

'The guards?' Who had told them? He could only think of one source: Edith, Sadhbh's miserable also-ran of a sister, with no looks, no academic prowess, no charm, no shape to her body, and no direction in life, but a reasonably refined accent and a bottomless well of bitterness to expend on him.

It must have been Edith, because Sadhbh had sworn blind she never told anyone else, and Edward believed her. Though the emails, that stupid, stupid error of judgement on his part ... How could Edith know that? No, she didn't, did she? The cops had discovered all this independently. Oh shit, shit, shit, shit.

'Isabel. You've known me for years. You were at my wedding. You can't believe I ...'

'Edward, I honestly don't know what to think.' Her tone had not warmed up. 'You're the one who pushed so vehemently for Sadhbh to be taken off her committee, de-selected, then expelled. And now I see you've been threatening her – just before she winds up dead?'

'You think I' – he dropped his voice – 'killed that girl? That's monstrous, Isabel. How dare you?'

'As I said already, Edward, I don't know what to think.' She was not backing down. This was not the Isabel who all those years ago had been considering running for the Dáil, the Irish parliament, and tentatively asked him his advice. A much younger Isabel, who knew him through a shared interest in horses and who nurtured at the very least a strong platonic fixation on him. Protestants both, if different sorts. Edward sighed and looked at the wall opposite. A small, framed picture of two shire horses hung there, one piebald, one black. Jane had put it up, slightly crooked. Edward found it endearing, had left it that way, but now was filled with an urge to straighten it. The horses presented their backsides to the artist, their tails swishing.

He needed to shut this down.

'If you recall' – and now he was icy as she – 'you came to me in tears after Sadhbh Drummond publicly gave an interview to the same journalist you're flaunting at me now. Dave O'Meara. She was still a member then, and you wanted her out, Isabel. And do you know what really got to you? When she said you were past it. Old. The editors put that right next to Sadhbh's photo, and yours.' A familiar rush of adrenalin overwhelmed him at his cruelty, that of a man escaping the disapproval of a woman he didn't want. 'So don't give me that bullshit about this being my idea. You hated her. You wanted her out. You couldn't stand the Green Maud Gonne stealing your thunder.'

He was panting now, audibly. There was a pause over the phone. A long pause. Then, unexpectedly, a chuckle. Isabel

Connolly was laughing. 'You don't know much about politics, do you?'

'No.' God, he was good and riled now. 'But I know your treasurer, Isabel. The party is in trouble, and frankly, so is your leadership. You're seen as weak, out of touch. There's talk you'll lose your seat next time. You can't afford to lose my goodwill. I've supported you from the beginning, long before anyone cared about environmental issues, and you were a joke in the polls.' He'd started drumming his fingers on the desk. He was glad Isabel Connolly could not see or hear how much he was shaking.

'That's as may be,' Isabel countered, 'but if this gets out, I can't afford to keep your goodwill. I can't waste party funds paying for a lawyer to sue the *Irish Examiner*. Christ almighty, we can barely keep the lights on in Wicklow Street! Edward, I'm sorry, but we've already agreed to terminate your position on the committee, and we're suspending your party membership. If the shit hits the fan, you're on your own. Sorry.'

She hung up.

TWENTY-ONE

2004

Their hands first touched under an electron microscope. He was watching her as she examined the muscular structure of *C. elegans*, more commonly known as a roundworm, in the college lab. The creature, just a millimetre in size, was still very much alive, but moving with infinite slowness so she could study its biological make-up on the screen above. The image was sharp, in black and white, and they were both bent over it.

'Yes, that's it,' he murmured as Sadhbh set the focus and the muscle tissue appeared on the screen like a spreading fan.

She exhaled, her left hand dropping down, and for that brief second his fingers brushed against that little space between her thumb and forefinger. The purlicue – that was what they called it. What an alluring word. *Purlicue.* A secret, giving, fibrous recess, where …

He had of course noticed her before then. But while she sat in his tutorials somewhere near the middle of the room, her hair cascading down her shoulders like a waterfall over rocks, her eyes blazing and fixed on him, he did not feel intimidated by her presence. Until one day when she came in early to a lab tutorial, headphones in her ears and an MP3 player in her back pocket. As she bent down to take out her materials, the small earphone in her left ear fell out and a sweet, high vocal spilled out. Edward looked at her and raised his eyebrows.

She laughed.

'Sorry, I should have taken them out.'

'No need. You're early anyway,' Edward said. 'What was it?'

She grinned. 'Have a listen.' She offered him the fallen left earphone, the other remaining in her own ear. He slipped it in.

What was he hearing? The background was ethereal-sounding: echoes, wind, the odd plink of a xylophone, slow guitar on reverb. A high voice singing foreign words. Sadhbh removed her right earphone and gently pushed it into Edward's other ear. He closed his eyes and relaxed into the music, forgetting the rows of white painted desks and the periodic table on the wall.

When Sadhbh finally removed the earphones, he started in surprise.

'Sorry, Prof. Thought I'd better sit down.'

'No, no, that's fine. It's ...' He was flustered. 'It's quite lovely.'

Her smile was wide as she looked down at him, her hair falling over her shoulders, barely an inch or two from his cheek. A quick flash of a vision assailed him, and he brought it forth: the warm, clean smell of her hair and his greedy hands tangled in its fronds as he pulled her close and— No!

'It's Sigur Rós.' Her smile was mischievous now, as if she guessed everything he was thinking. 'They're a band—'

'I've heard of them. Icelandic. My daughter has their CDs.'

'The song's been out a few years. I saw the video of it a while back. It's a group of dancers with Down syndrome; they move so slowly and gracefully in the fog ...' Her eyes grew distant. She raised one arm, bent in an arc, imitating the dancers.

Down syndrome.

'My brother had Down syndrome,' he blurted out.

Sadhbh let a gentle 'oh' escape her.

'He died in childhood.'

'I'm so very sorry.' The lightest of touches on his shoulder.

Edward rarely thought about Tobias, who had been sent away somewhere shortly after he turned three to a Church of Ireland institution with privet-lined gardens and grey limestone walls, never to return home. Died a few years later because the doctors didn't think the hole in his heart was worth fixing up. He had not attended his brother's funeral, and his parents had never mentioned Tobias again. No photos on the sideboard, no mementos of him anywhere. Every trace of him gone.

Edward's lack of emotion at the loss of Tobias was, in his own view, a personal failing, and he did not want to expose such an unattractive part of himself to anyone. Not even his wife, Maisie, whom he'd met at the Christian Union society in Trinity College when he was eighteen and she nineteen (they both admitted they only went for the free cake, which was superior quality, cream and jam.) Maisie, a stocky, square-faced, snub-nosed girl with a black bob and pretty, hazel eyes, had gently questioned him about it, but he had given little up, and she had soon dropped the subject.

That same night of the lab encounter, after his wife and children had gone to bed, Edward looked up Sigur Rós online. When he found the video, he saw the actors indeed had Down syndrome and were dancing in slow motion. They wore white robes, and their dance had the form of ritual: forming circles, breaking into statue-like figures. He imagined Tobias among them, and when the boy and girl in angelic robes slowly turned toward each other and kissed, languorously and with ease, tears finally gathered in his eyes for all that had been lost. He let them run down his cheeks and gather under his jaw without interruption.

Although he did not tell Sadhbh about this moment of catharsis, something changed in their interaction after that. There was that moment in the lab as they studied the insect. Then how he would specifically acknowledge her with a jerk of his head when their eyes met. Then how he observed her route. From the Environmental Science building across the river from UCC, it was a short walk to the bus stop at Victoria Cross, where Sadhbh had her bus stop. He still lived in Curraheen then, but 'it was no trouble' to wheel his bike while walking alongside her. It was 'on his way', after all. Just about. On the days when he drove in, he never offered her a lift, even if it was pelting down rain. There were some boundaries that had to be kept. Plausible deniability, to himself most of all.

Then Maisie got cancer.

Breast, of course; a lump silently suffered for months until courage was plucked up and she went to the GP. Who sent her on to the clinic where the bad news was duly delivered by a consultant, Edward sitting grimly by her side in that high-windowed, institutional room. 'Stage three,' said the consultant. The tumour was making inroads into the lymph nodes. Edward was no expert, but it didn't sound good.

Throughout the surgery, radiation and chemotherapy he was by her side, as she showed him her scar and wept, as her head was shaved, and she wept some more. He managed the teenagers, who feared their mother was going to die. He was not certain they were wrong.

As her treatment progressed, he felt ever more distant from her. Maisie refused to undress in front of him, would not respond to his occasional advances. At first, Edward reassured her, tried to hold her, told her she was still beautiful to him – but the longer it went on, the more her shame began to infect him, and he began to feel repelled at the sight of her. Why did she have to skulk around, her shoulders hunched? Why did she not just say 'Fuck it!' and mount him then and there, bald and titless? Death was taunting her; could she not at least try to raise some defiance? The worst of it was that Edward knew these feelings were thoroughly unworthy of him; that, in the language of the Billy Bunter books he'd read as a child, they made him a thorough cad. Or a bounder? He couldn't recall which.

But when she cheered up, it was even worse. Outside the bedroom, Maisie's mood was brisk. Brisk like a stew casseroling away in the slow cooker, brisk like shopping lists, frozen meals for mothers-in-law, defrosting thermometers, fabric freshener, cold cream for mature skin. That sort of brisk.

The kind of brisk that made people exclaim admiringly, how strong poor Maisie was.

Bad and all as tearful had been, it was nothing on brisk. Edward could not bear brisk. It made him want to run out onto the Glasheen Road and scream.

There was nothing brisk about Sadhbh Drummond.

One morning, Edward went to the Environmental Sciences building and was trying to get into his office when his key got stuck. He rattled and pushed and twisted lefty-loosey, righty-tighty, but still no luck. He banged his fist on the door in frustration. Then he heard a sound and looked down the dark, carpeted corridor. It was Sadhbh, a raffia bag on one shoulder, a folder under her other arm. Damn! He'd arranged to meet her at quarter past nine that morning to discuss … what was it? He couldn't remember.

'You OK?'

Her voice was soft and low. But something in it dislodged the last little piece of Edward's composure.

'Do I look like I'm OK, Sadhbh? I can't get the key in the damn door and my wife has cancer and she'll be probably dead in a year, and I must put on a brave face to everyone, including you, when I just want to put my key in the—'

He broke off, wild-eyed, horrified. Sadhbh stood there, a tourmaline scarf wrapped around her neck and tucked into her coat collar. Her deep, blue-green eyes were round with warmth and pity.

'I'm sorry,' Edward said shakily. 'I shouldn't burden you. Please forgive me, I'm under a bit of pressure …' He couldn't finish. Oh God, was he going to cry?

Sadhbh approached. 'May I?' Tugging the key out of the lock, she slipped it back in and twisted. The door swung open. She grinned sheepishly. 'My father always says there's a knack to these things.' Her fingers touched his arm. They burned through his suit jacket sleeve. 'You have nothing to apologise for, Edward. I'm so sorry you're going through this.' Then, a shy smile: 'I've always wanted to call you Edward.'

Something roared in his ears. He came alight. He, Professor Edward Fitzpatrick, was tinder, dry as bone, and those words – 'I've always wanted to call you Edward' – were the match. Spoken by that warm, generous mouth: the mouth he wanted to press his lips against – like the dancers did at the end of the Sigur Rós song. Not wanted, but *must*, and as he pulled her in to do so, her arm rose to him in accord. Their heads met on the level, their bodies entwined, and their lips met ... He pulled her inside, and this time when he turned the key, the lock clicked smoothly and the blind on the window went down without jerking, even though he was frantically tugging it while kissing Sadhbh so hard he was almost eating her alive.

She was the whole world, open to him, parched, exhausted, lonely. She was promise, forbidden fruit, the apple in the garden – and he was so frantic to possess her, he was unable to savour her. When their tongues touched; when he released one of her generous breasts from its plain white cotton bralette, beholding a dark, blood-red nipple, then touching it; when she slipped her hand under his belt and squeezed his buttocks – when each one of these things happened, he let out such a groan of passion and relief that she would have to put a finger either to her lips or his.

'Sssshhhh, Edward, it's all right.'

'I've wanted you,' was all he could say. 'So long.'

He would have had her then and there, on the office floor – he was that desperate. But when it was getting to that point, Sadhbh gently pushed him away. He stood there, swayed a little, suit jacket and shirt crumpled, still erect inside his olive-green Calvin Klein briefs. Sadhbh was almost as dishevelled, her cheeks flushed, her eyes full of laughter, one of her breasts exposed, her belly shapely and slightly rounded. And then that smile, full of gentle humour and patience.

'Oh, Edward.'

'Look at me,' was all he could manage.

She laughed. 'Oh, believe me, I am.'

According to the clock above Sadhbh's head, it was barely half past nine in the morning, and he had cheated on his wife with a girl younger than his daughter. One who confided in him that she had never done it before with a boy.

'Or a man.' Said again with a smile.

'Really?' He was more alarmed than aroused at that, though arousal would soon win out.

'I wanted to reserve it for someone worthy. Not just some boy.' She pronounced the word with soft contempt.

'But ... Sadhbh ...' He zipped up his fly and tucked in his shirt. 'You know my situation. I'm not worthy ...' He looked at her pleadingly. 'I've never done anything like this before. And with someone under my tutelage.'

That was when Sadhbh reassured him, in the kindest and most tactful fashion, that she understood. She did not in any way want to make his life more difficult. This did not need to be dramatic. It could simply move with the flow of his life – those were her words. And without once mentioning Maisie, she segued on to a story of herself and her friend Melanie, who'd had a rare bone cancer.

'Mel called me up one day. We knew the news wasn't good. I borrowed Dad's car and drove us out to Seven Heads, and we sat watching the migrating birds gather on the marshes. We sat on the beach wall and had ice creams from the van. Then we walked barefoot on the beach. We never said anything about Mel's illness. We didn't have to. She died a month later. Not that it's going to happen with you,' she added hastily.

And with that comment his heart melted, and he knew that he was a prisoner of his love for this artless girl.

Of course, none of it was artless. He found out much later that she had made it all up.

The next few months were a maelstrom of caring for Maisie and passionate hookups with Sadhbh: in the back of his car, in a tent on a field trip in the Burren, even, to his shame, in the lab cupboard after a lecture.

'Don't jiggle the formaldehyde!' Sadhbh had intoned in a Mrs Doyle accent, and they had laughed so much it nearly brought the whole act to a halt. They didn't go all the way for a while, until late in the autumn of 2004.

He had dropped Maisie off to the hospital for her oophorectomy, the surgery to have her ovaries removed. Their long-time friend Felicity Moore would collect her and bring her home. Then he had driven over to an agreed space out near the Lee Fields and waited behind the high stump of a recently felled tree for Sadhbh to approach from the opposite side, open the unlocked passenger door, and wait for him to emerge and pop in on the driver side. They drove fifty kilometres southwest to a small cottage near Kilbrittain. It was not new or fancy, but it had large windows looking out onto the long estuary of the Bandon river as it met the slow roll of the sea.

As he laid her down on the mattress, Sadhbh worried about messing the sheets, and he told her, kissing her ear, that nothing that came from her body could ever be dirty. Then, it happened. He tried to be as gentle as he could, but the touch of skin on skin, fleshy warm recess to jutting desire, giving mouth to probing tongue – she cried out, then buckled; he pushed on with frantic need, then felt stars burst, collapsed on her, ecstasy pulsing through him. In all his forty-four years, he had never felt it like that. She reassured him later that she was on the pill. Which turned out to be another lie.

Of course, Edward's guilt was immense. Towards Maisie for the most part, for being a shit to her when she was going through cancer treatment, but also towards Sadhbh. She was bright, ambitious, wanted to take part in research about what was more and more referred to as global warming. She had such a future ahead of her. He should not be a part of that, and yet he could not help himself.

His sole expiation was doing the thing that made him guilty. Only through possessing her, by falling on her bosom like a felled tree, could he feel the shame ooze out of him. Loving her, with all the smells and emissions and age difference and occasional laughter, was pure catharsis for everything.

Then it would start up again. The guilt. Nagging at him like a toothache.

He numbed it by convincing himself he was somehow honouring Maisie. Poor, doomed Maisie, who now with her ovaries gone and hormone tablets in full spate, was desireless – so much worse a fate than being undesirable. Maisie, soon to be no longer of this world, and therefore ethereal and tragic in the abstract, if tiresome in reality. While he and Sadhbh were at it like rabbits, he was mourning his lost wife in advance, or the ideal of her he kept in his mind. They almost mourned her together.

But then Maisie threw a spanner in the works. She didn't die.

The brutal treatment worked. Maimed, desexed, with body parts chopped off, but alive, Maisie soldiered on through that winter and the following spring, and the scans that month were clear. And as she did so, Edward was confronted with a problem. Now that she was recovered, now that he had done his part, Edward, realising that there was little left of the marriage, could leave her without guilt.

But Sadhbh Drummond was not the woman it was appropriate to leave Maisie for.

She was too young. She was his student. He was friendly with her parents, for God's sake; knew them slightly through biannual Arts Balls and charity events. Had even heard the tragic story about what happened to her father's family in the War of Independence.

At any rate, it would cause a scandal. And while he loved her passionately, she was not quite right. Not right enough to be worth the grief and pain. He could see that clearly, but unfortunately Sadhbh did not. That would not become clear until he attempted to extricate himself. Several times he tried and failed.

And then she got pregnant, and it all became very ugly. Threats to phone his home, tell Maisie everything. It took all his powers of persuasion to get her to understand that an abortion was for the best. He paid for everything. She wanted to fly, and he told her air travel was unethical. She told him he was a fucking hypocrite and burst into tears. Fair, but beside the point. He didn't have a spare €250 to pay for an Aer Lingus flight at short notice when Ryanair was all booked up that weekend.

Then there'd been that paper. The exams he had marked down. Sadhbh's brilliance, not a whit attenuated by the bitterness that had arisen between them. He almost admired her. He'd been presented with essays that he knew in his heart deserved a First. That should have ushered her into a doctorate. But no. Over his dead body would he let that girl work anywhere near him. She'd make his life a misery.

He graded one exam a third, another a 2.2. He hated himself for it, but it was the only way. He knew as he made the comments: 'Lacks distinctive flavour', 'Over-relies on Gee and Overton', that his treachery was unforgiveable, but if she were to join his department, his career was at stake. He could not afford mercy.

Sadhbh got a mediocre grade, did not attend her own graduation ceremony, and last Edward heard she'd gone to the Church of Ireland education college for her Masters, got a job teaching in Skibbereen and later married the local headmaster.

Five years after he ended his affair with Sadhbh, still married to Maisie, Edward had attended an inter-departmental academic conference in the Templepatrick Hotel just outside Belfast. He was alone, fidgety, unhappy. Then at the bar he met a reserved, dark-haired historian called Jane Lombard with pale Irish looks and a mouth small and neat as a bow. She was twenty-seven and wore an engagement ring, but within a month of that first meeting, the engagement was broken off, Edward had discreetly separated from Maisie – 'our lives had grown apart' – and when he married Jane, everyone congratulated him on his good fortune, even their friend, Felicity Moore, though she gave him that wry look once or twice that older women sometimes gave him.

Maisie was alive to this day and had never gotten over him. But Edward remained on good terms with his older children and delighted in the newer ones that came from his second marriage. Everything was perfect, for so long. But when you trash your environment, it catches up with you.

FOR THE NEXT HOUR, Edward prowled the house, snappish, unsettled, until Jane demanded to know what the hell was the matter with him, he apologised, and put his arms around her. Shortly afterwards, they went upstairs and made love with the curtains open. They climaxed together, and at that self-same moment, a starling perched on the gutter above let out a cheeky whistle.

'It's going to be all right,' he murmured into the whorl of Jane's ear.

'Why?' Jane was suddenly sharp. 'Any reason it wouldn't be?'

Naked, Edward panicked. 'Climate change.' He took her hand. 'Biodiversity loss. I try to block it out, but ...' He pulled the sheet up over his genitals.

'Oh Edward.' She softened, took his hand. For a moment, he thought of Sadhbh. *Oh Edward.*

'You know,' Jane said, 'I heard on a podcast that the Dalai Lama said you couldn't fight global warming if you were paralysed with anxiety over it. You had to transform anxiety into action. And we've done that.' She squeezed his hand. 'Haven't we?' Now she sounded less certain.

He squeezed her hand, looked away from her to the ceiling. 'Of course we have, my darling. We've done the best we can.'

TWENTY-TWO

Skibbereen, 4 May 2021, 11.30 a.m.

Staunton Davies' constituency office was on North Street, a few blocks down from the Chinese takeaway. The two police officers parked back at the hotel and walked up. Their mood was as hot and bothered as the weather. Kevin Xiao, in particular, was not in good humour.

He and Keane had been talking about Edward Fitzpatrick, and the conversation had moved on to privilege in general. Keane had declared that something was racist against white people, and Xiao had argued that wasn't possible. Things got very heated; Kevin Xiao got so annoyed that he nearly drove the wrong way up the town one-way system – again.

'Racism is privilege plus power,' Kevin said. 'What you maybe experienced was xenophobia. At best.'

Keane took that one in silence. Kevin didn't know what to make of him. He seemed to be happy with Kevin calling him 'Inspector', which felt clumsy, but Kevin had waited for the usual invitation to use first names, and it had never come. Mind you, he had nearly bitten the head off Keane when asked to give his Chinese name, so perhaps that was under-standable. It was at odds with the rest of his manner, though. Inspector Keane did not appear to be a man drunk on power, or devoid of humour. There was something else to him, something 'extra'. Kevin had learned almost by accident that Keane's name was ~~Gerry~~, but it was clear Keane didn't like to use it.

They made their way to the constituency office with its blue-flame Progressive Ireland logo and 'Staunton Davies' displayed in squashed-together cornflower blue capitals. Just inside the door they saw a row of plastic hard-backed chairs, some marked with 'Please respect social distancing'.

A girl with dark curls and a disposable paper mask sat at a small L-shaped table. The radio was on, and the soothing tones of veteran host Tom Walsh poured out as a wistful song faded. 'That was Tolü Makay. Beautiful voice, very talented artist. And now we have the prize for the National Recycling initiative against climate change. The winner will receive a €700 voucher to use at any Moran Oil station nationwide.'

'What the hell?' Keane exclaimed. 'Did I mishear that?'

Kevin had been thinking the same thing. It appeared not.

The constituency office was boiling. Even the open windows did nothing to alleviate the heavy stillness within, and under his mask, sweat gathered on Kevin's upper lip. Keane and Xiao showed their IDs and told the girl that they had urgent business with the Deputy, and could they be directed to his office? The girl looked like she wanted to demur, but a cop was a cop. She led them both to the inner sanctum.

If the outer chamber was a hothouse, Staunton Davies' inner office was a cauldron. Barefaced, wearing a short-sleeved shirt and with a fan running in the corner, he rose to welcome them, extending his hand before quickly snatching it back. 'Can't be doing that any more, can I?' he said with a grin. There was an open tub of own-brand supermarket hand sanitiser on his right which looked recently used. Well, he was a politician, and in Ireland, shaking hands was part of the business.

Introductions made, Davies snatched a mask from an opened plastic wrapper and slipped it on. 'When I'm on my own, I don't bother, obviously. I wait for the constituents to come in, then I stick it on. Thankfully, people are good; there aren't too many nutters. Welcome, in any case. Water's over there.' At this, the water cooler Davies was indicating at gave out an appreciative, mechanical gulp in acknowledgement. 'Help yourselves, officers.'

This man is nervous. That was Kevin's conclusion. He spoke with bonhomie, but too much of it, and he was grasping the table's edge until his knuckles were white.

'So. Sadhbh Drummond, I take it? Terrible news. So young. Your heart would go out to the family. Are you sure you don't need water?' They both declined. 'Right then. How can I help?'

He sat with his head forward so that Kevin could see the thinning top where his hair was receding. He had it cut quite sharply – what was left of it – which elongated his already ferret-like head. He had a sharp mouth and eyes that didn't quite meet yours for long enough to imprint themselves in your memory.

'Mr Davies,' Keane began, 'we're interested in the circumstances leading up to Sadhbh's demise. Not just the immediate hours and days, but the past month or so. Because we've gathered there was a lot of change in her life, and you were a part of that.'

Davies' expansive bonhomie immediately retreated to be replaced by a small, suspicious squint. 'Oh now, that wouldn't be the case. I didn't know her that well. To say hello to, that's all. After all, I'd hardly be looking for her vote, would I? We weren't exactly on the same page there.' He laughed, but nobody joined in.

'So, you never participated in any meetings with her?' Inspector Keane sounded surprised. 'I'm given to believe she was a prominent community activist.'

Davies squeezed out a glob of sanitiser and began to rub more on his hands. The unpleasant clinical smell filled the room.

'Look,' Davies said, 'we're all living in the real world, aren't we? The three of us. Well, then, you won't take what I'm going to say in the wrong way.'

Kevin Xiao tensed, felt the electricity go through him. That Davies man felt it too. Their eyes locked, for just a second.

'I don't go to those meetings. Extinction Rebellion and Climate Awareness and Zero Waste and the like. I want to talk to reasonable people I can do business with. Not head-bangers like ... Well, not Sadhbh, of course, God rest her, but the kind of people she'd spend time with. Crusties like that German fella, what's his name ...?'

'Peter Ludwig?'

'Ludwig, yes! He's a bad one and no mistake. If I showed up to any of those things with scumbags like him around, I'd get nothing but abuse. People shouting and yelling, saying I did nothing to stop climate change. I'm not here for that, to tell you the God's honest truth. I'm here to represent the people of Skibbereen and Drimoleague and Dunmanway, and that's it. I'm not here for head-the-balls being bussed in from abroad lecturing us about climate change and the like and having to give over an entire town to a fecking cycle lane.' His face was red. 'We have enough to be dealing with, never mind the roads and the broadband and— Did you know I was pivotal in the installation of the new broadband?'

'Congratulations.' Kevin could no longer restrain himself. Inspector Keane gave him a look. But Davies seemed not to notice, lifting his mask to take a drink from his plastic water bottle and continuing his rant. 'And these know-nothings who go on about renewable energy. Sure, hardly any of our supply comes from renewables. We need to be exploring the sea around here for more oil, and I'd certainly be delighted to do that. We're not going to be switching to feckin' wind power by 2030, I don't care what the Environment Party nutters say. We need transitional energy sources until we can find a way to make up the shortfall, and they can bleat on about Programme for Government all they want, I don't care. I'm here for common-sense, practical solutions.'

'Transitional oil and gas energy sources that could well end up becoming permanent?' The inspector felt as combative as Kevin did, obviously.

'And sure why not? These feckin' greenies, excuse my language, but they're not in the real world. I tell you what's real. Local jobs for local people.' He tapped the table sharply. 'And have you seen those turbines? Awful ugly-looking yokes, aren't they? You can't have a scenic area without them sticking up those yokes. Tell you something for nothing, you wouldn't see the Drummonds let any get built on their land, for all their organic talk.'

And there it was again. Land. The unspoken factor in all of this. When it came to Irish history, Kevin Xiao was no slouch. He'd read Roy Foster, Cecil Woodham-Smith, Diarmaid Ferriter. He knew enough to guess that Staunton Davies was probably the descendant of nineteenth-century strong farmers with a good package of fields – most Progressive

Ireland folks were – and yet still when he mentioned the Drummonds' land, the man's voice soured with jealousy.

'We visited Coláiste Íosagáin Naofa where Sadhbh taught,' Keane continued. 'We learned that the Board of Management was instrumental in her being fired six weeks ago. And your name is the first to appear on the list of board members. You're the most prominent person on it.'

'Oh no,' said Davies, his voice unctuous once more. 'You have that wrong. We don't have the authority to fire anybody. We can make recommendations, perhaps, but school procedures are not within our remit.'

'Are you suggesting,' Keane laughed mirthlessly, 'that Ronan Furlong took it upon himself to dismiss his own wife – with no pressure from you?'

'A meeting may have been held at a parent's request to discuss matters,' Staunton Davies said hotly, 'but we could hardly force such an issue.'

'When you repeat persuasion often enough,' Kevin jumped in, 'it eventually does become force. Did you frequently persuade Mr Furlong, by any chance, to dismiss his wife?'

'Now, that's enough!' Davies snapped to attention, an ugly look on his face. 'I can't speak for my fellow board members, but I conduct my affairs properly and any suggestion to the contrary …' He allowed the sentence to hang in the air, incomplete. 'Look, Sadhbh Drummond was a loose cannon. I had a discreet word in her ear one time. Told her to look sharp. People less nice than I might take against her. I mean, for God's sake. There was a badly needed housing development going up, and they were removing a tree beside the primary school. She went and videoed the children screaming and crying because there'd been a hawk living in the tree.' He rolled his eyes. 'Caused no end of trouble. We had to tell Ronan to make her take it down off Facebook and stop upsetting the kids. Then last year she told us all she was taking the Transition Years on an information tour and ended up bussing the kids to the refinery at Whitegate and getting them to sing 'Fuck You Very Much' outside the gates. I mean that's Not. On.'

Keane made a choking sound, and Kevin tried hard to keep a straight face.

'Do you think this is funny?' Davies was furious. 'We send our children to school to be educated, not indoctrinated. She's feeding them this … propaganda. It's unprofessional.'

'So, because she was telling the pupils facts that didn't suit you, first you directly threatened her—'

'I said I had a word—'

'—and then when she didn't back down, you leaned on her husband instead? Because it would be easier to get to him, wouldn't it? You and he being on the same level, socially. Sadhbh had too much social capital for you to dislodge her directly. You had to find the Catholic.'

Davies rose to his feet. 'How dare you! You get out of here!'

'Better be careful,' Kevin said levelly to his colleague, 'he might call the Guards.'

'You shut up,' Davies said sourly. 'Sure where do ye think all that coal burning and climate emissions are coming from? It's not Drimoleague or Skibbereen, I'll tell you that for nothing. Here we are being asked to kill our herd while the Chinese are out burning coal like there's no tomorrow.'

The malice in his comment was unmistakable, and Keane in turn, was on his feet. 'There's no need for that.'

'Really? It was just an observation,' Davies said primly.

Oh God. The inspector was going to take a swing at

Davies. Kevin could feel it in the body language. *Deep breath,* Kevin silently implored. *Back down.*

'All right, then. Let's move on.' Everybody sat back down again. 'Can you tell us where you were on the night of the 31st of May between the hours of six p.m. and twelve?'

From the dots of puce on his cheeks as he answered the question with injured self-pride, Kevin could tell Davies didn't like that one bit. That said, Davies had an alibi for the time of death, a pretty solid one involving a local Progressive Ireland cumann, and the interview concluded.

The detectives emerged from the broiling room back outside, where it was merely hot – the sky a roaring blue with barely a scrap of cloud. When Kevin Xiao opened the car door, Keane finally spoke.

'I'm sorry you had to deal with that. It was totally uncalled for.'

Kevin shrugged. 'I'm used to it. Usually, it's coronavirus or communism.'

Keane didn't speak again for a while. Perhaps he was revising his opinion of what racism really was after all. Then: 'Ronan Furlong did mention that other fella – his ex-brother-in law.'

'Diarmuid Savage.'

'And maybe Edward Fitzpatrick was involved too, somehow? That could be why Sadhbh was gunning for him.'

Kevin didn't reply. The Edward Fitzpatrick backstory was interesting, but privately he thought Keane was focusing on it too much.

'It's probably unnecessary to ask you what you think of Staunton Davies?' Said with the hint of a smile.

'I don't trust him.'

'Me neither.' The inspector drummed a rhythm on the dashboard while Kevin moved the key halfway to turn on the air conditioning. 'Right, who's next. Ah yes, Diarmuid Savage. Let's talk to him.' A pause. 'Kevin, are we going or what?'

Kevin tapped away on his phone. 'Five seconds, Inspector. I'm looking up something.' He screwed up his eyes and increased his phone brightness in the unrelenting sun, until he found what he was looking for.

'You recall Davies mentioning an incident with a tree and the children at the school? I looked that up and found the incident he was referring to. The proposed development was by Braiguemore Homes, of which, according the SoloCheck, one of three co-directors is ...guess who?' He opened the phone again and passed it over to Keane.

'Staunton Davies. Of course he is. Of course, he feckin' well is. This country.' Keane paused. 'Y'know what? Let's do a check on it. Good work, Kevin.'

Keane scrolled down through a bunch of numbers and dialled Anglesea Street, putting it on speaker. 'Put me through to Conall Flaherty, please. Thank you.' Dead air on the phone as they were transferred. 'Conall, hi, Keane here.' Conall acknowledged the call. 'Conall, can you investigate something for me? I'd like more info on Braiguemore Homes. B – R – A – I – G – U – E more. One of the directors being Staunton Davies, the TD. It's for the Drummond case.'

'Sure, no bother.' Conall was brisk, his Cork accent strong. 'Anything else?'

'Yeah.' It was slow, drawn-out. 'Can you do a check on any company where Diarmuid Savage has a beneficial interest? Based in Skibbereen, I'll give you his address in a tick.'

'No bother,' Conall said again, 'I know who you mean. He's a bit infamous around these parts.'

'Great. Thanks.'

They pulled out of the space and drove on.

TWENTY-THREE

Diarmuid Savage's insurance office, on the first floor of a newly constructed and near-empty office building on the N71 bypass, was closed, so they headed to his home further north, back inland. They drove a good ten kilometres before turning off onto a bumpy road just before the Union Hall turn-off. The car bounced around for another fifteen minutes, before the road smoothed out once more and the satnav finally intoned, 'You have reached your destination' outside a set of medium-height electronic gates with a wooden finish.

The inspector got out to press the bell while Kevin switched off the ignition and opened the driver door, turning out towards the blue of sky and sea. A wave of silence hit him. Fields ran all the way to a small marine inlet, and the hiss of the sea was barely audible yet permeated the air with its own quality. Few trees were to be seen. At his back, a yellow notice warning that 'THIS PREMISES IS MONITORED BY 24/7 SECURITY' was nailed to one of the gateposts. An insurance man being careful of his own property, naturally.

Kevin looked over the concrete wall. A huge lawn, recently mowed, stretched all the way from the boundary fence to the parking area in front of the house, almost two acres. The driveway, darkly tarmacadamed and smooth, continued in a straight line on one side of the lawn from gate to house, separated from the lawn by a fiercely trimmed box hedge with the occasional splash of privet and evergreen juniper.

The gates opened, Kevin got back into the car and they drove up to the house, which was what the inspector called, with a sigh, a 'McMansion' – a two-storey concrete lump with winged extensions and sashed PVC windows that briefly blinded Kevin when the sun shone on them from the south. When they got out, a huge Alsatian bounded into the driveway and barked several times before starting to growl.

'Kissy! Down now, good girl!' The voice came from the entrance, where a man, who was presumably Diarmuid Savage, had just opened the heavy louvred double doors. Kissy slavered a while longer, before eventually returning to her master, a plumpish man in his mid-fifties, clad in loose chinos and a short-sleeved light blue shirt.

'Come on in, guards. Never mind Kissy. She's friendly enough when she gets to know you.'

I wouldn't want to see what she's like when she's hostile.

They were ushered through an entrance hall with silver-grey walls and a shining parquet floor to a carpeted living room decorated in the same colour. A huge, gilt-framed square mirror hung over the fireplace and PVC French doors opened onto the back where a lawn of similar dimensions to the front one stretched in the opposite direction.

'Can I get you gentlemen something? A tonic water perhaps?'

This time, they both accepted, and Diarmuid Savage

disappeared briefly. When he returned, a young girl preceded him with a tray. They accepted their two glasses, tonics furnished with lemon and thin stirring sticks. Savage's water was lemon-free. The girl withdrew almost without a sound, the soft click of the latch the only audible indication of her exit.

'Well,' Savage said affably. 'I don't usually have the guards out to my house on a Tuesday morning. I'm presuming this is about poor Sadhbh Drummond?' He clicked his tongue softly. 'Una and I were shocked when we turned on the radio this morning and heard the news. We knew a body'd been found up in Knockalisha, but honestly, we thought it was a camper or some tourist or other. This is unbelievable.' He shook his head.

The inspector took a sip of the tonic water and put it back on the table. 'We understand you had dealings with her, Mr Savage. Through the school board.'

Savage nodded. 'Well,' he laughed, 'I doubt I can help you much in all honesty, but I'll tell you everything I do know.'

'That would be good, Mr Savage.'

'Diarmuid, please. When you're in my home.'

'We got a printout from a Ms Costello up at the school that Sadhbh taught at—'

'Triona Costello! Great lady, known her since we were knee high. She represents the teachers' interests on the board.'

'I see,' the inspector said. 'You're listed as being on that board too.'

'I am, indeed. Along with a whole host of others.'

'And I understand you complained to Ronan Furlong about aspects of his wife's conduct in her job?'

Savage sighed. 'Thought this might come up. Look, I'm not into conflict, I prefer the softly-softly approach, but Staunton Davies, he has a bit of a temper on him. He often butted heads with Sadhbh Drummond. He's a dairy farmer, so gets very touchy about the whole national herd thing and climate emissions. Of course, we've all got to do our bit,' he added meaninglessly.

Ah, the national herd. Farmers and environmentalists were at each other's throats about it. One crowd swore the belching cows were the number one contributor to climate change, while the other said the first lot were out to destroy Irish agriculture out of pure spite. Kevin had heard variants of it on the radio for the past few months, even in the canteen whenever he was up at Garda HQ and thrown in with some rural colleagues.

'Apparently things were said in class,' Savage went on. 'From what I heard, Staunton's son got uncomfortable, and it went back to his dad, and there were ructions, let us say. You know how these things start.' His grey fringe formed a lick in the middle of his head. He pushed it off his forehead. 'Sadhbh was going around implying his dad was responsible for climate change. You can see how that would be a bit much.'

Kevin, who understood perfectly well how cattle farming contributed to methane production and global warming, did not, in fact, think it was a bit much, but decided to hold his tongue.

'So Staunton Davies was gung-ho about getting Sadhbh Drummond sacked, but you were opposed. Is what you're saying?' Keane persisted.

'Well, I wouldn't say *opposed*.' Savage shifted his weight. He was beginning to look uncomfortable. 'I mean, I always considered Sadhbh Drummond a rather dangerous hothead. My kids are young still, and once they get to secondary school, I'd prefer them to be taught by someone sane. Someone who will tell them the facts without bringing emotion into it, you know?'

Savage continued to answer more questions with the same pleasant smile and blather. Among the mirror and the abstract, frameless paintings on the walls, Kevin spotted a row of photos behind a glass-doored cabinet made of modern fibreglass with a round plastic handle. One image stood out, sepia-tinted, encased in a gilt frame. It was the man's stare that drew Kevin's eye; the petulant, narrow-eyed look under a peaked cap. He was wearing a thick coat and carried a long stick-like object in his hands, which Kevin suspected from the man's expression was a weapon.

'That's my grandfather you're seeing there. We took his image out of his flying column and blew it up, so to speak, ha ha. Michael Savage. Flying column commander. We're very proud of him and the role he played founding the Irish republic.'

'I've heard of him,' the inspector said. 'Read about him in that book written by Dinny Geraghty—'

'Oh I wouldn't pay any attention to Dinny,' Savage chuckled, though a vertical line was deepening between his brows like a dropping barometer. 'Dinny Geraghty, God help him, lives in a shack down near the old church at Creagh and hasn't two cents to rub together. I helped him out a bit with the printing costs, you know – my name is in the acknowledgements. I was displeased when I saw how he paid me back. He doesn't source any of his material at all.' Savage hiccupped and touched his mouth briefly with his fingertips. 'He's mad as a box of frogs.'

'So you didn't like what he wrote about your grandfather?' Rosa tried to keep her tone light. She didn't want to put Diarmuid off from answering. But he seemed only too happy to elaborate, putting his hands on his hips and speaking to the room.

'Michael Savage fought for Ireland, but there are people

here who have sought to discredit him ever since. People he fought alongside, even.' For a moment, Savage's face contorted with disgust.

'But surely these people are deceased?'

'Their relatives aren't.' Savage looked thoroughly disgusted now. 'D'you know they tried to court-martial him for something he obviously didn't do? And they dropped the case. Of course, back then it was the law of the fucking jungle, wasn't it? That poor fella Erskine Childers shot by the Free Staters for having a pistol in his possession! A tiny yoke, something around the same size as that.' Savage gestured at the pearl-handled pistol next to his grandfather's photograph. It looked like it had not been fired in anger for quite some time. 'If they could come for Erskine Childers, they could come for him. He was lucky they had absolutely no evidence to try him on.'

'What did they accuse him of?'

At that question, Savage's bluster vanished and he became cagey. 'Doesn't matter. It was a long time ago.' He broke eye contact. Rosa was intrigued. Diarmuid Savage was obviously bothered by this whole exchange, and she was tempted to press him further on it. But what happened in 1921 hardly had anything to do with a murder in 2021. Or did it?

KEVIN WAS glad when it was over. Even with the cool hum of a discreetly placed air conditioner, he couldn't wait to get out of that house. Savage was standing at the window, making small talk with Keane, gesturing out. Keane asked him something about the garden, and he suddenly burst out, 'Well, you know, I'm just tired of them, all right? Trees.' Keane made a sound that might have been either yay or nay.

'Personally, I'd have every roadside tree cut down. The leaves and roots cause tripping, and the number of cases I've had to deal with where people have made ridiculous claims because they've fallen over one. Like, out there I had a couple of limes and a horse chestnut. They were just blocking the view and littering the lawn.'

There was a silence and then the inspector said, in a faraway tone, 'Thank you for your time, Mr Savage— Diarmuid. We'll be in touch if we need anything further.'

As the detectives got back in their car, and Kevin put it into first, circling back around the wide front area and heading down the driveway, Diarmuid Savage stood in the open doorway watching them go. His hand was on the gate button, waiting for them to reach it so he could release them. He could have just pressed the button and gone inside, but no, he continued to stare at them until the gates swung open and they left.

'I like him even less than Davies,' Kevin said flatly, when they were safely back on the N71. 'He gives me the creeps.'

Keane didn't answer. He was fumbling and fussing, rooting through pockets and glove compartments.

'Are you all right?' Kevin asked.

'I've lost it.' There was real panic in his voice.

'Lost what? Keys?'

'No,' Keane said tightly. 'My appointment card. It's gone from my inside pocket. I swore I had it there. I checked this morning before we went into the school.'

'Appointment? For what?'

'Medical.' Keane's tone discouraged further enquiry.

'Can you call the doctor? Check the time?' Honestly, why the fuss?

'You don't understand. I can't lose this card. I need to find out where I left it. We'll just have to retrace our steps, that's all.'

'You mean you want to go back to every single place we were this morning and ask them have they seen your medical records? You crazy?' What on earth could be the matter? Kevin rattled through all the possibilities: cancer, dementia? Huntington's chorea? Depression? Wryly he recalled how one of the worst of his tormentors in Shankill had a huge coffee mug that always had scum at the bottom and blared out 'YOU DON'T HAVE TO BE MAD TO WORK HERE BUT IT HELPS.'

'Turn the car around.' The inspector spoke with the same high, strangled voice. 'Turn it around and go back to Diarmuid Savage and ask him. Then if he hasn't seen it, go back to Davies. And to the school. Everywhere.'

Instead, Kevin flipped on his left indicator and pulled into what looked like a hard shoulder.

'That's the slow lane.'

'I don't care,' Kevin was exasperated. 'We're police. They're not going to bother us.'

About five cars overtook, and in spite of Kevin's reassurances, beeped loudly, some nearly crashing into the existing fast-lane traffic. 'I'm not moving till you tell me what's going on. Because what you're asking is ridiculous, Inspector. You know that.'

Keane sighed heavily. 'I know. But if I lose that card ...'

They were interrupted by the trill of the inspector's mobile. Kevin put the car back in gear and indicated out.

'Hello, Keane here. Oh hi, Sergeant. What? Sinead – the daughter? Christ. OK, we'll see you back for lunch.' Then, to Kevin, 'OK. Forget it, I was overreacting. You're right. We're heading straight back into Skibbereen. Sinead Furlong's showed up to the Garda station. She claims she's responsible for the second fire.'

TWENTY-FOUR

Goatenbridge, Tipperary, July 1921

Harry Keating crouched down at the entrance of the British Commonwealth war tent that Liam Lynch had stolen from Mallow Barracks, and looked down the Knockmealdown foothills towards the spread of fields around Clogheen. His tent was well concealed in the middle of a forest that stretched along the slopes of several hills above the Nire valley – Liam Lynch's stronghold. The peelers wouldn't bother him here.

He had just washed himself with Savelite soap in a rushing stream close to the break in the treeline. The water was cold enough to cut you in two, but he managed it. At his feet were the remains of a small fire he had lit with stray pine twigs earlier that morning. He had been scrambling the eggs a friendly civilian had left there from their farm. The fragrance the wood left after burning was fresh and sharp.

He'd gone to Lynch, via a network of associates, because he was the IRA commander of the whole region and Harry knew that he could trust him. Lynch was younger than Harry, in his late twenties, effetely handsome with thin lips, fair hair and thin, gold-framed spectacles. Even when wearing his IRA jacket, he looked like someone you'd find in the library, lamp lit, squinting over history books. He spoke in a slightly affected nasal tone with a pronounced Cork accent. In reality, he was as murderous and brutal as anyone who ever waged a guerrilla campaign against an occupying force.

Though even he had raised an eyebrow when he and Harry finally met. 'That raid on the Drummonds,' he commented as they shook hands. 'That was rough stuff.'

'It didn't go the way I wanted,' Harry said tersely, disliking the admiration in Lynch's voice.

'Well, it's done now.' And that was the end of it. Lynch disliked discussing operations. Loose talk cost lives. He was tight-lipped about his own life, too, only becoming expansive on occasions such as when Harry praised the two fine trout Lynch found for him.

'Caught them myself,' he answered proudly. 'When I had Major General Lucas held hostage, he taught me a few things about fishing. Told me how I should fix my bait.'

'You would have shot him in a heartbeat,' Harry retorted, but he had to admit that when gutted and set on the griddle later, the fish tasted pure delicious.

During Harry's cross-country trek, he'd been at the mercy of the wives of strong farmers in North Cork. They'd throw him their leavings of bread and soup, if they were bothered feeding him at all. Occasionally he dossed down in their outhouses and barns, until that time when a lurcher at the entrance of a barn had growled repeatedly until finally waking him up by barking in his face, teeth slavering. It wasn't friendly territory.

He had slept in cornfields, living on his wits, hitching lifts in hay carts and hiding in the straw whenever running into an Auxiliary checkpoint. The last few weeks had at least offered some peace and respite. And time to think.

What did it amount to, this fight for Ireland? He had land up in Knockalisha, next to the Drummond estate; his father, who had always farmed it, bought it back twenty years ago on a long lease mandated by the Wyndham Land Act. Harry wanted to build a homestead there; maybe even grow a few vegetables, along with the sheep and chickens. Make it a place he could live off in peace. He couldn't do that now, wandering around the country like a vagrant. Noreen was there now, but she was not from farming people, so he wasn't sure if she was coping.

Not to mention that decent job in the Munster and Leinster that Mr Blanchard had offered him just out of school. He'd turned it down: just the day before, he had seen the eviction of the Lehanes in Skibbereen, how they were marched over the bridge by the peelers, and he had decided to join the Fenians. Who would rather work in a bank, than agitate for Ireland's freedom? As it turned out, he would. Or even the Great War. King's shilling, but at least it would have paid, if he'd had guile enough to survive. He would have had his army pension and a bit of dignity.

In the end, he had given it all up for Mother Ireland. His own mother had been disgusted with him and bawled him out for three hours. Said he'd neither brains nor sense, to be giving up a decent life for some load of fol-de-rol he'd probably heard at the back of a pub. They had not spoken since. Another tie severed for Irish freedom.

A cuckoo-like whistle disturbed his reverie. Harry rose and stamped his boots, since his feet had got pins and needles from crouching so long. He knew that whistle. It was the code to indicate a trusted ally was in the area and coming to visit. He saw a man walking through the forest, his figure dappled and shadowy in the pine-filtered sunlight. He was stocky, and as he came closer, his thick moustache was visible. Harry didn't recognise him.

The man stopped just outside Harry's camp. Without preamble he delivered his message like a sentry. 'You were telling Liam Lynch you were planning on going home. I've come to tell you that you mustn't return to Skibbereen.'

Harry gave him a long look. 'Why?'

'It isn't safe.' A pause. 'That attack on the Drummonds ... I'm told it stirred up a lot of feelings.'

'I was thinking that myself,' Harry said, 'but we have the peace now.'

The man shook his head. 'It's nothing to do with that, Harry.'

Harry beckoned the man to sit beside him. But he demurred, staying rigid, to attention. Harry would be damned if he'd do the same. He plonked himself down on a tree stump. 'I don't know your name, but you know mine, it seems.'

'My name doesn't matter,' the man said, 'only that I'm a friend to Ireland.'

'And what does that mean any more?' At one of the Sinn Féin fundraisers he'd attended in Dublin the year before, a ball to fund a trip for de Valera to go to America for a bond drive, Harry had a brief fling with a wealthy English émigrée, who fancied herself a bit of a revolutionary. Unescorted by anyone, she was pretty and pert, with round eyes, hair in an up-do and pearly, cluttered teeth, the incisors almost hanging on her blood-red lower lip.

'I'm a friend of Ireland,' she'd whispered in Harry's ear as they spun around in a fast waltz. Later they kissed and kissed in an empty hall in Buswells Hotel where he had quickly spirited her off after it was obvious she wanted more than a dance. She was wearing some weird crêpe collar that crumpled when his chin met it, while the band next door played 'Dardanella', though they hadn't enough brass to get an ensemble for the melody line. The trumpet constantly went out of tune and Harry couldn't help but be annoyed by it, even as Esmée Cornell's tongue was insinuating its tip along his earlobe.

'I can make sure a message gets to your wife,' the unnamed man said. 'But you can't go home. And you can't stay here, either.'

So that was it. Liam Lynch, a fugitive, had had enough of Harry Keating, another fugitive. The man was right; his name didn't really matter. He was a functionary to give Harry his marching orders.

The sun had drawn in, a cumulonimbus dimming the light and making the forest cover seem dark and impenetrable. A stoat ran out with a rabbit in its jaws, then vanished into a hedge to consume its dinner. The man started slightly, but Harry, who had often seen that stoat, was undisturbed.

There was nothing more to be done now than politely see off that man, and mentally write off Liam Lynch for being such a coward. They exchanged a few more words and then Harry sat a while longer on his stump, watching the sunlight and shadow bathe the long plain below, with its patchwork of fields and the church bells at Fourmilewater striking two.

He would go home. The truce was imminent, and he could lay down his knife and gun, stop fighting, rest. Whatever else was to come could be resolved, he was sure. He needed to return to Noreen and the children. He needed to go back to the land, the very thing he'd turned his life upside-down fighting for.

That night, the weather turned. He slept badly as rain leaked into the tent's hide, and when he did get the chance to dream, all he could see was Theodore Drummond's upturned, crying face. He was just a boy ...

When he woke up on a grey, misty morning full of damp and chafing, soaking bedding and crazy abundant birdsong, a dank cough lodging in his chest, he recalled what the man had said on leaving. 'It was a worthy sacrifice, what ye did. Blood atonement for the wrongs inflicted upon us.'

All Harry managed in reply was, 'No, it wasn't. It wasn't at all.'

TWENTY-FIVE

4 May 2021, 2.30 p.m.

Dear Luke,

I'd say this is the first letter you've ever received from a holding cell in Skibbereen Garda station. The cops didn't seem to know what to do when I turned myself in. I had to do it, though. Because even though your dad is awful, he's your dad, and it's my fault he's being accused of something he didn't do.

I mean, the forest fire.

This place stinks and it's so hot. The tiny holding cell is right next to the men's toilets, on the other side of a steel wall. I can hear every shit, every fart, every flush, and – oh God! – the smell. In fairness, I asked for a pen and paper and water, and they gave me all of those. They offered to call Dad or a lawyer too. The Chinese fella told me I had to have Dad here because I was a minor, and I said, call Mam then, because I never want to speak to Dad again.

He says his name is Kevin, but I don't think that's his real name. I know you won't be jealous, but he's a ride. He was wearing short sleeves, and his arms are really toned. Had a wedding ring, though, sob sob.

The interview room isn't like what you see on the telly. The table's got a Formica top and one leg is wonky, so they've rolled a bit of the Irish Times *weekend supplement and stuck it under one leg to keep it stable. I think the leg of the table is smack bang in the middle of Sean Moncrieff's mouth and that made me laugh.*

Not that there's much to laugh about, really. Mam was all flustered and upset, saying how could I have done such a dreadful thing? Seeing her cry made me feel like utter shit. It reminded me of the time shortly before Dad left when he was picking at her about a new haircut she'd had to try and impress him. But he just said, 'It looks awful' and walked away. Then she broke down crying and begged him to be nicer to her. At the time I cringed for her, but now I feel ashamed of myself, knowing why he did it. Knowing he was banging someone else.

I remember you used to cry when you talked about your oul' lad, how he insulted you, smacked you around, did the same to your mam. You said I was the only one you could talk to. You were fed up with toxic masculinity, even wanted to be a feminist and work in a rape crisis centre. So you said. You would call around when I was at Dad's to hang out and chat, and I thought it was because of me. I thought confiding in me meant something.

My stepmother always insisted 'Feminism is for everyone,' but it isn't. It's for women like her. Women with beauty, time, class and money. Not for girls like me. Fat girls whose bellies bulge out and breasts bounce when running, so other girls laugh at them. Girls who bleed through their uniform. Girls who get picked last for the team. Girls whose fathers aren't there at night to hug them and talk to them and fight their corner because they're ball deep in some feminist who isn't their wife.

Remember that last summer, before the exams started, when we would sit in that wild bit of wood near the pylons, up the back of Hazelbrooke estate, and share a fag or two? I was never mad for the taste of it and dreaded Mam or Dad catching the smell, but I loved watching you smoke. You're looking out over the estuary and the houses and the green below, and you have your knees drawn up, and slowly expel a stream of it, as if you'd all the time in the world. I would shiver sometimes as the sun went down, and you'd take off your denim jacket and drape it over my shoulders. It was still warm from you and smelled of smoke. It felt like you were holding me close.

The fire I started up the hill, that smelled different. Heady at first as the gorse gave up its sweetness. Then charred and choking, the fumes awful. I nearly gave up, but the petrol can I nicked from my uncle's garage did a good job. The best bit was when that wooden post on the Drummond land saying 'Not in Our Lifetime – Eco Tree Planting Reserve' all went up in flames. I even took a few pictures, before I had to run to avoid getting burned myself. The guards were very interested in that, and they took the phone off me straightaway.

Her pride and joy. The one thing she clung onto during her endless rounds of 'eco-anxiety'. Oh God, we all got to hear about her eco-anxiety. Even my dad was getting a bit sick of it near the end. Her ranting and shouting, 'The planet is dying. How can you not care?' To be honest, I didn't, and I don't.

She used all that environment stuff to get at Mam half the time. 'Some of us might put the tumble dryer on for hours on end, but we don't do that in this house.' Fucking bitch. The hell with the planet. All I cared about was revenge on her. Because after you told me she was your real love, I swear to God, I could have burned down her family's entire estate and every wild animal in Cork, alive, and it still wouldn't have satisfied my desire to punish her.

But you can't hurt a dead person. I wanted her to know what I'd done. It pisses me off that she'll never find out.

But Luke, I didn't always hate Sadhbh. When Dad introduced us, I couldn't stop looking at her. She reminded me of the sun. She had a wide smile and big lips and a waterfall of golden-brown hair falling over her shoulders. Her hugs were warm and fierce. She wore tight tops with a silver curved pendant that would just nestle in her cleavage. It gleamed and glinted and when I asked her what it was, she said, 'It's the sign of Cancer. See those yin-yang things? They're crab claws.' Then she asked me when my birthday was and Dad said, 'July fifth'. I remember her smiling at me then, confidingly – her and me against all those Air and Fire signs.

I got my first period on one of my overnighters with Dad and she found out. I was embarrassed, but she smiled and said, 'Ah, Sinead, everyone goes through it. It's nothing to be ashamed of.' Turns out she'd got up a collection of reusable cloth pads and a mooncup in a small cotton bag. It was all in a beautiful cedar box that was scented with the same woody smell that exhaled from her skin. It was quite a bit fancier than the bargain packet of Kotex Mam had got for me for when the time came. Of course, that was the point. Everything nice she ever did to me was a subtle put-down of Mam.

It took a long time before I copped on to the truth.

I was in third year; it was break time and I was wandering around with some older girls – Cliona Dunne and them. It was a sunny day, and we were sitting on our Coláiste Íosagáin jumpers down on the sparse clumps of grass just above the car park. Some conversation was going on, I think about a celebrity getting a divorce. I said something like, 'Well, my parents divorced and everything worked out OK.' Cliona puffed out a big cloud of smoke from her Marlboros and said, 'Yeah, but your dad went off with Miss Drummond and your ma was pretty upset about it.'

'He didn't 'go off' with her.' I tried to sound lofty. 'Mum and Dad split up because they weren't getting on. Then, afterwards, Dad met Sadhbh and they got together.'

Cliona put down her cigarette and looked hard at me. I swear to God I saw pity in her big, baleful eyes. 'If you say so,' she said then, and took another drag of her cigarette, before returning to the earlier conversation she was having. But I wasn't finished.

'What, then? Are you saying Dad had an affair?'

'Jesus Christ,' she said, throwing down her cigarette, 'how would I know?'

'Because you just said.'

'Sinead, can we stop, please? I don't want to know about your family business. Especially when it's teachers.' She mimed vomiting.

'But you said —'

'Jesus, Sinead. Cop on. Are you nine years old or what?'

Actually, I was ten when Mam and Dad sat down and told me they weren't getting on so well any more, and we would be moving to another house, but we would see Dad every second weekend and during the week. It was all very civilised. Though, looking back, I could see Mam trembling a bit.

'So, you're saying you don't know what happened'

You're just making it up, Cliona Dunne.' I felt the sun redden my face. My eyes were burning too.

'Oh kid,' she said then, her voice all full of patronising pity. 'Men don't leave to be on their own.'

'But what if it's a mutual decision? They're both breaking up with each other?'

'Looking at him – and Miss Drummond? Ah, Sinead.'

Another of the girls, Olwyn Doyle, started making spastic noises at me. She was the worst of the group, and she had a face like a rat. I started arguing again, and Cliona got up and stared at me. Her face was like a gate; she was really annoyed. 'For God's sake, I'm not your therapist, all right? Will you just forget I said anything? I don't know what's going on any more than anyone else. You need to talk to your parents.'

I left them. As I trudged away, my shoes scuffing the grass, I could hear Olwyn Doyle's mocking tone: 'She's so naive.' And then, as I got further away. 'Ungh. Spa.'

That's what hurts the most. That when I finally told you about how girls like Olwyn bullied me, you put your arm around my shoulders and told me, 'You're worth a thousand Olwyns,' and gave me a peck on the cheek. When I went home that night I was in heaven. I started to let myself hope. Of course, you never in a million years would have thought of me that way. Who was I kidding? I was just a conduit to get to Sadhbh.

When you suddenly got weird with me and told me we couldn't meet any more, I think my heart just broke. I'd told Audrey O'Keeffe in confidence about you saying I was worth a thousand Olwyns and giving me a kiss. I said it to her several times not to tell anyone, and she nodded her head, all wide-eyed, and said she wouldn't tell a soul. It was all around the school the following day. Cliona Dunne even asked me about it, and I smiled and tapped the side of my nose, thinking I was all sophisticated.

Your disgust that afternoon when we met at Hazelbrooke completely stripped me of any of that. You asked me why I blabbed a private moment between friends all over the place. That us meeting was nobody else's business. Because I'm needy, all right, Luke? I'm not poised enough to have the attention of somebody like you and be blasé about it. But when you grabbed my wrist with your nails digging in and looked at me with your mouth twisted with rage and derision and uttered those words, 'Did you tell Sadhbh?', then, finally, the penny dropped.

'Don't bother contacting me again,' you said. And last night my dad told me and Mam the same thing. I remember Mam as she got in the car, turning on the windscreen wipers with shaking hands, as if she were confusing her own tears with the weather, before turning them off and putting her head and elbows on the steering wheel and breaking down crying – loud, heaving sobs. Then I remembered the *look on Lorraine Twamley's face, when Sadhbh came up to her in the playground and told her to stop shouting at her little fella, because it wasn't proper parenting. Lorraine's not the sharpest tool in the box, and she probably does shout too much at her kids, but Sadhbh broke up my parents' marriage! Who is she to tell anyone they're a bad mother?*

That's when I realised there would be no point in time when that whore Sadhbh Drummond would stop hurting other women. And getting away with it.

That's why there's one thing I didn't tell the Guards, Luke.

A while before she died, maybe a few months ago, Sadhbh got kinda obsessed with some title deed or legal document or something back from the 1920s. You know, that time her people got their house burned down because they were our fucking oppressors. She kept talking about it to Dad when they went to bed at night. Anyway, I eavesdropped, because by then I knew what she really was and I figured anything she was so fixated on that wasn't the planet Earth (boke) could be interesting information.

There was something about a will. Harry Keating's will. Yes, your great-grandad, Harry, who you kept slagging and calling a terrorist. Kept hearing the name Hugh as well. I've no idea who that is. But Sadhbh cared enough to go look up the National Archives about it. She'd go on and on about it and Dad would be like, OK. Then there was some affidavit. That's the word I heard a lot – affidavit, affidavit. Telling the truth about what happened, she'd say. I'd hear stuff like the War of Independence, Sing Sing, all sorts of talk about her ancestors. And something called a Medal of the Children of Mary. Not sure why they were fixated on that, given she was Protestant, but there you go.

It was all to do with the Not in Our Lifetime project she wanted to start. Your da was trying to block it.

Anyway, I kinda mentioned it to Mam, casually because I knew she didn't want to hear too much about that wagon, but I thought it might be an interesting bit of information. Anyway, Mam's face went all weird – not the way she usually looked when I mentioned Sadhbh, but more frightened than upset. Her lips went all in on themselves and she ran into the hall and was on the phone to Uncle D, pacing up and down like a lunatic.

I remember watching her through the shitty marbled glass door of that shitty house, Mam being bent over her mobile. She was nodding her head like a puppet each time she spoke: 'Yes. Yes. At Knockalisha, yes.'

Then I heard her say: 'Look, I don't know what to do now. I can't get involved, Dee. I just can't.' Then, 'Yes, I know it's not just about the company. It's about the reputation. Losing it all. I understand, yes. The reputation.' She kept saying that word. I swear to God, she was nearly in tears. After saying that, she looked up and I had to scarper.

I thought hard about telling the guards, but after everything Mam's been through, I won't let her suffer any more. Besides, what did she do only make a phone call? She lost everything when Dad went away. And never a bad word about Sadhbh, not once. She had no hand or part in whatever happened that day.

Anyway, I just wanted you to know all that. Also, I need to say it. I love you, Luke. I know that means nothing to you, but it's the truth.

SINEAD

TWENTY-SIX

By the time they had got Sinead's mother in, then her father, argued with the latter about Sinead's bail, which he was at first unwilling to pay, then dealt with the solicitor Ronan had called as an emergency, and then authorised her release with a pending court hearing in train, it was near five in the evening and Rosa's head was as melted as the Solero she'd bought earlier en route back from Diarmuid Savage's house and immediately forgotten about.

Before she could draw breath, her phone hummed again. It was Maura Casey from the State Pathologist's office. This meant they had the autopsy results in.

'Evening,' Maura said cheerfully when Rosa answered, 'I heard they put paid to your day off yesterday.'

'They did indeed, the bastards,' Rosa laughed. 'Have you news?'

'I have.' Her tone became serious. 'Are you alone?'

'It's OK, I'm in the car. Here, I'll put you on speaker.'

'All right,' Maura's voice rasped out as Rosa set the phone

on the holder. 'As we initially suspected, Sadhbh Drummond did not die from burning, charring or smoke inhalation. We are ninety per cent sure she was not asphyxiated either as the hyoid bone is intact. Indentations and fractures would indicate that she was subject to quite a savage attack before whoever it was tried to burn her body. Evidence of blunt trauma to the skull. Right temple looks smashed in. The pattern of injuries would indicate a struggle, and that death was not instantaneous. Best guess for a time is between six thirty and eight pm that night.'

Jesus. Not a nice way to go.

'You still there?' Maura's voice wavered through the dodgy West Cork signal.

'Yeah. Yeah, of course. Sorry. Was just thinking that was nasty.'

'Nasty indeed.' Maura's tut and inhalation over the speaker sounded ghostly. 'At a guess, it was the head injury that did for her. But it's hard to tell. There wasn't enough to work on to give a definite conclusion.'

There wasn't enough to work on. That was a euphemism if ever she'd heard one. What Maura meant was that the corpse was too badly disfigured for much evidence to be left. All that beauty ... Rosa felt a sudden rush of sadness.

'Thanks, Maura. Guess at the murder weapon?'

'Something very large and blunt, I'd say, if the skull injury is what we're talking about. A hammer, possibly even a brick. But then again ...'

'Not much to work on. I understand. DNA?'

She laughed shortly. 'On the body? Only her own, unfortunately.'

'No problem, I understand. Are you ready to release it for the funeral?'

'Well, the coroner has to finish up the inquest, but then,

yes. We're not going to get much else out of what we have.' Maura was brisk. 'I've emailed you on the official findings.'

'Thanks, Maura. And look, didn't you lose your day off too?'

'Sure it comes with the territory.' Maura laughed lightly. 'Speak to you later.'

After she ended the call, Rosa checked that Xiao had heard everything, then leaned back in the passenger seat and closed her eyes. God, it had been a nightmare of a day. Her anxiety was rattling inside her like a loose part of an old car engine. The loss of her appointment card – how could she have been such an idiot? – had exercised such a grip on her mind that it was almost impossible to think of anything else.

Putting her hand in her pocket to check it was still there, and finding empty air instead, had given her such a shock she had almost buckled on the spot. The fear. You couldn't describe it. It had been all she could manage not to scream there and then. Where had the damned thing gone? Was it in the school where Triona Costello would frown and tut-tut before putting it into a file somewhere? Was Diarmuid Savage perusing it with his tonic and lemon? Was Dinny Geraghty having a read of it to put in his next blasted book? Had it fallen out in the street?

Xiao had been annoyed when she begged him to turn the car around. And well he might have been – she was not being rational. But the fear of discovery scrambled Rosa's logical mind. Her biggest desire – to be known as she truly was – combined with her greatest dread.

Signing with her government name had been a strategic choice. She knew that the Gender Care Clinic waiting times were treacherously long, and if you put a foot wrong, they would make you wait at least a year longer. Also, she'd heard tell of a woman years into transition who had needed to vote for Repeal but had not yet got her name changed on her birth cert and the electoral register. That unfortunate woman had dug out a men's suit, wiped her face clean of any make-up, and walked down to the polling centre to vote using her old name. If that woman had sacrificed so much to engage with the state, Rosa, too would want to mind her Ps and Qs. So she had written down 'Gerry Keane' on the form. That decision, so careful at the outset, had now proved to be a mistake. Because if that card got in the wrong hands ... if everyone knew what Louise knew ...

With her estranged wife, there was a stalemate. If Rosa lost her job, Louise would lose the money lodged in her account every month, Muireann would lose her pony lessons, and even the house in Glanmire would probably go. And fat lot of good being on the moral high ground would do her then. That, Rosa was convinced, was the only reason Lou kept quiet.

Her mobile rang again. Eames. Wanting to know how it was going. Such a question from a superior was never innocent. Rosa relayed him Maura's findings and Sinead Furlong's confession.

'Well, Gerry,' Eames said, 'you know this is getting a lot of media attention, don't you?'

Rosa did. They'd popped into a petrol station on the Bandon relief road to fill up and she'd gone into the shop for a can of Coke. Newspapers blared out the headlines: 'WHO KILLED THE GREEN MAUD GONNE?' and 'ECO-ACTIVIST BURNT BODY FOUND IN FOREST.' The words that sprung out to her anxious eyes were 'Gardaí are keeping an open mind'. Way to let everyone know they hadn't a clue. That bombshell from the Furlong girl had really thrown the cat among the pigeons. If Tom Keating hadn't started the fire, then it was less likely he was the killer.

'So,' Eames said, 'the focus is sharp on this, you know?'

Rosa said nothing.

'Look, I heard you had to let Tom Keating go. Are you managing all right, you and …?' He'd forgotten Kevin Xiao's name. Christ almighty, the man had been outside his office on desk duty for at least a month.

'We're all right so far, Super. Though if you have a few more uniforms to do a bit of questioning, that would be appreciated. And maybe allow us expenses so that we can stay in Skibbereen for a few days more?'

'OK. I'll authorise that. But, Gerry, I'm feeling a lack of urgency here. I mean, you haven't even found that German fellow yet.'

'Ludwig? We're on it.' Eames's needling along with the endless ~~Gerry~~ing made Rosa anxious, which in turn made her voice veer from its usual low baritone into a nervy mid-contralto, far closer to the voice she heard in her own head.

And they were by no means on it. Ludwig had managed to survive his suicide attempt, but had been too unwell for questioning. As Eames knew.

Eames harangued her some more in his oh-so-reasonable way before eventually hanging up. Kevin, bless his socks, made no comment whatsoever on the call, so Rosa could switch her concentration to an email that had come through to her work account.

It was a transcribed voice note from Conall Flaherty, subject 'Braiguemore Holdings, and other info'. Conall had been a law clerk in a previous life, and was Rosa's go-to guy for any information she could not get off Google. The voice note was because Conall was dyslexic, and writing was his pain point, hence his abandonment of the law. But the same dyslexia also seemed to give him a 'big picture' memory that could conceptualise multiple gangland murders and evidence trails all in his mind. For seeing the link between seemingly unrelated entities, or suspecting its presence in the first place, there was no officer of the peace more suited than Conall Flaherty.

Not to mention he was an inveterate gossip.

Braiguemore Holdings was indeed a construction company, Conall noted, specialising in luxury second homes and retirement centres. Its first named founder was Staunton Davies, with an address in Skibbereen. 'Busy man' commented Conall, 'since he owns and manages two hundred acres of dairy farm near Drimoleague as well as his public representative role.' The other two directors were his wife, and someone called Matt Toner. Conall had managed to dig up the tree-by the-school affair and verified that a complaint had been made by Sadhbh Drummond to Sergeant Connolly on the grounds that Davies et al had not bothered to procure the obligatory arborist's report before cutting down the tree. No further action had taken place on foot of the complaint.

Matt Toner, Conall had added as a by-the-way, had children at the primary school who would have been in classrooms with a direct view of the tree. So that explained the video being taken down off Facebook.

But that was not all. Braiguemore Holdings was a minority shareholder in another, affiliated company, FEC Ltd. This company, about which little information was available online, appeared to be in the business of selling gravel and sand wholesale to garden centres, construction companies and activity parks. They had procured land in various agriculturally poor but minerally rich parcels of land around West Cork to mine the stuff, which would mostly then end up as cement.

FEC in turn was one of the companies belonging to the

Liss Ard Group, a portfolio owned by no less than Diarmuid Savage.

'God,' Rosa said aloud, 'it's like *Kind Hearts and Coronets*.'

'Huh?' Kevin looked nonplussed

'It's a black-and-white film from the late 1940s. Alec Guinness plays eight roles in it.' She sighed. 'I'll explain later.'

'No problem,' Kevin said impassively, 'I can always look it up.'

As they approached the Ballinhassig junction a few miles out from Cork City, it occurred to Rosa that calling his group Liss Ard was one more inventive way Diarmuid Savage had found to spit in the eye of Sadhbh's murdered ancestors and their ruined house.

TWENTY-SEVEN

Later the same day

By the time they returned to Cork City, then Anglesea Street to drop off the car, Rosa was happy enough to exchange the briefest of goodbyes with Kevin before gathering her belongings and returning to the house on South Douglas Street. She'd kept it together for the rest of the journey, but her nerves were shot. After the shock of losing her card, she needed to be alone.

By seven o'clock that evening, all the windows of the house on South Douglas Street were curtained, all blinds drawn down. Inside, the nondescript living room with its mustard-coloured, tufted chintz couch and empty glass cabinet, the small kitchen with its off-white vinyl floor and gently humming fridge, the bedroom with women's dresses, blouses and underwear strewn all over the bed and floor – in any of these rooms it might as well have been the dead of night outside, even though it was still bright. The bathroom door was open, and the fan still hummed as the air cooled from a recent shower. The smell of Marks & Spencer Royal Jelly and Honey was blown across the dimly lit room.

Rosa, in a grey silk slip, was standing at the chest of drawers near the en-suite door, peering into a round, self-supported mirror backlit by a Tiffany lamp balanced on the unit's corner, and carefully applying a jet-black, wet, gleaming curve to her left eyelid. She'd ordered a rake of products, including both pencil and gel liner – had gone mad online buying stuff, truth be told. Then she'd tried the pencil, and it had been a disaster – her skin was too dry – so had gone with the gel instead. You wouldn't want to be drunk doing this, that was for sure. Drunk, or just back from a day and a half investigating a murder case where no headway had been made, and half the town seemed to be a suspect.

Day cream. Foundation. Blusher. Eyeshadow. Mascara. Eyeliner. Done, finally, after much smudging, cursing and looking up 'how to fix eyeliner mistakes' on her phone. (Turned out you needed to dip the eyeliner pen in warm water and then draw that over the offending bit.) Then lipstick, in a shade called 'Red Hot Susan' she had also found on the internet – but Red Hot Susan was a bit too red and hot for Rosa's taste. She blotted some of it off. God, this was complicated. There was no guidebook, no manual called 'How to Transition' that helped you find the happy medium between vamp and twinset-and-pearls. 'Being in the Guards, a lot of it is learning on the street,' Eames had told her once. And here she was again. Learning on the street.

The short walk home from Anglesea Street had felt ominous. Lockdown and good weather meant the streets were crowded and people were drinking openly, coming out of the offices and the Spar with cans, wandering around aimlessly in the city centre, which had been defensively designed so that nobody could sit anywhere. Heaven forbid even one homeless person might get a bit of kip. Normally, Rosa would take the chaos in her stride. Today, with the whole lost card fiasco, she felt exposed, no matter how much she told herself that nobody knew who she really was.

But it wasn't just the chaotic atmosphere and the spilled outdoor pints and discarded masks and puke that made her feel on edge. Since she'd left Anglesea Street, Rosa had the distinct impression that she was being followed.

While passing the old Model School on her right, now a courthouse, she had become aware of two men in casual clothes on the other side, tracksuit and hoodie. There was something in the pattern of their movements that marked them out to her, a feeling of mirroring. They were constantly on the edge of that point between sight and blindsight, until she turned around to look, when they would melt in behind other walkers.

Paranoia, she told herself, widening her stride and increasing her pace. And sure enough, as she turned the corner onto Copley Street, the hoodies vanished. They were probably going elsewhere. But as she came back onto the river at Union Quay, Father Mathew Church looming up in all its mock-Gothic sandstone grimness, they returned to her blindsight once more. There weren't so many people walking along Union Quay; Rosa knew that if she turned around, she would see them. When she was a teenager, she had read *The Hounds of the Morrigan* where the children could only flee the Mór-Ríoghan if they didn't run. Once they turned around, looked at the hounds and started running, the dogs would be on them right quick.

Somewhere near the Palestinian café, the men disappeared again, but Rosa was ill at ease taking the now-familiar left turn up the quays towards Nano Nagle Place. It all might have been coincidence, but ...

She looked round several times before even approaching her front door, let alone putting the key in the lock, but the street was empty. Quickly, she closed it, set the chain latch on, and set about drawing the blinds and curtains on every window in the place. The house smelled of dust and lack of occupation, even though she'd only been gone one night. It would never be home. There would never be the sound of children's laughter and fighting in these rooms. Lou had made that clear. Rosa was in no position to argue one whit about custody – not in this case. Lou had her in a vice.

It must be a miserable existence for her, Rosa sometimes thought, but it was hard to be sympathetic. Imagine keeping her apart from the kids just because you were bitter; just because you could. Strange to think she and Lou had once been friends and allies, had once loved and understood each other.

But now was not the time to cry, not with eyeliner, eyeshadow and mascara setting, and foundation at risk of getting smudged. Now was time to pull her thinning hair back into a tiny, painful ponytail and set the ash-blonde wig she had bought online from Vibes & Scribes on top of the flat-tened grey-dark strands. Now was the time to spritz her silk-covered body with Fleurs de l'Himalaya, around her neck, shoulders and wrists (*they're rather too wide*, her inner voice might whisper) then slip on the dress. Or wrestle with it, to be accurate. Choosing the right outfit had been a challenge – there had been a beautiful red diamante dress on Depop, but it looked like something the drag queen Panti Bliss would wear. Rosa admired Panti immensely and respected her courage – but unlike Panti, she was not in drag. She was dressing as herself.

She had finally found it – a green cotton maxi dress with an empire line and long, flowing skirt. It had a check pattern with some lace detail around the neck and flounces on three-quarter-length sleeves that jazzed it up a little. Slightly girlish, but not garish, and that was the main thing.

Then it was time for the earrings – clipped on because Rosa had lacked the nerve to go into Wilton shopping centre, sit down in Claire's Accessories amid the My Little Pony hairclips and frosted pink combs and, as ~~Gerry~~, request a piercing. Next came rolling on a pair of tights and shoving her recalcitrant feet into a pair of dark blue patent leather high heels. Eugh! They hurt. Rosa often remembered waking up in the night when Lou came back from a girls' night out, the digital clock closing on 1 a.m., her wife throwing off her heels and massaging the balls of her toes by the anglepoise light near her bed, reeking of CK One and cigarette smoke. The sigh of relief and liberation as the shoes rolled away and she put on a pair of freshly laundered cotton pyjamas. 'You're lucky, ~~Gerry~~' – the murmured words rolled across the bed – 'you don't have to worry about stuff like that.'

Outfit complete, Rosa 'took a turn around the room'. Her phone, flat on the bed, seemed to wink at her in the light, telling her what to do next. She picked it up and took a quick selfie, careful to dip the left side of her face and relax her mouth. She looked feminine, but out of focus. Try again. Good. Now she would allow herself her one transgression – get it, ha ha ha, *trans*gression? Oh never mind …

Twitter. Under that account that nobody in her real life – her ~~Gerry~~ life – knew about. @rosabk1975 only betrayed her age, nothing else. Even location was switched off. Many of the people she followed were trans women, who unlike her, were out and proud. She admired them, but had no idea how they dealt with the abuse. She saw that Laura Wilson had locked her account again. Not surprising, after being featured in an exhibition in the National Gallery called 'Warrior Women', she'd been swarmed by nasty comments.

'Not in our name. We won't validate his fetish.'

'Disgusting man with a midlife crisis.'

And the evergreen one: 'It's the wife and children I feel sorry for.'

And then a load of cranks all hit the socials with the same pseudo-academic wording. They called Laura an 'autogynephile.' What in God's name was that? It sounded like a word Philip K. Dick would have made up for an app to remote-control your home heating.

Turns out it meant falling in love with yourself as a woman. Some quack had decided that being a trans woman was nothing more than a sexual fantasy of having the body you desired and called it 'autogynephilia'. Which was fine and well for about five minutes of the day, Rosa wanted to argue, but what about when you weren't thinking about sex, when you needed to put bleach in the toilet, or put the green bin out, or the many other mundane tasks in life? Were you supposed to be in some sort of permanent orgasmic thrill every minute of the day, thinking of your ladylike thighs? It didn't make sense.

Dara Mulvey had been the one to stir it up, of course. That poet and playwright who since his BAFTA award had for some reason turned against trans people and liked nothing more than to make their lives hell, urging his followers on to terrorise people like Laura and Rosa. Mulvey and his minions were clever, too. Dressing up their hate as concern, as advocacy for women, descending into Jesuitical, hair-splitting discussions of what was a woman and what wasn't, adorning their arguments with respectable language, until a trans woman went 'too far' – i.e. existed without apology – and then the snarling hounds were loosed.

Where did it come from, this fanatical rage? With Mulvey, it was clear enough – in the same play that won him the award, he had given an offensive quip to one of his characters, had been told it was hurtful to trans people and had maintained a hefty chip on his shoulder ever since. But in the last few years, something had turned. His views were no longer isolated. More people than ever were joining in: newspaper columnists, novelists, politicians. Particularly in Britain. Not to mention that there was a fine, eight-hundred-year tradition of Brits exporting their crap across the water, with Irish turncoats like Mulvey only too happy to help them.

And what, if they turned on Rosa, could she say in her own defence? Nothing more than what Martin Luther had said centuries before: 'Here I stand, I can do no other.'

Time to go out.

TWENTY-EIGHT

Even at ten o'clock at night, it was not yet fully dark. The air was still, laden with the heat the buildings had absorbed all day and now let out. Rosa had checked for people sitting outdoors. She had seen nobody – her road was a rat-run and the footpaths narrower than a duck's arse – but God, she was nervous. Finally, tentatively, she closed the door behind her and faced the world as herself.

Walking like this felt strange and familiar at the same time. Strange because the shoes were not made for walking, the dress felt oddly light against her legs yet constricting against her waist. And the underwire in her bra …that was weird. Yet, Rosa felt more free than she had in a while. She quickened her pace a little, felt her confidence grow. People called this a fetish? How could she make them understand that the only bondage in her life was being saddled to a false body she longed to cast off?

From the top of the road emerging onto the quays, voices called out. Sudden loud guffaws, braggadocio. The smell of the

River Lee settled in, slightly sweaty, damp, with a hint of seaweed. To distract her nerves, Rosa thought about Edward Fitzpatrick. She'd already got Eames to send out some other detectives to question him. They were all closing in on the professor: guards, papers, even the Environment Party would surely begin to distance themselves once the truth was out. Question was, what truth was that? A long-ago, sordid MeToo style case, or something far worse than that? Fitzpatrick would be desperate to hide it at any rate, and might well have resorted to desperate measures when it came to Sadhbh Drummond.

He lived upriver, Rosa knew – Sunday's Well. The river flowed faster there, more herons and otters about. Here it was brown and shallow, culverted tributaries spilling in. Someone kicked a can down a lane behind her. It clanked and rattled, before settling on the edge of the path. She stopped and looked down at it: beer spilling from its open slit, frothing into the gutter. Then, when she straightened up, gently adjusting her wig, she sensed it again. That presence in her blind side.

She turned around. The street was empty. One sodium orange light blinked and fizzled. A breeze blew, sending goose pimples across her arms. She pulled the small black bolero she had stolen from Louise's wardrobe tighter around her chest.

Shivering slightly, she headed on towards the brighter streets on the quays. Check your walk, sway a bit, but don't exaggerate the hip movement; don't hunch your shoulders – it will only emphasise their shape. Oh, who was she kidding? It was obvious she was trans – a body like hers did not pass that easily. This was like the early days of learning to drive a car, when you constantly had to think about changing gears and finding biting point on a bloody hill start without conking out the engine. Perhaps she was better off sticking to the side streets.

She did not even hear footsteps before the blow came swiftly to the back of her head. The coloured lights turned black and white, the laughter surged and faded like white noise. The pain beneath her skull radiated out like electric waves. Somebody grasped her from behind, pressing a gloved hand to her mouth and nose. The smell was salty cowhide and dirt. Rosa lifted her foot to give her assailant a good kick in the shins, but before she knew it, she was pulled around a corner, lifted up, and then flung head first to the ground, the grit lacerating her forehead as it violently met the tarmac. Then a rustle of leather and now-audible footsteps. Quick glance, but they were masked. One was raising a base-ball bat in their hands.

Then it started in earnest. It seemed she was no longer in normal time, because it went on and on, even though thinking about it later, it couldn't have lasted more than about two minutes. Her unknown assailants kicked her, stamped on her head and rained blows on her bruising flesh with the bat. All this they did in almost perfect silence, other than the creak of leather, the thump of weapon against skin and bone, and the grunts as they took turns to kick her. Rosa tried to remember her training. Don't fight back, curl tightly, protect your head – but she didn't have the chance to do much of it. She was at their mercy. One booted kick had her tasting blood, and a tooth felt loose.

Am I going to die? The sentiment was disgust rather than horror. She'd be buried with 'Gerry' on her headstone, her estranged wife and children mourning the man who had, in truth, died long ago. She knew people did that, erasing the truth. Had read about it happening to trans kids who killed themselves. The parents would put up funeral notices with their deadnames and misgender them all the way through.

No. I won't let them do that to me.

One of the men kicked her harder than expected in the stomach and she expelled air sharply, doubling up in pain. She held herself and moaned in agony, shoes dangling off her feet, dress torn and mangled, face smeared with road grit and God-only-knew what sort of dirt. She just wanted it to stop. Oh God …

Then as suddenly as they had begun, they stopped.

One of the men bent down to her ear and said in a low, firm voice with a trace of a Cork accent: 'Leave that West Cork business alone. Stop poking and interfering. Stay in Cork. We know you're a pervert, so your card is marked.' He flicked a finger against her ear and then through one eye – the other was too bruised – she saw two figures quietly flee back around the corner towards Nano Nagle Place.

She tried to raise herself to her hands and knees but moving was too painful. She tried to call for help, but her jaw ached and burned; her mouth was metallic with blood, and only a low, almost guttural, baritone moan came out. Just metres away, people drank and laughed by the riverside. Metres? It might as well have been miles.

Rosa closed her one working eye. Surely someone would come? She was getting weaker, she knew it. A car swept by on the quay, its headlights just missing her. It was surely only a matter of time before one swept down here and just ran over her almost prone body, a heap of glad rags and gewgaws, handbag scattered. But then the engine idled, and she could hear the click-click of hazards and a car door open and close, followed by soft exclamations.

'Are you all right?' The accent was metallic, Chinese, instantly recognisable. *Oh shit.*

'Kevin?' Rosa could barely get the word out. It sounded more like 'ke'in'. But her colleague – for it was he – did not miss it.

'Inspector?' The astonishment in Kevin Xiao's voice was unmistakable. Then, pushing back a strand of Rosa's wig, a shocked 'My God.' She heard Xiao inhale deeply, then enquire in a more normal tone, 'Can you hear me, Inspector?'

'Yesh.'

'I need to move you to safety. Is that OK?'

Rosa gestured at Xiao's car, driver door open, headlights still on, engine running. Even though it wasn't that large, it blocked the laneway for traffic. 'Car.'

'Don't worry about it.' Xiao stood up and called in a firm, loud tone, 'Can anyone come and help me please?'

In no time at all, a young man and two girls were on the scene, still holding their warm plastic takeaway pints, only relinquishing them when Xiao gave directions. Before she knew it, Rosa felt a warm, strong pair of hands under her back and shoulders and an exhalation of beery breath as her carefully prepared hair slipped entirely off her head.

'Fuck, it's a wig. Jesus, it's a man in drag. What ha—'

'Please,' Xiao interrupted. 'Just help me. It doesn't matter who she is.'

She. Even in her desperate state, Rosa felt her heart blow open. Xiao could come across his superior officer badly beaten on a public road and clad head to toe in women's clothes and still accept her presentation. That was something else. That was almost like love.

She tried not to scream with pain as the two men lifted her up and carried her into the back of Kevin's car, depositing her supine on the seat. Throughout, Kevin kept up a constant stream of instructions – 'Keep her back flat.' 'Don't move her head.' 'Careful!' She was far too tall to lie down fully, and her stockinged feet dangled out the doorway. The car was clean and soft, and smelled of deodorant and chlorine.

'What do we do now? Should we call the guards?' That from one of the girls.

'No.' Kevin responded. 'This is ... delicate, you understand?'

'Delicate? How did you get here so fast, like?' The youth sounded sceptical, almost sneering. 'What's going on here?'

Rosa tried to indicate that it was OK, that Xiao had not in fact beaten her up, but it came out like the lowing of a cow. Thankfully Xiao managed to placate the others' suspicions with a well-delivered, utterly reasonable response. After ascertaining, with a couple of brief, light touches – accompanied by an apology for each one – that no bones had been broken and no spinal injury had taken place, he then, with the gentlest of pushes, set Rosa's stockinged feet at an angle to the door, pushing her knees slightly upwards. Clicking it shut, he thanked his helpers, slid into the driver's seat and moved off towards Nano Nagle Place, then manoeuvred adeptly through the warren of tiny one-way roads, finally emerging at the junction with Turner's Cross. Rosa could not see from the road, but she could tell from the position of the lights and buildings that they were now on South Terrace. She was too exhausted to tell Kevin they had left her house behind. As they approached the traffic lights, the old synagogue on their left, Kevin spoke for the first time.

'You're in a bad way, si— Inspector.' Again, that self-correction, such a small thing, yet it made an exhausted and vulnerable Rosa want to weep like a child. 'Shall I take you to the hospital?'

'No,' Rosa gasped. 'I'll have to give ... my name. They'll know.'

Kevin thought a moment. 'I have a pair of tracksuit

bottoms in my bag. I always bring a spare. I don't know if you have a T-shirt or something? That might make things easier for you.' He paused awhile on 'easier'. He was calculating how far the dressing-up went; whether she was wearing Y-fronts or boxers or the pair of black, cotton, size 16 women's knickers she'd picked up in Dunnes last week. God help the poor man, trying to navigate this nightmare.

'No.' Rosa was clearer and firmer. 'I can't risk it. I'd rather go home. Please.' Slowly she pulled herself up to a seated position, coughing and then holding her ribcage straight afterward because her chest hurt with the effort.

'If you are sure about the hospital, I'll head back into the city,' Kevin replied, coolly enough, flipping on the indicator. The lights turned green. 'I was only over this side of town for my night swim. I go three times a week, when I'm not training.' That would explain the chlorine smell.

'My house—' Rosa began.

But Kevin cut her off. 'You are coming home with me. You should not be on your own tonight, Inspector. Not after such a brutal attack.'

'But I am disturbing you – your family?'

'My wife will not mind.' Kevin turned onto Penrose Quay, the bridge at the next junction lit up in coloured lights. 'I am going to call her now. Hey, Siri!' The phone sounded a note. 'Call Yu-lin.' Siri, in its female voice, complied, and soon a conversation took place entirely in Cantonese. Rosa wondered how Xiao would explain the spectacle he had encountered to his wife, and was thankful she couldn't understand a word they were saying.

The call ended. 'All good,' according to Kevin.

'I can't meet your wife like this.' But Kevin waved his hand, presumably to indicate Rosa's appearance wasn't relevant. Rosa was of a contrary opinion. She could still feel the foundation and blusher heavy on her cheeks, the weight of the mascara on her eyelashes – presumably all stained and smeared now. If only she had brought one of those many hand mirrors she kept face down in the drawer. She did have some wet wipes in her handbag, which Kevin had thoughtfully left on the floorboard within her reach. It hurt to stretch from her seated position, and she had butterfingers trying to get the clasp open, but eventually, she was able to pull the packet open and wipe down her face, neck and eyelashes. Her tights had laddered badly, so she pulled them off, her wig having already given up the ghost. Both were stuffed into the handbag, the humiliating remnants of her attempt to be Rosa on the outside as well as the inside. Hot, fat tears came to her eyes and threatened to spill down her cheeks. What a fool she had been. She was ~~Gerry~~ in a wig and a dress and make-up, nothing more.

'Kevin, I … just want to tha—'

Kevin cut across her. 'You don't need to thank me for showing some basic humanity, Inspector.'

He switched on the radio. It was one of those commercial stations that announced the news with dramatic music and transatlantic accents. There was the usual Covid update, with the familiar back-and-forth between the National Public Health Emergency Team and the government and the Licensed Vintners' Association and …

Then the truth struck Rosa like a hammer blow: her attackers had not just come up right then and there. They'd been following her all day. Like the para gang who had beaten up that liquidator fella in Monaghan and carved letters on his chest – someone was paying them. Someone who wanted her to back off. As long as Kevin was associated with her, he was in danger too.

'*It is reported that as many as 26,000 emperor penguins in the*

Antarctic have died en masse from starvation and drowning, due to melting ice and rising global temperatures,' the brash announcer's voice interrupted. *'Scientists have warned that we are running out of time to—'*

Rosa put her hands over her ears. Usually when the climate change stuff came on the radio, she would switch it off or change the channel – but this was not her car. It was all just too much, so she chose not to deal with it. In the end, if it wasn't in your face like coronavirus, or getting beaten up, what point was there in driving yourself mad with anxiety about it? She could do nothing to help the drowning penguins, the burning koalas, the thirsting flamingos. She no longer had access to her daughter, to pour false reassurances into her ears when she woke up in the middle of the night in tears about turtles choking to death on plastic. She had to detach. Sadhbh Drummond hadn't. She'd poked her nose in to try and change things – and look what had happened to her.

The news moved on to something else, and Kevin turned off the quays, gears sputtering, roaring and complaining as he pointed the car up one of Cork's most vertiginous hills. The large period houses at the base made way for close, nineteenth-century terraces as the road narrowed, then climbed past a church at a junction.

Cresting the hill, just at the start of the descent towards Mayfield, Kevin turned and parked outside a small, three-storey cluster of apartments that had been shoehorned into a space next to a garage on one side and a health centre on the other. The car park was just six spaces, and there was little in the way of even token shrubbery as Kevin put his arm around a limping, wincing Rosa and escorted her into the tiny lobby before guiding her, step by painful, jolting step, up the carpeted stairs to the second floor.

'No elevator.' That comment by way of apology was the first thing he'd said since the start of the drive. *You call it 'lift' here*, Rosa wanted to say, but given Kevin's extraordinary generosity, she kept her mouth shut.

The door opened immediately and Kevin's wife, Yu-lin, welcomed them both in without surprise. Kevin removed his shoes at the door; Rosa's high heels had already been long abandoned in a southside gutter. He led Rosa into a small sitting room with a gas fireplace and a tiny kitchenette at the back with an open doorway. At the far end, past the sofa, a desk against the wall was piled with papers and a pigeonhole file system, as well as a laptop and a large monitor. A few large, glossy textbooks in Chinese and English were stacked in the shelf below. Rosa read one of the titles: *Clinical Guide to Antineoplastic Therapy*. Whatever that was, when it was at home. A cloth decal, picturing an ox and some Chinese characters, hung on the wall above. Rosa remembered from her frequent drop-ins to the Jade Palace near Turner's Cross of an evening that 2021 was the Year of the Ox.

Usually, she'd barrel in there with Darragh McClure after a few pints. They'd order sweet-and-sour chicken with noodles and a side of spring rolls, and carry off their booty in steaming plastic meal boxes, while the spring rolls would be swaddled in white wrapping paper. Then, in the back kitchen in Rosa's house, they'd scavenge for functioning cutlery – 'Jesus, did Louise not even leave you a fork? Harsh, man' – and pile onto the couch in the small living room that faced onto the street, turning on the telly and extracting each box from the large plastic bag as if it were a treasure chest of wonders. They would watch back-to-back old episodes of *Scandal*, not a word passing between them for two hours, until Darragh would burst out, a la Olivia Pope, 'It's handled!' and they would both collapse into laughter. Sometime later, Darragh would declare it was time to go and weave drunkenly to the door, waving away Rosa's concerns.

'Don't worry, ~~Gerry~~,' he would slur; then, discovering the rhyme, chant over and over, 'Don't worry, ~~Gerry~~, don't worry, ~~Gerry~~ ...'

Yu-lin Xiao brought Rosa a mug of green tea. She did not look Rosa in the eye, whether for cultural reasons or because of Rosa's appearance, Rosa didn't know. Yu-lin's face was almost a pure oval. Her hair was cut in a bob just above her shoulders, and when she half-turned, her fringe obscured her cheek. If Rosa had had enough hair, in an ideal world she would have tried that style herself. But thinking of that reminded her once more of her current situation: that this strange woman, and near-stranger colleague, knew her deepest secret.

This was not like watching *Scandal* drunk with Darragh McClure. This was awkward.

'Drink it,' Kevin insisted, looking at the green tea mug Rosa held onto like a talisman. It had no handles, so she let her palms heat up to the point of discomfort before tilting the thick ceramic lid to her lips. It was too hot, and tasted of nothing much, but there was something calming about the rising steam and the gentle herbal kick. While she drank, Kevin and his wife left the room for a moment. Rosa heard some rattling around, then Yu-lin emerged with a tin box filled with bandages, plasters, TCP and Savlon cream. She switched on the main light, and the glare hurt Rosa's eyes.

Yu-lin smiled. 'Don't worry. I am qualified first aid.'

'She is a student oncology nurse.' Kevin smiled, not hiding his pride. That would explain the textbook.

There proceeded an exceedingly painful sequence of pressing, dabbing, dressing, disinfecting, and in one case, bandaging of Rosa's cuts, bruises, injuries and ailments. At one point, Rosa felt a pang of embarrassment when she realised she must have bled all over Kevin's car. Like that second-hand thrill of mortification she felt when Louise told her about when she was eleven and her first period came on suddenly when she was staying at a friend's house and she left a stain on the sheet.

When Yu-lin told her to open her mouth and put a swab into a gap where a tooth had been, Rosa flinched. Something about losing a tooth felt primal. A gap-tooth – how would she explain that to her colleagues, or the dentist? There was a measure of comfort in that the gap was just out of view, so if she was very careful about her facial expression, she could hide it. Rosa's mind whirled with these thoughts as Yu-lin tended to her. Sick leave was out of the question. She had to go back, that she knew. No matter what the risk.

Kevin and his wife talked in Cantonese for a few minutes before he turned back to Rosa. 'I am sorry we only have this fold-out bed, but it is very comfortable.' Then, after an awkward pause, 'We – Yu-lin and I – were wondering what happened with your injuries? Do you know who attacked you?'

'You mean you want to know why your boss was caught beaten up in the street wearing a dress and make-up? I don't blame you, Kevin. I'd be more than curious in your position.'

'Um ...' Kevin was struggling, Rosa saw. Poor fellow was out of his depth here. He looked at Yu-lin, who said a few soft words. Then, to Rosa, 'Inspector, your private life is not relevant to me. I will not ask about it.'

'But it is relevant, Kevin.' Rosa was harsh. 'Remember I lost a medical letter in Skibbereen and panicked about it? That was my gender clinic appointment card. It was addressed to my deadname, and somebody found it. As far as I'm concerned, the name everyone calls me isn't mine any more, but until I come out officially, that's what I have to use. They got some people to follow me to Cork and tell me to stay off the Drummond case or else.'

'So,' Yu-lin said gently, 'you're a woman? Transgender?'

Rosa gripped hard onto her green tea mug, letting her fingers settle in its cooling ridges. 'I know, it sounds ridiculous. But, yes, I am. My name is Rosa.'

Kevin took a gulp of his tea in turn. 'If it is all right with you …' the pause seemed to last an age '… may I still call you 'Inspector'?'

Rosa laughed, though it hurt her belly to laugh. 'You can, indeed, if you want. Anything rather than—.' She did not say the name.

'So, Rosa.' Kevin tried it out. It sounded fine. 'Do you think you were attacked because of the case?'

'I don't think it. I know it. They told me to drop the West Cork business. Obviously, the threat is that if I don't, I'll be outed against my will. I think they expect me to go on leave and tell the Super I can't be involved. Slow the whole thing down.'

'I would say more than that.' Kevin frowned. 'I would imagine they want you to persuade Eames to drop the case.'

Rosa stared at him in horror. 'I can't do that!'

'We have a suspect already,' Kevin said. 'There are ways and means of producing evidence in retrospect and wrapping things up quickly.'

'Evidence in retrospect?' Rosa began to feel ill. 'Kevin, are you suggesting we hang it all on Keating and fix the investigation?'

'I'm not suggesting anything. I'm saying it's been known to happen when a garda is compromised.'

Yu-lin had not left the room. She sat in the armchair next to the couch, pyjama-clad legs drawn up on the seat, chin in hand, listening gravely. When he and Darragh used to talk shop, Lou would always leave – at the beginning, when Rosa had asked her to, then later of her own volition. Kevin obviously confided in Yu-lin about everything. This was against the rules, but in fairness, showing up at her door with her husband late at night, clad in ruined mascara and a bloody dress ...? Rosa was not in a position to pontificate about any rules right now.

'That's what they want you to do,' Kevin continued, then put his palms on his knees. 'But I don't think that's possible now, even if it were ethical. Not after the stepdaughter's confession.'

Rosa blinked. That felt like years ago already, and it had been only yesterday.

The thought of going to work tomorrow, Kevin driving silently and knowing, was unbearable. The fear that those bastards would attack her again, knowing full well she could never tell her colleagues the reason why. The Irish police did not have one single transgender officer, male-to-female or vice-versa. There would be no flowers or celebrations. She'd be out on her ear ... and that was another thing she had meant to say ...

'I owe you an apology.'

Kevin raised his eyebrow very slightly. 'What for?'

'For all that guff about white privilege and the like. When you had to go through that tribunal and face the officers who slagged you off like that. I read about it when I looked you up. It must have been hell.'

Kevin nodded. 'It wasn't nice, that was for sure. So,' and now he did smile, 'if you admit you have white privilege, I will admit I have cis privilege, and we can call it quits. What?' – he smiled at Rosa's incredulous look – 'You think I don't know what 'cis' means? Do you think I don't read the news? Look at Twitter?'

'Well, I ...' Rosa fumbled for words. She felt extraordinarily happy and grateful.

'On Chinese television,' Yu-lin said, 'there is a talk-show host called Jin Xing. She is pua – seng – yan.'

'Transgender.' Kevin nodded. 'She is very famous. Even my mother watches her show.'

'But they put her in prison,' Yu-lin added sadly. They began talking again in Cantonese, leaving Rosa to listen to their back-and-forth without understanding. She wondered if Kevin had spiked the green tea with valerian or some other substance, because her eyelids felt heavy, and she suddenly just wanted to sleep the sleep of the dead.

'I should go home,' she said, but neither Kevin nor Yu-lin would hear of it.

'You're in no state to go anywhere. And I don't want to hear about you coming into work first thing tomorrow.' Kevin raised a hand to prevent Rosa's protest. 'I understand you don't want people to know. I respect that. But if you are not going to seek medical attention, you need to rest. I will tell the Super.'

'No,' Rosa said, tiredness overwhelming her as if she were five and up past her bedtime. 'No, if anyone is going to tell him, it has to be me. Let me handle it, Kevin.'

'If you promise to rest and sleep.'

'Pinky promise.' The words came out of her before she could stop herself. That was what she always said to Muireann when she was a small child: 'pinky promise', and they would link their little fingers together. Once again, tears pricked her eyes. *Everything I have lost, was it worth it? For this notion that I am Rosa?* The dull magnolia walls and the low beige ceiling seemed to crowd around her as she let tears run down her cheeks. Yu-lin searched in her handbag for a tissue but her husband touched her arm and said something again in Cantonese, and she stopped.

Kevin and Yu-lin extended the couch into a futon, and fetched sheets and pillowcases. They would not hear of Rosa helping them. When they were finished, they both left the room with quiet goodnights, leaving Rosa a white T-shirt and a pair of cotton boxers. As she undressed, piling her now-unwanted clothes at the side of the futon beside her shoes, she bit her tongue whenever she felt a stab of pain. She did not want to bother the Xiaos, who were getting ready for sleep next door, their conversation and bathroom trips all audible through the thin walls. Urination, toilet flushing, the quick blast of the tap, the drone of an electric toothbrush … all the sounds of domesticity.

She slipped into the makeshift bed. The counterpane was light and soft, and had a faded pattern of blue squares with a white background. Everything felt cool, and smelled clean, and as her cheek hit the pillow, slumber overcame her like a wave, and she surrendered to it.

That night she dreamed of burning forests, fleeing animals, and Tom Keating coming forward to rip her dress. He sounded like Louise: 'freak', 'disgusting'. She turned to run away, but then Sadhbh Drummond loomed before her, hair flying, eyes blazing. 'Rosa,' she called out. 'I know. I have always known. I would have fought for your right to live in peace. Don't leave me here. Don't leave me.'

TWENTY-NINE

Wednesday, 5 May 2021, 9 a.m.

The grubby PVC-framed window was thrown open to the countryside, and the phone was hooked up to a Bluetooth speaker playing Dermot Kennedy's 'Giants' at full volume.

Luke Keating knelt on the floor, methodically packing clothes into a small backpack, his dark hair catching the glint of the sun. He'd just had a shower and had been about to let the fan run, before realising it didn't matter any more, and switching it off.

The clothes were folded and rolled neatly, to take up minimum space. By the backpack's side was a clear plastic travel wash kit which contained a travel toothbrush head, a small tube of toothpaste and a 30 ml bottle of decanted shower gel. The washcloth was rolled up separately. There were pockets for the laptop, its charger, and the phone charger. The phone would go in last, just after his packet of cloth masks.

Anything not needed went in the bin. Mixed in with the banana peels and cigarette butts were the torn fragments of a letter that had been ripped to pieces within moments of being read. The little scrap with 'Love, Sinead' on it floated on the top, refusing to sink to the bottom of the pile. It caught Luke's eye as he packed, so he paused to look around for an empty can of Tanqueray and orange and pushed down the fragment with it.

A noise downstairs – his mother closing the microwave door. She had made him a cup of tea earlier and he hadn't drunk it, so she was probably warming it up again. Sure enough, her voice sneaking up the stairs like weak tea itself: 'Luuuuuuuuke ...'

He put the volume up on his phone and picked a rockier track from the album. Something with a lot of guitar. Then a quick text.

Ollie, it's on. I've got to come up.

A reply quickly flashed up on the screen.

No worries, bud. I getcha.

I'll have to take the bike, because it's lockdown. I'm really sorry putting this on you while you're social distancing and all.

Jeez. Don't worry about that, just mask up. Nobody will know you're there in the basement. Is there nobody who would drive you up? You can't cycle to Dublin!

Luke rocked back on his heels for a moment, put the phone down and sighed heavily as the guitar hit a high point. Then he picked it up again and typed:

No. Can't trust anyone here now.

I hope you're not in some sort of trouble?

The 'rolling on the floor' emoji at the end did nothing to dispel the static of worry behind the words. Luke typed:

I'm not sure

Then he backspaced the message, hoping Ollie could not see he was typing and deleting. Ollie had an Android and Luke's mobile was an iPhone so that meant Ollie wouldn't be able to see the dots, but Luke couldn't be certain. Quickly, he texted:

Nah, nothing like that. But I need to get away from the old man.

Cool.

On impulse, Luke added:

My heart's in bits, Ollie. I'll never be the same now she's gone.

But no, that couldn't be let through. His anguish must be private now. He had to hit the road – like his great-grandad Harry.

'That Sadhbh Drummond's gentry scum. Your great-grandad Harry knew her type,' his dad once told him, when they were having a row about him spraying Roundup on everything that moved and most stuff that didn't.

At which point Luke had said, 'Fuck Great-grandad Harry.'

'Y'what?' Tom's pause was brief, dangerous.

'You heard, Dad. Fuck him. He's no hero. He liberated nattin' and nobody. He killed an innocent man and his young fella, and he got what he deserved.'

But that was then. Now things were different. Sadhbh was dead, and he wasn't safe.

His mother had given up on the tea, presumably, and retreated to the kitchen. She would be making his da and the contractor some sandwiches, concentrating on the cheddar cheese, making sure she had the cheese knife at exactly the right distance. Too thick, and it would enrage. Too thin and it would break into pieces, and also enrage. And if she went and just lashed on a cheese slice, he'd go mad. It had to be cheddar with the ham. Between the margarine and the cheese, her pass rate was something like fifty per cent.

It was time to go.

Like the Beatles song, Luke thought wryly, slipping out the side entrance and wheeling his bike out from the shed. Past the concrete yard, where the guard dog howled, dying slowly of stomach cancer because Tom wouldn't do the decent thing and put her down. Past the sheds full of broken, rusting machinery that held not a single swallow's nest because Tom ranted and raved about the bird shit and knocked them out with a broomstick. Out the gate where, for metres around, every blade of grass and wildflower had been sprayed with the Roundup Luke and Tom had been arguing about, until it turned the stones black and the grass and flowers into something burnt-looking and lifeless.

'You're very bright, Luke,' Sadhbh had told him. 'You deserve better.'

Time to go before his da or the Guards got after him. When they'd announced Sadhbh's death during assembly, he'd broken everything up. Rage had made him do things that horrified him, and he had to flee, whatever bullshit he'd told Ollie. Unfair of him to lie, but escape was more important. A few yards later, Keating land ended, and the verges were uncut and unsprayed once more, spilling out with crocosmia and fuchsia, dandelions bringing up the edge. The air even smelled different. Sweeter. It filled the lungs better. Luke felt something lift as he mounted his bike and started the long freewheel down Knockalisha Hill, but also a knot of sadness too.

Because this had been Sadhbh's country, and he was leaving her behind for ever.

THIRTY

Wednesday, 5 May 2021, 10 a.m.

It was no great hardship, Kevin Xiao reflected, to be on the road again. He'd come into Anglesea Street with a sinking heart about having to finesse Rosa's absence. Eames demanded to know why Keane was calling in sick, and did he have 'It'. Kevin, still reeling from the previous night's revelations, took a while to realise what Eames was talking about.

'No, sir,' he told him then. 'The inspector does not have coronavirus.'

'Oh for God's sake,' Eames had snapped. 'Why is he out then? I can't spare anyone – we've got the anti-mask lunatics converging on City Hall today. Mary Fehily is spurring them on from her channel. This is bloody inconvenient.' He looked at Kevin with rheumy eyes. 'I guess you're in charge, Detective. Congratulations.'

'Sir.' The irony in Eames's tone undermined the compliment, but it didn't matter. Kevin was in charge, and heading cross-county to Bantry, because Sean Connolly had phoned

Anglesea Street to let them know that Peter Ludwig had regained consciousness and was able to answer questions.

Terry Bailey was with him. She spent most of the drive on the phone to her childminder. He missed the inspector and his— *her* silly faux pas – and even the history lectures. Terry was his age, younger by far than Keane, but she had a racist puss on her that made her look a decade older and declined to put on a mask to conceal it. 'A puss on her' – that was one of the expressions he had learned back in Kilsheelan, from another rookie garda who turned out also to be racist. But never mind that. It was a turn of phrase that fitted Terry's expression very well.

It did not help that the road was in turns boring and poor quality, sometimes both at once. To have taken the Skibbereen route then gone along the coast would have been nicer, but they'd have landed in Bantry sometime next Thursday, so that was out. As it was, they had to go through a series of towns in North Cork, and one or two traffic snarl-ups, before finally emerging onto the N71 and into Bantry town, which turned out to be quite lovely, situated in the snuggest corner of a large ocean bay. Kevin had never been to Bantry before, so he obeyed the phone's directions as he had done in Skibbereen. These brought Kevin and Terry uphill, along the appropriately named Hospital Road to their destination.

They asked for Peter Ludwig at the main desk and were directed to the mental health facility just beside the main building.

'I guess after they fixed him up physically, where else would they put him?' said Terry. Then she added, 'When I think of little kiddies with cancer and what they go through. It's pure self-indulgence. They take up beds and never care about the people they leave behind.'

Kevin considered telling her that if a person had died by

suicide and left people behind, logically, they would not be taking up a hospital bed – since they were dead. But in the end, he was too disgusted with her to bother. He'd heard enough of that rubbish in his country of origin.

Peter Ludwig, it turned out, was outside; he was sitting at a picnic table in a large, paved patio area dotted with planters and a small lawn on one side. The sky was blue and scudded with only tiny clouds. It was hot out, but Peter was wearing a hoodie. He had his head in his hands and elbows on the table. Even with that, it was impossible to ignore the thick, heavy bandages on his wrists.

'We're here to talk about Sadhbh Drummond.' Kevin did not bother with a greeting. Depressed the man may be, but he still called officers 'pigs', and he might well have been the last person to see Sadhbh alive.

'We know that you and she communicated in the hours before she was killed and that you probably met. We also have reason to believe you were in a secret relationship.'

Peter looked at them blinkingly, like an allegator. Then he said slowly, 'I was not the one who wished to keep it secret.'

'You wanted to her to leave her husband?' Terry broke in, interested in spite of herself.

'Of course.' Peter briefly glanced at the decal behind him on the fence, one of many put up around the garden's perimeter. It said, 'If you can change your mind, you can change your life.'

'What bullshit,' Peter commented acidly. 'As if mental illness has nothing to do with the sick capitalist society we live in. We are being indoctrinated like sheep. The sheep we let tear down every trace of wildlife on these mountains. Sadhbh knew. She warned you. And you killed her.'

'Try a communist society and see how you get on,' Kevin snapped. He hated tankie nonsense like this from Westerners.

Terry put a hand on his arm and gave him a nauseating, condescending smile. Kevin wanted to shake it off in a rage. How dared she put her hand on him like that?

'I find it interesting that you accuse us of killing Sadhbh,' he said, 'when you are the one whom the evidence places closest to her when she died. Are you sure you're not projecting, Peter? We see you attempted to take your own life. Were you avoiding arrest? Are you such a coward?'

Peter made a noise that sounded a bit like a cough combined with a sob, but which turned out to be a long laugh.

'Oh Guard, thank you so much, it's been ages since anyone has told me such a good yoke. *Joke.*' He corrected himself. 'You think I tried to end my life because I'm afraid of you? Or because I ended Sadhbh's life and couldn't face myself? No. That was not why.' Sombre again, he looked down at the table. 'The truth is more embarrassing. I wanted to leave this life because I could not live without her. That meeting you speak about, that was me begging her one last time, 'Please change your mind; please come away with me. Leave your husband, give up on this godforsaken country which hates you so much and will never change.' But she got angry. Told me if I ever bothered her again, she would contact you people. So – finished.' He pursed his lips surlily. 'Our affair was a passionate spree of unreason. Many would say it was doomed from the beginning. But I loved her more than life itself. More than Ronan who took off his Fitbit every time he made love to her. She hated that. Hated that he was still treating her like a shameful affair long after they were married.'

'Because it started as an affair, right?' Terry seemed to be more interested in getting the gossip than figuring out if Peter were the murderer.

Peter moved to fold his arms, but presumably his injuries prevented him, as he moved them back again. 'That's the kind of scurrilous talk I wanted to protect her from. Sadhbh was not like that. She had a pure, childlike wulnerability ...' He sighed, letting the slip go by. 'She was so misunderstood.'

Kevin remembered Yu-lin telling her about a friend's divorce back home, about how her friend's husband spouted similar guff about his mistress. But he sensed Peter wanted to talk. 'Tell me more about her,' he said in his softest tone.

Thankfully Terry kept her mouth shut and didn't ruin the moment, because Peter was more than happy to talk. To the despised members of the constabulary avidly listening, he poured out the saga of his relationship with Sadhbh, how it started in 2018 when they met in Cork at an Extinction Rebellion protest to enforce the traffic ban on Patrick Street on Sundays – the 'Pana ban' whose observance was chiefly honoured in the breach. How he'd stood in front of a car for five minutes refusing to give way until Sadhbh gently took his hand and led him to the footpath. How they made such a team and had been arrested in Bantry at the fish farm protests; how they'd nearly been injured sabotaging a hunt near Ladysbridge in east Cork. How he thought he was doing these things for the planet, but it became more obvious he was doing them for her.

Then, those blissful months when they finally admitted their feelings for each other, making love for hours on end, most often in his Abbeystrewry caravan. The scent of her: deep, salty, of the earth, and yet clean, with lemon vervain. How her long, thick hair engulfed him. How there was no anxiety about his Fitbit because: 'I do not use those capitalist spyware products.'

He was quite the one to share, was Peter Ludwig.

She had sent him away for a while to do voluntary work

in a refugee camp near the English Channel, to work on her marriage, she said – but then, when he'd been on the verge of getting together with a French girl, she'd messaged him on Facebook – a quote from Yoko Ono: *'I am a cloud. Watch for me in the sky.'* – and it had all come to an end. He had rushed back to her, and their affair ('I hate calling it that') had resumed, shortly after Leo Varadkar had called for the first coronavirus lockdown in March 2020.

Terry was goggle-eyed. To her, this was probably better than every gossip site online. A murder, landed gentry shagging a German migrant, Fitbits, Yoko Ono – she was eating it up. Kevin was more interested in getting Ludwig nice and relaxed, so that he could incriminate himself. He was torn between asking the man if he wanted a cold drink or even an ice cream, and not breaking the spell being woven. Besides, he'd have to ask Terry to do it, and that would go down like warmed-up sick.

'And did other people notice?' he asked, as Peter seemed to have tired of talking.

'Yes.'

'Such as?'

Peter fidgeted. He looked uncomfortable. 'After that time we were caught at Liss Ard, things changed. Sadhbh began to go cold on me. Said she couldn't turn her back on her rewilding project. I think she still had some strange attachment to Ronan.'

'He was married when they met. He was more of a prize because she got him off someone else,' Terry cut in.

Kevin didn't check her words, because she was right. Instead, he moved in close to Peter, eyeballing him. 'Who caught you?'

'Luke Keating.' It was a hiss of contempt. Kevin pulled back in surprise. That name he had not been expecting.

'Go on.'

'Sadhbh and I met at Liss Ard in the ruins – as a sort of homage I suppose. Don't believe the lies that anyone tells you in that town. The hurt that was done to her family never went away.'

'And Luke caught you … presumably, in a compromising position?'

Peter frowned. 'We didn't know it was him. We were … finished, but still, you know, wrapping things up.' Kevin nodded. Wrapping things up presumably meant Peter figuring out what to do with the condom, since he could hardly throw it away and look Sadhbh in the eye afterwards. 'We heard a rustle somewhere, and then a twig snapped. But he did not confront us.'

'So how did you know it was him?'

Peter pointed to a bruise on his face which Kevin thought had been part of his suicide attempt. 'He came to my caravan the next day and beat me black and blue. I was in nearly as bad a state as when I tried to kill myself. He told me to stay away from her if I knew what was good for me.'

'Why?'

Ludwig rolled his eyes in disgust. 'Because he was in love with her too.'

Ah. Kevin remembered Triona Costello saying something about Luke earlier, that he had been very upset when Sadhbh was killed.

'He was angry that she would pick me. I first noticed it when Sadhbh brought him along to a protest against cutting hedges in nesting season. We were in her car, and I put my hand on hers when she was changing gear. He noticed it and looked at me like pure poison.'

'Were there witnesses?'

'Yes! Murt Phelan was there and Jane Deasy too. They're

both in the environmental WhatsApp circle. OK, I was indiscreet, maybe. But they saw how cold Luke was. And there is CCTV evidence of the beating he gave me.'

'Oh really?' Kevin perked up. All this time, he only had Peter Ludwig's word that any of this was true, but this changed things.

'Yes. I had Danil fix some outside. I hate surveillance, but the caravan had been broken into and attacked before. Ever since I got with Sadhbh. People were after me.'

'And where is it now?'

'I texted Danil this morning and asked him to collect the footage. I was scared someone would try steal it. He's got it all safely. I'll give you his number.'

Kevin had gone into that interview determined to arrest Peter Ludwig. Now, as they said their goodbyes, and he paused at the vending machine for the long-awaited tea to pour into the little cup that automatically dropped down, he called Sean Connolly. 'Can you bring in Luke Keating, please? We need to speak to him.'

THIRTY-ONE

Wednesday, 5 May 2021, 12 p.m.

Sergeant Connolly stuck his head around the door of the incident room. 'I'll be ready in ten minutes, OK?'

Kevin Xiao was on his second coffee in spite of the heat, and his head was nearly hitting the desk with tiredness. He had just arrived in Skibbereen after over an hour's drive from Bantry. Adding that to this morning's trip, he'd done a round trip of the largest county in Ireland. Much to his relief, he'd said goodbye to Terry in the Maritime Hotel, where she was going to have lunch and get the bus back.

Kevin had stopped in Ballydehob to get petrol and bought himself a 99 at the service station to cheer himself up. He ate it leaning against the wall beside the shop window, gazing at the forecourt and the cars lining up at the pumps, their engines echoing against the roof and the concrete floor. Across the road from the station, a long viaduct from an abandoned railway stood guard over a playground. Beyond that were the islands of Roaringwater Bay. Apart from the drone of the engines and the gasoline sneaking up his nostrils, it was peaceful here, a million miles away from murder enquiries and climate anxieties.

It gave him a little time to wonder what the inspector's predicament meant for the investigation. Never once did it occur to Kevin Xiao to dispute the inspector's evaluation of herself. He knew enough of human nature to know that such things happened. That said, Kevin feared for Rosa Keane's future – and feared there might be a point where he would have to put his own career first.

Now here he was, back in Skibbereen and sitting in the middle of the incident room – if you could call it that – drinking godawful powdered-instant black coffee. That, the Ballydehob 99, and the earlier tea in the mental health unit at Bantry hospital were the only fare he'd enjoyed that day. He was spoiling for some sour jellies, but Yu-lin would kill him if she found out he was eating sweets like a 'fat Westerner'. She had already made her feelings clear about his sneaky 99s.

The fan was already on, its shadow thunk-thunking the opposite wall. Pictures and arrows of the investigation danced before Kevin's exhausted eyes, the red marker on the whiteboard drawing connections between Sadhbh in the centre – a still of her on the podium, zoomed in to the point where she had finished her speech, exultant – to a picture of her husband, squinting in the sun with a grim look on him. Then her stepdaughter, her face as there-and-square as a potato. SÍNEAD written below, with the accent on the wrong letter, the 'i' instead of the 'e'. Irish people, in Kevin's experience, were very creative when it came to misspelling their own language.

The photos were all cut out of papers or printed from scanned images and stuck on with gobs of Blu Tack. Sadhbh Drummond, Ronan Furlong, Tom Keating: victim, witness, suspect, suspect, suspect, suspect... Luke Keating was not on it yet, but it was only a matter of time.

His phone vibrated, and he fished it out of his pocket.

'Inspector.'

'Hello, Kevin.' Keane sounded happier than in a while. 'Just wanted to check how things were going.'

'Never mind that, how are you?'

'Just up. Had the best night's sleep in a long time. I feel a bit sore and wonky, but miles better than last night. What did you tell Eames?' Kevin didn't reply. 'Never mind. Probably better to text me.'

'I'll do that, sir— Um, sorry, Inspector.'

'Don't be worrying about that. I'll be incognito awhile yet,' Rosa chuckled. 'Do you know, your wife made a lunch for me? The most gorgeous collection of grub I ever did see. Some dumplings to heat up in a bit of soup, and then the sesame toast, and the little crunchy things ... what d'ye call 'em? Wontons, that's it. I must confess I ate the lot for my breakfast. They were gorgeous. And the fish ...'

A door opened. The sergeant was back. He rapped at Kevin on the glass panel of the half-open door with his car keys.

'I'll give you a lift out to Deirdre now.'

'Is that Connolly?' Keane said. 'Tell him I'll be back in action as soon as I can.'

Kevin quickly concluded the call and followed Sean Connolly out. He was in shirtsleeves, but once again, the car was boiling hot. He wound down the passenger window and masked up, passing a spare one to Connolly, who waved it away. 'Sure we have the window open, we'll be grand.'

'Ye get used to driving in a rural society.' Connolly took the turn signposted Bantry and Killarney. 'Not so many paths and buses. Jesus, 'tis hot.'

'Any sign of Luke Keating yet?'

Connolly frowned. 'Last I heard, the boy went out of his parents' place up at Knockalisha, and there was no sign of him. Half his room cleared out, bike gone. His mother was going on about making him tea, and he was playing music.'

'Maybe he's just gone out somewhere.'

'If he has, they haven't located him yet.'

This was not good. Luke could be anywhere.

Connolly turned up the air conditioning to 4 as the road widened and off-white concrete walls rose either side of them, like battlements cutting off the town. 'It narrows here in a bit.'

It did indeed narrow, passing a playground and a group of small bungalows, followed by hedgerow, until it descended to the bridge at the river Ilen, with Abbeystrewry famine cemetery just on the opposite bank.

Half an hour down the road, on this side of the bay, the German woman had been bludgeoned to death in a remote cottage on the way out to Mizen Head. That was the case that Eames had warned Keane about on Monday when giving the briefing. There wasn't a guard west of Clonakilty that wasn't nervous about that case, and the mess they'd made of it.

Connolly turned left at a church and followed a signpost to 'Heir Island Pier'. As they approached the sea, the road deteriorated and the car's suspension began creaking and groaning as it made its way through rocky fields and fiercely cut hedges before pulling in at a modest whitewashed cottage with a low stone wall and a half-door painted red.

The tarmac path bisected a fledgling lawn and ran parallel with a small flowerbed filled with heather and the kind of shrubs one might see in a corporate car park: waxy, durable, not given to over-ambitious flowering. A large bag of moss peat compost leaned against the wall near the door. Before the sergeant could raise his hand to the black wrought-iron knocker, both doors opened and a short, oblong figure of a woman emerged wearing a loose red T-shirt and cream slacks. Deirdre Twamley would, Kevin guessed, be somewhere in her mid to late forties. Her hair was cut short and a lick of it seemed glued to her forehead.

'Come on in, lads. Don't mind the cat.' And Kevin noticed the creature for the first time, sinuous and quiet, just about brushing his leg as it stalked past them onto the lawn, tail in the air, looking for birds, no doubt.

They were ushered into a room on the right, dusty and unused, unpleasant in the heat. It was the usual format of the Irish 'good room' – cabinet packed with forgotten trophies, chintzy couch, nondescript coffee table and a large-screen television. Photos that nobody looked at, old schoolbooks that never got read. Some historical biographies: *Patrick Pearse: The Making of a Revolutionary*, and *1916: A History of Ireland from the Rising to the Present*. All the sort of books that would be expected in the household of a member of Muintir na hÉireann.

Over the years, Deirdre's party of choice had gained a somewhat unfair reputation of coming up with extra-judicial solutions to common problems. Though recently they had laundered some of their past misbehaviour by dint of vigorous rebranding and playing a role that positioned them as a party of the people rather than of guns, the whiff of cordite had never quite deserted them, north or south of the border.

Deirdre re-entered with the customary cups of tea, even though the room offered no respite from the heat. She sat down opposite them.

'Well, boys, what can I do for you?'

'We're here in connection with the murder of Sadhbh Drummond.'

Deirdre's hand flew to her forehead and shoulders in an automatic sign of the cross. 'The Lord have mercy on her. 'Twas shocking.'

Kevin decided not to waste any more time on pleasantries. 'It is shocking. But leading a protest outside her family home, banging on her car window when her children were present, just weeks before she died – that is shocking too, wouldn't you say?'

Deirdre flushed red very quickly. 'And what's that to do with anything? We have our constitutional right to protest. If you've something to say, Guard' – an ugly look crossed her face – 'you'd better come out and say it. You forget I was at the 'Right to Water' protest right here and chained myself to a manhole.' This directed at Connolly, who very clearly had not forgotten at all and shifted uncomfortably on the couch.

Kevin was unbothered by Deirdre Twamley. As people had never stopped reminding him ever since he'd set foot in Dublin Port, he wasn't from around here. He didn't care if a local councillor from Skibbereen didn't like him. 'Ms Twamley, can you tell us where you were on the evening of May 31st between five and eight p.m.?'

'I was at home. Are you insinuating I had something to do with all that?'

'At home.' Kevin wrote a note on his alibi list. 'Will anyone confirm this?'

'My son Tadhg. He's eleven. His sisters are too little. And Emer Hession, a neighbour of mine who dropped in. I have her number here on my phone.'

'Sure, I know her well,' Connolly cut in, just as Kevin was laboriously searching for his pen. 'I'll have a word with Emer.'

'Did you receive any communications that might have led you to believe Ms Drummond's life was in danger?'

'Communications? And what do you mean by that? Why would I hear anything?'

'Ms Twamley. Come on, please. You are a member of a party that, let's say, has a tradition of sorting things out without bothering us or the courts.'

'I'm a democratically elected representative, and I take offence at your line of questioning.' Deirdre Twamley was prim, arms folded, lips thinned.

'I don't care.' Kevin didn't bother hiding his exasperation. 'According to a witness, your sister makes a gesture at Ms Drummond six months ago like this.' e drew his finger across his throat. 'Subsequently, you lead a group of people outside her house banging on her car windows, threatening her in front of her kids. Then, weeks later, her burned body is found in a forest. If you don't want to be offended at my line of questioning, Ms Twamley, you and your relatives should not have committed offensive actions in the first place that might lead us to your door.'

Sean Connolly looked up, his eyes widening in alarm, a flaming blush overtaking his freckles. 'Go easy, there now, Kevin.'

It took a few seconds for the cannonball of rage that hit Kevin in the chest to diffuse all through his body, sending such a shockwave that his skin prickled and he felt a frisson so cold that his teeth almost chattered. He gripped the sides of the armchair and saw his knuckles whiten. Connolly had chided him in public. While interviewing a possible suspect. In front of her. When he had been brought in to keep an eye on them.

He'd never have done that if Kevin Xiao were white. Not in a million years.

All the bullshit from the gardaí in Shankill began to rico-
chet in his head. They'd abuse him behind the counter, but
whenever reporters queried diversity stats, they'd wheel him
out and slap him on the back. Kevin was fed up with the
disrespect of being told that the daily insults were nothing to
do with race.

But for now, Kevin Xiao would have to bite back his anger
and focus on the matter at hand. Which was that he had a
very un-cooperative interviewee, and he was finding it hard
not to sneeze his head off in the stagnant air and the tight face
covering.

'She was no angel, you know.' Deirdre's reply startled him
out of his reverie.

'Who?'

'Sadhbh Drummond.' She almost spat the name. 'You call
me an extremist? If anything, I was trying to calm things
down. It wasn't just the objections, though. I had enough
constituents complaining about those. It was her behaviour.
She hurt a lot of people, the way she carried on with Ronan
Furlong behind his wife's back.'

'Yes, but that was ten years ago,' Kevin objected. 'Ronan
and Sadhbh were married with children. Surely everyone
would have got used to it?'

Deirdre laughed slowly. 'Doesn't matter how long ago.
Look at Princess Diana and Camilla Parker Bowles. People
remember how it started – that's what matters.' She cleared
her throat. 'They remember the 'lady of the manor' swan-
ning back from fancy school and university, and just taking
her man like he belonged to her. Like poor Jeanne didn't
matter. I confronted her once, you know. Told her she had no
business telling people what to do with their plastic bottles
when she had gotten Jeanne and the kids kicked out of their
house. She laughed in my face. Told me I was a bitter

woman who knew nothing about passion and real life. I said to her, I said, 'Sadhbh, I see plenty of real life and passion in my constituency office every week. I see its broken consequences. I see people on their knees going to the food kitchen in Clon. I see things that you will never see because you are never connected to that world.' But she didn't understand. She was all about the animals and plants, but I don't think she ever understood how to make a real connection with a person – one that didn't depend on beauty or power.'

She paused, her face flushed, then got up and wrestled with the window latch until it loosened. She gave it a shove and it flew open. The hot air that leisurely wafted in from outside brought little relief to that small inferno.

'You were talking about Lorraine, Guard. She has her problems, you know; her husband is a no-good. In the before days, she couldn't even go out for a drink with friends – not without him texting her every minute, wanting to know where she was and who she was with. I've told her she should leave, but she feels tied with the babbies, you know? Ciaran, now, he's a lovely little fella, but he's like all one-year-olds, full of mischief. She was trying to get him back into the buggy and he started fighting her. Yes, Lorraine let out a roar at him, like. But there's no badness in her. It wasn't on for a fast piece like Sadhbh Drummond to tell her she was abusing her son.'

'I imagine that must have been hurtful.'

'Hurtful – and untrue! Lorraine loves her little boy, and what that woman did to her, shaming her like that – after the way she'd behaved to Jeanne, to the community, thinking we'd forgotten – the nerve of her!'

'Was there a chance that Sadhbh might have been genuinely concerned?' Kevin asked, making a mental note to follow up with social services on Lorraine Twamley, if that was her name, and her husband.

'Not a bit of it,' Deirdre said in disgust. 'Lorraine's little fella is the happiest, most loved boy you've ever seen. All their appointments kept. Happy and healthy. 'Lady' Drummond had no interest in doing a thing for Lorraine. That woman' – here Deirdre's voice dripped so corrosively that Kevin could almost see the acid drops burn the table – 'only cares about herself. That was the day I decided to go ahead and ring around, and organise the march. Finally do something about the deluge of complaints I had about her, while the fury was on me. Mind you, I wish I'd done it differently.' She folded her hands on her lap and squeezed the fingers of one hand with the other. 'I have great respect for Ronan, you know. Just because he's in the EP and I'm in Muintir na hÉireann doesn't mean we hate each other. There's a lot of cross-party goodwill at local level. He taught my eldest and gave him extra time when my marriage broke up and his marks went down. He's a good man. Quiet about it, never ostentatious. Of course, we don't speak now.'

Kevin wondered about the circumstances of Deirdre Twamley's marriage break-up. If her husband had left her for someone younger, it might account for her animosity towards Ronan Furlong's second wife. Because it was odd to have her speak so warmly of Ronan when he was the one who had left, while excoriating Sadhbh.

'We always had an understanding in the council chambers that personal life was off limits. It was decency; something we all understood and didn't breach. Ronan may not have been on the council, but he was a long-time Environment Party member, and we'd work with him a lot on school traffic and that. So you can see why I held off criticising his wife in public, for a very long time.'

'Until Ronan's protection wasn't enough to shield her any more.'

'Nobody could shield her.' Deirdre was exasperated. 'She was the kind of person who you'd give an inch to, and she'd take a mile. Indoctrinating the kids and taking them off on climate protests and telling them all about how they were doomed because of older generations. Giving them nightmares and sending them home crying and arguing with their parents. They're just kids! It was completely unprofessional, and what with the objections she kept lodging and how she poked her nose into people's business ... it was only a matter of time.'

'Before?' Kevin said sharply.

'Before she used up people's goodwill.' Deirdre put her head in her hands. 'Look, it was dreadful what happened to the woman, don't get me wrong. But don't ask me to shed any tears for Sadhbh Drummond. Just don't.'

Even with the window open in early summer, and the gorse and ragwort flowering, there was not an insect to be heard buzzing. The silence was unbroken apart from the faint echo of a jet engine trailing a blue sky far above. There was something wrong about that silence.

'Thank you, Ms Twamley,' Kevin said softly, 'for your honesty.'

'You're welcome.' She looked near tears – the tears she had sworn just moments ago that she would never shed.

'Can I ask,' Kevin continued, 'if anyone approached you with plans to attack Ms Drummond? Did anyone confide in you? Or use you in their plans? Someone who might have known how deep your antagonism towards her was?'

Deirdre shook her head.

'I promise you, Deirdre, we will treat any disclosure with absolute confidence. If you feel more comfortable talking to me personally, or Inspector Keane when they come back, that can be arranged. Sometimes it helps to speak to someone who isn't local, and it won't get back to anyone.'

Connolly flinched, and Kevin had his revenge.

Another silence lengthened in the room as Deirdre contemplated his question. The sun emerged and hit Kevin right in the face, so he squinted. When he opened his eyes again, everything unfolded for a second in bright technicolour.

'No, Guard,' Deirdre said, after far too long a deliberation. 'Nobody ever spoke to me about anything like that.'

THE DRIVE back was a silent one. Kevin used the opportunity to read through his list. Deirdre Twamley's alibi seemed solid, though they would check for sure. That was one thing about this lockdown – when everyone swore they were at home all evening, it was a plausible excuse rather than a suspicious coincidence. Of course, everyone was so tight in this town that she could be ringing up Emer Hession right now demanding the woman lie for her.

'There was no need to be like that.' Sean Connolly stuck out his lower lip as he turned into the Garda station and parked the car.

'Like what?'

'Disrespectful.' The sergeant frowned. 'All that 'if you don't feel comfortable talking to local people' stuff. That was aimed at me.'

Kevin struggled to keep his temper. 'Sergeant, I came here with Inspector Keane to oversee this case. We are partners. Anything I request, presume it has their blessing.'

'I get you, but you need to understand this town, and its ways. Like someone who is from here.'

Kevin was spared a response by the welcome vibration of his mobile. 'Kevin Xiao speaking.'

'Hello!' It was Keane again. 'Is now a good time, Kevin? I can call back later.'

'No, now is perfect.' Kevin watched as the sergeant went inside, his feet crunching lugubriously on the gravel. 'How are you, Inspector? I hope you're relaxing and taking it easy. You can stay as long as you—'

'Relaxing!' Keane cut in with a short laugh. 'Would you get out of that. I'm in Rosscarbery.'

'Inspector, you're not well enough.' Though Keane did sound more himself. *Herself.* It was hard to reconcile the timbre of voice with the Inspector's freshly declared identity.

'I'm a bit smashed-up, but your wife did an excellent job. And was so kind about it. I'll never forget.' A pause on the line, a dragged-out sigh. 'Anyway, I thought it would be better to keep an eye on things. I've every confidence in you, Kevin, don't get me wrong. But you're on your own with that crowd, and they're slippery as eels.' Kevin had never heard Keane be so talkative before. It was as if having revealed themself the night before had loosened them up considerably. 'Anyway, look, you didn't find out any more about who might have found that card, did you?'

'I haven't started looking yet,' Kevin admitted. 'We were interviewing Peter Ludwig today, then Deirdre Twamley.'

'Oh, the Muintir na hÉireann woman. I suppose she had an alibi?'

'She did. And it checks out one hundred per cent. Her friend uploaded a TikTok, and it's clearly Deirdre's house in the background.'

'A TikTok!' Keane chuckled. 'I've heard it all now. And Ludwig, what about him?'

'Not so much, but he was very helpful to enquiries.'

'Was he now?' Rosa did not hide her amusement. 'Fuck the police, except when I need 'em?'

Kevin filled her in on Peter Ludwig's account, and his encounter with Luke Keating.

Rosa tutted. 'That family are really something else.'

'I need to go now. Sergeant Connolly just came back.'

'No problem. And Kevin?'

'Yes, boss.'

'It is so refreshing to be able to talk to you as my real self. I cannot tell you how much lighter I feel.'

'Good.' Kevin felt slightly uncomfortable at Rosa's effusiveness, but could not deny he felt a little touched as well.

Just as he ended the call, Connolly charged over to him. 'They've found Luke Keating's bike. Down by Knockalisha, on the famine road near the lake. There's car tracks there and one of his shoes on the road. But he's disappeared.'

Kevin swore in Cantonese. It truly never rained but it poured.

THIRTY-TWO

Wednesday, 5 May 2021, 1 p.m.

'*This call will be recorded*' the tinny computer voice announced as Isabel Connolly's face loomed and clarified on Rosa's laptop screen.

Connolly was in an office with a floor-to-ceiling window in the background which had a view of the Liffey. The Dáil – parliament – was in session that day in the Conference Centre. They'd moved there for the duration of lockdown. The sky was oppressively blue, and the odd seagull could be seen wheeling around. Probably desperately thirsty for water that didn't have salt in it.

Rosa was in the tiny spare bedroom in her home on South Douglas Road, but kept the background blurred. She didn't want to go back in yet. Not when her face still looked like a bit of a war zone.

Even Isabel noticed. 'Are you OK, Detective Inspector? I'd offer you a glass of water or something but ...' She grinned and made a gesture to indicate 'you're over there and I'm over here'.

She was a square-jawed woman in her early fifties with small hazel eyes, a wide forehead and hair tied back in a ponytail with the odd tendril escaping. It was a young style for a woman her age, and she made no attempt to hide the greys at her temples, but somehow it worked. She was wearing a high-collared shirt, a navy suit jacket and just a dash of lipstick. From time to time, she drank out of a shimmering water bottle with a steel neck.

'I'm OK, thanks, Minister.' Rosa had done her research on Isabel, even though she was a well-known public figure. She had picked up a copy of *The Phoenix* magazine, the Irish equivalent of *Private Eye*, and there had been pages and pages about rows between her and Sadhbh. Apparently, Isabel had been overheard saying, 'There's not an original thought in Lady Muck's arsenal. That stuff about old, white men pissing away the future? Stolen from Orna Logue down in Cork South East, and God knows Orna and I aren't friends.' This was a reference to the last election. Connolly had taken her party into a government coalition and a good few councillors, even a member of parliament, had left in protest.

'Talk to me about Sadhbh Drummond and where she fitted into the party structure.' Rosa leaned back before remembering she was using a straight-backed chair to keep her upright. Damned painkillers. She needed to be on top for this.

'I was shocked when I heard she died.' Isabel's eyes went dark and soft. 'I nearly dropped my phone when Dave McGill rang and told me the news. It's dreadful. Just appalling.' She took a gulp of water and wiped her mouth. 'Look, it's no secret we didn't see eye to eye. When she put out that article just after the election, I was taken aback. But this is heartbreaking. I knew she had threats, but ...' Isabel gestured in front of the camera, her hands surprisingly elegant. 'This is a gut punch to all of us.'

Rosa nodded. 'I read the article. It was very strongly worded. She called you a traitor, by name. That must have hurt you.'

'Well ...' Isabel looked uncomfortable '... there were strong feelings circulating at the time. We were trying to negotiate with the coalition partners. There's a faction in the party that don't want to sully themselves with the dirty work of politics and compromise. They'd rather hurl on the ditch.'

'Sadhbh said that you were weak on red line issues and would let the other parties walk all over you. That your approach made you a traitor, whether you liked it or not.' Isabel's lips thinned, but she said nothing, and Rosa continued. 'Then she said – and I quote –'the party had a serious problem with misogyny, particularly towards young women, and the leadership is no ally to them."

Rosa paused, and Isabel Connolly took another gulp from her water bottle.

'It did hurt, Detective, you're right,' she said, quietly enough that Rosa had to turn up the volume to hear her. 'I've given my entire life and career to doing the best I could for the people who voted for me and the planet. And apart from personal feelings, it broke party discipline.'

'Was that why you expelled her?'

Isabel shook her head. 'It wasn't just down to me.'

'But you're the leader.'

'Decisions like that are never made by just one person. The committee makes the call.'

'So, a committee decides to suspend Ms Drummond? I'm asking because a month later, she lost her job at the school where she teaches, and two months later, she was dead.

That's all I care about, Minister. We can't understand the actors if we don't know the play.'

'Detective, we're in politics, so whatever the play is, it's probably Beckett.' Isabel grinned wryly. 'Talking and talking about agriculture subsidies and pleading for bike lanes while we're being buried up to our necks in plastic and drowning in an overheated sea.' For a moment she sounded younger and fiercer, more like the activists she was condemning. Rosa wondered what the years of compromise had cost her.

'Sadhbh thought I was solely responsible for her expulsion. That's not the case. I even wanted to bring her back, to be honest, but there was strong feeling on the EC that it wouldn't be a good idea.'

'EC?'

'Sorry. Executive committee. For a smallish party, we have a lot of committees. And policy groups.' For a second, Isabel Connolly looked bewildered at how the Environment Party had mushroomed – as if she'd had no hand in it. 'Thinking back on it now, I think she wanted out. 'Blueshirts on bikes', she called us. Like I enjoyed voting down the anti-hare coursing bill and letting the other parties kick out tenants for no-fault evictions.' She rolled her eyes. 'The problem is every decent Irish person wants to save the planet, but they don't want to get out of their cars or stop eating beef or take a ferry instead of Ryanair or do the slightest thing that might impinge on their sense of personal entitlement and convenience. So they blame us, and expect us to court them.'

Rosa decided to get the discussion back on track. 'It is not a Beckett plot we are looking for here. More like a Shakespearean tragedy. You say there was 'strong feeling' against Sadhbh in the committee. Who were the people with strong feelings? Did they know Sadhbh or was this just loyalty to you?'

'Some of it was loyalty,' Isabel admitted. 'We are very divided at the moment. But Edward Fitzpatrick, now, he's a long-time committee member, knew Sadhbh from way back, and he was particularly forceful on the matter.'

She had brought him up herself. That would make things much easier.

'Professor Edward Fitzpatrick, head of biosciences at UCC, and long-time Environment Party member? Who is going to be profiled in the *Examiner* for his role in Sadhbh Drummond's life?'

Isabel nodded. 'It's a shitshow, Detective Inspector. Excuse my language. It's really going to damage the party. Dave O'Meara has a spread on it all ready to go, blast him. We have a statement ready, but we have a bill coming into law about zero VAT on solar panels and this will destroy the publicity.' She was looking at Rosa, and there appeared to be an implicit plea in her gaze – delay going public until we get the bill through.

Rosa ignored it. 'Damage the party? Why?'

'Well, if you know about the *Examiner* exposé, you'll know why.'

'I'd like to hear it from you, Minister.'

She sighed. 'They had an affair. Decades ago. It was messy.' Isabel's mobile began trilling cheerful, churchy arpeggios. 'I can't now, Rob. I'm with the Guards. Yes, yes, it is. No, everything's fine. See you later.' She rang off. 'Sorry about that. Yes, Edward got very emphatic about expelling Sadhbh from the party. He said it was because she was attacking me in public.'

'Are there notes to the meeting?'

Isabel looked shamefaced. 'Edward specifically told us not to minute the notes. He isn't normally very forceful, so we did as he asked.'

Rosa shook her head and tutted. 'Did you even record it?'
Isabel cast down her eyes.

'Was that all he said about his reasons for wanting her
out?'

'He said he knew her when she was a student, and she
was volatile and manipulative. 'She could be a serious
liability to you, Isabel.' Yes, that was it. She was mentally ill
and could turn on you. She would tell lies about people.'

Rosa sucked in her breath. 'And you never asked him
what he meant by that?'

'It didn't occur to me. I was surprised at how insistent he
was that we expel her. But he was always a wise voice in the
past. If it were between him and Sadhbh ...' Isabel exhaled
deeply. 'I would have trusted him.'

'You trusted him so much that you agreed to his request to
keep the entire conversation off the record?' Isabel was silent,
her head half-turned from the screen. 'And yet Sadhbh must
have known about it to contact Edward, after all this time.'

She still did not turn to face the screen. 'I told my policy
assistant, Dave McGill. He and Sadhbh were once close –
before she married. I'd say he told her. Or told someone who
would.'

'So, by telling him, you were giving Sadhbh a heads-up,
weren't you? That didn't have to come from you. Because you
didn't trust Edward, did you, deep down?'

'I did. Up till Dave O'Meara sent me on his piece. The one
you fed him.'

Rosa shook her head. 'Wasn't us.' That had come straight
from Edith. Though she wouldn't care if it had been them.
She had no deep compulsion to protect the lecherous silence
of a middle-aged male academic.

'It's been difficult.' Isabel dropped her tone, and even in
the variegated composition of the laptop camera, Rosa could

see she was ashen. 'He's been a mainstay for the last twenty-five years and is very popular on all sides. If he backs you, generally you'll win. He's got very elevated connections, though he never flashes them, and he keeps out of party squabbles. He's old money, you see. God, I know this sounds terrible, Guard, I'm so sorry.' Isabel put her hand to her mouth.

It did sound terrible, but it was useful.

'I appreciate your candour, Minister. It makes things simpler. Now I'd like to discuss the affair Fitzpatrick conducted with the victim. Which, according to witness testimony' – Rosa quickly glanced at the notes made during her interview with Edith, meticulously transcribed on her phone – 'began in late 2004. Sadhbh was just nineteen and his student. Up till then, she had gained high marks in her examinations but at the last, she graduated with a mediocre degree.'

'I could imagine she'd be distracted,' Isabel agreed.

'I am told that the distraction was not the reason why her grade was so low.'

'You think Edward gave her a low mark deliberately?'

'That's what has been suggested to us, yes. And that he might well kill to keep it a secret.'

'I suppose,' Isabel said, as if the possibility had just occurred to her, 'that could have happened. Though apart from the mental illness stuff, he didn't mention anything else about that time.'

I'll bet he didn't. A seagull flew by, its head and wing marking a brief shadow, its call mournful. The sun went in and the light-shadow effect on the minister's face was less defined. She sounded softer too. 'Believe it or not, I liked Sadhbh. She was sassy and determined and unafraid. And so inspiring! She reminded me of how I was starting out – before all this.' Isabel gestured to the office, the desk, the shelves with statutes and periodicals. 'But it's not natural to stay there. To be fixed in a place of constant rebellion and opposition.'

'It's not natural to be murdered at thirty-six either.' Rosa was sharp.

'God.'

The woman's face sagged, dimples pixelating. *And well she might be nervous*, Rosa thought. Isabel Connolly, Environment Party leader and minister, was far too close to a man who had good motive to kill Sadhbh Drummond. And her protests that she knew nothing of what was going through his mind were not convincing.

'I should have helped her, yes.' Isabel rubbed her eyes. 'But that's it, isn't it? Internalised misogyny. Refusing to believe or help another woman because I'm fighting her for crumbs of the patriarchy. I'm beginning to understand why Thatcher pulled up the ladder. Excuse me.' She got up so her long, narrow body briefly took up the whole screen, then vanished and reappeared as she opened a desk drawer and took out a tissue, dabbing the corner of her eye. 'Yes, Sadhbh was a troublemaker. But she was the beating heart of the movement, and I left her out there in the wind.' Isabel heaved a sigh that sounded like interference on the microphone. She looked anguished.

'You might not believe this, Detective, but we weren't so different, she and I. We wanted the same things: an end to fossil fuels, restoration of biodiversity, a better future for us all. We just couldn't agree on how to do it. I didn't give her the time I should have done. It's a tragedy, and if I could take back my part in all this, I would. In a heartbeat.'

THIRTY-THREE

Anglesea Street, Cork, Thursday, 6 May 2021, 11 a.m.

Kevin was looking at files again.

Beside him was the stack of documents they had recovered from Sadhbh's home. Ronan had raised no objection when they took out the boxes from the rather disorganised study that looked out over Sadhbh's vegetable garden and dumped them into the car.

Kevin had his cloth mask on this time, plain black. Poker face. There had been no updates with either the Drummond case or Luke Keating's whereabouts. The lads in Dublin had got hold of Luke Keating's friend, Oliver Tiernan, whose family had moved to Dublin. Oliver had agreed to illegally have Luke stay in his basement during sheltering-in-place, but as it happened no law had been broken because Luke never turned up.

'I'm worried about him,' Oliver had told the sergeant. 'He seemed on edge. Like he'd done something wrong. His da knocked him about, but that wasn't all of it. He was mad into that teacher who died. Like, a bit stalkerish.'

A lot of the material Kevin had to work with was nothing more than recycle-bin-in-waiting: health insurance reminders with thick glossy booklets, quarterlies from the teaching union, reminders of unpaid fees – wasn't there email for this sort of thing? – then bank statements; at first, too far back to be much use, then closer to the time, then closing in April and May. Kevin read them carefully, but there was very little that looked untoward. Ronan continued to pay his annual Environment Party sub; Sadhbh had not. It was mostly food and clothes shopping, except for one large payment every month for two thousand euro and a second for half that. The second was labelled 'MORT. TOE HEAD', which meaning was clear enough. The first had only a stream of numbers and letters. It took a few moments for Kevin to realise what it was: maintenance.

Kevin whistled. Two thousand euro. That man must have felt guilty. Or perhaps the judge in the family court felt guilty on his behalf. Either way, to not even name the payment …

It was a joint account. Kevin wondered how Sadhbh must have felt, seeing that sum of money go out month after month. And according to his daughter's letter to Luke Keating, Jeanne Furlong was broke. This did not make sense. She was working, on top of the maintenance. Even with tax, you could live decently on that. He made a mental note to investigate it further and carried on.

As he liked to do when he was engaged in a long, satisfying task, Kevin slipped in his earbuds and hit play on Spotify. This was his happy place, where he could enjoy the songs he loved and cool didn't get a look in. First up, Candi Staton's 'Young Hearts Run Free'. Kevin was not even aware he was singing aloud until a female uniformed guard, unknown to him, popped her head round the door. She had honey-coloured dyed hair and looked to be in her mid-thirties. Her perfume was strong, but not unpleasantly so. He pulled his headphones out of his ears and asked if he could help her.

'Jaysus. I was wondering who that was. You're back!'

Kevin looked at her questioningly.

'I used to see ye here all the time. Typing away outside his office.' She jerked her head to indicate she was talking about Superintendent Eames. 'We had bets on whether you'd go postal before the month was out.'

He smiled thinly. 'I did not, as you can see, go postal.'

'Well, it's nice to hear you singin' now. You look more cheerful, if you don't mind me saying so.'

'I decided to cheer up. Because you know it might never happen.' His sarcasm was not missed on the woman, and she laughed raucously.

'Well, it's good to hear. I mean, that you're in better form. Not the singing, now, that's terrible.'

'Thanks,' Kevin said. 'I've been told that before. It doesn't discourage me, sadly.'

'I'm Valerie, by the way.'

'Kevin.' He rose to shake her hand.

'Whatcha doing back here anyway?'

'Reading through documents for a murder investigation.'

She raised her eyebrows. 'That'll be your woman in Skibbereen, won't it? Need a hand? I'm not particularly busy right now. I was going to knock off, but ...'

Kevin was going to tell her everything was fine, he had it in hand, but Valerie pointed out that the pile of documents on the left, the ones he had looked at, was far smaller than the pile on the right, and there was another box on the floor.

'Ní neart go cur le chéile,' she remarked cheerfully. 'We learnt it at school. It means there's no strength until we work together.'

Kevin enunciated the Irish words slowly and carefully. Valerie nodded enthusiastically, but not to the point of being patronising, which was a relief. It occurred to Kevin that Valerie was right. He'd never get through all this lot working on his own. Candi Staton could wait until later. He and Valerie took a box each, sat at each edge of the small desk, and got to work.

It did not take long for her to find the handwritten letter, on legal stationery from Tynan and Cowley Solicitors, dated 17th February 2021.

'Kevin, c'mere. This looks interesting.' Valerie passed it over to him. Tynan and Cowley was the name of the firm whose logo was embossed at the top, and their address was in North Road, Skibbereen. Kevin did not remember them specifically, but there were a few law offices there near the town hall. Kevin struggled to read the writing, even with his reading glasses on.

DEAR SADHBH AND RONAN,

THANK *you very much for your recent submission of documents from the National Archives. I read both the will and affidavit with great interest. That certainly casts a different light on matters. If these can be established as genuine, and the intentions of Harry Keating confirmed – to wit, that Mrs Furlong's grandfather, Hugh Drummond, was named as a tenant in common – there is a good chance of your objection standing. The main justification for the application to quarry limestone on Forestry Department land and an Area of Outstanding Natural Beauty hinges on TK's ownership of the land. This entire document, along with the companion affidavit, throws that into question.*

. . .

HOWEVER, *regretfully by itself it does not suffice to have his application thrown out.*

THESE DOCUMENTS ARE A MIMEOGRAPHED *fair copy made at an uncertain date by, we believe, the descendants of Ernest Jennings. We need sight of the originals if at all possible. It is unclear why they are not already in the National Archives' possession given they were allegedly drawn up well after the burning of the Four Courts on 28 June of the same year.*

NOR DOES *the cessation of ground rent payment carry any weight here, since this happened sixty years ago when Harry Keating's youngest son Maurice was the property owner, his other siblings having died in a tragic house fire. Had Hugh Drummond intervened to secure this rent, it would keep the matter 'live' but regrettably he did not do so.*

IN ORDER TO *safeguard the Not in Our Lifetime project, I will need you to supply me with the original copy of the will and the corresponding affidavit. That will be the clincher, if you can find it. I understand the witness to the will, who later became a commander in the fledgling Garda Síochána, wrote a private memoir that is also in the Archives? Anyway, we can discuss this in person next week.*
    Best,
    Clifford.
    'So, this Hugh Drummond thing? What's going on here? Do they still own Tom Keating's land?' Kevin frowned, looking at the sheet.

'I just can't believe ground rents are still a thing.' Valerie said. 'Did a law degree before I ended up here, and to be honest, I think it's all nonsense. People shouldn't own land. That's where it all went wrong. Shooting trespassers and the like. It should be held in trust for future generations, like the Australian First Nations peoples, say. Or we could all go communist maybe and have collective farms.'

'Oh, don't do that,' Kevin grinned. 'Been there, done that, worn the Revolutionary Guard T-shirt.' Though he hadn't. It would be more accurate to say his grandfather had done, but the consequences had lasted generations, so it was not altogether a lie.

Valerie continued, 'It looks like your man is after putting in an application thinking he's away and good, and not realising there's a piece of paper dated from 1922 which could wreck the whole thing. Quarrying, though? In a location like that? What put that idea into his head?'

Kevin put up a finger, a 'hold on' signal. Something was stirring in his memory. Braiguemore Holdings. FEC. Diarmuid Savage.

'Gravel.'

'What?'

'He wants to make gravel out of the side of Knockalisha. Diarmuid Savage.'

Valerie frowned, uncomprehending.

'It can't be a coincidence.' Kevin stood up, began pacing around the room. Keating and Savage, the sergeant had told him and Rosa. They're all in together.

'We need to find out if it's FEC Ltd. The company. Savage wants to use Keating's land to do it.'

'I tell you what,' Valerie said, suddenly animated, 'can we not look up the application on the county council map?'

Kevin, who had not been involved with planning

applications for some time, was unaware that was possible, but Valerie soon disabused him, pulling her chair closer to the desktop screen. 'They've got all the layers on the map and everything! Look.'

She typed some search terms into the ancient browser – Internet Explorer 6, no less – and a map of County Cork soon materialised. 'Can't believe they have it on this prehistoric system,' Valerie commented. 'It's new and all. OK, let's zoom in. Hang on, we can search by application number, have we got that?'

'No, afraid not.'

'Well, bad cess to Clifford the solicitor not to even reference the case he's talking about,' Valerie grumbled. 'OK, let's see if we can zoom in. Ah shite!' The map of Ireland shrank and disappeared from the screen. 'Let's try refreshing.'

Eventually, after much refreshing and swearing, they were able to zoom in to the area around Skibbereen. It was riddled with small dots, each of which displayed an information label when Valerie hovered the mouse above them. 'Every planning application since 2000,' was her comment. 'We've got a lot to look at.'

'We want here.' Kevin pointed to the zone around Knock-alisha Hill.

'On it.' Valerie zoomed in. 'Shouldn't be many, since it's a forest park. Ohhhh wait. There we go.' Right on the lower slope of the hill, a dot. Click. 'Got it.'

Valerie smiled in satisfaction. She read aloud: 'The proposed development will authorise the extraction and processing of rock at the c.151.97HA quarry along with ancillary work, including landscaping and rehabilitation of the quarry. The proposed development seeks authorisation for a welfare type office along with modifications to the site entrance, to include a new internal road, internal roundabout, weighbridge and wheel wash, along with ancillary drainage works.

'What on earth do they think they're playing at?' She broke off, staring at the screen. 'How do they imagine they'll ever get permission for that? They haven't even included an environmental assessment.'

Kevin shrugged. 'Pulling a stroke.' That was a handy bit of Hiberno-English he had learned early on in his Garda training. He felt a stirring of pride at being able to use it with such efficacy.

Valerie sighed heavily. 'I suppose. Does Tom Keating have friends in the county council?'

'Not friends. More people who would be nervous about crossing him. If you know what I mean.'

Valerie did know. 'People like him normally don't ask permission.'

Kevin shrugged. 'Tourist area. It would attract a lot of negative attention.'

'It's going to anyway, if it goes ahead.' Valerie frowned. 'It says 'pending' here, so nothing yet. I imagine there will be a list of objections as long as your arm.' She drummed her fingers on the desk. 'So, it's this FEC company putting up the money for this?'

'It must be. Tom Keating doesn't have that kind of money himself. CAB ran a check on him and didn't find anything.' The Criminal Assets Bureau were nothing if not thorough. Had there been anything to ferret out, they would have managed it.

'I wonder—' Valerie began, but was interrupted by another guard popping his head around the door. Tousled hair, roguish dark eyes, but he was not smiling.

'Sorry,' he said coldly, withdrawing. It felt as if he were Valerie's husband and she had just been caught in flagrante with Kevin.

She sighed. 'I'd better go. He's my lift.'

'Of course. Thank you for your help. It's wonderful.'

'Ah, not at all. I'll come back tomorrow if you need more.' She picked up her small bag and headed to the door. Then turned around at the last minute. 'The lads told me to stay away from you. Said you'd ratted out your colleagues and you couldn't be trusted. More shame to me, I believed them.' Before Kevin could respond she disappeared into the corridor, leaving Kevin feeling gratified, but with a still-intimidating pile of papers to get through.

He read again the handwritten legal letter, his head swimming with planning application numbers and ground rent legislation and what Valerie had just told him. He lifted his mask for a few seconds and breathed in deeply, the air dry and unsatisfying, and decided to head out for an iced coffee. There was a good place near the corner of Anglesea Street: Cork Coffee Roasters had just opened, takeaway only, naturally.

Ten minutes later, Kevin was sitting at one of the street tables, sipping a large carton of iced mocha with a straw. It was still hot, but overcast. These new paper straws were tricky too. They were more likely to sag and crumple on the lips. But then again, there was not much justification for what their firmer plastic counterparts were doing to marine life.

It was like that now. Every transaction was weighted with this knowledge. The act of buying an iced coffee in a plastic domed cup with a straw could no longer be done unthinkingly.

It was while his thoughts were diverted that Kevin recalled something about the note. There had been a lot of talk about the ground rents between him and Valerie, but there had been a crucial part left out: a will – 'if you can find it'. Somewhere along the line this document had been lost, and nothing had indicated that it was ever found again. Eric Drummond had dismissed the idea of Harry Keating's will as nonsense – an old woman's hallucination.

But more than one person believed it was not lost and might be found again.

PART 2

THIRTY-FOUR

Knockalisha, 8 May 2021

The grille above his head opened, and daylight was briefly obscured as the water and lunch were hurled in without ceremony and landed in his lap, the full water bottle hitting him smack in the groin and making him squeal. Luke immediately recognised the ham and cheese sandwich, wrapped in cling film: it had been bought in the petrol station just out on the Baltimore Road, just like all the others. It had no branding, only a price sticker, that was how he knew. Their sandwiches were always crap; the ham would be gristly, the chicken too dry and the cheese sliced poorly, thick as a book. But it was all that was on offer, so he took it, along with the own-brand mineral water and Double Decker chocolate bar.

He had to bite back the automatic 'thanks'. Every time. Even though the man feeding him this stuff didn't deserve a thank you. He'd kept Luke in this cell for three days with nothing but a grille at the top which let in daylight and allowed him a sense of time, and a bucket in the corner for ...

Well, the stink from it told its own story. His clothes, too, were smelly; he'd been wearing them since he'd arrived here. He couldn't take them off as there was only a dirty blanket on the ground to sit and lie on. His belt had been removed; presumably to prevent him using it to reach the skylight.

He never saw the man's face. Through the grille he saw only a pair of eyes, the rest was covered in balaclava.

He was exhausted. He'd shouted and screamed and roared for help, but nobody had heard him, or if they had, had paid no mind to it. He had no idea where he was, and no visual or audible clue apart from the movement of the clouds and the occasional whisper of tall trees. But he suspected he wasn't far from home, even though he'd been driven around for miles, bound, gagged and blindfolded in the sweltering, almost airless boot of the hatchback he had seen just before the man had knocked him off his bike.

He just asked the same question he always did when the man arrived. 'When are you going to let me out of here?' Usually, he got no reply, once or twice he'd got a box in the face, and once he was told, 'That's up to the boss.' To his question 'Who's the boss?', he again received no answer.

He had tried escape, several times. But the grille was too high. He'd jumped up a couple of times, desperate to get a grip, but nearly broke a nail on one of his attempts and gave up.

'I wouldn't bother with that,' the man had said in the same flat tone, once he saw the disturbance and guessed what had caused it. 'It won't end well for you.'

'The guards will be on to ye,' Luke said, his voice wavering a little.

The man laughed shortly. 'Not gonna happen.' And with that, he left, leaving Luke on his own in this cell once more.

Hours, days, nights had gone by. A bird sang; Luke didn't

know which one. To his father, they were all pests. Until Sadhbh had entered his life, he'd known nothing about birds. With her gone forever, he had no reason to bother remembering a meadow pipit from a curlew, or a nightingale from a blackbird.

Before Sadhbh, Luke Keating had been nobody going nowhere. He smoked behind the sheds, mitched off school, dealt some blow, and when he bothered to turn up to school, he would torment the teachers for months until the inevitable suspension. The only one who was a match for him was Mr Furlong, that cold dryshite of a man. But while he could sneer Luke into submission, he couldn't make him learn.

Then Miss Drummond arrived. From the very start, she made it clear that they weren't going to just learn whatever was on the curriculum. Geography, it turned out, was not merely the study of dead minerals. Sadhbh never talked down to them. She never held back. Unlike all those other bullshitting teachers, she told them the truth about what was in store for Luke's generation: climate breakdown, the burgeoning Anthropocene, the decimation of wildlife, drought and starvation through fire, floods. All of it coming from human greed.

She told them of how unnamed officials in the Department of Education had watered down the section of the geography syllabus related to climate change because – 'who knows? It's always a good idea to know which tail wags the dog, and which powerful lobbies influence our government.'

One day she took them all to a slaughterhouse as part of their module about the impact of agriculture. Luke had steeled himself to watch the parade of cows on their way to the stun gun and the neck slash. My God, the smell of the place. It was indescribable. Stayed on his clothes all the way home and he'd thrown them all in the washing machine in one go.

Sadhbh was not bothered by Luke's insolence, never tried to take him on, or best him. But the one time she did ask him something, and he didn't know the answer, she just shook her head and smiled. 'Oh, Luke. You're not ready for the revolution, are you?' And the entire class burst their piss laughing at him.

That was the day Luke Keating realised that even if he didn't know what it was about, he damn well wanted to be ready for the revolution. He would take a bullet for this woman. She was too beautiful to spend her nights lying in bed with that dull, *dull* Mr Furlong. Leaving Sinead's mam to be with Sadhbh Drummond had been the most exciting thing that long drink of water of a man had done in his life. It was a miracle he hadn't had a heart attack with the excitement. Luke could imagine her dancing naked in the glow of a night-light, effortlessly beautiful, and that boring fucker lying back with a book-light on, reading something by Kant, or, oh Jesus, maybe *Silas Marner*. He didn't deserve her.

That was the day Luke Keating started to get his shit together. He worked hard, not just for Sadhbh, but for all the teachers. He wanted to get a better grade so that he could get enough points to get into Politics at UCC. Or maybe Environmental Sciences. He didn't know which yet, but he was going to excel. Around the same time, he'd gotten friendly with Sadhbh's stepdaughter, Sinead. She was good for him, if a bit precocious and priggish; kept him on the straight and narrow, and was a good way to get to Sadhbh. He stopped selling drugs. He tidied himself up.

Then the summer before lockdown, he bumped into Sadhbh at the Saturday farmer's market, and she'd invited him to come with her on a protest against hedge cutting. He'd agreed immediately, but when they met in the church car park that afternoon, Sadhbh's small car was packed with people, two of them Environment Party members, and the last one, this German fellow, Peter Ludwig, who looked at Luke as if he were shit on his shoe. They'd driven up near Knockalisha and parked by a boreen. That scumbag Ludwig had been fondling her the whole trip. When he put his hand on hers as she changed gear, Jane Deasy sucked in her breath and Murt Phelan, the lad nearest the window, shook his head with a quiet, 'Jesus'.

Once they got out, Sadhbh managed to get some posters out of the boot – how, Luke had no idea. It was like the Tardis in there. These were crudely painted in red and green; some cloth, some plywood, all in the same stencilled capitals.

'44 MILLION SONGBIRDS GONE' read one.

'STOP CUTTING DOWN OUR TREES!' cried another.

'HEDGEROWS ARE OUR HERITAGE' was the one Luke was left with. HERITAGE did not fit; the 'E' was squashed in at the end.

Then his father had come across them.

That was his Toyota truck. The way one headlamp dangled off the front. That crack in the windscreen wipe and the whine in the engine. And Tom had his red gardener's gloves on the steering wheel, and in the back of the truck a stepladder and Black & Decker trimmer-chainsaw. There was a rough look on him.

Luke would never forget that awful day, Sadhbh standing by the hedge waving her poster; Tom menacing at her with the live chainsaw, whirring and roaring. Luke frozen and helpless as his father roared the saw between Sadhbh's legs, close to her groin. How in the end he'd gotten her out of the way and started cutting, a sweet aroma hitting the air as the flowers all came off and scattered on the road. Her scream of anguish as the nest was exposed, with the tiny necks and beaks of baby birds, as their parents flew out and chirped in panic, uselessly beating their wings. The baby birds screaming and screaming, but Tom Keating cared nothing for any of that, for he drove his strimmer in even further until they toppled out and the nest fell to pieces.

And then he smiled. 'Job well done. Nice and tidy.'

Over the last few days, being imprisoned in this place, Luke had had plenty of time to remember that day. Any love or respect he might have had for his father had died like the baby birds. From then on, it was only a matter of time before he chose to leave Knockalisha behind.

He wondered if his own father had kidnapped him. It seemed like overkill, but that evil fucker was capable of anything, Luke knew. Or was it something to do with the interminable phone calls Tom had been making, pacing back and forth, in the far field where he thought Luke couldn't hear him?

'I told ye, I haven't got it, I haven't a bull's notion. No, look, I'll do me best.' He had sounded stressed, but when you hung around with the kind of people Tom Keating did, that was par for the course. Luke had been wakened at midnight a lot as a child.

Or maybe it was to do with him beating the living daylights out of Peter Ludwig that day after he'd spied on them fucking in the woods near Liss Ard. He'd been following Sadhbh around a lot lately – jealousy had spurred him on. And in spite of all his protestations, he felt his father's rage rise in him when he saw them copulate at dusk. He wanted to kill Peter, naturally; but he also felt so, so angry at Sadhbh. 'Disgusted grief' was the best way he could describe it, rising through the back of his throat like chips after too much cider. That the woman he had put at the centre of the world turned out to have the morals of an alley cat. That she'd throw him over for that German prick.

I could break his neck, Luke thought. *And hers.*

Maybe somebody knew the extent of the badness in him. Maybe somebody knew what he had done.

Then he heard the clink and slow drag of the grille being pulled aside. The man again, wearing jeans and a workman's shirt along with his balaclava. But this time he was jumping in using a rope, with what looked like a toolbox in his hand. He pointed at Luke 'Boss hasn't got what he wanted. That's bad news for you.' Before Luke could say anything else, the man dragged him towards the wall with his hands clasped together and expertly bound them to a hook about a metre up. Luke could not kick back because the man was pressing his legs towards the wall in a grotesque imitation of sex. Then he tied his feet up as well. Luke, weakened by his time in captivity, started to feel very scared.

'I'll need a light for this,' said the man, switching on an LED emergency torch that shone right in Luke's eyes so that Luke could not see, but only hear the man rifle around in his toolbox. Then he did see, and he opened his mouth in horror to scream.

The man had taken out a hammer and a chisel.

Luke felt a sharp blow across his face as the man slapped him. 'Stop that noise. Nobody will hear you.'

Then he grasped and tugged at Luke's ring and pinky fingers and started hammering.

The pain was indescribable. But it was the fear, the loneliness, knowing that nobody was there to protect him, love him, remove this horror. Over and over, he screamed and screamed, and pissed himself, and cried, and bled. It was done slowly, and Luke was sure he would die. And then he saw that thug lift his own two fingers, severed from his hand.

'The boss will have these delivered with a note. Next time, it will be worse for you.'

And as he switched off the torch, untied Luke and slithered up out of the grille hole, dragging it shut with a series of grunts and curses, Luke sat in the gloom and wept with fright.

THIRTY-FIVE

Knockalisha, 30 September 1922

When Harry Keating finally made it home, there was no parade to welcome him, or old guard to stand him a drink. When he alighted from the bus outside the Elgin Hotel and blinked, looking around as the crowds moved on market day, nobody called out to him. And why would they? Nobody knew he was there. Even his wife did not know.

Hard to believe that just over a month ago, Michael Collins had stopped at this very spot to make a rousing speech, then motored up the back road and got ambushed at Béal na Bláth. Shot dead. A dirty business in a dirty war.

As he walked down the road, he saw that the Minehanes' house was burnt out, the roof with a hole in it and the windows boarded up. Harry felt a queasy sensation in his stomach. He'd heard stories of the Black and Tans torching people out after finding out they harboured fugitives. Could be them, or the Irregulars maybe. He hoped the Minehanes were still alive but had heard no news.

How did whoever it was know about them and me? he

wondered. It nagged at him, like a brace of sore teeth in his jaw, that his most secretive movements were watched and recorded. Someone had told. Someone close to him.

He'd needed to borrow a bicycle to get out to Knockalisha. He'd gone to the Savages' yard first, but when he asked for Terry, he was told by a young lad he didn't know that 'the manager was busy'. There was a sidelong glance when this communication was made, one that made it clear they had been instructed not to deal with him. Then he had tried the Rooneys, but Stephen's mother had chased him out, declaring he had brought nothing but trouble on them all with his murderous ways, and he should count himself lucky she didn't set the peelers on him.

He eventually cadged a Raleigh off Mossie Geraghty at the post office who knew him fadó fadó. Mossie's teenage son Jerry used it for his rounds, but he was away on 'a weekend'. Harry didn't care. He just wanted a sturdy bike for the long, steep climb up Knockalisha Hill to where the Keating land lay, hardly a stone's throw from what was left of the Drummond demesne.

Past the famine road, built out of unimaginable suffering as a patronising project by the very social order that kicked his people as they starved. Robert Delacour Beamish had his patsy land agent evict out the Widow Ganey from her hovel near Creagh. She and her baby were starving, and she tried to go after the land agent to plead with him, but collapsed on the road, her baby in her shawl. Both died like animals. No. Not animals, because Robert Delacour Beamish would never have let his animals suffer that much. That was within living memory, Harry reminded himself, just about. If there were ever proof of no God, it was that Beamish died in his bed, at eighty-six, in 1877.

Then he passed the lake. It was saltwater, yet almost fully

contained. When he was a lad, he'd sometimes gone down to the small pier and swum there with his friends. Perhaps Theodore and Arthur had done so, too.

Perhaps the last thing the Widow Ganey had seen was this clear, beautiful lake, untouched by farmer or oppressor, where starfish, sponges and top shells could live in relative peace. Full of sparkling blue water that neither she nor her baby could drink.

As he passed 'Sing Sing' and remembered the events of the year before that had sent him into flight, Harry got off the bike and wiped his brow. This was the point where the hill got particularly steep, but it was a good opportunity to pause and listen to the birds, the gentle hiss of waves in Lough Ine below – and the silence that enveloped that famine road. Audible silence – the idea seemed a contradiction, but Harry had become accustomed to seeing land in the context of absence: that abandoned farm, those evicted labourers on the road, that field whose soil was too rocky and thin to give a decent crop. That road, deep in the valley, was enveloped in its own, terrible quiet.

Eventually, he made it to the other side of the hill, and to the gates of his small farm. And what he saw there had him fall to his knees, scuffing them on the rough stony surface as he cried out to God.

The front field adjoining the gate was now scorched, blacked stubble, with a few late flowers poking through, stunted and timid in their spots of green. The ground was almost dead, and so was nearly everything on it. There was no gentle rustle of the wind through the long grass he would have expected from a fallow field, no 'crex, crex' of a mating corncrake. The hedgerow too was an abject skeleton, the hawthorns and rowans bare and seared, the remains of their barren twigs jutting lifelessly in the air.

Somebody had burned it all down.

Heart filled with foreboding, Harry walked his bike up the bumpy driveway, barely more than an old cow track. He couldn't hear the chickens squawking and fussing, and he knew Noreen had kept them.

There was little to be heard other than the steady tread of his boot on the lumpy ground, the tick-tick-tick of the bike wheel as he pushed it on. Harry could hear no sounds of children, or of his wife. When he reached the house, he saw it was intact, but there were burn marks against the whitewashed walls. Something was badly wrong. Fear rose in him then, roaring in his ears along with his heartbeat.

He wheeled the bike into the yard and set it against the far wall, and by instinct looked around for Freddy, the Airedale guard dog, to run up to him. Nothing. A brief flash of another dog at another home, and the quick deployment of his knife, entered his brain and exited it almost as quickly. He pushed at the main door; he had his keys, but it was open.

Inside, the house appeared untouched. Everything was the same, the entrance corridor, the carpet, the little Sacred Heart on the whitewashed wall just past the door, the small pile of turf in a basket. It was as if he had walked out in late 1919 when Noreen was stirring the pot of stew and returned in 1922 when she had finished it. But the Aga was bare, its door open and only ashes in the grate, and there was still no sign of his wife. The place felt and smelled, Harry realised, as if nobody had been there for a while. The clock on the high shelf had not been wound up for a long time, its hands at ten to three. A patina of dust covered everything, making him cough.

'Noreen!' he called out, then his children's names. Nothing.

My God, he thought, *where are my children?* He shouted

their names louder, sweat prickling on his back, his heart knocking about in his chest. The silence was awful.

He went to the tiny back parlour, brushed aside the cobwebs that had sprung up on the entrance and looked out the small window at the valley below. The sun came out behind a cloud from the southwest, over the Atlantic Ocean, which lay beyond his view. The entire slope lit up, the gorse bright yellow, the heather a blaze of pinks and purples. Beyond and above the Keating homestead, a tiny plantation of conifer seedlings clung precariously to the mountain's edge; the newly fledged Forestry Department's attempts to set right the centuries of plunder of Irish wood for English armadas, merchant ships and towns.

A donkey cart was making its way down the hill, empty. Harry knew whose it was and knew that, come late evening, it would travel back up full of bales of silage. Within five seconds he was back out the door and down the road, hailing the driver, Malachi O'Donovan. Malachi, with admirable sangfroid, brought his ponies to a halt and let Harry up on his cart.

'Well, good afternoon, Harry Keating. It's been a while, for sure.'

Harry was in no state for pleasantries. 'Malachi, where are my wife and children? What's happened to them?'

Malachi looked away, out over the valley. 'You haven't heard, so.'

'Tell me, Malachi. Are they all right? Where have they gone?' Harry had to suppress an urge to shake Malachi by the shoulders. He knew it would only frighten the horses.

'The children are with their grandmother,' Malachi said slowly.

'And Noreen?'

'She's in the county home, Harry.' Malachi was gentle. 'After what happened a month gone, she went downhill.'

Harry had to straighten himself then, gripping the edge of Malachi's cart until his knuckles went white. 'What happened ...?'

'Ah, sure, lookit,' Malachi sighed, 'will you let me stop at yours on the way up. 'Tis not a story to be told on the road.' Harry nodded, unable to speak, and Malachi did a smart right turn up the bóithrín where Harry had wheeled his bike just minutes before.

'Did nobody tell you?' Malachi said, then answered his own question. 'Ah, of course they couldn't. Sure nobody knew where you were. There were rumours you were hiding with the Irregulars. Among others. Rumours that did you no favours.' His tone was severe.

As Malachi pulled into the yard, Harry suddenly felt a thirst overcome him like no other. He longed to slake it with a gallon of warm tea. Not water or even whisky; no, tea, weak and milky. He offered to put the kettle on for Malachi, but the latter declined. 'I can't leave me horses,' he declared, but Harry had the feeling that he didn't want to stay too long at that wretched homestead, and that the ponies, who stood docile, were just a pretext. Something dreadful was going on, Harry knew it. And Noreen in the county home! What in God's name had happened?

He ushered Malachi into the kitchen and made a small pyre of turf in the grate, lighting it with a sliver of wood from the silver birches he'd cut down on Drummond land a year and a half previous, and left to dry all this time. Even with the neglect and damp, the tinder leapt into flame and the turf cuttings soon took fire. A sweet smoke billowed into the room and dirtied the window, as Malachi shifted his weight in the kitchen chair and coughed. He was a non-smoker, Harry remembered, as well as a pioneer. And never troubled any authority about anything, which was probably why he had lived so long.

'We tried as best we could to clear up after it happened,' Malachi began, obviously nervous.

'It ...?'

'The National Army came that night.' Malachi coughed again. 'They ransacked the place, I mean, really trashed it. It was just after Collins was shot, you know. Feelings were high. Drink had been taken. Then afterwards, they set your fields alight.' He paused again. Harry, hearing Malachi's throat gone dry. made a move towards the kettle, but Malachi shook his head. 'You'll never get that heated up in time, and I hafta tell this now before I lose my nerve. There were three of them, in guns and uniform. Now I'm only telling this third hand, because it was Noreen's mother that was there. She'd often stop by, just to keep Noreen some company and look after her, you know, with Noreen being on her own with the childer.'

Malachi looked away. There was a space here for Harry to feel ashamed, and he quietly took it.

Then Malachi continued, 'They kept shouting at Noreen about your whereabouts and that she had given hang sang-widges and water to some Irregulars who were hiding out in hill country near here. She denied it all.'

'She was telling the truth.' Harry was brusque. 'I told her it was too dangerous.'

'Indeed, and it was. But when she kept saying she didn't know anything about anything, the lads got angry. They tied up the mother and childer, shot the dog – we buried it just out there' – Malachi gestured towards the front field – 'and dragged Noreen off into another room. Then, as I'm told, there were … outrages.'

'Outrages?'

'They raped her, Harry.' Malachi did not attempt to touch him, even lightly on his hand, which he might have done. His eyes were level with Harry's. He was watching every move on the other man's face, Harry could tell.

'All three of them?' he rasped. Slowly, Malachi nodded. Harry leaned forward and put his head in his hands, so far, he nearly toppled his stool over on the uneven floor. It was not a large house, and while the outer walls were thick and strong, the inner ones were paper thin. The children would have heard everything. Noreen's mother, too. A slow, anguished groan escaped him, like a cow being slaughtered. Noreen, alone while he was out gallivanting. Noreen, the mother of his children, subject to this brutality ... Had he been there, he could have defended her. The hell with the RIC, or whatever they were called these days. The hell with the National Army, Irregulars and the whole damn lot. He could have fought them off. Or at least done damage trying. Anger stirred in him, but mostly directed towards himself. What had all that striving been for?

'I don't understand, Malachi. Why Noreen? She never harmed anyone. And I never had quarrel with the Free State. My fight was for Irish independence. This whole dirty business ... I played no part in it. And they've destroyed my land. Why, Malachi?'

'I need to be getting back now.'

Harry rose quickly, staring the other man down. 'Not till you tell me who did this – and why. Because you know, Malachi. I can see it in your eyes.'

The tinder spat in the grate and the turf took the flame easier now: no more smoke and a sweeter odour. Apart, of course, from that smoke which rose through the chimney and perhaps signalled to possible enemies that somebody was there. He considered putting it out, but Malachi was beckoning him to sit back down again.

'I can't exactly say as to who, Harry, but from what Bridget told me I can maybe tell a bit as to why. Normally, even when feelings are high, the women are left alone. But with Noreen – well, it was personal.'

'Personal about her?'

'No, personal about you, Harry. About the Drummond business.'

Harry was nonplussed. 'So – they attacked in reprisal?'

'Not exactly. Even the Free Staters aren't that violently concerned with Protestant lads.' Malachi chuckled bitterly. 'It was more about the rumours you'd been spreading afterwards.' Harry's eyebrows shot up. 'That it wasn't you who was responsible for killing Arthur and Theodore, as well as the Frost lad.'

'Oh, it was me all right, Malachi, I've never denied it, but it was a dirty business, and 'twas only because—'

Malachi put a finger on his lips. 'Harry. Them's the rumours I'm talking about. That's the line that will get you in trouble. People don't like being blamed by association. It can make them very angry.'

Harry licked his dry lips. 'These men – the ones who attacked Noreen – they're local?'

Again, Malachi slowly nodded his head.

'I need a glass of water.' Harry went to the sink.

'The water'll be off. Switched off after they left.'

'Christ!' Harry was not a man who swore liberally, but it was all too much for him. He sat back down again and thought about what he had been told. He knew that even since the War of Independence, the Savages had courted both Liam Lynch's forces and Michael Collins's. They gained business and influence by doing deals with the local anti-Treaty forces, which were in the ascendancy here in West Cork, while they were also in cahoots with the National Army and even lent them a few trucks. The Savage dynasty was not overburdened with principle, and would take sides with whomever suited themselves. Michael Savage had hated him ever since that night at Liss Ard. He'd been only biding his time.

'And ... nothing will happen to these bastards? To ...' He didn't say the name, but they both knew whom he meant.

Malachi tch-ed gently at his language. 'There's talk of court-martialling them. The government are bringing in emergency powers, so they'll be tried under military law. Might be a stricter penalty for that, than for a regular court. But to be honest ...' He shrugged. 'It's doubtful they'll have enough evidence. They'll probably walk. And take the boat to Australia, if they've any sense.'

The flame leapt in the grate just as the sun broke out again and a breeze blew through the small windowpane Harry had opened. That little fire seemed so cosy and harmless, and yet a month ago a similar flame had turned into a malicious inferno. The breeze and the light played dappled shadows on the far wall, and if Harry screwed up his eyes, he could imagine they spelled something out. If only he could read it as the prophet Daniel had done for Belshazzar in the Bible.

Malachi got up to leave, wiping his hands on his trousers. He hadn't even removed his flat cap. It occurred to Harry then that his presence on the hill had not been an accident. That he or someone else had been watching Harry since his arrival, and Malachi had been sent out to warn him. That far from being the simple farmer he made himself out to be, Malachi O'Donovan was knee-deep in it.

'Can I not see her, Malachi? Or the children?'

Malachi's mouth was set in a grim line. 'Better not. Poor

Noreen, her mind is gone. It would only confuse her now, and the nuns have her well cared for. And sure, lookit, Harry, I know you'll want to be taking the law into your own hands. If I were younger, and it were my family, I would do the same. But you're not supposed to be here. You're not safe.'

'Even with the Brits gone?'

'Especially with them gone. The Free State'll catch ye, and they'll put ye on trial for the Liss Ard murders. You'll swing if you don't get out on the next ship out of Queenstown – Cobh, as is now. Jesus, I can't be keeping track of all the name changes.' He paused. 'Noreen was good to me. And some of my people when they were in need. What you heard about the water being given out wasn't a lie, even if you did warn her. It's a shame, but ...' He went to the door. 'The horses will be gettin' restless.' He tipped his cap to Harry, climbed back into the cart, then smartly wheeled his cart back down the hill.

As Malachi disappeared from view, Harry paced the rooms of the abandoned house, kicking anything in his way that he couldn't see in the gloom. Into one of the small bedrooms where it had happened. He was interrupted from his thoughts by something on the threadbare carpet glinting in the half-light from the windows. He bent down and picked it up.

It was the silver Children of Mary medal Michael Savage always wore.

THIRTY-SIX

National Gender Service, Loughlinstown, 10 May 2021, 10 a.m.

THE SMALL RADIO in reception with its cute little retro arial was broadcasting the news loud enough for Rosa to hear, even though she was at the far end of the waiting area.

'Gardaí in West Cork are still searching for Luke Keating, who has been declared missing on Friday after failing to turn up at a friend's house in Dublin. According to Superintendent Colin Eames, they believe the disappearance may be connected to the murder of local activist Sadhbh Drummond on Monday, May 3rd. Luke's father, Tom Keating, has been questioned in relation to the murder but released without charge. Superintendent Eames has called for anyone who might know of Luke's whereabouts or his last known movements to contact them in confidence.

'Sadhbh Drummond's funeral takes place today. Her family have asked media to respect their privacy.'

The news faded into music, much to Rosa's relief. She shouldn't really be here, not with all the goings on down in

West Cork. She hoped her appointment, already delayed half an hour, would not take too long. It was hot again that day, and the clothes she was wearing, while adequate for the judgement of cis medical practitioners, were also an absolute sweat trap and she already wanted to leave the room to spray herself with deodorant. But the fear of losing her slot was far, far too deep for her to even contemplate getting out of her seat.

Even though it was only ten in the morning, every designated seat was occupied. Only the continuing restrictions prevented the room from being more crowded. Not a single transgender person in that room was going to breach coronavirus restrictions, no matter how stringent they might be. They'd stand for hours rather than dare.

The fear of being sent to the back of the queue was reflected in the dress of the people around her. They dressed according to their gender identity, but conservatively, the trans men looking like they would sweat in their tweeds. Rosa wondered wryly if they'd had to change in the car park like she had, last minute. She wondered if some of them were married with children and had tied themselves in knots making up lies to get here. Most people were still working from home, so 'the office' was no longer the excuse it would have been in the past for clandestine affairs – or gender clinic appointments.

Many of the younger trans women were also heavily made up, sporting floral and printed maxi dresses. But a few wore jeans and a T-shirt. They were obviously veterans, with less to prove.

When the nurse in wine-coloured scrubs called her by her deadname, her voice was soft and apologetic. She directed Rosa into the second of a series of cubicles off the corridor beyond the waiting area. Her name was Colette, and she was going to weigh her and take her blood pressure. 'Just pop on the scales,' she said. Rosa guessed she was in her thirties, hair dry and straight, tied back in a scrunchie and bunched in a hairnet. As she set up the pump, Rosa noticed Colette wore compression socks. 'Must be tough having to stand around all day.'

'Oh, *tell* me about it,' Colette laughed, pushing up Rosa's sleeve and securing the straps, all the time deftly pumping up the machine with her foot until electricity took over and it started to close in on Rosa's arm with a loud noise. Then three beeps. 'That's grand. Textbook blood pressure.'

'You wouldn't think it, with my job,' Rosa laughed, then worried about Colette asking her what her job was, then wondering if she were 'out' there, and wishing she'd kept her mouth shut. But Colette didn't enquire. She just told Rosa to go back to the waiting area, take a seat, and the psychiatrist, Professor Gilmartin, would be with her soon.

In her respectable court pumps, Rosa hobbled back to her seat and tried to distract herself by scrolling on her phone. She was worried about the time; she'd thought once she was called first, that would be it. Sadhbh's funeral was at 3 p.m. and Protestant churches didn't tend to start late.

She scrolled through endless clips of people recommending how to get up at 4.30am, or bullet-journal their entire day, and a man who stealth-camped on a roundabout in a Canadian business park. It took another half an hour's wait, but eventually Colette called her back, by her proper name this time.

The consulting room was bare of any furniture, apart from a medical table, a sink and foot-pedalled bin, and three chairs, one empty, the other two occupied by a man in a navy two-piece suit and a nurse in purple scrubs. The man introduced himself as Professor Gilmartin, the consultant psychiatrist.

Miss Caldwell, the social worker, smiled thinly and dipped her chin, reminding Rosa of a nun who used to teach at her sister's school. Gina, her sister, had always complained that the nun would say in a creepy, hissing tone, 'Now, Miss Keane, where should you be?'

Bloody good question, mind you. Where should she be?

'Why don't we begin?' Prof Gilmartin began, pleasantly enough. 'Can you tell us why you're here?'

As her daughter Muireann would have said, well *duh*. 'Because I'm Rosa?' She could not prevent the question mark coming up at the end of the sentence. Doubting herself. 'I'm Rosa,' she repeated, more firmly.

'OK.' The consultant's tone was still warm and benign. 'I understand that, but Rosa didn't come from nowhere. Why don't you tell us your journey?'

So Rosa told them. About how she had known since she was four or five years old that the body she was born in was not the one she felt right in. How she loved Barbie dolls and frocks but sensed an unsaid prohibition. How, on the morning of her wedding, she had looked at her face in the mirror and could not comprehend the pale, wretched face of the man staring back at her. Her blank look to her brother as he straightened her bowtie and smoothed down her suit, not leaving her alone for a minute. That perhaps this need of hers would go away; that it was false.

The more she talked, the more emotional Rosa became. In that hot little room, she poured out her heart to these gate-keeping strangers. She even admitted how she had been discovered – first the reading of the her diary, then being caught rolling on a pair of Louise's tights over her Marks & Spencer rose-patterned bra and knickers. Her wife's appalled stare quickly turning to flinty disgust. Her uttering of one, contemptuous word: '*You*.'

Rosa wasn't sure why she had told the doctor and nurse this humiliating fact. She knew she was supposed to present a façade of respectability, dignity. Not the break-up of a marriage, the distress of her daughter, who hadn't seen her for a year. The mention of underwear, suggesting sex as a motive. But as she talked, she felt lighter. Ms Caldwell kept her head bowed, and as the minutes rolled by, Rosa felt less self-conscious. By the time she finished, she had a raging thirst on her. Professor Gilmartin himself filled her tumbler from the water filter outside. She thanked him a little over-profusely.

'Very moving.' His tone was hard to decipher. Not as friendly, but not sarcastic either. 'You haven't had an easy time of it.'

'No,' Rosa said, trying to stop the unbidden tears. 'I haven't.'

'And in a job like yours,' Miss Caldwell looked straight at Rosa, her light blue eyes with pupils like pinpricks, her voice sharp and rural. 'I can't imagine it's going to go down well at the station. Detective Inspector, am I right?'

'Yes.' Rosa's fear returned, her feet and hands feeling inexplicably cold. 'I'm actually working on an important case at present. Sadhbh Drummond.' She realised how she must have sounded, blabbing this stuff just to impress the woman, who remained impassive.

'Anyway,' Professor Gilmartin seemed to want to return to the matter at hand, much to Rosa's relief. 'Thank you for that … er … Rosa.' Was she mishearing, or had Miss Caldwell just let out a *tch* under her breath?

Gilmartin asked her a few questions about her background that Rosa had not managed to supply in her earlier monologue. Questions about school, about her parents, what her home life had been like. Questions that could be readily answered, and were, but which didn't seem to have much to do with getting a hormone prescription for transgender women.

Rosa gulped down another tumbler of water. This whole experience was bizarre. That said, it looked like they were past the worst bit. A silence descended as Gilmartin finished making his notes. All she had to do now was smile, collect her prescription, and get the hell out of this place and back down the M8 to Skibbereen ...

'How often do you masturbate?'

Rosa was so shocked she nearly spilled the remainder of her water over her lap. Had she heard Miss Caldwell correctly? 'Excuse me ... what?'

'I think you know what,' Miss Caldwell said pertly. 'How often do you masturbate? Answer the question, please.'

Rosa looked wildly at Gilmartin for help. 'I'm not answering that.'

'Oh yes, you are.' Suddenly Gilmartin's smile was a lot less benign. Fuck. He and Caldwell were doing good cop, bad cop. And to think she, a cop herself, had not figured it out the minute she entered the room!

'We cannot arrange for hormones until we know all the sexual patterns and habits of our clients, to determine what is clinically appropriate for their future treatment.'

'How the hell is this 'clinically appropriate'?' The more Rosa lost her temper, the louder and deeper her voice. She knew those two were clocking it. 'What does ... that have to do with ...?' Being myself? Being a trans woman?

'Questions like this are important,' Professor Gilmartin insisted. 'If you can't give an honest answer, we'd have to question your motives.'

'But ... you can't just— What about personal boundaries?'

'We have to be sure,' Caldwell responded. She was

smiling but her eyes were like ice. 'It's our professional duty, for the patient's welfare. And for society.' And then Rosa saw it. The small necklace with a cross Caldwell wore.

The message was clear. If Rosa wanted to leave this clinic with an oestradiol prescription in her hot hands, she would have to subject herself to this hazing ritual.

If she drowns, she's a refugee; if she floats, she's an economic migrant.

Over the next hour, twitching with humiliation, Rosa stammered out the answers to all their intrusive, prying, prurient questions. What did it feel like when she had an erection? What sort of porn did she watch? Why that particular preference? Had she ever been sexually molested? Raped? How did she have sex? Was there penetration? Ejaculation? Anal? What was her relationship with her mother like, and before she could answer, why was it dysfunctional? How aroused was she by women's clothing? Had she sought treatment for that? How did it feel when she got a blowjob?

On and on it went, feeling like a strip search as every fig leaf of Rosa's dignity and autonomy was peeled away, smilingly, with gentle contempt, until there was nothing left of her constructions and she was only ~~Gerry~~ Keane, a man in his late forties, sitting in that stifling foundry of an office sweating under her ridiculous getup, stammering out details about blowjobs while Gilmartin and Caldwell remained cool and efficient, untroubled by the heat, so above it all.

By the end of it all she was shaking uncontrollably, her fingers beating a rhythm on the chair's steel and rubber arm. She couldn't drink any more water because she couldn't even hold the tumbler without spilling it. She was a wreck.

'Thank you for doing this for us, Rosa,' Gilmartin said in a gentler tone. 'We know this isn't easy.'

She didn't answer. Her throat was closed up.

Could they not see? How shredded she was before them. That enormous price she had just paid, small pennies to them. Of course, they'd heard and seen it all before. People like her would do anything, say anything, to hold that prescription in their hot hands. And yet Gilmartin seemed kind and even Caldwell had not said anything mean to her apart from those questions. *This is just the dance that needs to be done.*

'Right,' Gilmartin wrote a few more words in his pad. 'I think we have all we need here. We'll be in touch.'

'In touch?' Rosa's voice felt faint, raspy. What did he mean? She pressed on. 'I should tell you which pharmacy I'm using? I don't think that's in my notes?'

'Pharmacy?' Gilmartin was all warm, disengaged puzzlement now. 'Why?'

'For my prescription?'

Gilmartin shook his head with another of his handsome smiles. 'Oh no, that's not in the pipeline yet. We have to read up on our notes and decide if it's suitable to go forward before we arrange another appointment.'

Rosa felt a sudden downward lurch in her stomach. Was she in hell?

'And how long will that take?'

'It will take as long as it takes.' Gilmartin was stern now. 'Do you not understand? Hormonal treatments are not a magic bullet. Not when there are underlying mental health issues that need to be treated first. That's why we have to review everything before us so we can come to a decision that's best of your welfare. We need to winnow out the people who genuinely would benefit from them.'

'Certainly we do.' Caldwell nodded her head, and it bobbed up and down like a toy woodpecker. 'Genuine people.'

Gilmartin nodded too, firm and solemn. Rosa was dismissed.

Three minutes later she was back in her car, fan on full blast, engine idling, the exhaust sending more fumes into the already heavy air around the hospital car park. Her mind was blank. She was spent of all energy. She rested her head on the steering wheel, leaving a smear of make-up all over it.

Christ, she had to go to Sadhbh Drummond's funeral now. And the traffic would be murder. Appropriately enough.

Slowly summoning up a bit of presence of mind, she rummaged around for a small tub of Nivea face cream and a packet of tissues and started to wipe her hands, which were sweaty and covered in foundation from where she had put her hands to her cheeks during that hellish interview.

What was the next right thing to do?

Muireann, a fan of *Frozen*, had often sung the song 'The Next Right Thing' when she was smaller, traversing the house in Glanmire and delivering it full blast to everyone who cared to listen and quite a few people who didn't. Rosa didn't know what Muireann sang now. She hadn't seen or spoken to her since Louise had kicked her out.

Suddenly, she ached for her daughter. Her laughter, her weird common sense, her earlier fixation on stuff like *My Singing Monsters* and horror videos on YouTube and the like. Before she could stop herself, Rosa punched out the familiar number. One of the last things she'd done before discovery and eviction was to get her daughter a mobile.

'Hello?' Muireann's tone was breathy, excited.

'Hi, Muir … It's me.'

'Dad?' In a disbelieving tone.

'Yes, love. I just wanted to … see how you were doing.' Rosa had to blink and swallow several times. Her eyes were overflowing with tears.

'Dad, it's been ages.' The hurt in her daughter's voice pierced Rosa like a rapier sword.

'I know, love, I'm so sorry. It was beyond my control, I swear.' Rosa breathed in deeply. 'How are you, pet?'

'I'm OK.' Muireann paused a moment. Her breath, too, sounded ragged. 'Got picked for the Under-18s.'

'Oh, that's fantastic news. That's my girl.'

But then a voice in the background. *Louise.* 'Muireann? Muireann, who are you talking to?' Then. 'Give me the phone.' Cold as cold meat. 'Give me. NOW.' Sound of a door closing. Then, close into the microphone. 'Don't. You. Ever. Do a thing like that again.' The line went dead. Muireann was gone.

Rosa put the phone back in its cradle, plugged it back in like a robot, folded her arms onto the steering wheel and wept.

THIRTY-SEVEN

Portlaoise, 11 May 2021, 11 a.m.

Rosa and Laura Wilson had agreed to meet at an out-of-town garden centre near Portlaoise, which was as far south as Laura, who lived in Dundalk, could manage, and as far north as Rosa dared to go without taking too much time away from the case. Rosa was unsure about how she should dress and afraid to ask for fear of causing offence, but Laura put her at her ease without any prompting.

Feel free to present however, she DM'd. *I'll be in my glad rags. As per usual.*

As Rosa took the motorway north, there was still no sign of rain. The plants and trees that had been enjoying the continuous heatwave were now beginning to look wilted. Earlier that morning when she'd checked her social media, amidst the 'wash your hands' warnings and headlines about Israel forming a new government, it had been full of wildlife activists begging people to leave out water boxes lest the birds and wild animals die of thirst. Rosa didn't have a garden any more – she'd left that behind in Glanmire – and she wondered if Lou or the kids would bother. But thinking about them was too painful. Having that brief call with Muireann stopped, and the inevitable fusillade of abusive texts, had almost broken whatever was left of her after Gilmartin and Caldwell tore her apart. It had been hard to focus.

Something had to break, she thought. *It's not natural to keep going on like this. Just like it had to rain, surely, sometime, and break this heat dome?*

Sadhbh's funeral had been exhausting. Or rather, Sergeant Sean Connolly's blow-by-blow reactions to it. 'That was something,' he'd kept saying on the way back to the station, sniffing loudly as he did so. When nobody reacted, he elaborated:

'I thought it was a bit off. To be honest. That sermon.'

Kevin, it appeared, had no interest in rising to the bait. Rosa would have to do the emotional labour. 'You mean by Father Browne? I thought it was quite powerful.'

Father Browne was a Catholic priest, but had been invited to speak at the service. He had laid into the congregation for their arrogance and hostility towards Sadhbh, not to mention how they turned their backs on their own Pope and ignored his epistle *Laudato Si'*, concerning the state of the environment. It was shameful, he had declared, that a Protestant woman had paid more attention to the spirit of the letter than they had.

The sergeant clucked disapprovingly. 'There was no call to be using the occasion to give out to people. He has to see a lot of his congregation on Sunday. You're not from the area, though.' He was sullen, resentful at being supervised by blow-ins. 'The whole thing was an insult to Sadhbh, to be honest. Ludwig showed up, did you see that?'

'No.'

They'd had to let Ludwig go, in the end, after prolonged questioning.

'Not in the church. Fighting at the graveside. With Ronan Furlong.'

'Jesus.' Rosa sighed. 'Why didn't you tell us, Sean? We could have found something useful there, I'm sure.'

'I was going to intervene, but they seemed to sort it out amongst themselves, so I let it be.' The sergeant allowed himself a smug smile. Infuriating, but she'd have to leave it for now. A fight between a husband and a lover was not, in the grand scheme of things, all that surprising.

Rosa arrived early, bringing Dinny Geraghty's book with her for light reading. She went to an outdoor table for the fancy café and ordered a coffee and apple pastry. The green plastic tables and chairs were on that fake grass stuff that was rolled out on the ground. Little flecks of bird shit dotted them here and there and a blackbird with some opinions to share was sounding off from the top of a *Buxus* plant for sale in a terracotta pot. The sun kept beating down on the asphalt car park just in front of them, while motorway traffic hummed constantly in the background.

She opened a random page, and the words loomed in front of her:

It was often told that any person missing from the hinterlands around Skibbereen and Baltimore would be at the bottom of Lough Ine, and that if they were, their bodies would eventually be washed up on the little island ...

Her email pinged and she closed the book. It was Kevin. He was talking about some county council shenanigans involving Sadhbh and Tom Keating. Rosa scrolled through. It was interesting stuff and worth looking into, especially that missing file, but she couldn't focus on it right now.

Eames had picked up on her state. Had pulled her in to

the office last week and asked was '... *everything OK at home; you seem distracted*'. The way he said 'OK' with that northern lilt – 'Ouuuu – kye' – Rosa knew he was not violently concerned for her welfare.

'You need to pull it up, ~~Gerry~~,' he'd concluded.

Colin Eames, Garda Superintendent and mental health expert.

'Rosa?' The voice was a soft, high tenor. Laura eased in opposite her. Rosa could not help but smile to see that oft-clicked profile there in front of her in the flesh: black curly hair flecked with grey, firm jaw, grey pantsuit and lipstick.

'I confess the book came in handy. You'd see it a mile off.' She also had a northern accent, but it was softer, more border than Eames's high Protestant. 'What do you recommend I order?'

'Nothing. The coffee is watery, and this pastry feels like cardboard.'

'Oh aye,' Laura said. 'Doesn't surprise me. Americano, they call it. H2O, more like. I'll try a flat white. They don't usually mess those up. Back in a minute.' She rose and made her way to the counter, leaving Rosa to wonder at her nonchalance in going about her business as a trans woman, without worry or fear. When Laura returned, she said as much. But Laura's face darkened immediately. 'Believe me Rosa, it's an act. Getting out of bed in the mornings requires all my confidence these days. And it's getting harder, not easier.' She sighed and pushed in her chair. 'Why don't you tell me everything?'

In a low voice, Rosa proceeded to tell Laura Wilson the whole story, about how she had always known she was trans-gender, then her marriage break-up and the recent beating. When she went on to mention the gender clinic, Laura imme-diately sucked in her breath and let it out as a tut between her lips. When Rosa told her about Caldwell and Gilmartin's interrogation, Laura sighed heavily, 'Jesus Christ', and fiddled with her silver lady's watch.

Families passed them by, an exhausted mother chiding her son, 'No, Louis, I said *one* cookie. One. Now please don't run off, I need to look at these geraniums— *Louis.*' Geraniums were forgotten as she chased her toddler through the corridor that led to the portacabin sheds in a separate section round the back.

Laura Wilson put her hand on Rosa's. 'You poor creature,' she said, 'you've really been through the mill, haven't you?'

Her compassion brought unexpected tears to Rosa's eyes. Her hand was soft. Feminine. There was even the delicate citrus smell of some hand cream that left the slightest residue on Rosa's skin when Laura withdrew her hand. But Laura's eyes were kind.

'Thanks for listening to all that,' Rosa gulped as Laura handed her a tissue. 'And for coming in the first place.'

'Sure after everything I've been through myself, if I can make life easier for anyone else, I'll do my best.' Laura set down her flat white. 'I'm telling you, Rosa, I wouldn't wish it on my worst enemy. Being transgender. If there was any other way I could conduct myself in this shitshow of a world, I surely would.'

Laura must have seen how crestfallen Rosa looked at that, because she smiled gently, her lips almost disappearing. 'People like us don't really have the choice. That's the pain of it, and it's the cure at the same time. Because life becomes much simpler when you know yourself.'

'Yes,' Rosa exclaimed. 'That's exactly how it is.'

'And your Chinese friend – he accepted you.'

'He's not really my friend; he's just a colleague. I don't know him all that—'

'Rosa,' Laura cut in, 'if you are going to walk this path, you don't get to pick and choose.' She took a bite of her croissant and continued talking even as she ate. 'If you find someone who accepts you as you are, then you hold onto them, you hear me? You don't get the luxury of not having them in your life. Not now. It's never been rougher for trans folk than it is now.'

Rosa contemplated having Kevin as a friend. The idea did not seem as preposterous as it would have done a few weeks ago. Kevin had, after all, seen her at her lowest and not judged or tattled. He had offered her his home and hospitality. And his wife was a sweetheart. But—

'God,' she muttered, 'I don't know where to start.'

Laura laughed. 'You've got to stop thinking like a cis man, Rosa. Y'know, the one who'd rather have a gastric ulcer than talk about feelings? God forbid you'd mention anything personal or let your guard down.'

'In fairness,' Rosa laughed, 'I am a guard.'

'Fuck the police,' Laura said amicably, as if she were talking about the weather. 'Sorry. I hang around a lot of radical ACAB sort of people. Nothing personal.'

'No offence taken. I'm not a bastard, though. Neither literally nor figuratively.'

'Haha, fair enough. Another coffee?' Rosa shook her head. 'I'll be honest with you, I've a low opinion of the guards, but it's not them. It's the media. In the *Irish Times* and *Independent* any day of the week – nearly a foot's worth of column inches about how their transphobic bullshit is being silenced.' She sighed. 'I've been targeted many times. They send messages to my workplace calling me a pervert and an autogynephile.'

'Good God.' Rosa's throat nearly closed over. The thought of people ringing up the Super and telling them she was a pervert and a ... she still could not pronounce that word.

Imagine Eames saying it in his cold northern accent: 'Au – to – gay – ne – feel'.

'What did your employers do?'

'They're behind me one hundred per cent.'

'Thank God for that.'

'I'm lucky, though.' Laura frowned. 'I work for a multinational, and I'm in IT. Permanent, not contract. It's quite another thing if you're on one of those zero-hour contracts. Precarious labour. Then you're fucked.' She bit off another piece of croissant. 'Those ones are always mank. On the display for less than two hours and they're stale.'

A few metres away from them, a garden hose lay uncoiled on the ground, like a lazy snake. It was hitched up to a water tap at the side of the building, and on the other side, fed a sprinkler which one of the workers brought to life by turning on the tap. Arcs of water gushed out and caught the sun, spattering the leaves of the geraniums Louis's mother had forsaken, not to mention the antirrhinums, nasturtiums and cheerful petunias. Rosa looked at the plants with envy. She wanted to run under the sprinkler. But Laura was unimpressed.

'What a waste. When you think of climate change and water getting scarce. There are entire continents becoming unliveable and still we have sprinklers.' She sighed. 'I really want to get more involved with the environment and activism. Like your murder victim.' She laughed mirthlessly. 'But it seems that once you're trans and out, you can't have any other story. You can't even go for a swim or to the jacks without it being a political gesture. To be honest, if I ended up in her position one day, I wouldn't be surprised. I'm sorry to be this grim about things, but there are people who really hate us. Not mildly dislike. *Hate*. They want us gone.'

Rosa looked at the red of the geraniums, the garish flamboyant purple of the petunias. Their close, dense odour released by the pattering drops. Consider the lilies ... though there weren't any on that shelf. The flowers, they were just able to be themselves. Watered by the sprinklers and urged on by the sun. Whereas she and Laura were on barren, hostile ground.

'Do you regret coming out?' she asked.

Laura's response was instantaneous. 'Never.'

'Even though you fear for your life?'

'I'd rather die looking like this,' Laura declared, fishing in her black faux-leather handbag, 'than live looking like *that*.' She showed Rosa a photo of a shy-looking man in an Aran cardigan and thinning hair. 'I know it looks odd, me carrying around a picture of my former self. But I keep it there so I can remind myself how far I've come in the meantime. There's nothing wrong with him – I still carry a lot of him with me and that's fine – but God, I wouldn't go back. Not for all the tea in China.'

'Or crap coffee in a garden centre off the M7.'

Laura chuckled. 'Exactly.'

'So, it looks like I'm never going to get my meds, isn't it?'

Laura tutted again. 'Gilmartin is a cunt, God forgive my language. I've heard so, so many stories from other trans people. Fuckin' gatekeeper of everything. He acts like a pater-familias, this godlike doctor who says 'No' to desperate people, just because he can. Loves nothing more than firing legal letters about to shut us up, too. And that Caldwell wan – I haven't met her myself but I've heard stories. Gilmartin enables her, though. He lets her toy with us, then moves in for the kill.'

'Yeah.' Rosa sighed. 'I noticed that dynamic all right. Should have done earlier, given my line of work.'

Again, at the allusion to the guards, Laura darkened. But

she merely commented: 'It's such hypocrisy when people say Ireland has self-ID and is better than the Brits. When they make you wait and beg for basic healthcare.'

'Did you come across them yourself, when you were ...?' Rosa asked.

'No, thank Christ.' She was about to say more, and then stopped.

'You mean you ordered the meds online?'

Still, Laura said nothing.

'Laura,' Rosa laughed in exasperation. 'Honest to God, I don't care. There's enough proper crimes about.'

Laura's mouth was a thin line, only discernible by her vermilion lipstick. 'How do I know you're not undercover?'

Rosa guffawed at that. 'Because, for fuck's sake, wouldn't I have invented any other job than being a detective sergeant in Cork? I'd have been ... I dunno ... a dog beautician or something.' It was the first thing she remembered from the careers list at school.

Laura laughed. 'If I ever give up IT and the full-time job of being trans, I'll consider becoming a dog beautician myself.'

This feels nice, Rosa thought. Just chatting to this woman and laughing and being friendly. And Laura seemed to have mellowed too, because she muttered, 'Here,' and passed over a plain card with only a web address written on it. 'Look them up. They'll give you what you need without the Gilmartin and Caldwell crap. It won't be cheap, but it'll be easier than all the palaver here.'

Rosa looked at the card.

'And look, you're not on your own, ever. OK, so I might have scared the bejaysus out of you today – but you can always talk to one of us, closeted or not. We don't judge because we know how God-damn hard it is, especially now.'

She extended out her hand. 'Welcome to the club, Rosa Keane.'

'Thank you for this,' Rosa said fervently. 'I needed it. I just … after that gender clinic thing. For some reason that upset me more than those goons who beat me up.'

Laura nodded. 'That tracks.' She fiddled again with her watch, which was tight on her wrist. 'That book looks gorgeous, by the way.'

'It's by a local historian in Skibbereen. When he saw me and my colleague out the other night, he insisted on giving it to me. He published it himself.'

'He did a better job than a lot of regular publishing houses,' Laura commented, opening the book at where Rosa had left her jacket flap and running her finger along the page. 'Look at that paper quality! And the photos are beautiful. Wonder if they were taken by a drone?'

A drone …

'Rosa – are you OK?'

The words loomed in front of her again, undeterred by the sun's gleam on the glossy page:

It was often told that any person missing from the hinterlands around Skibbereen and Baltimore would be at the bottom of Lough Ine, and that if they were, their bodies would eventually be washed up on the little island …

'Wait a minute,' Rosa said aloud, just as the sprinklers suddenly stopped. 'Wait … a … minute.'

'Don't worry, I'm not going anywhere.' But Rosa was not listening. She was in that liminal place where connections are made and stories converge. That exciting moment of finding the solution, or at least the way forward to it.

'Laura. I'm sorry, but you'll have to excuse me. I need to make a phone call.'

Laura rolled her eyes. 'I take it's about your case?' Then

she smiled and briefly took Rosa's hand one last time. 'The truth about you, Rosa Keane, is that whatever else you are, first and foremost you identify as cop.'

Back in her car, Rosa picked up her phone, starting the engine at the same time, and rang a number in Athlone.

'Get a sub aqua team down to Dineen's Creek on the north-western side of Lough Ine. We need to find a drone.'

THIRTY-EIGHT

Cork City, November 1922

The Bridewell prison near the riverbank was in poor enough condition that Harry might well have tried to escape, if he had a mind to do so. The paint on the fine windows was peeling and the holes in the brickwork IRA prisoners had made punching their way out in the past had not been repaired. Little effort had been made after the RIC had handed the place over last year.

But Harry, stuck in the damp basement, his cell window seeing only the boots of passers-by, could not take advantage of the building's decrepitude, nor could he rely on anyone to help him get away. He had lost all friends in the movement, but more importantly, he had lost his spirit. They had broken Noreen and broken him through that. The land he had sworn to restore was wild and burnt. And now, a death sentence, administered by a kangaroo court. The new Garda force had caught up with him in Rosscarbery, hauled him into an old Ford they'd inherited from the RIC, and driven like the clappers all the way to Cork.

By then, Harry had heard the news about Erskine Childers, hauled in front of a firing squad for possession of a pistol, his last words encouraging the distraught executioners to fire straight. Harry hadn't liked him much, but he had been a man in his final hours, and besides, shooting someone on a technicality? That was not the way a proper country was run.

He was roused by the rattle of the grille being pulled back. A voice barked, 'You've a visitor,' and the tall, stooping form of the solicitor Ernest Jennings eased its way in through the doorway before it was banged shut behind him.

Harry rose and moved to shake Ernest's hand, but Ernest, who was wearing a greatcoat and galoshes, clasped Harry's hand in his and pumped it forcefully, while his satchel hung off his other elbow. Pity radiated out of Jennings' long frame. He had the aura of a priest about to deliver the last rites, which Harry found grimly amusing since he knew Jennings was most definitely a left-footer. Unitarian, or something – but as far as Harry was concerned that meant Protestant.

They engaged in a bit of small talk before Ernest finally said, 'So, you want your will witnessed?' Harry nodded and handed over the crumpled sheet of paper to Ernest, who smoothed it out and moved over to the dim light from the grille to read it properly. 'Power out again?' he asked rhetorically as he scanned through, murmuring the words that Harry knew backwards.

I, *Harry Keating, am of sound mind and of suitable age. This is my last Will and Testament as signed and witnessed on the 29th August, 1922. It is also a Letter of Intent to indicate where I wish to bequeath my assets and possessions. Firstly, in the matter of ground rent, I wish to reinstate the annual payments to Penelope Drummond, which I ceased to pay in January 1918, and revert the land to*

her and her descendants to use as she sees fit, subject to the safe
housing of my children Patrick, Katy and Maurice. I wish to make
reparations for the harm done, which I never intended and was
beyond my control, and furthermore –

Ernest looked up. His forehead was furrowed with lines
all the way up to his bald skull. 'That ground rent provision is
hardly applicable. You already have your lease on the land.
And this paragraph here about the Drummonds' – he tapped
it – 'it really isn't relevant and could muddy the waters. Not
to mention ...' He scanned downward again, the lines
furrowing even deeper. What's this about your wife and
Michael Savage and a religious medal, and ...? Look, Harry, a
will is not the place to make allegations like this. You will
cause your family nothing but trouble.'

'But I've made provision for them.'

'Making provision in this context means absolutely nothing.' Ernest had raised his voice and it echoed along the cell
walls. He murmured an apology before continuing. 'I know
it's an emotional time but try to think a little more logically
about it all.'

'Hard to be logical when you're going to be swinging
from a rope.' Ernest flinched at Harry's bluntness. 'Look, I
want it known what really happened. Otherwise, I'll be
remembered for life as the man who killed that innocent boy.
I don't want Michael Savage and his descendants to go about
their business in peace and sleep well in their beds at night.'

The cell was silent for a moment apart from the wash of
rain on the footpaths, the dripping of an unseen pipe, and
some shouting outside in the corridor. The whole place
smelled of river water. Harry felt one of those surreal
moments that sometimes came on him since they'd banged
him up: that he was outside his own life, that this sentence
was somehow unreal. Imposed on someone else.

'If that's what you really want,' Ernest said quietly, 'I know a better way to do it.'

Harry breathed in, and returned to earth, his situation, the solicitor and the bare dimensions of his cell. 'All right. I'm listening.'

Ernest tapped the sheet. 'Everything you have put here about Michael Savage – all the vile things you are sure he has done – belong in a sworn statement that I can ratify here and now. It's called an affidavit, Harry. You write it, sign it in my presence, and I sign it below. It's there as a piece of insurance in case Michael Savage or any of his associates try to go after your family. Then we sort out this will. May I suggest that you name your children and the child from the Drummond family, the one whose father you killed ...'

'Hugh.'

'Hugh, that's it. Name him and your children as tenants-in-common. That gives your children the right to use the property themselves or for income.'

'But not without his agreement?'

'No, not without his agreement.'

Harry nodded slowly. What Ernest said made sense. He had been so obsessed with making sure that his testimony not be erased from the record, he had not considered his family. 'We'll do that, so. Can you ask the rozzers to give us a little more time so we can write the new bits?'

The extra time granted, they worked on the documents, Harry balancing the page on his knees as he wrote, his neck bent forward as he laboured at the work, his pen digging into the headed paper Ernest had provided. He passed the affidavit to Ernest who looked through it briefly.

'This will suffice, I think. Though, this medal ...you don't happen to have it with you, by any chance?'

'Thought you'd never ask.' Harry grinned, slipping it out

of his pocket. The silver flashed briefly in the weak light from the grille. Ernest pocketed it in turn.

'How on earth did you get this past the checks?'

To which Harry only responded. 'You don't want to know, Ernie. Seriously.'

Ernest flinched again, shaking his hand fastidiously as if trying to dry it. 'Good Lord. Perhaps not.' But he manfully continued with signing the affidavit before handing it back to Harry. Reading the words set out in front him, Harry felt a deep relief wash over him, leaving pinpricks of sweat on his back.

Then it was time for the will, and somebody to witness it. Harry couldn't think of anyone else, so Ernest rattled on the grille and shouted for the warder to go get Constable William Eames.

'He's not from round here,' Ernest said. 'He's a northerner. But he's the most trustworthy person I can find right now.'

Harry reflected that under normal circumstances Noreen would be the witness, or maybe the executor? Either way, she would be there. Not broken and lost in a home, her body violated, her memory gone. Harry had not been the best of husbands, nowhere near, but it broke his heart to think of her.

Constable Eames was a short, slim man with a clipped moustache and a Belfast accent that could cut rocks it was that harsh. He witnessed Harry's signature on the document without looking at Harry until he was done, at which point he shook Harry's hand and looked at him with piercing grey eyes. 'Glad to be of service, sir.' Then he cast his eye on the second document, which Ernest was stuffing into his briefcase. 'Did we miss a page?'

'Er ...no, that's a separate matter.' Ernest looked flustered, though God knew why. They had done nothing wrong, and even if they had, it hardly mattered at this stage.

'I see,' said Eames, and looked like he'd like to say more, but thought better of it. He sounded as if he'd caught them both smoking in an English public school, but Harry knew that Eames would be present at his execution – an event he could not think about without feeling dizzy.

The business concluded, Ernest Jennings slowly put on his coat and put the battered will in his satchel. 'I won't be able to pay the bill,' Harry joked weakly, but Ernest tutted at his gallows humour.

'Don't worry about that at all, Harry, that's fine.' As if Harry were worried! Where he was going there would be no debt given or taken.

When Ernest Jennings had gone, Harry stamped his feet for a few moments. He needed to feel something. The dissociations were getting worse, to the point where he nearly felt his soul exit his body through his head. Granted, his circumstances were dire, but the unreality of it spooked him.

These were his last days on earth. He wanted to feel every tread, smell every dank reek off the walls and sewage from the river, even the purging feeling of taking a shit in the latrines.

He would also have liked to make love to a woman. God, any woman, but what were the chances of that?

He did what he often did when he needed to steady himself. He imagined his last day. The sun would be weak and tremulous, like milky tea, the clouds scudding over. They would call him from his cell and escort him out to the small courtyard. The building would be a little island among the quays and streets, as people walked or cycled by, splashed in puddles, unaware of what was happening inside.

In the courtyard would stand a gallows and noose. Constable Eames, he imagined, would be standing to one side, one crease on his brow, his eyes glazed to hide whatever emotions lay behind them. The sergeant would be alongside, and the hangman, brought over from England especially. Were executioners hired on a daily rate? Harry didn't know.

And of course, the priest, that sleeveen, with his long robes blowing so hard in the wind that you could see his tuppence-ha'penny cambric trousers beneath. A round head like a large cricket ball and eyes that positively bounced in it, they were so goitrous. To call him a vulture would be an insult to that fine bird.

They would walk Harry up to the platform. The priest would say a few words. He would feel the rough cords of the rope around his neck. Horsehair, maybe? He wasn't sure. Tightening, more words, then quick as you like the trapdoor releasing under his feet and – cracking, blurring, constriction, his body a marionette he could not control, the longing to breathe, the inability, bowels loosening, the smell everywhere, the people's faces blurring, pain, choking, lungs unable to gasp, everything going black and white, then fading. His mother, wife, children laughing, younger than they truly were. Oh, the agony …

Then oblivion.

THIRTY-NINE

Lough Ine, Wednesday, 12 May 2021, 5 a.m.

It was a cool sunrise, the dappling light bobbing up and down on the saltwater lake, the remains of Knockalisha forest still greening the foreshore. At the pier a few early morning swimmers had quickly dispersed at the sight of the Garda Sub Aqua Unit's van arriving. Rosa, already parked by the low wall east of the pier, leaned against the Garda-marked hatchback and sipped on coffee. Kevin was there too.

The unit was based in Athlone, so they had a four-hour drive to get there, never mind the effort involved setting up the equipment. They must have been driving all night. Rosa hoped she hadn't given them a wasted journey. She knew Kevin was sceptical, but something about Dinny Geraghty's book drew her in. A fanciful streak maybe, a mercurial, whimsical inclination to put more weight on folk tales than they deserved. If nothing was found, Eames would do his nut.

Rosa had not slept well. Late last night, she got an email to her work address. Subject heading: '*you are a tranny*'. All in lowercase, it simply said:

we know what you are and have alerted your boss you will never work again after this, you should have left well alone in skib, now you're done for.

Accompanying this were several close-ups of Rosa battered on the ground, a bit blurred but clearly recognisable, zoomed in on her lipstick, her skirt, her tights, her heels. One of the men must have filmed her when the others were beating her up.

She'd thrown the phone on the living room couch, run to the kitchen sink, and vomited. Then she had to clean up, pouring bleach down the sink, as if she could scorch away the evidence, sterilise her own soul.

Afterwards, she felt empty and still. So, now Eames would know. Would he protect her, throw her under the bus, send more forces after the people who'd brutalised her? Or worst of all, see her as a liability and take her off a case she was – she was sure – close to solving?

She watched as a female garda in waterproofs and a Helly Hansen jacket directed two male colleagues in wetsuits into a small boat with a five-horsepower engine. Powerboats were banned on the lake usually, but nobody was going to stop a Garda unit at ridiculous o'clock in the morning. The woman pushed the boat off the shore, leaped in, and pulled the cord to start the motor. Off they put-putted towards Dineen Creek, the narrow passage between the island and the mainland. Halfway there, she stopped the motor, and the men adjusted their headgear and oxygen cylinders and dived in. Instead of waiting for them, she continued to the island. Her name was Natalia Rochford. Rosa had spoken to her briefly when they arrived, apologising for the unsociable hour, but she just laughed. Her last job, she told Rosa, was hunting for the dismembered remains of a gangland kingpin down in the Drogheda sewage network. Lough Ine would be a welcome break.

Twenty minutes went by, but it was impossible from Rosa's vantage point to see what was going on at Dineen's Creek. She could have walked around, but it was a bit of a trek. She wandered over to a small hillock on the grassy pier and found a rock to sit on. She had a few plain digestive biscuits in a sealed bag and nothing much else. Wryly, she thought of what Darragh McClure had said to her recently when he saw her with the plain biscuits. *I bet Louise took the chocolate ones.*

Rosa nearly inhaled them, then wished she had made a flask of coffee, because she was craving some more. She was just about to get up and see if she could have a closer look when the powerboat came back into view with all three members aboard. The divers had removed their helmets and were balancing the boat on either side, while Rochford, the cox, was making a beeline for the shore they had left barely half an hour ago. Spotting Rosa, the woman raised her arm in the air. At first, Rosa thought she was waving, then realised Rochford was holding something aloft – something that caught the light as she waved it around.

They had found the drone.

FORTY

Skibbereen, 9 May 2021
Marked: FRAGILE – DO NOT BEND
Dear Tom,
My apologies for keeping you waiting so long for this letter. I know you wanted it urgently, but as it happened, I combed the whole office for it and there was no sign of it whatsoever. It was driving me a bit mad because my grandfather was a meticulous man, very aware of the status our family had in Cork at the time. Had to be in the times he was working in. He would not have misplaced a will. I thought for a moment that I'd mislabelled it when we collected it from the basement in the old Cork office, but after looking high and low, I realised there was no sign of it at all. There were terrible floods in Cork the previous year as I am sure you have heard. Some files were indeed lost and I feared Harry Keating's was one of them.
But then – hallelujah! – I remembered that my grandfather had an odd quirk my father told me about; when he did not have the original of a document, he would open a new file for the copy. He kept these copies in a separate compartment also in the basement

but in a back room rather than in the main room at the front. This room managed to avoid the worst of the flooding and so the copy of the will was preserved with a handwritten note to say that Ernest had spoken to Bridget Keating, mother of Henry Joseph Keating, in her capacity as the will's executor; in that same capacity, she tore up the will on the spot and cautioned Ernest that it would result in further ruination for Harry's family. Questions would be asked, and she would have to bear the brunt of them and be shunned in the town. This speech obviously deeply troubled my grandfather as he added a note saying that he would not press Bridget to execute the will or challenge her in probate. For Ernest Jennings not to execute a lawful document, the pressure must have been extreme. I do not envy him having to operate in such difficult and belligerent times.

Obviously, I felt moved to read it myself and immediately saw why Mrs Keating would have been so troubled at the terms of the will. Harry left his property to his three children and Penelope Drummond's son as tenants-in-common. I must emphasise that Mrs Keating's objections, in so far as I can gather their nature, were not based on personal avarice but on the conspicuous nature of the decision. She admitted to being terrified of people noticing it, since a will is a public document, and Ernest noted that 'regretfully the affidavit did not reassure her, much less the medal.'

At first, I was unsure of what he meant, but then I saw that there was a second document in the file, written by your grandfather himself, and an original document rather than the copy Ernest kept – and I must admit that I found the contents quite shocking. If true, and if the descendants of all parties are still living in the town, I can see why it would be seen as necessary to suppress it.

It also, I'm afraid to say, shines a new light on the death of your father's three older siblings in a house fire in 1931, leaving the property to Maurice, the youngest son, since Noreen Keating had also since died. This was always viewed to be a tragic accident, but Maurice's paternity being now in question, a different and more sinister motive may now arise. I hasten to add that I have no doubt your father was ignorant of this.

I will stop now as, understandably, as an amateur historian, I have rather developed a fixation on this whole subject, even though it is not my story to tell – rather, it is yours – and my wife has threatened to sign me up to the local golf club as a more productive use of my time.

I attach the copy of the will and accompanying original affidavit. Should you prefer an electronic copy, please let me know.

Kind regards,

Timothy Jennings

FORTY-ONE

Skibbereen, Wednesday, 12 May 2021, 9.30 a.m.

They gathered in Connolly's cramped office, huddling around his 2012-issue Windows 8 laptop. By rights the machine should have gone to computer heaven, but nothing else in the station had a suitable USB outlet to connect the large spider-like object that sat on the desk beside it, cleared of all the sand and seaweed, still blinking.

The eagle had taken the drone down to the lake, presumably to feast on it before realising it was inedible. A particularly vigorous spring tide had saved it from the worst of the saltwater, washing it so far up Dineen's shore that the later surges had not reached it. According to Natalia, the divers had not been needed. It had been there, hiding in plain sight, covered in a mound of seaweed.

Thank God for that eagle, Rosa thought. *And may she rest in peace. She deserved a better fate than being poisoned by hill farmers. Clodagh is right – why* are *we Irish so backward?*

Connolly sat on the one chair, while Rosa and Kevin

flanked him on either side. Flanking them in turn were Niall and Paraic, the other local guards, while Clodagh Duffy and Philip Moulton from the Forestry Department stood behind Connolly, leaning over to see the results.

'Why's it taking so long?' Kevin fretted, watching the hourglass turn and listening to the laptop's small motor whirr.

'It's based on map data,' Clodagh explained, 'and that's very heavy to process. You have your map layer, then all the others. You know how on Google maps you can select satellite or terrain? Well, we've six different layers to choose from for our forestry maps, and then the little computer is putting the visual data on top. Of course, when the eagle took out the satellite communication, we lost that reference, so there's a whole lot of orphaned data it can't relate to anything. So, you get error messages. If you get anything at all. I think yiz are being optimistic, to be honest.' She ran her hand through her hair, which hung loose and free. She hadn't brushed it, and her clothes were in a state. They'd rung her at six and she'd had to leap in the car and drive three and a half hours from her home in south Wicklow to get here.

'Seems you're right,' Connolly commented. A slew of white boxes had blizzarded the screen with helpful messages like '*Object of 'longitude' could not be found.*' There was no option but to click OK for each one. After twenty clicks, and ever more boxes showing up, Sean Connolly looked around and said, 'It's going to just keep doing this forever, isn't it?'

'Keep going,' Clodagh said, and now her tone was intense. Sean clicked away again twenty more times until Kevin said, 'What happens if we hold down the shift key?'

Sean told him, 'Don't be daft,' but Kevin leaned across and pressed three keys with one hand, clicking OK on the next box. Then the boxes disappeared, the laptop whirred some more, and the ARC GIS logo showed up. Several held breaths released at once.

'Good work!' Rosa exclaimed.

'I used to run an Access database, because PULSE was—' Kevin stopped. No Garda could willingly admit to outsiders that PULSE, the Garda software system running on two servers in Visual Basic, a language deprecated twenty years ago, was pure grinding shit. 'Whenever it got stuck, if you held down the shift key, you could log in and fix it.'

'Is it ever going to stop loading, though?' Sean Connolly stared at the unresponsive screen, the logo and hourglass.

'I wouldn't write it off yet,' Philip reassured him. 'Even on a good day it can take up to five minutes.'

'Five minutes!' Sean cried good-naturedly. 'Anyone fancy a coffee?'

But nobody moved. The seconds on Kevin's watch ticked by as they waited and waited.

Then the screen went black.

'Shit!' Rosa groaned and Clodagh put her head in her hands. Sean hit the keys repeatedly, but nothing happened. The LED on the drone still flashed on and off, the computer was still on, but there was no sign of any heavy activity.

'Of all the times for my laptop to break,' Sean moaned, but then it was whirring again, and the blackness was replaced by something blurred and moving, something that looked like …

The top of a mountain.

'Oh my God,' breathed Philip. 'It kept the footage.'

'Can we rewind this?' Rosa asked. 'Look, there's a play button down there near the bottom.'

'Yes, but it's nearly at the start,' Clodagh said. 'Probably the rest was downloaded to our servers. Its instructions are to download as soon as it finds a secure connection. There isn't one up here, so it never transferred.'

The eagle was wrestling with the drone, and it soon turned skywards. Weird whooping sounds came out of the laptop's speakers as the drone was turned and pulled at. The wind blowing and crackling.

'Christ,' Philip muttered, 'there won't be much left out of that.'

Back downwards it swung, and suddenly, the whole of Knockalisha hilltop was clearly in view. And on the top right-hand corner, a digital clock. It said 18:10. Was it possible?

Then the drone suddenly veered off course, down the hill towards the lake. As fast as the team's spirits had risen, they fell with the falling camera. It was down further now, and circling the other side, nearly at the road—

'Hold on a minute.' Kevin grabbed the mouse and clicked the pause button. 'Is that ...?'

Sure enough, on the frozen footage, it was possible to see the dipped headlights of a white van heading up the hill from the lake. If the van had come from Skibbereen, it could have turned off earlier and passed the lake before ascending Knockalisha Hill to rejoin the Baltimore Road.

'Can you magnify?' Philip was hoarse.

Rosa and Sean managed between them to screenshot and expand the picture until the registration plate was just about legible. They wouldn't even need OCR for it.

Rosa nodded. 'It matches Tom Keating's.' She hit Play once more, barely daring to hope they might have more. But the eagle decided to carry the unfortunate drone back up the hill again and the van disappeared. It was passing the trees far below – trees that had barely survived the second fire that had raged moments later, but in that footage were still verdant and lush. The eagle soared, the drone footage moved up, and the van rematerialised, driving into the same laneway that Kevin and Rosa had taken on their initial scouting. Then it stopped and far below, a figure hopped out of the driver's side.

'Screenshot. Now.' Rosa hissed. Clodagh did so. 'From here on we screenshot every few seconds. OK, now continue.' Her mouth was so dry her tongue nearly stuck to the roof of it.

Play was pressed again. The van's back doors opened. The figure was pulling something out, something wrapped in black bags. Slinging it over his shoulder. And God bless that eagle for having one last bout of curiosity and flying low, because now there was no need to expand the picture.

'Screenshot,' Rosa commanded again, but Kevin had already grabbed the laptop and was capturing and saving the footage. Then back to the media file again. The figure, short and ungainly, was carrying the bagged object in a fireman's lift, so it was obvious what – and who – it was. The film began to veer from side to side, but still they could see: one arm wrapped around the legs, the other around the torso. And all along, Kevin pausing and saving each frame.

'*Bingo*,' Rosa said in a whisper. 'We've got them.' No sooner had her words been uttered than the screen went blank for the last time and a polite white box popped up: *File Not Found*.

And Clodagh, leaning in, exclaimed in wonder, 'All along I was wrong. I was convinced I was right. So sure.'

'Well, lads.' Sean stood up and closed the laptop. 'Well, I'd never have thought it—'

But he was interrupted by a scuffle at the door. Paraic went out to see who it was, and soon re-entered with a distressed-looking Tom Keating in tow.

'You need to come now. He has Luke. I'm after getting two

fingers in the post. That will my granda Harry wrote.' He stood in the doorway, panting, red-faced, beads of sweat on his forehead.

Sean got up. 'Hold on, Tom. Back up a little. What will, and who are we talking about?'

'Savage.' Tom grabbed an open bottle of water on the desk and swallowed half of it. 'The will. He wanted it shredded. He wanted it gone because Sadhbh was after it, so he wanted her gone too. And my granda's affidavit. He wanted her dead and he wanted my land. And like the fool I was, didn't I nearly go and give it to him.' His eyes were wild with fear and panic, his cheeks flared. He breathed heavily. 'I know you won't believe me, but ...' He thrust forward what looked like a small flimsy gift box, but the stench that came from it was appalling and Clodagh recoiled. Then Rosa looked inside and saw two severed fingers, the flesh turning rotten under the skin.

Rosa Keane had seen a lot in her career but the sight of that nearly made her vomit.

'Tom,' she said, 'we have him carrying Sadhbh's body on camera from the Forestry Department's drone. We've got him.'

Tom sagged down on the sergeant's chair. 'I thought she was the enemy. Spent all my time fighting her. Blamed her for everything. I didn't have to cut those hedgerows, you know. Coulda left them alone.'

'What'll I do with these?' Connolly said aggressively, swinging the box about.

Philip said something under his breath, then piped up. 'I'll take them out. I don't think we'll be regrafting those when we find poor Luke.'

Rosa turned her chair to face Tom. 'Look, what happened before. None of that matters. We have him, but we want to get Luke out safely. We'll need your help for that.'

Tom's response was immediate. 'What can I do?'

'Call Diarmuid Savage, tell him you have the will. And the affidavit. Ask him to return Luke and you'll give it to him. We'll do the rest.'

FORTY-TWO

They walked Tom Keating through what he needed to say on the call. He was compliant and attentive, scribbling notes onto a ruled page provided for him.

Sean Connolly kept shaking his head. 'It's like he's a different person,' he whispered to Kevin as Rosa guided Tom through what he needed to say. 'Whenever I've had dealings with him, he's roared at me like a bull. And now look at him.'

'Seeing your son's severed fingers in a box will do that to you,' Kevin answered grimly.

It was true. Tom Keating was a changed man. He looked older, less forceful. He seemed to realise it himself, repeating, 'I don't know who I am any more.'

'Take your time, Tom.' Rosa tried not to sound strained. Time was something they were running out of, but they couldn't upset Tom. They had to do this right. For Luke. For Sadhbh.

'He burned my land, you know.'

'Who? Diarmuid?'

'His grandfather.' Tom exhaled, making a huffy sound.

'When Harry was on the run, Savage burned his land. And what he did to my grandmother Noreen ...' Anguish twisted his features. 'She never recovered, Inspector. Michael Savage was so brutal with her. They put her away. Because she had lost her senses, but really because of the shame.' He bowed his head. 'My father was born in 1923. After they hanged Granda late the year before and Granny Noreen never even laying eyes on him. And the other children died.'

Rosa sucked in her breath. *That* was a discovery. Tom Keating had hung his lifetime's reputation on being Harry's grandson. Destroying this belief would certainly have done something to him.

I know what it's like not to be who you thought you were.

'I needed Diarmuid,' he went on. 'I had debts like you wouldn't believe. And not to banks neither.' Tom stopped. Then, realising that nobody was going to enquire where he had his debts, he continued. 'He promised me a load of money once they got the scheme up and running. But when he heard the Drummonds were looking for Harry's will and that there was information in it that would keep the ground rents and even return the land, he got antsy. He went on and on at me to find it so he could shred it. I told him it was nothing more than a rumour. I never thought it was real.'

He entwined his fingers, cracking them. Sean and Clodagh both winced.

'I can't believe any of this is real. I love my son. And I've done nothing but drive him away.' His eyes filled with tears. 'And burning my own land, just like Savage burned it for me during the Civil War. What in God's name was I thinking?'

Tom was wandering. He no longer seemed to distinguish himself from Harry, Diarmuid Savage from Michael.

'We can't change the past, Tom, but we can get Luke for

you. But we need you to work with us.' Impulsively, Rosa took Tom's hands. 'Can you do that?'

Tom sniffed loudly, swiped his arm across his nose, and mumbled, 'OK, yeah. Shall I put him on speaker?'

'No. Do as you'd normally do. We don't want him getting suspicious.'

He scrolled down his phone, found Diarmuid Savage's contact details, and pressed Call. 'Hiya. Look, I've got a bit of news for you.'

'I hope you've found that item we were discussing, Tom. I really do.' Diarmuid Savage's smooth, bland, insurance-man voice was distinctive even with speaker off. 'If you haven't got it, I'm afraid to say it won't be good news for you.'

'As it happens, I have.' And Tom went on to talk about some local historical society and someone called Timothy Jennings. Rosa seemed to recall that in Dinny Geraghty's book there had also been mention of someone called Jennings, a prosperous merchant family in Cork. Tom stood up and put the phone to his ear, keeping his other arm up protectively to shield himself.

'Nah, no, not out and about. I'm at home. My wife's upset, you know. She doesn't understand. She's worried, y'know.' Another pause, Tom nodding. 'Yes. Uhuh. I understand.'

What a hold Diarmuid Savage must have had over the man, Rosa mused, that he would speak so softly to him when his own son's life was in danger.

'Right. Right, OK. Meet at where? Liss Ard. The Drummond ruin? You sure that's …Yes, of course. Five is fine. So I give over the will and you'll burn it? OK. No, I've no copies. No, of course I'd never do a thing like that.' Rosa could hear the genuine terror that underlay Tom's conversation. Diarmuid Savage badly wanted that will gone.

Tom hung up and slumped into a chair, the phone skeetering across the floor as it left his grip. Clodagh wordlessly handed him a bottle of Ballygowan and he slugged it back.

'Well done, Tom. Good job.' Rosa turned to Kevin. 'Can you get on to Eames and tell him we need the ERU and back up for Liss Ard estate, right at the house. Seventeen hundred hours. Hostage situation with a minor. Give him the co-ordinates off the map but tell them not to park nearby. Sean, can you rendezvous with them as you know the estate well. You and you' – she gestured at Sean Connolly's two underlings – 'you're coming with me. Kevin too, once that phone call's done. Right.' She gave Tom a wire. 'Put that on. We'll be paying attention to everything you say.'

Tom smirked. 'Well, I never thought I'd end up being an informer for the peelers, but sure the wheel has come full circle now.'

FORTY-THREE

As much as Rosa wanted to, she did not put on the siren. Its loud keening wail would alert every badger and fieldmouse on the route, let alone the bandits that Tom Keating and Diarmuid Savage did business with. They wanted as little fuss as possible.

They headed south-east to Liss Ard, Rosa tearing through the country roads so fast that the ageing, unmarked Opel almost flew into the air, flinging the passengers against the windows, in spite of their seatbelts, the hedgerows too harshly cut back to brush the side of the car as it veered past. Niall looked as if he were about to be sick out the window.

Rosa hoped to God the Emergency Response Unit would be quick off the mark. They were the only section of the Gardaí who were fully armed, but after the absolute mess they'd gotten into with Tomi Obasanjo, people had been leery of them. The lad was having a bad episode, but the ERU'd mistaken it for a hostage situation and took him out in a hail of bullets.

God, she was nervous.

There was little to hand in Skibbereen Garda station, but she did feel the reassuring bulge of the Smith and Wesson, now on her belt. Not loaded yet, but it soon would be. She remembered that poor garda up north who had accompanied a woman out of the house during a domestic, only to have her IRA man husband shoot him dead on the spot, before turning the gun on himself, the despicable coward.

Terrorism was in Diarmuid Savage's blood, too. Rosa had no doubt that if cornered, he would do the same to her. She would need every piece of ammunition she had, especially as Kevin didn't have anything, even though he ranked as a detective. Months behind a desk meant it had been taken off him.

Earlier on, and then during the journey, Tom Keating continued to talk about Diarmuid Savage, who, it turned out, had been in far rougher financial straits than his opulent home and *flaithiúlach* manner had indicated. He had been expanding so far that he had become involved in something called 'contracts for difference' which Rosa vaguely recalled from the 2008 crash. Weren't they some sort of financial instrument that mortgaged the mortgages?

His core firm was in danger from all his extraneous borrowings and investments, so he had, in the way a gambler does, decided to recoup it all by investing it in the ample mineral reserves that lay below the poor soil on Tom Keating's land. He knew it was a sure thing – if only he could get his hands on it. That was the obstacle. The land on Knockalisha Hill was divided up between the Forestry Department, Tom himself, and the remnants of the Drummond estate that belonged to Eric and Olivia, and which Sadhbh was using for her Not in Our Lifetime project.

He had been in the middle of an elaborate scheme to push the county council along with the Office of Public Works to obtain a CPO, as well as the planning application. Staunton Davies had been the one he'd asked to bat for him.

'The fella took a bit of persuading,' Tom roared over the wind. 'Even he's aware of the special conservation issues. It would be fierce unpopular, but Diarmuid had a hold over him of sorts. He's good at finding out your private business, is Diarmuid.'

Rosa remembered how those strangers had emerged from the corner when she had been out as a woman. They had known who she was, where she would be. She must have dropped that blasted card in Diarmuid Savage's house.

'Anyway, they were getting very close to finalising it when Sadhbh got wind of the whole thing and started poking about in them files. And then the Furlong wan, her step-daughter, got wind of it and passed it on to her ma, who told Diarmuid. And that's when he started leaning on me hard.'

Then Tom Keating started recanting his past evils, swearing if he got Luke back, he'd never start another fire again. Rosa wasn't sure he was sincere. But it didn't matter. They only had to be on the same page for a few hours.

Rosa was so fierce in concentration that it took the others yelling at her to realise she had overshot the gates. Slowly, she pulled onto the right-hand side of the road, so the car was pressed against a plethora of whitethorn and nettles, and two of the lads in the back had to get out to allow Tom to leave.

'Fuckin' guards can't park for shite,' Tom muttered, but did as he was told.

'You have it on?' Niall had a quick look at the apparatus while Rosa and Kevin put on a set of headphones each. 'Just say something so we can hear.'

'Éirinn go brách' Tom declared. Paraic rolled his eyes at Niall, but the sound over the speakers was clear. Tom put a sleeveless, padded jacket on over his short-sleeved shirt to hide the wire. 'Right.' He looked around at them uncertainly. ''Tis a bit hot.'

'Off you go, Tom. Good luck. We'll just be in the lawn perimeter, behind the trees. You go forward.'

Tom smiled grimly. 'Like Stephen Rooney the day that army lad shot him point blank. Jesus, I'm sweatin' buckets with this yoke.'

The detectives hung back as Tom walked alone up the driveway. Kevin whispered to Rosa, 'Inspector, this whole place gives me the creeps. Feels like eyes everywhere.'

They walked on through the long grass, the sun advancing in the sky and catching their shoulders and the pale backs of their necks. Never mind that Rosa had left her factor 50 suncream at home. Her neck and face would be like a beetroot by the time this was over. If she got out all right.

Keep going. Now they were in the thicket past the east end of the house. Rosa tried to keep them under tree cover. Niall stepped on a stick. The crack echoed like a gun, and they all turned on him with furious shushing noises. Then they heard voices. Young, hoarse, crying. A 'please'. Rosa's throat nearly closed over.

It was all down to Tom now. Only he could put an end to this eye-for-an-eye local war.

The radio crackled to life. It was beginning.

FORTY-FOUR

The first they heard over the wire was the sound of Tom crashing through undergrowth and breathing heavily. Rosa motioned Niall and Paraic to move towards the gaping open window hole. Kevin had already intuited where to go and was right at her side. There, they could at least see what was going on, as well as hear.

The floor level of the ruin's basement was below ground level; Tom gasped as he hit the ground, several feet down. Following him, the guards moved towards the gaping window hole.

A cracking twig, some feedback. Then, 'Hello, Tom. 'Tis yourself.' Diarmuid Savage, bland and agreeable as ever.

'Sure who else would it be?' Tom now, so clear and loud that the headphones nearly buckled, although he was talking at a normal pitch. Then he added, 'Hello, Luke.' Luke, wherever he was, made no response. Presumably unable, or too frightened.

Rosa was impressed at Tom's composure. So, it appeared, was Diarmuid, because his next comment was, 'I'm glad you're being reasonable about this, Tom. So are the lads.' There was meaning in his voice. Evidently the guards weren't the only people who had called for backup. Shit. Rosa and Kevin exchanged a glance. She prayed this wouldn't turn into a gun battle.

'Well, I didn't have what you were looking for, but then I got it from Timothy Jennings.' There followed a long explanation on Tom's part about how he had managed to source the document from some fellow in the local historical society who happened to be Ernest Jennings' grandson. All to play for time, give the forces a chance. For someone who despised being a grass, Tom was good at it.

'Well, that's a meeting you could have told me in an email,' Diarmuid Savage joked. 'I would have thought you'd be keen to get this out of the way.'

'I am! Sure, here's that document and all. The family will never see it now.' For a moment, silence. Diarmuid Savage was obviously investigating it. Rosa wondered if he had known the truth all along about his grandfather. Or would this be a shock to him? Would he be enraged by what he discovered? That had not occurred to Rosa, but given how cherished his ancestor was to Diarmuid, she could not rule out his going nuclear. Double shit.

But Savage didn't seem angry. 'Right. That's grand. You don't have copies, by any chance, Tom? Ones you might have kept without telling me?' A muffled squeal over the radio. Was that bastard hurting Luke?

Keep calm, Tom, Rosa silently begged over the wire. *Don't rise to it.*

'I told Timothy Jennings I just wanted the original document, nothing more. I've made no copies. Sure, I don't have a photocopier out in the middle of the mountains.'

Diarmuid laughed. 'Ah Tom. Sure all you have to do is

take a photo on your phone.' Another squeal, and a hardening at the end in Diarmuid Savage's voice. 'We wouldn't want that, would we?'

'Diarmuid, I swear to you, I've no copies, no photos, no nothing.'

'Oh, I know ye don't. But just in case, why don't you hand over your phone, like a good man.'

There was a rustle as Tom fished the phone out of his pocket. This was all fine. They had planned for this.

'Don't I know well you could have deleted it?' Diarmuid Savage's voice was getting harsher now. Rosa looked around for backup, any signs in the undergrowth. Nothing as yet.

Keep it going, Tom, as long as you can.

'I swear I wouldn't do that!' Tom cried. 'I only want to go home with Luke. I don't want to be giving my land back to the Drummonds, for God's sake. I'm happy for the FEC development, Diarmuid. You know I am. Please now, be reasonable.'

'I can't afford to.' Savage's voice was gravel. 'If this fuckin' thing ever surfaces, the whole thing is jeopardised. Ronan Furlong and Eric Drummond will file their counterclaims, and there won't be a damn thing you or I could do about it. We'll be ruined, Tom.'

'And your reputation too,' Tom answered thoughtlessly, 'with your Granda Michael. And everything.'

Silence. Then a slow ominous, 'What do you mean by that, Tom?' Over the radio, Rosa heard another muffled squeal and winced. What was going on? She couldn't see and didn't dare move. Shapes had begun to materialise, dappled shadows behind the laurels and hedges, but they were Savage's men, not hers. She motioned to Kevin: *keep down.* The two of them bent low, but the men passed by without detecting them. They were wearing balaclavas. Oh God, this might well be a gun fight. If the ERU ever turned up. Where the *hell* were they?

'My grandad Michael Savage was a warrior and a patriot,' Diarmuid hissed, close to Tom's wire, 'and yours was a gurrier. Nothing more. And his wife—'

Suddenly, he was cut off. Had Tom finally been wound up enough that he couldn't keep his already volatile temper in check? Rosa heard a rustle and some grunting. She looked at Kevin. Did they need to break cover? Just as Rosa feared the worst, Tom's voice came back on again. 'I wasn't looking to push ye Diarmuid. You have it all wrong. Ye have the will and the affidavit now, and there are no copies, I swear it.' His unsteady breathing filled the microphone. 'Can Luke come home with me now? C'mon, Luke.'

'Dad!' It sounded as if the boy had been released.

'Not so fast, pet.' Diarmuid Savage again. 'You're going nowhere quite yet.' More scuffling, Luke swearing. Kevin whispering into Rosa's free ear, *Should we go in?* Rosa shaking her head. *Not yet.*

A small, welcome breeze soughed through the treetops, those birches allowed to grow tall and free, with a few stumps from those cut down. Rosa looked up and saw how the pattern of the heart-shaped leaves danced with the sunlight. Week after week of relentless heat, they had stayed green. But it would only be a matter of time before they, too, would shrivel. The ground underneath was dry and hard and even the breeze did not stay long. The wild garlic that grew everywhere and infused the place with its scent would give up the ghost.

'Your grandfather let mine down and blackened his name,' Savage snarled, 'and I'm not a man to forgive easily.'

'That was a hundred years ago, for Christ's sake!'

'Y'know, Tom,' Savage continued in a more pleasant tone.

'It's roasting out, isn't it? I'd imagine you'd have that jacket taken off long ago.'

'Well, now, I don't—'

'Take off your jacket, Tom, why not? You must be sweating.'

He'd guessed. Damn it, they were running out of time, and still no sign of backup! Rosa slowly pushed the magazine into her pistol until it snapped into place with a gentle click, then she pushed the slide forward. Loaded. She put her hand on Kevin's arm. He gave her the thumbs up, then signalled to the others.

'Pearse, you can help our friend Mr Keating here.'

Now.

They charged out, Rosa in the lead, crashing down through the last of the undergrowth and out on the western lawn, heading through the archway, leaping down the same way Tom had done. They had to get there fast and get Tom out, Luke too.

Savage had three others with him, not counting Tom and Luke, both of whom were pinioned in the arms of the men in balaclavas. Rosa couldn't see if they were armed or not, but they had to take the risk. She went straight for Savage, firing at him and getting him in the leg, as she had planned. Then she barrelled down on him, bringing him to the ground. He fell with a soft grunt. She was so close she could smell the man's shower gel, and his stinking breath, and could taste the morning's coffee repeating on her own. She could hear Kevin shouting at Luke's captor, grabbing him, trying to twist his arms behind his back.

'Help him!' she called out, hoping the others would intervene. Kevin was young and strong, but even he could not fight all those fellows off on his own.

She had Savage supine, but his hands were still free. She needed to grab his arms and pinion them—

Rosa suddenly felt an impact on her side, and a pain like she had never known before, not even when those thugs were beating her up. The power went out of her arms and her body slumped over Diarmuid Savage's, her cheek brushing and touching his. She heard him *tch* in revulsion. God damn it, the bastard had a knife all along!

Savage got to his feet and loomed over her. She felt warmth spread on her pelvis. Blood.

Diarmuid Savage put his hands on his hips and sighed. 'The guards don't send their best down from Cork, do they? A pervert like you in women's knickers and a Chinky? Youse really thought you could take me on?'

Rosa frantically looked around for Kevin; there he was, in the corner of her eye, still and cold, at the point of a gun, Tom beside him. Both held onto by the same balaclavaed figure. Rosa's pistol lay useless in the long grass a few metres away where Savage had thrown it.

'Was it for this, Tom? 'Tis a terrible disappointment for you to turn informer.' Savage sighed and clucked. 'You let me down, Tom. When push came to shove. We were almost there, you and me, but you had to go involve people in our business.'

He's going to kill us all, Rosa thought, as a weird metallic taste filled her mouth. *He's desperate.* She was too weak to move with this bloody knife stuck in her, and if she managed to pull it out, she'd haemorrhage to death right there.

A huge shadow passed over the unrelenting sun, for what seemed the first time in forever. The air began to change, humming with expectation, moist, gathering. Was this the change before death? Rosa wondered. For the blinding light to go out of her eyes, everything fade to black? In the end she would die as ~~Gerry~~. Be waked and buried and memorialised as ~~Gerry~~. But that wouldn't be her concern any more. In death, she could relinquish him. Finally.

Then she felt the first drop on her cheek.

And another.

And yet another.

Soon it was a fusillade and torrent, a roar of water, hissing on the birch leaves, belting the stone walls, splattering on the weeds. A gunshot rang out, Savage leapt to his feet and swore, and the ground began to sigh with relief.

'I told ye not to fire in the fuckin' rain!'

His hapless goon had meant to shoot Kevin but had ended up hitting one of his own. Rosa had spent some time in the artillery range at the Glen of Imaal, firing at targets along with a bunch of rain-sodden cadets, and she remembered well what Savage was talking about – bullets fired in heavy showers had a significant yaw from their target. Kevin had been able to move just in time.

It wasn't death. It wasn't the end. It was only rain.

Kevin had already disarmed his would-be attacker as his mate lay screaming on the ground, blood gathering in the crook of his shoulder, and then turned the gun on Savage. 'Don't move,' he said calmly. 'Are you all right, Rosa?' He dropped to his knees, not releasing his hold on the gun for one moment.

'Rosa!' Diarmuid scoffed.

'I told you. Not. To. Move!' Kevin barked at him.

'That's a Glock 19,' Rosa said dreamily. 'Powerful yokes.'

Kevin ignored her. 'Can any of you attend to the inspector, please?' he called out, his voice hoarse in the rain. 'My hands are full. Come over and I'll cover you.'

Paraic ran forward and dropped to his knees beside Rosa

while Kevin looked from Diarmuid Savage to the goon who had shot him with a challenging stare.

Rosa winced as Paraic examined the wound.

'Lost a bit of blood there,' he said, 'but I think it's superficial. He got you in the abdomen, but you had enough fat to shield it.' Rosa had to smile. She didn't mind the lad's tactlessness.

'OK, deep breath,' Paraic instructed, taking hold of the knife handle. 'I'm gonna take it out. Look away now; you'll feel a bit of a pinch.'

Rosa felt considerably more than a pinch. She roared as Paraic pulled the knife out. Christ, that hurt! He nodded approvingly. 'Not much blood left there.' He was interrupted by a kerfuffle behind him and Kevin shouting, 'Damn!'

Diarmuid Savage was running away, crashing through the cluster of brambles at the south side, limping from the bullet Rosa had inflicted on his left, his pale-pink-clad arse bobbing through the long grass. Rosa took a deep breath and jumped to her feet, breathing through the pain.

'Don't fire,' she told Kevin, 'This one's mine.'

'You sure?'

Rosa nodded.

'Good luck then, Inspector.'

There wasn't time to grab her gun. She managed a jog through the fog of pain, pure adrenaline overruling it all. Savage was easy pickings to take down to the ground once more, punching him in the stomach so that she could feel pleasure in the *uuuuhhh* of how easily it yielded. She hoped it hurt.

'Diarmuid Savage,' she called out in a voice that sent crows flapping, 'I'm arresting you for the murder of Sadhbh Drummond and the false imprisonment of Luke Keating—'

A shot rang out, and almost instantly afterwards a new

pain flowered in her left midsection. Kevin yelled in despair. Nettles stung her cheek as once more she collapsed on Diarmuid, pressing into him as if they were lovers.

'Get off me,' Diarmuid muttered in disgust, pushing her away from him. She collapsed on her back, moaned with agony as she sank back into the brambles, her clothes sodden with rain and blood. *Where was Kevin? What was going on?*

Diarmuid rose slowly, the rain plastering his smoothly combed hair into a skullcap. 'Look at you,' he declared, as loudly as Rosa had a moment ago. 'Arresting me, hah? Like you're anything more than a nonce? 'Twasn't clever of you to leave that card lying around, *Gerry*. D'you think you'll be allowed around children? The shame. You don't need to say another word.'

Savage disappeared briefly before emerging again, armed, with the very gun that Kevin had pointed at him before.

I should have let Kevin take him down, Rosa thought disconsolately. He aimed it at her face.

Then he began a monologue of hate. Called Rosa every insult under the sun. The T word, of course, and that he would shoot her in the mouth, like he shot his dogs, except he would put them down more kindly. His face was contorted with hate and flecks of spit gathered in the corners of his mouth.

'You won't get away with this. Let me tell you—'

A sudden, sharp outbreak of shots flew over Rosa, and Diarmuid Savage's expression changed. The gun dropped out of his hands, spread in front of him with a look of astonishment. From his hip, blood gathered. A loudhailer crackled, and suddenly, everything got busy. Armed guards running everywhere, sirens wailing. Diarmuid turned around, wounded and snarling, to face them.

Was Savage going to charge at them? One last glorious suicide run?

No, he was not. Not on her watch.

Like she had to Kevin, Rosa called out to the ERU officers, 'This one's mine!'

Rising, limping with pain, not sure if she would even manage to make it over, she approached Diarmuid. Softly, so only he could hear: 'I think you'll find it's *you* who doesn't have to say another word.'

And as everything went black and white, the skies wheeling, the sirens at high-doh, and the wild garlic beginning to exult and let out its scent in the rain, she managed to finish the incantation before she fell:

But anything you do *say ...*

PART 3

FORTY-FIVE

Knockalisha Forest, September 2021

Ronan was surprised to see the crowds gathering on the forest road, above the still-blackened ruins from the fire, though the rainy August had softened the harshness a little. He hadn't been sure they would come. Continuing the Not in Our Lifetime movement after Sadhbh's lifetime had ended so violently had been a gamble.

His ex-wife had been released from custody for her trial hearing for failing to disclose a crime and was on bail awaiting trial later in the year. Ronan felt profound relief that she wasn't there. That the sentiment in the town no longer silently backed her. Too late, of course, but there you go.

Sadhbh would probably have seen the humour in it, he decided. She always had a great understanding of human frailty. *Look at them all,* she would say, *that motley crowd, the usual pillocks of the community. Hated me alive, can't get enough of me now I'm safely dead.*

She would have been glad to see a group of Travellers there. Just a few weeks after she died, two feuding families had presented Ronan with a wreath, saying that when the whole town had tried to run out their halting centre, Mrs Furlong had stood firm and had none of it.

'She always had time for us,' Jack Nevin declared. 'When everyone else in the town would cross the street to avoid us, she treated us with dignity.'

Oh, he missed her so much. The slight breeze sighed her name. The tender little shoots that had come up over the scorched earth somehow seemed to bring her back to life. But it was an illusion; she was gone forever. Not all damage and destruction could be healed.

Catriona was keeping an eye on the little ones. She was a lot gentler with him these days. 'I can't believe Jeanne knew and said nothing,' she had admitted to Ronan by way of apology. 'And all to protect her brother.'

Ronan knew it was a failing in him that he could not bear to think about Sinead. That while she was in juvenile detention, he had managed to visit her only once. He could not, as a father, love her the way she wanted. Sadhbh, God bless her, had tried. But that was Sadhbh in a nutshell: she had always tried, and usually got it wrong, and look how Sinead paid her back! The petty cruelty of it.

He was fed up with her false maturity, her spite and bottomless well of need. If that reflected badly on him, to hell with it ... He sighed. It wasn't entirely Sinead's fault. He was blaming her for his own incapacity to love fairly, equally. In truth, he feared he could only love the children in the same proportion he loved their mothers. That said, things with her full sister, Jennifer, were better. She was Jeanne's daughter too. That, he could hold on to.

Press photographers gathered at the margins, snapping away at the people on the hillside. Just down the hill, in front of the trees and the shimmering blue of the lake, Ronan recognised Fergal Heeny, the RTÉ man, his cameraman carefully positioned on a sloping bit.

A large black shape dived down from the blue sky towards the reporter, getting just metres from the ground before climbing once more in an arc that would do any airshow pilot proud. A buzzard, possibly mistaking the sound engineer's boom mike for a rabbit or bird. A century before, they'd been hunted to extinction. Harry Keating and Michael Savage would not have seen them on their way to exact vengeance for the killing of Stephen Rooney.

Some stragglers made their way up the exposed forest path. One of them was the detective inspector who had interviewed Ronan on that terrible night after Sadhbh had been found. God, he'd been in shock back then. Had gone completely into headmaster mode before having a complete meltdown at Jeanne and Sinead. And all the time Inspector Keane had been a closet transgender woman!

Ronan had seen some of the headlines while paying for petrol. SECRET TRANS COP MAKES ARREST along with a blurred image of Keane taking down Savage. Diarmuid Savage appeared to have imagined he'd get a reduced sentence, because the arresting officer was, in his words, 'a fuckin' transvestite'.

Brave of her to show up for me, that gentle voice chimed in his brain. *I hope she knows I appreciate it.*

Ronan's eyes pricked with tears. Because that wasn't just his brain. Those words had to come from Sadhbh herself, not his imagining of her. He wasn't generous enough to think that himself.

I wish you were here. I wish I'd been a better man.

The reporter was speaking. Ronan could imagine what he was saying, what the headlines would report: '*After a horren-*

dous murder, a community gathers in hope.' Well, most of the community. There were a few other prominent absences.

Staunton Davies had angrily refused to resign after his role in the Knockalisha consortium became clear. His Progressive Ireland colleagues had 'persuaded' him to step down. He would be fine. He'd live to fight another day, him and his seven hundred cows and his polluted streams and his hedgerows stripped raw and stubbly like waxed female genitalia. He'd probably go in as an Independent. Older voters, farmers and bourgeoisie, would entertain his repeated assertions that climate change was a scam. Probably enough to vote him in for one more election cycle before they died off for good.

Before the planet died off for good, maybe.

Speaking of farmers, Luke Keating was there too, as was his mother. She looked haggard and used up. Shortly after Diarmuid had been arrested, she'd come home after shopping to find the Alsatian shot to death in the yard, Tom slumped beside it, nothing much left of his face after he had done similar to himself.

There had been talk on the grapevine of Tom's father being the product of rape by Michael Savage on Noreen Keating. For Diarmuid, Ronan mused, this revelation would hurt almost as much as the prospect of being banged up for quite some time. Yes, he had been in a financial hole, but at heart he had wanted to protect Michael's legacy more than anything. Ronan didn't like the man, but he had studied him enough to know his weaknesses. All that work to shield his grandfather, and all for nothing. Sadhbh had been right; the truth always came out. Like the poisoned body of the eagle, like the nitrates polluting the river – everything that was done in secret would eventually be revealed. And a country like Ireland, one that had kept going on secrets for so long, could barely take it. Tom, too, had been unable to live with the guilt of what he had done to his son, not to mention he was Michael's descendant too. Ronan had no love for the man, but it was tragic all round.

Peter Ludwig wasn't there either; he had left some time ago. He was finished with Ireland, he said. Oddly, given the circumstances, Peter and Ronan had established some sort of rapport after their tussle over Sadhbh's grave; it was to Ronan, over a post-lockdown pint in Kiely's, he revealed this information.

'It's failed,' Peter'd said gloomily. 'It's all failed. The push for a better future, the anti-capitalist movement. Ireland will never be free of Civil War parties and big business. And the agri-dynasties that own half the hospitals.'

Ronan had wiped the foam off his upper lip with a tissue and smiled grimly. 'You could have stopped at Civil War.'

'I won't judge when it comes to war.' Peter allowed himself the ghost of a smile.

'Haha! Fair. I'll get us another.'

Peter shook his head. 'Not for me. I have an early start. Taking a ferry to Le Havre and a train to Calais. To help the refugees again. Then after two weeks I go home.'

'I thought here was your home.'

Peter shook his head. 'No. Not since …' He broke off, tears filling his eyes. Ronan, unused to comforting other men, particularly someone who had cuckolded him, clapped him lightly on the shoulder.

This was weird, he thought, *but it feels right.*

'Why do you stay when she is gone?' Peter said, after a moment. 'You could start a new life.'

Ronan shook his head. 'This is my land. My home is here.' A Kavanagh poem he had learned at school resonated in his mind, particularly a line about the poet's mother looking up eternally, from the ground. His Sadhbh, her lustrous eyes, her wide, generous, laughing mouth, the one he'd kissed until it almost bruised sometimes, when he forgot himself. This was her land too.

The breeze stirred and Ronan caught a waft of pine from the trees below. Colm Fenton, that wheezy bore of a Progressive Ireland councillor, was giving the introduction. He claimed to have taken up travelling by bike and cutting down on meat. 'I won't lie, Sadhbh and myself were often at cross-purposes,' he declared, 'but after everything... I want to do better.'

Applause broke out and Colm Fenton flushed red from his chin to his shiny bald head. 'But less about me,' Fenton continued, 'and now to hand over to somebody who I'm sure needs no introduction – Ronan Furlong, Environment Party stalwart, school principal and Sadhbh's husband.'

Ronan was surprised to find himself nervous. He hadn't addressed an assembly in quite some time. When a voice from the crowd shouted in an adolescent tenor, 'G'wan Mr F!' and a small group cheered, emotion almost overcame him.

'I'll keep it brief. Thanks everyone for coming, it really means so much.' Pause, a deep breath. 'We all know I'm a poor substitute for the woman herself. This was Sadhbh's brainchild to be started on her land, and expanded into state forest lands, if a deal could be reached. Unfortunately, some people did not want that to happen.' He paused awhile and the crowd was silent. Some of the Travellers crossed themselves. 'Sadhbh was a force of nature, and she lived for nature. It would be some restoration of justice for her to be remembered not for how she died, but how she dreamed – the simple idea that we plant trees we will never see come to maturity and do it for the next generation.' He was sweating hard, even in the wind. 'And so, for the first planting for Not In My Lifetime, I would ask Oisin to come forward.'

His little boy stepped up, holding an oak sapling in a plastic pot, an anti-deer barrier wrapped around its tremulous stem. Clodagh Duffy from the Forestry Department had given it to him. She was there too, as was Philip Moulton. Oisin had clasped it close to his chest the entire time, determined not to drop it. Ronan was so proud of him.

Behind them hovered Triona Costello and Tammy Kelly, the new teaching assistant for French and History. She wore a T-shirt saying 'Nevertheless, she persisted'; her hair was in braids, her eyes a warm brown. She was heavily involved in her local animal rescue too. Triona Costello caught Ronan's eye, then looked meaningfully at Tammy, then back at him. Ronan acknowledged the look with a brief dip of his head.

Throughout his adult life, he had never been alone. Austere or not, he was no hermit. His natural need for comfort, Tammy's youthful enthusiasm – he felt from the conversations they had, they would eventually, gently, find each other. Sadhbh would understand, he thought; she, like him, had never left one relationship without moving to another.

Oisin stepped over to the shallow hole in the ground. Solemnly, delicately, he set the sapling into the soft, peaty, mountain soil, before patting around with a spade to set it in. The breeze blew the serrated leaf edges as Ronan bent down to whisper in his ear, 'Well done, Oisin,'

The little face crumpled up. Oisin was confused. They were all talking about his mummy, but they told him his mummy was dead, and he missed her cuddles. Tammy saw the child's tears and gently enveloped him in her arms, kissing him on the cheek. 'Good job, Oisin! We're all very proud of you.' Oisin brightened up again, and everyone clapped hard. Triona and the other teachers began planting their saplings. All native woods: hawthorn, oak, birch, sally willow.

I'm sorry about the tree, Sadhbh. More sorry than I can say.

When Sadhbh had first moved into his home, she had brought an apple tree cutting from the dower house orchard, from a tree that was a hundred years old. Every year, as it grew, it blossomed in the spring and the white petals had covered the mossy grass below. Over time, he had fashioned a little seat for her, a modest piece of woodworking, and loved nothing more than to watch her sit and read under the growing tree's shade. He often thought of Yeats's line when first meeting Maud Gonne – *a glimmering girl with apple blossom in her hair.* The tree had suffered the attacks of climate change driven storms, some years only yielding a few apples. And yet it had stayed up and flowered every year, even so.

Until he'd found out about Peter Ludwig and cut it down in a fit of rage.

He'd read the texts a few days earlier. She was discreet, but Peter was not. He wanted— Well, Ronan wasn't sure what he had wanted, he was so demented with rage. But then a desire clarified itself. He would destroy that tree. It was a nuisance, threatening to break the window, and the apples were cookers. He knew that it would hurt Sadhbh, but damn, she started it. At the very time Diarmuid Savage, unbeknownst to him, was beating his wife to death, he had the chainsaw out and oiled, driving into that old bark, so soft and yielding, so easy to destroy. And the gladness he felt when he saw it crack and fall. Of course the guards hadn't seen all of that when they found the spike on his Fitbit. God, why had he been so obstinate, not to tell them? His own pride risked putting him in a cell.

Perhaps, he thought, it was because of this: while he was

not the murderer, that day he had killed something. Something in himself. He had fallen headfirst into the maw of brutal spite that enveloped so many of his countrymen, maddened them into destroying beauty for its own sake. Sadhbh had strayed, but the tree had done nothing wrong.

Oh Ro, the voice returned, *look at our boy planting. Look to the future now.*

'What do you reckon?' Ronan heard Philip murmur to Clodagh.

'Some of them might take,' she murmured, 'but hardly more than a quarter I'd say.'

'A quarter is enough,' Ronan turned around, smiling. 'Believe me a quarter is better than none.'

EPILOGUE

January 2022

The long beach is greyish white in the winter light. Mostly rock when the tide is in, but when out, as it is now, exposing a long seam of glowing swamp as the sea retreats to Ballycotton Lighthouse. A nippy breeze plays on the sand heaps, on the waves and on Rosa's skin. As she hugs her forearms, she cannot stop shivering. Goose pimples gather on her thighs, her knock knees converge. Her modest, black swimming costume, a one piece with shorts, barely shields her from the cold. Up in the indifferent sky, clouds race in front of a washed-out egg blue.

Conditions for swimming are good, in spite of the time of year and the empty beach. In all ways, she reminds herself, she is allowed to be here.

When Rosa messaged Laura to say: *I'm gonna go for it. Am I completely crazy?*, Laura offered to come with her, for moral support. Rosa thanked her, but said she needed to do this alone, and Laura understood.

Since separating from Louise, Rosa has not exposed any

part of her body to the full glare of daylight, apart from her arms and face. Now, attenuated by six months' worth of oestradiol, it feels the cold far more. The chill gets right to her bones. Her breasts have a new tenderness to them, both alarming and affirming. It cannot be denied; they fill out the top half of that costume. Those little messengers, those hormones, have brought new tenderness to her heart as well. Those pills and injectables, furtively ordered online under Laura's guidance. Payment arranged via someone else's credit card, cash changing hands – Gilmartin, the gatekeeper and poacher finally bypassed and conquered. For the first time in her life, she feels fully human. Every emotion opens out in front of her like a fan.

For the first time in eight months, she has been able to take a break. After arresting Diarmuid Savage, the rest of the year was a blur. From being manhandled into an ambulance by fully masked paramedics and driven all the way to Cork at high speed, to the bizarre aftermath a month later in Eames's office, where he was more interested in the transgender stuff than the Distinguished Medal of Service she had earned, on to a fully paid leave of absence 'to recuperate' – though Rosa suspected more to 'change her mind'. After that first discussion, nobody mentioned her gender again and no discussion was held about what she should do about it next, though some old friends were markedly colder to her than before. Darragh McClure had blanked her twice.

Kevin, by contrast, stayed loyal and respectful. Poor man had been so upset about losing the gun. Blaming himself for being distracted, for leaving Rosa vulnerable.

'It was my duty,' he said, awkward by the hospital bed, looking at his hands while the fan roared white noise near the nurses' station. 'And I failed you.'

'Kevin, I was the one who wanted to bring him in. If I'd let you do it, we wouldn't have had the problem in the first place.'

Kevin shook his head. 'You could have been killed.'

'And instead I'm here reading headlines about me being a transgender cop.'

Kevin reminded her that they'd put her in the men's ward.

'Well,' Rosa said, 'they didn't know I was transgender in the ambulance, and I didn't want to make a nuisance of myself correcting them.'

Kevin sat up very straight and looked at her sternly. 'Inspector, you need to listen. You must make a nuisance of yourself. You will have to tell them over and over that you are a woman, and you are valid. I don't know a lot about transgender issues. But I do know what it's like to be 'not conventionally Irish'.' He wiggled his fingers in quotes. 'Your existence is a battleground now.' He saw her dismay and softened a little. 'You won't be alone. Many, many people are here to help. Me included.' He smiled then, and it was so warm and genuine that Rosa had to look away briefly, brush her hand across her eyes. In the months to come, with the hormones she'd taken, there had been more tears, and less embarrassment about shedding them. That was nice.

Another thing had happened in the hospital. She got a text from Louise. It said:

Saw the news. Nice work, ~~Gerry~~. All over Twitter too. My Insta is flooded with DMs about you!

Thanks. I'm Rosa these days, btw.

Rosa??!! It was far from Rosa you were reared, you absolute gobshite. Could you not have picked something like Siobhán? Hope you're doing OK.

Thanks Lou. Appreciate the moral support as always.

You're welcome, gobshite. Btw Muireann says she wants to talk to you. Give her a ring when you have a minute.

Sure. Thanks.

It is a détente of sorts, though almost as fragile as Harry Keating's battered will. The wounds still run deep there. The mocking words, the hatred directed Rosa's way – that will not be easily forgotten. There will be other arguments, other moments of pain and lashing out. Rosa can only hope they will be shorter, blow over sooner, be taken less personally, until eventually they fizzle out. Even though she and Lou are enemies, there is no one else who has fought in that trench.

As she picks her way painfully over the small stones, mussel shells and slippery seaweed, sure enough the voices start in: voices that might have belonged to Louise, or Mulvey, or random TERFs on socials, but which she has now taken to her heart:

You look absolutely ridiculous. Pretending to be a woman. You're a joke. A man in a dress, and now in a swimsuit. Invading women's spaces. Wearing bras, the state of you. You're a man. A fat, middle-aged, midlife foolish man. Hormones? That's nothing. You can never know what it's like to be a woman.

'Fuck off,' Rosa says, clearly and firmly, still stooped, her words not quite whipped away by the wind. A seagull wheels an arc on the same south-westerly gust, using it as leverage to bat an oblique way to its destination, a small rock a few metres out. Rosa does not straighten up. She keeps going forward.

Another few steps out. *Christ, it's cold.* Not too late to turn back and dry her feet. Not too late to go home and make a hot water bottle. But she keeps walking until the cold waves lap at her ankles, then at her shins, blotchy from homemade shaving, then lumpy knees, then thighs, then – oh Jesus, the churning cold of that seawater shrivelling up the controversial bits so much that surely even the most roaring TERF must admit—

She stubs her toe on a stone, loses her balance and falls in with an almighty splash. *Aaaaagggggh, Christ,* she did not think her tits would get so cold! And it's while she is kicking and struggling and swearing and trying not to take in a mouthful of water that she realises it's supporting her. The water.

She is swimming.

She rights herself with a gasp and immediately plunges in again. Alongside the agony, she feels a surge of exaltation like nothing she has known before. Rolling briefly onto her back, she finds that she can float. The sun comes out, bright and fractured in her water-speckled vision.

For a moment she senses Sadhbh nearby. It feels like the same energy that was in the air back when they were protesting the incinerator and she looked straight at Rosa, woman to woman, except now it's more like one of the waves Rosa surfs, cold and smiling. *I had the measure of you then, Rosa Keane, and I have the measure of you now.* Fading again, the whisper of a wave breaking and hissing on the shore.

What's causing this feeling of euphoria to course through her? Is it the hormones? The high of transgression? Extreme cold?

Or is it that she is life: woman, mammal, fish; all curve and wave, softened like a glass pebble carried by the sea for hundreds of years and gently left on a beach to glint brown or aquamarine; mermaid, transformed back to what she always was: pure foam, no longer forced to walk on blades? Is it that the sea bears her weight, her marked body, her censured shape, without judgement and all is renewed once more? Or that the same sea, worn out with human ordure and human poison and human, life-choking plastic – miles and miles of it – can still find room for another human, still among all the mess and acidifying heat and relentless statistics, somehow make one anew?

Is it that she is allowed to be here, as Rosa herself?

Sadhbh died violently, but she did not die in vain.

Her imperfect body kicking a lopsided breaststroke through an imperfect sea, Rosa swims on, feels as if she could swim to the horizon and beyond, and perhaps find a world where human touch is kinder and more merciful, and where the gods could not just forgive her transformation, but hasten it.

Sooner or later, it will be time to come ashore.

But not yet.

AFTERWORD

While I have taken liberties with both the geography and history of County Cork in this book, not to mention the weather, most of the events in both timelines came from true stories. Harry's assassination of the Drummonds and Herbert Frost is loosely based on the IRA assassination in Dunmanway of Herbert Wood and James and Samuel Hornibrook in 1922. All the victims were Protestant, suspected by the IRA of being informers to the British government, and this sparked off a spate of sectarian murders in the area.

'Sing Sing', where the Drummonds are imprisoned in 1922, and Luke in 2021, was a real place of detention for the IRA during the War of Independence, an underground cell located in an ancient crypt in Knockraha, Co Cork. For narrative convenience, here it is featured on the slopes about Lough Hyne. While these are designated with the fictional name Knockalisha and are geographically different from the real slopes, the marine lake itself is real, and was designated as a nature reserve in 1981.

In spite of this, Lough Hyne too has become polluted by

the scourge of Ireland – agricultural run-off containing excessive levels of nitrogen which kills off the rare species of sea-urchin within it. Sadhbh would have been outraged, and would have pushed for action, but she probably would have been ignored, since the lobbies and vested interests which protect this practice appear to be more powerful than any voice raised for nature.

Many of the incidental occurrences mentioned in the book such as the threat to beat bats to death, Diarmuid Savage's comments on trees, and the felling of a tree outside a classroom window are also based on real events which I heard about from the news and fellow Green Party members. The excoriation of Sadhbh in a public meeting by Tom Keating and other goons is also sadly common – in 2023 during a farmers' meeting about the EU Nature Restoration Bill, an audience member suggested that the then Green Party leader, Eamon Ryan, be 'thrown off the cliffs of Moher.'

The epilogue of the novel first appeared in print as a flash fiction in *Channel* magazine in 2023, titled 'Rosa at Garryvoe, January '22'.

I am grateful first and foremost to the people who saved my life in 2023 – if you want to write books, being alive is a plus. Surgical consultants Paul Redmond and Norma Relihan at the Orchid Breast Cancer centre in Cork University Hospital, as well as the medical oncology team and Carol McGibney and the Glandore radiotherapy centre, have ensured that I will be around to be a thorn in the side to the Irish literary consensus for many years to come. Thank you all.

Bernadette Kearns edited this novel and helped marshal it into coherence after many years of struggles. The suggestion that Sergeant Connolly would be the kind of man to wear his covid mask beneath his nose is one hundred per cent her idea and shows her humour, empathy and engagement throughout. Thanks for collaborating on this project with me, Bernadette!

A shout-out also to the unnamed reader at Faber Academy who read an earlier version of the manuscript and gave me a lot of clear suggestions and directions and reactivated my faith in *The Planter's Daughter*.

Aoife Martin brought her knowledge and awareness to the novel to ground and clarify Rosa's journey with her gender identity. I'm grateful to Aoife for her engagement and it was a pleasure to engage with her advice and comments.

Thanks to all the authors who lent their kind words to the book, including Ronan McGreevy, Awais Khan, Michelle McDonagh, Maybelle Wallis and Byddi Lee. Byddi in many ways was my pathfinder in this journey of writing climate-adjacent fiction and I hope that our work will resonate more as the years go by and the weather invariably gets worse. (I would prefer if the weather did not get worse and we sorted ourselves out, to be honest, but...)

To those in the Irish Green Party, present and former, who were supportive of my writing journey, and of me: Hazel Chu, Cliona O'Halloran, Louise Jordan, Lorna Bogue, Mary Ryder, Liam Quaide, Roisin Cuddihy, Alan O'Connor, Monica Peres Oikeh, Dan Boyle, Moggy Somers and many others.

To the writers who have cheered me on: Shirley Benton, Kemi Tijani and once again Byddi Lee. Both of you understand all too well what it is like to be 'outside the system' wearied from the endless, tedious gatekeeping therein. Madeleine d'Arcy and Danielle McLaughlin's Fiction at the Friary project was always fun to attend on the last Friday of each month. Both successful writers themselves, they created a wonderful space to nurture talent in Cork.

A special shout-out to the 'Pally squad' – wonderful

people in Gaza I've had the pleasure of getting to know over the past few months. In spite of living through unspeakable horror, they've never hesitated to offer encouragement and love. Wafaa, Hamza and Kholoud, and your families, I pray for you all the time. You are legends.

My mother-in-law, Lil O'Neill, left this earth in 2022. She was a lioness, and I miss her. She loved *White Feathers* and got everyone she knew to buy a copy. I hope she would have enjoyed *The Planter's Daughter*, even though there is quite a bit more swearing in it. I'd like to thank all the Lanigans for their support, my friends who have stood by and uplifted me through good times and bad, and of course Jonathan and Luca, my whole world.

ABOUT THE AUTHOR

Susan Lanigan is the author of *White Feathers* (2014), *Lucia's War* (2020) and *Unfortunate Stars* (2021) Her first novel, *White Feathers*, was a Novel Fair winner in 2013 and was shortlisted for the Romantic Novel of the Year Award in 2025 and her short fiction has been published in variety of outlets, most recently Channel Magazine and Overtly Lit.

She lives by the sea in Cork with her family.

SD - #0127 - 271025 - C0 - 216/140/26 - PB - 9612907000024 - Matt Lamination